Overload

Arthur Hailey, storyteller *extraordinaire*, has become one of the most widely-read writers of all time. His books are *Flight into Danger* (with John Castle), *The Final Diagnosis*, *In High Places*, *Hotel*, *Airport*, *Wheels* and *The Moneychangers*. They are published in thirty languages, his worldwide fans number millions.

Arthur Hailey was born and educated in Luton. He was an RAF pilot during World War II and afterwards emigrated to Canada where he met and married his wife Sheila, also an emigrant from Britain. Now the Haileys' home is in Lyford Cay, Bahamas, from where they visit Britain frequently.

Sheila Hailey recently wrote and published her own frank, forthright account of life with Arthur – *I Married A Best Seller*.

Arthur Hailey

Overload

Pan Books London and Sydney

First published in Great Britain 1979 by
Michael Joseph Ltd in association with
Souvenir Press Ltd
This edition published 1980 by Pan Books Ltd,
Cavaye Place, London SW10 9PG
5th printing 1980
© Arthur Hailey 1979
ISBN 0 330 25948 2
Printed and bound in Great Britain by
Richard Clay (The Chaucer Press) Ltd, Bungay, Suffolk

Author's note for this edition

The words 'public utility' and 'utility', as used frequently in this story, refer to a commercial company which produces and distributes electricity and gas.

In the United States most such 'utilities' are large, private-enterprise corporations, their shares publicly traded on the nation's stock exchanges.

Unlike other commercial companies, however, the activities of 'public utilities', including the rates they charge customers, are closely controlled by regulatory boards appointed by state and federal governments.

Each 'public utility' serves a limited area – a portion of a state or, in some cases, a single large metropolis. The US has no national electric grid system – great distances make it impractical – although most 'utilities' are linked to others by high-voltage transmission lines and can buy and sell each other's surplus power as need dictates.

Let your loins be girded about, and your lights burning.
St Luke, xii, 35

O dark, dark, dark, amid the blaze of noon . . .
John Milton

Since . . . 1974, the rate at which new electrical generating capacity has been built in California has fallen to less than half of the 1970–74 level. As a result, the threat of an economically ruinous power crunch by the 1990s is very real; and there is already apprehension over the danger of brownouts and blackouts in the 1980s . . .
Fortune magazine

Part One

1

Heat!

Heat in stifling blanket layers. Heat that enveloped all of California from the arid Mexican border in the south to majestic Klamath Forest, elbowing northwards into Oregon. Heat, oppressive and enervating. Four days ago a hot, dry thermal trough a thousand miles long, three hundred wide, had settled over the state and sat there like a brooding hen. This morning – a Wednesday in July – a Pacific frontal system was supposed to shove the heat wave eastwards, introducing cooler air, with showers on the north coast and in the mountains. It hadn't happened. Now, at 1pm, Californians still sweltered in temperatures from ninety degrees to well over a hundred, with no relief in sight.

Throughout cities and suburbs, in factories, offices, stores and homes, six million electric air-conditioners hummed. On thousands of farms in the fertile Central Valley – the richest agricultural complex in the world – armies of electric pumps gulped water from deep wells, directing it to thirsty cattle and parched crops – grain, grapes, citrus fruits, alfalfa, zucchini, a hundred more. Multitudes of refrigerators and food freezers ran unceasingly. And elsewhere the normal electrical demands of a pampered, spoiled, convenience-oriented, gadget-minded, power-guzzling populace continued unabated.

California had known other heat waves and survived their consequences. But in none had demands for electric power been so great.

'That's it, then,' the chief electric dispatcher said unnecessarily. 'There goes the last of our spinning reserve.'

Everyone within hearing already knew it. And everyone, in this case, included regular staff and company executives, all crowding the Energy Control Center of Golden State Power & Light.

Golden State Power – or, more often, GSP & L – was a giant, a General Motors among public utilities. It was the wellspring which produced and distributed two-thirds of California's electric power and natural gas. Its presence was as familiar in the state as sunshine, oranges and wine, and usually taken just as much for granted. GSP & L was also rich, strong and – by self-description – efficient. Its all-pervasiveness sometimes earned it the sobriquet 'God's Power & Love'.

The Energy Control Center of GSP & L was a security-restricted, underground command post, once described by a visitor as like a hospital operating theatre mated with the bridge of an ocean liner. Its centrepiece was a communications console on a dais two steps above floor level. Here the chief dispatcher and six assistants worked. Keyboards of two computer terminals were nearby. The surrounding walls housed banks of switches, diagrams of transmission line circuits and sub-stations, with coloured lights and instruments announcing the present status of the utility's two hundred and five electrical generating units in ninety-four plants around the state. The atmosphere was busy as a half-dozen assistant dispatchers monitored a constantly changing mass of information, though the sound level remained low, the result of engineered acoustics.

'You're damn positive there's no more power we can buy?' The question came from a tallish, muscularly built, shirtsleeved figure standing at the dispatch dais. Nim Goldman, vice president, planning, and assistant to the chairman of GSP & L, had his tie loosened in the heat and part of a hairy chest was visible where the top buttons of his shirt were open. The chest hair was like that of his head – black and curly with a few fine wires of grey. The face, strong, big-boned and ruddy, had eyes which looked out with directness and authority and most times – though not at the moment – with a hint of humour. In his late forties, Nim Goldman usually appeared younger, but not today because of strain and fatigue. For the past several days he had stayed at work until midnight and been up at 4am; the early rising had required early shaving so that he now had the stubble of a beard. Like others in the control center, Nim was sweating, partly from tension, partly from the fact that the air conditioning had been adjusted several hours ago in deference to an urgent plea – originating here and transmitted through TV and radio to the public – to use less electric power because of a grave supply crisis. But, judging by a climbing graph line of which everyone in the centre was aware, the appeal had gone mostly unheeded.

The chief dispatcher, a white-haired veteran, looked offended as he answered Nim's question. For the past two days two dispatch aides had been continually on phones, like desperate housewives, shopping for surplus power in other states and Canada. Nim Goldman knew that. 'We're pulling in every bit we can get from Oregon and Nevada, Mr Goldman. The Pacific Intertie's loaded. Arizona's helping out a little, but they've got problems too. Tomorrow they're asking to buy from *us*.'

'Told 'em there wasn't a snowball's chance,' a woman assistant dispatcher called over.

'Can we make it through this afternoon ourselves?' This time it was J. Eric Humphrey, chairman of the board, who turned from reading a situation report developed by computer. As usual, the chairman's cultured voice was low-key in keeping with his old-Bostonian aplomb, worn today as always like a suit of armour. Few ever penetrated it. He had lived and thrived in California for thirty years but the West's informal ways had not dulled Eric Humphrey's New England patina. He was a small, compact person, tidy in features, contact-lensed, impeccably groomed. Despite the heat, he wore a dark business suit complete with waistcoat, and if he was sweating, the evidence of it was decently out of sight.

'Doesn't look good, sir,' the chief dispatcher said. He popped a fresh Gelusil antacid tablet in his mouth; he had lost count of how many he had had today. Dispatchers needed the tablets because of tensions of their job and GSP & L, in an employee-relations gesture, had installed a dispenser where packets of the soothing medicine were available free.

Nim Goldman added, for the chairman's benefit, 'If we do hang on, it'll be by our fingernails – and a lot of luck.'

As the dispatcher had pointed out moments earlier, GSP & L's last spinning reserve had been brought to full load. What he had not explained, because none there needed to be told, was that a public utility like Golden State Power & Light had two kinds of electrical reserve – 'spinning' and 'ready'. The spinning reserve comprised generators running, but not at full capacity, though their output could be increased immediately if needed. The ready reserve included any generating plants not operating but prepared to start up and produce full load in ten to fifteen minutes.

An hour ago the last ready reserve – twin gas turbines at a power plant near Fresno, 65,000 kilowatts each – had had its status raised to 'spinning'. Now the gas turbines, which had been coasting along since then, were going to 'maximum output', leaving no reserves of either kind remaining.

A morose-appearing, bulky man, slightly stooped, with a Toby jug face and beetling brows, who had listened to the exchange between the chairman and dispatcher, spoke up harshly. 'Goddammit to hell! If we'd had a decent weather forecast for today, we wouldn't be in this bind now.' Ray Paulsen, executive vice president of power supply, took an impatient pace forward from a table where he and others had been studying power consumption curves, comparing today's with those of other hot days last year.

'Every other forecaster made the same error as ours,' Nim Goldman objected. 'I read in last night's paper and heard on the radio this morning we'd have cooler air.'

'That's probably exactly where she got it – from some newspaper! Cut it out and pasted it on a card, I'll bet.' Paulsen glared at Nim, who shrugged. It was no secret that the two detested each other. Nim, in his dual role as planner and as the chairman's assistant, had a roving commission in GSP & L which cut across department boundaries. In the past he had frequently invaded Paulsen's territory, and even though Ray Paulsen was two rungs higher in the company hierarchy, there was little he could do about it.

'If by "she" you mean me, Ray, you could at least have the good manners to use my name.' Heads turned. No one had seen Millicent Knight, the utility's chief meteorologist, petite, brunette and self-possessed, come into the room. Her entry was not surprising, though. The meteorology department, including Ms Knight's office, was part of the control centre, separated only by a glass wall.

Other men might have been embarrassed. Not so Ray Paulsen. He had climbed up through Golden State Power & Light the hard way, starting thirty-five years before as a field crew helper, then moving up to lineman, foreman and through other management positions. Once he was blown from a power pole during a mountain snowstorm and suffered spinal injuries which left him with a permanent stoop. Night college classes at the utility's expense converted young Paulsen to a graduate engineer; across the years since then his knowledge of the whole GSP & L system had become encyclopedic. Unfortunately, nowhere along the way had he acquired finesse or polished manners.

'Bullshit, Milly!' Paulsen shot back. 'I said what I thought, just like always – and would about a man. You work like a man, expect to be treated like one.'

Ms Knight said indignantly, 'Being a man or a woman has nothing to do with it. My department has a high record of forecasting accuracy – eighty per cent, as you perfectly well know. You won't find better anywhere.'

'But you and your people really screwed up today!'

'For Chrissakes, Ray,' Nim Goldman protested. 'This isn't getting us anywhere.'

J. Eric Humphrey listened to the argument with apparent indifference. The chairman never said so specifically, but sometimes left the impression he had no objection to his senior staff's feuding, providing their work was not impaired. There were some in business – presumably Humphrey was one – who believed an all-harmonious organization was also a complacent one. But when the chairman needed to, he could cut through disputes with the sharp knife of authority.

At this moment, strictly speaking, the executives now in the control centre – Humphrey, Nim Goldman, Paulsen, several others – had no business being there. The centre was competently staffed. Actions to be taken in emergency were well known, having been worked out long ago; most were computer-activated, supplemented by instruction manuals conveniently at hand. In a crisis, however, such as the one GSP & L was facing now, this place with its up-to-the-second information became a magnet for those with authority to get in.

The big question, still unresolved, was : would demands for electric power become so great as to exceed the supply available? If the answer proved to be yes, entire banks of sub-station switches would necessarily be opened, leaving segments of California without power, isolating entire communities, creating chaos.

An emergency 'brownout' was already in effect. Since 10am the voltage supplied to GSP & L consumers had been reduced in stages until it was now eight per cent below normal. The reduction allowed some power saving but meant that small appliances like hair dryers, electric typewriters, refrigerators were receiving ten volts less than usual while equipment wired for heavy duty was being deprived of nineteen to twenty volts. The lower voltages made everything less efficient, and electric motors ran hotter and more noisily than usual. Some computers were in trouble; those not equipped with voltage regulators had already switched off automatically and would stay that way until normal voltage was restored. One side effect was to shrink television pictures in home receivers, so that they failed to fill the screen. But over a short period there should be no lasting damage. Lighting, too – from ordinary incandescent bulbs – was slightly dimmed.

An eight per cent brownout, however, was the limit. Beyond that, electric motors would overheat, perhaps burn out, creating a fire hazard. Thus, if a brownout was not sufficient, the last resort was load shedding – committing large areas to total blackout.

The next two hours would tell. If GSP & L could somehow hold on until mid-afternoon, the time of peak demand on hot days, the load would ease until tomorrow. Then, assuming tomorrow was a cooler day – no problem.

But if the present load, which had been climbing steadily all day, continued to increase . . . the worst could happen.

Ray Paulsen did not give up easily. 'Well, Milly,' he persisted, 'today's weather forecast was ridiculously wrong. True?'

'Yes, it's true. If you want to put it in that unfair, ugly way.' Millicent Knight's dark eyes flashed with anger. 'But it's also true there's an air mass a thousand miles offshore called the Pacific High. Meteorology doesn't know very much about it, but sometimes it throws all California forecasts out of whack by a day or so.' She added scornfully, 'Or are you so wrapped up in electrical circuitry you don't know that elementary fact of nature?'

Paulsen flushed. 'Now wait a minute!'

Milly Knight ignored him. 'Another thing. My people and I gave an honest forecast. But a forecast, in case you've forgotten, is just that – it leaves some room for doubt. *I* didn't tell you to shut down Magalia 2 for maintenance. That's a decision *you* made – and you're blaming me for it.'

The group by the table chuckled. Someone murmured, 'Touché.'

As they well knew, part of today's problem *was* the Magalia plant.

Magalia 2, part of a GSP & L facility north of Sacramento, was a big, steam-driven generator capable of putting out 600,000 kilowatts. But ever since it was built some ten years earlier, Magalia 2 had been a source of trouble. Repeated boiler tube ruptures and other, more serious malfunctions kept it frequently out of service, most recently as long as nine months while the superheater was retubed. Even after that, problems had continued. As one engineer described it, operating Magalia 2 was like keeping a leaking battleship afloat.

For the past week the plant manager at Magalia had pleaded with Ray Paulsen to allow him to shut down number 2 to repair boiler tube leaks – as he put it, 'before this jinxed teakettle blows apart'. Until yesterday, Paulsen had adamantly said no. Even before the present heat wave began, and because of unscheduled repair shutdowns elsewhere, Magalia 2's power had been needed for the system. As always, it was a matter of balancing priorities, sometimes taking a chance. Last night, after reading the forecast of lower temperatures for today, and weighing everything, Paulsen gave approval and the unit was shut down immediately, with work beginning several hours later when the boiler had cooled. By this morning, Magalia 2 was silent and leaky pipe sections had been cut from several boiler tubes. Though desperately needed, Magalia 2 could not be back on line for two more days.

'If the forecast had been accurate,' Paulsen growled, 'Magalia wouldn't have been released.'

The chairman shook his head. He had heard enough. There would be time for inquests later. This was not the moment.

Nim Goldman had been conferring at the dispatch console. Now, his forceful voice cutting clearly across others, he announced, 'Load shedding will have to begin in half an hour. There's no longer any doubt. We'll have to.' He glanced towards the chairman. 'I think we should alert the media. TV and radio can still get warnings out.'

14

'Do it,' Humphrey said. 'And someone get me the Governor on the phone.'

'Yes, sir.' An assistant dispatcher began dialling.

Faces in the room were grim. In the utility's century-and-a-quarter history what was about to happen – intentional disruption of service – had never occurred before.

Nim Goldman was already telephoning Public Relations, over in another building. There would be no delay about warnings going out. The utility's PR department was geared to handle them; although, normally, the sequence of power cuts was known only to a few people within the company, now they would be made public. As another point of policy, a few months ago it had been decided that the cuts – if and when they happened – would be known as 'rolling blackouts', a PR ploy to emphasize their temporary nature and the fact that all areas would be treated fairly. The phrase 'rolling blackouts' was a young secretary's brainchild, after her older, more highly paid superiors failed to come up with anything acceptable. One of the rejects: 'sequential curtailments'.

'I have the Governor's office in Sacramento, sir,' the dispatch assistant informed Eric Humphrey. 'They say the Governor is at his ranch near Stockton and they're trying to reach him. They'd like you on the line.'

The chairman nodded and accepted the telephone. His hand cupping the mouthpiece, he asked, 'Does anyone know where the chief is?' It was unnecessary to explain that 'chief' meant the chief engineer, Walter Talbot, a quiet, unflappable Scot now nearing retirement, whose wisdom in tight situations was legendary.

'Yes,' Nim Goldman said. 'He drove out to take a look at Big Lil.'

The chairman frowned. 'I hope nothing's wrong out there.'

Instinctively, eyes swung to an instrument panel with the legend above it: *La Mission No 5*. This was Big Lil, the newest and largest generator at La Mission plant, fifty miles outside the city.

Big Lil – Lilien Industries of Pennsylvania built the huge machine and a news writer coined the descriptive name which stuck – was a monster delivering a million and a quarter kilowatts of electric power. It was fuelled by oil in enormous quantities which created superheated steam to drive the giant turbine. In the past Big Lil had had its critics. During the planning stages experts argued it was sheerest folly to build a generator so large because too much reliance would be placed on a single source of power; they used a non-scientific simile involving eggs and a basket. Other experts disagreed. These pointed to 'economies of scale', by which they meant: mass-produced electricity is cheaper. The second group prevailed and, so far, had been proved right. In the two years since it began operating, Big Lil had been economical compared with smaller generators, magnificently reliable, and trouble-free. Today, in the Energy Control Center, a strip chart recorder showed the heartening news that Big Lil was giving its utmost, running at maximum, shouldering a massive six per cent of the utility's total load.

'There was some turbine vibration reported early this morning,' Ray Paulsen told the chairman. 'The chief and I discussed it. While it probably isn't critical, we both thought he should take a look.'

Humphrey nodded approval. There was nothing the chief could do here, anyway. It was simply more comfortable to have him around.

'Here is the Governor,' an operator announced on Humphrey's telephone. And a moment later a familiar voice: 'Good afternoon, Eric.'

'Good afternoon, sir,' the chairman said. 'I'm afraid I'm calling with unhappy . . .'

It was then that it happened.

Amid the bank of instruments under the sign *La Mission No 5* a buzzer, urgently insistent, sounded a series of short, sharp notes. Simultaneously, amber and red warning lights began blinking. The inked needle of No 5's chart recorder faltered, then descended steeply.

'My God!' someone's shocked voice said. 'Big Lil's tripped off the line.'

There remained no doubt of it as the recorder and other readings slid to zero.

Reactions were immediate. In the Energy Control Center a high-speed logging typewriter came to life, chattering, spewing out status reports as hundreds of high voltage circuit breakers at switching centres and sub-stations sprang open at computer command. The opening of the circuit breakers would save the system and protect other generators from harm. But the action had already plunged huge segments of the state into total electric blackout. Within two or three successive seconds, millions of people in widely separated areas – factory and office workers, farmers, housewives, shoppers, salesclerks, restaurant operators, printers, service station attendants, stockbrokers, hoteliers, hairdressers, movie projectionists and patrons, streetcar motormen, TV station staffs and viewers, bar-tenders, mail sorters, wine makers, doctors, dentists, veterinarians, pinball players . . . a list ad infinitum – were deprived of power and light, unable to continue whatever, a moment earlier, they had been doing.

In buildings, elevators halted between floors. Airports, which had been bursting with activity, virtually ceased to function. On streets and highways traffic lights went out, beginning monumental traffic chaos.

More than an eighth of California – a land area substantially larger than all of Switzerland and with a population of about three million – came abruptly to a standstill. What, only a short time ago, had been merely a possibility was now disastrous reality – and worse, by far, than feared.

At the control centre's communications console – protected by special circuits from the widespread loss of power – all three dispatchers were working swiftly, spreading out emergency instructions, telephoning orders to generating plants and division power controllers, examining pedal-actuated roller system maps, scanning cathode ray tube displays for information. They would be busy for a long time to come, but actions triggered by computers were far ahead of them now.

'Hey,' the Governor said on Eric Humphrey's telephone, 'all the lights just went out.'

'I know,' the chairman acknowledged. 'That's what I called you about.'

On another phone – a direct line to La Mission's control room – Ray Paulsen was shouting, 'What in *hell* has happened to Big Lil?'

2

The explosion at the La Mission plant of Golden State Power & Light occurred entirely without warning.

A half hour earlier the chief engineer, Walter Talbot, had arrived to inspect La Mission No 5 – Big Lil – following reports of slight turbine vibration during the night. The chief was a lean, spindly man, outwardly dour, but with a puckish sense of humour and who still talked in a broad Glaswegian accent, though for forty years he had been no nearer Scotland than an occasional Burns Night dinner in San Francisco. He liked to take his time about whatever he was doing and today inspected Big Lil slowly and carefully while the plant superintendent, a mild, scholarly engineer named Danieli, accompanied him. All the while the giant generator poured out its power – sufficient to light more than twenty million average light bulbs.

A faint vibration deep within the turbine, and differing from its normal steady whine, was audible occasionally to the trained ears of the chief and superintendent. And eventually, after tests which included applying a nylon-tipped probe to a main bearing, the chief pronounced, 'It's naething tae worry over. The fat lassie will gi' nae trouble, and what's necessary we'll see to when the panic's bye.'

As he spoke, the two were standing close to Big Lil on metal gratings which formed the floor of the cathedral-like turbine hall. The monstrous turbine-generator, a city block in length, sat perched on concrete pedestals, each of the unit's seven casings resembling a beached whale. Immediately beneath was a massive steam chest with high pressure steam lines going in from the boiler and out to the turbine, as well as other service facilities. Both men were wearing hard hats and protective ear pads. Neither precaution, however, was of help in the explosion which occurred with a deafening roar an instant later. The chief and Plant Superintendent Danieli took the secondary force of a dynamite blast, originating beneath the main hall floor, which initially breached a three-foot diameter steam line, one of several running from the boiler to the steam chest. A smaller lubricating oil line was also pierced. The explosion, combined with escaping steam, produced an overwhelming noise, deep and thunderous. Then the steam, at a thousand degrees Fahrenheit and under pressure of 2,400 pounds per square inch, rushed through the gratings on which the two men were standing.

Both died instantly. They were cooked, literally, like vegetables in a steamer. A few seconds later the entire scene was obscured by dense black smoke from the ruptured oil line, now burning – ignited by a spark from flying metal.

Two plant workers, painting on a scaffold high above the turbine room floor and in danger of being overcome by the rising black smoke, tried to clamber blindly to a walkway some fifteen feet higher. They failed, and fell to their deaths below.

Only in the plant control room – two hundred feet away and protected by double doors – was total disaster averted. The fast reactions of a technician at No 5's control panel, aided by automatic devices, ensured that Big Lil was shut down without damage to the turbine-generator's vital components.

At the La Mission plant it would take several days of inquiry – a painstaking sifting of debris by experts and questioning by sheriff's deputies and FBI agents – to discover the explosion's cause and circumstances. But a suspicion of sabotage would emerge quickly and later be proved true.

In the end, the accumulated evidence provided a fairly clear picture of the explosion and events preceding it.

At 11:40 that morning, a white male of medium build, clean-shaven, sallow-complexioned, wearing steel-rimmed glasses and in the uniform of a Salvation Army officer, approached the main gate of La Mission on foot. He was carrying an attaché-type briefcase.

Questioned by the gate security guard, the visitor produced a letter, apparently on Golden State Power & Light stationery, authorizing him to visit GSP & L installations for the purpose of soliciting funds from utility employees for a Salvation Army charity – a free lunch programme for needy children.

The guard informed the Salvation Army man that he must go to the plant superintendent's office and present his letter there. The guard gave directions on how to reach the office which was on the second floor of the main powerhouse and accessible through a doorway out of sight from the guardpost. The visitor then left in the direction indicated. The guard saw no more of him until the visitor returned and walked out of the plant about twenty minutes later. The guard noticed he was still carrying the briefcase.

The explosion occurred an hour later.

If security had been tighter, as was pointed out at a subsequent coroner's inquest, such a visitor would not have been allowed into the plant unescorted. But GSP & L, like public utilities everywhere, faced special problems – a dilemma – in matters of security. With ninety-four generating plants, scores of service yards and warehouses, hundreds of unattended substations, a series of widely scattered district offices and a central headquarters comprising two connected high-rise buildings, provision of strict security, even if possible, would cost a fortune. This, at a time of soaring fuel, wage and other operating costs, while consumers complained that bills for electricity and gas were already too high and any proposed rate increase should be resisted. For all these reasons security employees were relatively few, so that much of the utility's security programme was cosmetic, based on calculated risk.

At La Mission, the risk – at a cost of four human lives – proved to be too high.

The police enquiries established several things. The supposed Salvation Army officer was an impostor, almost certainly wearing a stolen uniform. The letter he presented, while it may have been on official GSP & L stationery – not difficult to come by – was a fake. The utility would not, in any case, allow its employees to be solicited at work, nor could anyone be located in the GSP & L organization who had written such a letter. The La Mission security guard did not remember a name at the bottom of the page, though he recalled the signature was 'a squiggle'.

It was also established that the visitor, once inside the powerhouse, did not go to the superintendent's office. No one there saw him. If anyone had, the fact was unlikely to have been forgotten.

Conjecture came next.

Most probably the bogus Salvation Army officer descended a short metal stairway to the service floor immediately beneath the main turbine hall. This floor, like the one above it, had no intervening walls so that even through a network of insulated steam pipes and other service lines, the lower portions of the

20

several La Mission generators could be clearly seen through the metal grating floor of the turbine hall above. Number 5 – Big Lil – would have been unmistakable because of its size and that of the equipment near it.

Perhaps the intruder had advance information about the layout of the plant, though this would not have been essential. The main generating building was an uncomplicated structure – little more than a giant box. He might also have known that La Mission, like all modern generating stations, was highly automated, with only a small work force; therefore his chances of moving around without being observed were good.

Almost certainly, then, the intruder moved directly under Big Lil where he opened his briefcase containing a dynamite bomb. He would have looked around for an out-of-view location for the bomb, then would have seen what seemed a convenient metal flange near the junction of two steam lines. After actuating a timing mechanism undoubtedly he reached up and placed the bomb there. It was in this choice of location that his lack of technical knowledge betrayed him. Had he been better informed, he would have located the bomb near the monster generator's main shaft, where it would have done most damage, perhaps putting Big Lil out of action for as long as a year.

Explosives experts confirmed that this indeed had been a possibility. What the saboteur used, they decided, was a 'shaped charge' – a cone of dynamite which, when detonated, had a forward velocity similar to that of a bullet, causing the explosion to penetrate whatever was directly ahead. As it happened, this was a steam line leading from the boiler.

Immediately after positioning the bomb – the hypothesis continued – the saboteur walked unaccosted from the main generating building to the plant gate, leaving as casually and with even less attention than when he arrived. From that point his movements were unknown. Nor, despite intensive investigation, did any substantial clue about identity emerge. True, a telephoned message to a radio station, allegedly from an underground revolutionary group – Friends of Freedom – claimed responsibility. But police had no information as to the whereabouts of the group or knowledge of its membership.

But all this came later. At La Mission, for some ninety minutes after the explosion, chaos reigned.

Fire fighters, responding to an automatic alarm, had difficulty extinguishing the oil fire and ventilating the main turbine hall and lower floors to remove the dense black smoke. When, at length, conditions were clear enough, the four bodies were removed. Those of the chief engineer and superintendent, scarcely recognizable, were described by a horrified plant employee as 'like boiled lobsters' – the result of exposure to superheated steam.

A quick assessment of damage to No 5 revealed that it was slight. A seized bearing where the lubricating oil supply was cut off by the explosion would require replacement. That was all. Repair work, including replacement of broken steam lines, would take a week, after which the giant generator could be back in service. Ironically, in that time, the slight vibration which the chief engineer had come to inspect could be corrected, too.

3

'An electrical distribution system that's gone into a widespread, non-scheduled blackout,' Nim Goldman explained patiently, 'is like the kids' game of "Fifty-two Pick up". One minute you're looking at a full deck, then the next – without warning – a floor littered with cards. They have to be picked up one by one and the whole thing takes a while.'

He was in an observation gallery, slightly above and separated by a glass wall from the Energy Control Center, to which reporters from newspapers, TV and radio had been admitted a few minutes ago. The reporters had been dispatched hastily to GSP & L from their various news centres, and the utility's PR vice president, Teresa Van Buren, had appealed to Nim to be the company's spokesman. An impromptu press conference was the result.

Already some of the press people were antagonistic because of what they saw as a paucity of answers to their questions.

'Oh, for God's sake!' a reporter from the *California Examiner*, Nancy Molineaux, protested. 'Spare us that homespun analogy crap and tell us what we came to find out. What went wrong? Who's responsible? What, if anything, will be done about it? When will the power be back on?'

Ms Molineaux was intense, attractive in a severe way – high cheekbones made her face seem haughty, which she sometimes was – and her usual expression was a mixture of curiosity and scepticism bordering on disdain. She was also chic, wore good clothes well on a willowy body, and was black. Professionally, she had achieved a reputation for investigating, then exposing, venality in public places. Nim regarded her as he would a needle-sharp icicle. Her reporting in the past had made clear that GSP & L was not an institution Ms Molineaux admired.

Several other reporters nodded agreement.

'What went wrong was an explosion at La Mission.' Nim controlled an impulse to snap back angrily. 'We believe that at least two of our people have been killed but there's an oil fire and dense smoke, and so far there are no more details.'

Someone asked, 'Do you have names of the two dead?'

'Yes, but they can't be released yet. The families must be informed first.'

'Do you know the cause of the explosion?'

'No.'

Ms Molineaux injected, 'What about the power?'

'Some power,' Nim said, 'is already back now. Most of the rest should be restored within four hours, six at the outside. Everything else should be normal by tonight.'

Normal, Nim thought, except for Walter Talbot. Word of the chief's involvement in the explosion and his assumed death had reached the Energy Control Center with shattering suddenness only minutes earlier. Nim, a longtime friend of the chief's, hadn't had time yet to grasp the reality of the news, or to grieve, as he knew he would later. Nim had known Danieli, the La Mission plant superintendent, only slightly, so that his loss, while tragic, seemed more remote. Through the soundproof glass partition separating the observation gallery from the control centre working area, Nim could see urgent activity continuing at and around the dispatch console. He wanted to get back there as quickly as he could.

'Will there be another blackout tomorrow?' a wire service correspondent wanted to know.

'Not if the heat wave ends, as we understand it will.'

As questioning continued, Nim launched into a description of peak load problems in unexpectedly hot weather.

'So what you're really saying,' Nancy Molineaux suggested tartly, 'is that you people hadn't planned, hadn't foreseen, hadn't allowed for anything which might jolt you out of the ordinary.'

Nim flushed. 'Planning can only go so . . .'

The sentence was never finished.

Teresa Van Buren, the public relations director, came into the gallery, from which she had been absent for several minutes. She was a short, plump, bustling woman in her mid-forties who invariably wore rumpled linen suits and sensible brown brogues. Often she was untidy and uncombed, and looked more like a harried housewife than the experienced corporation executive she was.

'I have an announcement,' Mrs Van Buren said. Her voice was emotional and a paper in her hand was shaking. The room fell silent.

'We have just learned there have been four deaths, not two. All of the dead are company employees who were working at their jobs at the time of the explosion. Their next of kin are being informed now and we'll have a list of names for you, with brief biographies, in a few minutes. I'm also authorized to say that, while there is no proof at this moment, sabotage is suspected.'

Amid the fusillade of questions which followed, Nim eased his way out.

Step by step, directed by Energy Control, the disrupted distribution system was returning to a state of order.

At the communications console the chief dispatcher, juggling two telephones and manipulating a battery of buttons, was issuing fast, low-key instructions to switchmen, in an attempt to restore interconnections with other utilities; these had separated automatically when Big Lil tripped. When the Pacific Intertie was re-established, the dispatcher leaned back in his grey metal swivel chair and released an audible sigh, then began pushing buttons to start restoring load. He glanced sideways briefly as Nim returned. 'We're halfway home, Mr Goldman.'

It meant, Nim realized, that nearly half the total area affected by sudden blackout had full electric power restored and the process was continuing. A computer could, and did, shut down the system faster by far than any human agency. But it took direct switching by technicians, supervised from Energy Control, to put the system back together.

Cities and towns had priority and, district by district, were coming electrically alive once more. Suburbs, particularly those with concentrations of industrial plants, were next. Country villages would follow. Outlying rural areas, at the bottom of the power totem pole, would be last of all.

A few exceptions were made. Hospitals, water and sewage treatment plants and phone company installations rated special preference because of their essential nature. It was true that such institutions usually had standby generators of their own, but these carried only a partial load and outside power was essential for normal functioning. There were also, here and there, pockets of special consideration for individuals.

The chief dispatcher had transferred his attention to an unusual wiring circuitry map which he was discussing on one of his telephones. The map had a series of coloured circles dotted over it.

Waiting for a pause in the phoning, Nim asked, 'What's that?'

The dispatcher looked surprised. 'You don't know that one?'

Nim shook his head. Even a vice president of planning could not assimilate, or even see, the thousands of minutely detailed charts in an operation as large as GSP & L's.

'Life-sustaining equipment in private homes.' The dispatcher beckoned one of his assistants and moved out of his seat as the other replaced him. 'I need a break.' He ran a hand through his white hair in a gesture of tiredness, then absently popped another Gelusil tablet into his mouth.

Freed from pressures for the moment, the dispatcher positioned the circuitry map between himself and Nim. 'Those red circles are iron lungs – respiratory equipment, they mostly call it nowadays. Green is kidney dialysis machines. This orange circle is an oxygen generating unit for an infant. We've got maps like this for every division and we keep them up to date. Hospitals, who know where the home equipment is located, help us.'

'You've just filled a gap in my education,' Nim acknowledged.

He continued to study the map, which fascinated him.

'Most people relying on life-sustaining equipment have the kind that switches over to batteries in emergency,' the dispatcher continued. 'Just the same, when outside power fails it's traumatic for them. So what we do, if there's a local outage, is check quickly. Then, if there's any doubt or problem, we rush in a portable generator.'

'But we don't have that many portables – surely not enough for a widespread outage like today's.'

'No, and there aren't many crews available either. But today we were lucky. Divisions have been checking. No users of life-sustaining equipment at home were in trouble.' The dispatcher indicated the map. 'Now, in all these spots we have power back on.'

The knowledge that a human element so small in numbers was being watched and cared about amid vaster concerns was moving and reassuring. Nim studied the map, his eyes roving. He found a street intersection he knew well. Lakewood and Balboa. One of the red circles marked the site of an apartment house he had driven by many times. A name beside it read *Sloan* – presumably the iron lung user. Who was Sloan? Nim wondered. What was he like?

His musing was interrupted. 'Mr Goldman, the chairman wants to speak to you. He's calling from La Mission.' Nim accepted a telephone which a control room assistant offered.

'Nim,' Eric Humphrey said, 'you knew Walter Talbot pretty well personally, didn't you?' Despite the crisis, the chairman's voice was urbane as usual. Immediately after first reports of the explosion, he had summoned his limousine and left, along with Ray Paulsen, for La Mission.

'Yes,' Nim said. 'Walter and I were good friends.' He was conscious of a catch in his voice, with tears not far away. Almost since Nim's recruitment to Golden State Power & Light eleven years ago, he and the chief engineer had shared a mutual liking and habitually confided in each other. It seemed inconceivable there would be no more confidences ever again.

'And Walter's wife? How well do you know her?'

'Ardythe. Very well.' Nim sensed the chairman hesitate, and asked, 'How is it out there?'

'Grim. I never saw bodies of men burned by superheated steam before. I hope I never do again. There's virtually no skin left, just a mass of blisters with everything underneath exposed. Faces are unrecognizable.' For a moment Eric Humphrey's composure seemed to waver, then he recovered it. 'That's why I'd like you to go to Mrs Talbot as soon as possible. I understand she's taken the news badly, which is not surprising. As a friend you may be able to help. I'd also like you to dissuade her, if you can, from viewing her husband's body.'

'Oh Christ, Eric,' Nim said. 'Why me?'

'For the obvious reason. Someone has to do this, and you knew them both, apparently better than any of us. I'm also asking a friend of Danieli's to go to his wife for the same purpose.'

Nim wanted to retort: *Why don't you go – to the wives of all four men killed? You're our commander-in-chief, paid a princely salary which ought to compensate for an unhappy, messy duty once in a while. Besides, doesn't dying in the service of the company merit a personal call from the man at the top?* But he didn't say it, knowing that J. Eric Humphrey, while a hardworking administrator, purposely kept a low profile whenever he could, and this was clearly one more occasion, with Nim and some other unfortunates acting as his surrogates.

'All right,' Nim conceded, 'I'll do it.'

'Thank you. And please convey to Mrs Talbot my deep personal sympathy.'

Nim brooded unhappily as he returned the telephone. What he had been instructed to do was not the kind of thing he was good at handling. He had known he would see Ardythe Talbot eventually and would have to grope emotionally for words as best he could. What he hadn't expected was to have to go to her so soon.

On the way out of Energy Control, Nim encountered Teresa Van Buren. She looked wrung out. Presumably her latest session with the reporters had contributed to that, and Teresa, too, had been a friend of Walter Talbot's. 'Not a good day for any of us,' she said.

'No,' Nim agreed. He told her where he was going and about the instructions from Eric Humphrey.

The PR vice president grimaced. 'I don't envy you. That's tough duty. By the way, I hear you had a run-in with Nancy Molineaux.'

He said feelingly, 'That bitch!'

'Sure, she's a bitch. She's also one spunky newspaperwoman, a whole lot better than most of the incompetent clowns we see on this beat.'

'I'm surprised you'd say that. She'd made up her mind to be critical – hostile – before she even knew what the story was about.'

Van Buren shrugged. 'This pachyderm we work for can survive a few slings and arrows. Besides, hostility may be Nancy's way of making you, and others, say more than you intend. You've got a few things to learn about women, Nim – other than callisthenics in bed, and from rumours I hear, you're getting plenty of that.' She regarded him shrewdly. 'You're a hunter of women, aren't you?' Then her motherly eyes softened. 'Maybe I shouldn't have said that right now. Go, do the best you can for Walter's wife.'

4

His substantial frame jammed into his Fiat X19 two-seater, Nim Goldman wove through downtown streets, heading northeast towards San Roque, the suburb where Walter and Ardythe Talbot lived. He knew the way well, having driven it many times.

By now it was early evening, an hour or so after the home-bound rush hour, though traffic was still heavy. The heat of the day had diminished a little, but not much.

Nim shifted his body in the little car, straining to make himself comfortable, and was reminded he had put on weight lately and ought to take some off before he and the Fiat reached a point of impasse. He had no intention of changing the car. It represented his conviction that those who drove larger cars were blindly squandering precious oil while living in a fool's paradise which would shortly end, with accompanying disasters. One of the disasters would be a crippling shortage of electric power.

As Nim saw it, today's brief power curtailment was merely a preview – an unpalatable *hors d'oeuvre* – of far graver, dislocating shortages, perhaps only a year or two distant. The trouble was, almost no one seemed to care. Even within GSP & L, where plenty of others were privy to the same facts and overview as Nim, there existed a complacency, translatable as : *Don't worry. Everything will come out all right. We shall manage. Meanwhile, don't let's rock the boat by creating public alarm.*

Within recent months only three people in the Golden State Power & Light hierarchy – Walter Talbot, Teresa Van Buren and Nim – had pleaded for a change of stance. What they sought was less timidity, more directness. They favoured blunt, immediate warnings to the public, press and politicians that a calamitous electrical famine was ahead, that nothing could avert it totally, and only a crash programme to build new generating plants, combined with massive, painful conservation measures, could lessen its effect. But conventional caution, the fear of offending those in authority in the state, had so far prevailed. No change had been sanctioned. Now, Walter, one of the crusading trio, was dead.

A resurgence of his grief swept over Nim. Earlier, he had held back tears. Now, in the privacy of the moving car, he let them come; twin rivulets coursed down his face. With anguish he wished he could do something for Walter, even an intangible act like praying. He tried to recall the Mourner's Kaddish, the Jewish prayer he had heard occasionally at services for the dead, said traditionally by the closest male relative and in the presence of ten Jewish men. Nim's lips moved silently, stumbling over the ancient Aramaic words. *Yisgadal veyiskadash sh'may rabbo be'olmo deevro chiroosey ve' yamlich malchoosey* . . . He stopped, the remainder of the prayer eluding him, even while realizing that to pray at all was, for him, illogical.

There had been moments in his life – this was one – when Nim sensed instincts deep within him yearning for religious faith, for identification, personally, with his heritage. But religion, or at least the practice of it, was a closed door. It was slammed shut before Nim's birth by his father, Isaac Goldman, who came to America from Eastern Europe as a young, penniless immigrant and ardent socialist. The son of a rabbi, Isaac found socialism and Judaism incompatible. He thereupon rejected the religion of his forebears, leaving his own parents heartbroken. Even now, old Isaac, at eighty-two, still mocked the basic tenets of Jewish faith, describing them as 'banal chitchat between God and Abraham, and the fatuous fairy tale of a chosen people'.

Nim had grown up accepting his father's choice. The festival of Passover and the High Holy Days – Rosh Hashanah, Yom Kippur – passed unobserved by the Goldman family and now, as an outcropping of Isaac's personal rebellion, a third generation – Nim's own children Leah and Benjy – were removed from Jewish heritage and identity. No bar mitzvah for Benjy had been planned, an omission which occasionally troubled Nim and prompted the question: despite decisions he had made about himself, did he have the right to separate his children from five thousand years of Jewish history? It was not too late, he knew, but so far Nim had not resolved the issue.

As he thought of his family, Nim realized he had neglected to call Ruth to tell her he would not be home until late. He reached for the mobile phone to his right below the instrument panel – a convenience which GSP & L supplied and paid for. An operator answered and he gave her his home number. Moments later he heard a ringing tone, then a small voice. 'Goldman residence, Benjy Goldman speaking.' Nim smiled. That was Benjy all right – even at ten, precise and systematized, in contrast to his sister Leah, four years older, perennially disorganized and who answered phones with a casual, 'Hi!'

'It's Dad,' Nim said. 'I'm on mobile.' He had taught the family to wait when they heard that because on a radio-telephone conversations couldn't overlap. He added, 'Is everything all right at home?'

'Yes, Dad, it is now. But the electricity went off.' Benjy gave a little chuckle. 'I guess you knew. And, Dad, I reset all the clocks.'

'That's good, and yes, I knew. Let me talk to your mother.'

'Leah wants . . .'

Nim heard a scuffling, then the voice of his daughter. 'Hi! We watched the TV news. You weren't on.' Leah sounded accusing. The children had become used to seeing Nim on television as spokesman for GSP & L. Perhaps Nim's absence from the screen today would lower Leah's status among her friends.

'Sorry about that, Leah. There were too many other things happening. May I talk to your mother?'

Another pause. Then, 'Nim?' Ruth's soft voice.

He pressed the push-to-talk bar. 'That's who it is. And getting to talk to you is like elbowing through a crowd.'

While talking, he changed freeway lanes, manoeuvring the Fiat with one hand. A sign announced the San Roque turnoff was a mile and a half ahead.

'Because the children want to talk, too? Maybe it's because they don't see much of you at home.' Ruth never raised her voice, always sounding gentle, even when administering a rebuke. It was a justified rebuke, he admitted silently, wishing he hadn't raised the subject.

'Nim, we heard about Walter. And the others. It was on the news; it's terrible. I'm truly sorry.'

He knew that she meant it, and that Ruth was aware how close he and the chief had been.

That kind of understanding was typical of Ruth, even though in other ways she and Nim seemed to have less and less rapport nowadays, compared with how it used to be. Not that there was any open hostility. There wasn't. Ruth, with her quiet impertur- bability, would never let it come to that, Nim reasoned. He could visualize her now – composed and competent, her soft grey eyes sympathetic. She had a Madonna quality, he had often thought; even without the good looks she possessed in abundance, char- acter alone would have made her beautiful. He knew, too, she would be sharing this moment with Leah and Benjy, explaining, treating them as equals in that easy way she always had. Nim never ceased to respect Ruth, especially as a mother. It was simply that their marriage had become uninteresting, even dull; in his own mind he characterized it as 'a bumpless road to nowhere'. There was something else – perhaps an outgrowth of their mutual malaise. Recently Ruth seemed to have developed interests of her own, interests she wouldn't talk about. Several times Nim called home when normally she would have been there; instead, she appeared to have been out all day and later dodged explaining, which was unlike her. Had Ruth taken a lover? It was possible, he supposed. In any case, Nim wondered how long and how far they would drift before something definite, a confrontation, had to happen.

'We're all shaken up,' he acknowledged. 'Eric has asked me to go to Ardythe and I'm on my way there now. I expect I'll be late. Probably very late. Don't wait up.'

That was nothing new, of course. More evenings than not, Nim worked late. The result: dinner at home was either delayed or he missed it entirely. It also meant he saw little of Leah and Benjy, who were often in bed, sometimes asleep, when Nim arrived. Sometimes Nim had guilt feelings about the meagre amount of time he spent with the children and he knew it troubled Ruth, though it was a rare occasion when she said so. Sometimes he wished she complained more.

But tonight's absence was different. It needed no further explanations or excuses, even to himself.

'Poor Ardythe,' Ruth said. 'Just as Walter was getting near retirement. And that announcement just now makes it even worse.'

'What announcement?'

'Oh, I thought you'd know. It was on the news. The people who planted the bomb sent – a communiqué I think they called it – to a radio station. They were boasting about what they'd done. Can you imagine? What kind of people must they be?'

'Which radio station?' As he spoke, Nim put down the phone with a swift movement, snapped the car radio to 'on', then scooped up the phone again in time to hear Ruth say, 'I don't know.'

'Listen,' he told her, 'it's important I hear. So I'm going to hang up now and, if I can, I'll call you from Ardythe's.'

Nim replaced the phone. The radio was already tuned to an all-news station and a glance at his watch showed a minute to the half hour when he knew there would be a news summary.

The San Roque exit was in sight and he swung the Fiat on to it. The Talbot's home was just a mile or so away.

On the radio, a trumpet blast punctuated by Morse code announced a news bulletin. The item Nim had been waiting for was at the top.

'*A group calling itself Friends of Freedom has claimed responsibility for an explosion today at a Golden State Power & Light generating plant. The blast claimed four lives and caused a widespread failure of electric power.*

'*The disclosure was in a tape recording delivered to a local radio station late this afternoon. Police have said that information on the tape points to its authenticity. They are examining the recording for possible clues.*'

Obviously, Nim thought, the station he was listening to was

not the one which received the tape. Broadcasters didn't like to acknowledge a competitor's existence and, even though news like this was too important to be ignored, the other radio station wasn't being named.

'According to reports, a man's voice on the tape recording – so far unidentified – stated, quote, "Friends of Freedom are dedicated to a people's revolution and protest the greedy capitalist monopoly of power which belongs rightfully to the people." End quote.

'Commenting on the deaths which occurred, the recording says, quote, "Killing was not intended, but in the people's revolution now beginning, capitalists and their lackeys will be casualties, suffering for their crimes against humanity." End quote.

'An official of Golden State Power & Light has confirmed that sabotage was the cause of today's explosion, but would make no other comment.

'Retail meat prices are likely to be higher soon. In Washington today the Secretary of Agriculture told a consumers . . .'

Nim reached out, snapping off the radio. The news depressed him with its sickening futility. He wondered about its effect on Ardythe Talbot, whom he was soon to see.

In the growing dusk he saw that several cars were parked outside the Talbots' modest, neat two-storey house with its profusion of flower beds – a lifelong hobby of Walter's. Lights were on in the lower rooms.

Nim found a spot for the Fiat, locked it, and walked up the driveway.

5

The front door of the house was open and a hum of voices was audible. Nim knocked and waited. When no one answered, he went in.

In the hallway the voices became clearer. They were coming

from the living room to the right, he realized. Nim could hear Ardythe. She sounded hysterical and was sobbing. He caught disconnected words. '. . . those murderers, oh my God! . . . was good and kind, wouldn't harm anyone . . . to call him those filthy names . . .' Interspersed were other voices, attempting to bring calm but not succeeding.

Nim hesitated. The living room door was ajar, though he could neither see in nor be seen. He was tempted to tiptoe out, leaving as unnoticed as he had come. Then abruptly the living room door opened fully and a man came out. Closing the door quickly behind him, he leaned back against it, his bearded, sensitive face pale and strained, eyes shut tight as if for a moment's relief. The closed door cut off most of the sound from inside.

'Wally,' Nim said softly. 'Wally.'

The other opened his eyes, taking a few seconds to collect himself. 'Oh, it's you, Nim. Thanks for coming.'

Nim had known Walter Talbot Jr, an only son, almost as long as he had been a friend of the dead chief. Wally Jr, too, worked for GSP & L – as a transmission lines maintenance engineer. He was married, with children, and lived on the opposite side of the city.

'There's not a helluva lot anyone can say,' Nim told him. 'Except I'm sorry.'

Wally Talbot nodded. 'I know.' He motioned with an apologetic gesture towards the room he had left. 'I had to come out a minute. Some damn fool put the TV on and we heard that goddamned announcement those murdering bastards made. Before that we'd calmed Mother down a bit. It set her off again. You probably heard.'

'Yes, I did. Who's in there?'

'Mary, for one. We left someone with the kids and came on over. Then a lot of neighbours have been coming in; most are still here. I guess they mean well, but it isn't helping. If Dad were here he'd . . .' Wally stopped, forcing a wan smile. 'It's hard to get used to the idea he won't be around any more.'

'I've been feeling that way, too.' It was clear to Nim that Wally Jr was in no shape to take charge of what was happening in the house.

'Listen,' Nim said, 'it can't go on like this. Let's go in there. I'll talk to your mother and do the best I can. You and Mary start easing the others out.'

'Okay, that makes sense. Thanks, Nim.' Obviously, what Wally had needed was a lead.

There were perhaps ten people standing or seated in the living room as Nim and Wally went in. The room was bright and comfortable, normally spacious, but seemed crowded now. It was also hot, despite air conditioning. Several conversations were being conducted at the same time and the TV had been left on, contributing to a general hubbub. Ardythe Talbot was on a sofa, surrounded by several women, one of whom was Mary, Wally Jr's wife. The others Nim didn't recognize. Presumably they were the neighbours Wally had spoken of.

Though Ardythe was sixty at her last birthday – Nim and Ruth had attended a party to celebrate it – she remained a strikingly handsome woman with a good figure and a strong face only lightly marked with beginning lines of age. Her stylishly short auburn hair was streaked naturally with grey. Ardythe played tennis regularly and the effect showed in radiant good health. Today, though, her poise had crumbled. Her tear-stained face appeared drawn and old.

Ardythe was still speaking as she had been earlier, her voice choked, the words disjointed. But she stopped when she saw Nim.

'Oh, Nim.' She put out her arms and the others made way as he went to her, sat beside her on the sofa and held her. 'Oh, Nim,' she repeated. 'You heard the terrible thing that happened to Walter?'

'Yes, dear,' he said gently. 'I heard.'

Nim observed Wally, across the room, switch off the TV, then take his wife aside and speak to her quietly. Mary nodded. Immediately the two of them approached others, thanking them, ushering them out one by one. Nim continued to hold Ardythe, not speaking, trying to calm and comfort her. Soon the living room was quiet.

Nim heard the front door close behind the last of the departing neighbours. Wally and Mary, who had gone out to the hallway, came back. Wally ran a hand through his hair and beard. 'I could use a stiff scotch,' he announced. 'Anyone else?'

Ardythe nodded. So did Nim.

'I'll get them,' Mary said. She busied herself with glasses and mixes, then ashtrays, tidying the living room, removing its signs of recent occupancy. Mary was slim, gamine and businesslike.

Before her marriage to Wally she worked on the creative side of an advertising agency and still did freelance work while also caring for her family.

Ardythe was sitting up unaided now, sipping her scotch, some signs of composure returning. She said suddenly, 'I expect I look a mess.'

'No more than anyone would,' Nim assured her.

But Ardythe had gone to a mirror. 'Oh, my goodness!' She told the others, 'Have your drinks, I'll be back soon.' She left the living room, carrying her scotch, and they could hear her going upstairs. Nim reflected with wry amusement: few men are ever as resilient or strong as women.

Just the same, he decided, he would tell Wally first of Eric Humphrey's warning that the family should not view Walter's remains. He remembered, with a shudder, the chairman's words '. . . *virtually no skin left . . . Faces are unrecognizable.*' Mary had gone to the kitchen. While the two men were alone, as gently as he could and omitting details, Nim explained the situation.

The reaction was immediate. Wally tossed back the remainder of his scotch. With tears in his eyes he protested, 'Oh Christ! - it's bad enough to hear. I couldn't tell Mother that. You'll have to.'

Nim was silent, dreading what was to come.

Fifteen minutes later Ardythe returned. She had made up her face, rearranged her hair and changed from the dress she had been wearing into a smart blouse and skirt. While her eyes and demeanour revealed grief, superficially she was closer to her normal, attractive self.

Mary, too, had returned to the living room. This time Wally replenished the drinks and the four of them sat, uneasily at first, uncertain of what to say.

It was Ardythe who broke the silence.

She said firmly, 'I want to see Walter.' Then, turning to Wally, 'Do you know where your father has been taken, what . . . arrangements have been made?'

'Well . . . there's a . . .' Wally stopped, got up and kissed his mother, then, standing where he did not have to meet her eyes, continued, 'There's a problem, Mother. Nim is going to talk to you about it. Aren't you, Nim?'

Nim wished he were somewhere, anywhere, else.

'Mother, dear,' Wally said, still standing, 'Mary and I have to go home to the children for a while. We'll come back. And one of us will stay the night with you.'

As if she had not heard, Ardythe intoned, 'What problems? ... Why can't I see Walter? ... Someone tell me.'

Wally went out quietly, Mary following. Ardythe seemed unaware they had gone.

'Please ... Why can't I ... ?'

Nim took her hands and held them between his own. 'Ardythe, listen to me. Walter died suddenly. It was all over in less than a second. He didn't have time to know what was happening and there could have been no pain.' Nim hoped it was true. He went on, 'But because of what happened, he was disfigured.'

Ardythe moaned.

'Walter was my friend,' Nim persisted. 'I know how he thought. He wouldn't have wanted you to see him as he is now. He would have wanted you to remember him ...' He stopped, choked by his own emotion, not sure that Ardythe had heard or, even if she had, had understood. Once more they sat in silence.

More than an hour had gone by since Nim arrived.

'Nim,' Ardythe said at length. 'Have you had any dinner?'

He shook his head. 'There wasn't time. I'm not hungry.' He was having trouble adjusting to Ardythe's sudden changes of mood.

She got up. 'I'm going to make you something.'

He followed her into the compact, orderly kitchen which Walter Talbot had designed himself. Characteristically, Walter had first made a time and motion study of functions to be performed, then positioned everything for maximum convenience and a minimal need to move around. Nim seated himself at an island worktable, watching Ardythe, not interfering, reasoning she was better off with something to do.

She heated soup and served it in earthenware mugs, sipping her own while she put together an omelette, seasoned with chives and mushrooms. When she divided the omelette between them, Nim discovered he was hungry after all, and ate with enjoyment. Ardythe made an initial effort, then left most of her portion. They followed the meal with strong coffee which they took into the living room.

Speaking quietly and rationally, Ardythe said, 'I may insist on seeing Walter.'

'If you do,' Nim told her, 'no one can stop you. But I hope you won't.'

'Those people who planted the bomb, who killed Walter and the others. Do you think they'll be caught?'

'Eventually. But it's never easy when you're dealing with crazies. Because they aren't rational, it makes them harder to catch. But if they try something similar – which they probably will – the odds are on their being caught and punished.'

'I suppose I ought to care about them being punished. But I don't. Is that bad?'

'No,' Nim said. 'In any case, other people will take care of that.'

'Whatever happens, it can't change anything. It wouldn't bring Walter . . . or the others . . . back.' Ardythe mused. 'Did you know we were married thirty-six years? I should be grateful for that. It's more than many people have, and most of the time was good . . . Thirty-six years . . .' She began crying softly. 'Hold me, Nim.'

He put his arms around her and cradled her head on his shoulder. He could feel her crying, though not hysterically any longer. These were tears of farewell and acceptance, of memory and love; gentle and cleansing tears as the human psyche began its healing process – as old, unexplainable and wondrous as life itself.

Holding Ardythe, Nim became aware of a fragrant, pleasing perfume. He had not noticed it when they were close together earlier, and wondered when she had put it on. Probably when she went upstairs. He switched his thoughts away.

It was getting late, Nim realized. Outside it was fully dark, the only exterior lights from occasional passing vehicles. But the street was secluded and quiet, with traffic infrequent. Inside, the house had settled down, as houses do for the night. and was silent.

Ardythe stirred in Nim's arms. She had stopped crying and moved closer. He breathed the heady perfume once more. Then, to his consternation, he discovered his body becoming aroused, and an increasing awareness of Ardythe as a woman. He tried to divert his mind with other thoughts, to control and negate what was happening, but without success.

'Kiss me, Nim.' She had moved so their faces were close. Their lips touched, gently at first, then strongly; Ardythe's mouth was seductive, warm, demanding. As he felt sexual excitement surge in them both, he asked himself: *Can this be happening?*

'Nim,' she said softly, 'turn out the lights.'

He complied, a part of him urging: *Don't do it! Go! Leave now!* But even while despising himself, he knew he wouldn't leave, and that the inner voice was a token protest only.

There was plenty of room on the sofa. While he had turned out the lights, Ardythe had removed some of her clothing; he helped her with the rest and swiftly shed his own. As they reached out, then held each other, he found her eager, excited and experienced. Her fingers, travelling lightly, deftly, sought to please him, and succeeded. He responded in kind. Soon, Ardythe moaned, then cried aloud, 'Oh God, Nim! Don't wait any longer, please . . . please!'

He had a last, vague stirring of conscience and a sudden, dismaying notion that Wally Jr and Mary might return, as they had said they would, and walk in. Then that and all else dissolved as pleasure and passion engulfed him.

'You're troubled, aren't you?'

'Yes,' Nim admitted. 'Troubled as hell.'

It was an hour later. They had dressed and the lights were on. A few minutes ago Wally had phoned, announcing that he and Mary were on the way back and both would stay the night.

'Don't be.' Ardythe touched his arm lightly and gave a swift, shy smile. 'You've helped me more than you know.'

Nim's instincts told him she had left something unsaid: that the compatibility they had just shared was discovered rarely by two people and, in all probability, the experience would be repeated. If so, there was now a dual worry: not only had he behaved shamefully on the day of his good friend's death, but an additional complication had entered his own life – one he didn't need.

'I'd like to explain something,' Ardythe said. 'I loved Walter dearly. He was a sweet, kind, gentle man. We had fun together; he was always interesting to be with. Life without him . . . well, I can't begin to think about that yet. But Walter and I hadn't had sex together for a long time – it must be six or seven years. Walter simply couldn't manage it any more. That often happens to men, you know, much more than to women.'

Nim protested, 'I don't want to hear . . .'

'Whether you do or not, you're going to. Because *I* don't want you leaving here tonight all mixed up and miserable. I'll tell you something else, Nim. You didn't seduce me just now; I seduced you. And I knew what was going to happen, what I wanted to happen, long before you did.'

He thought: the perfume. It acted on him like an aphrodisiac. Could Ardythe really have intended it that way?

'When a woman is deprived of sex at home,' Ardythe went on firmly, 'she either manages or goes elsewhere. Well, I managed. I settled for what I had, which was a good man I still loved, and I didn't go elsewhere. But it didn't stop my wanting.'

'Ardythe,' Nim said, 'please . . .'

'No, I'm almost finished. Today . . . tonight . . . when I realized I'd lost everything, I wanted sex more than ever. Suddenly all that missing seven years swept over me. And you were here, Nim. I've always liked you, maybe a little more than "liked", and you were here when I needed you most.' She smiled. 'If you came to comfort me, you did. It's that simple. Don't make it more complicated, or feel guilt where there should be none.'

He sighed. 'If you say so, I won't.' It seemed an easy way to put conscience to rest. Perhaps too easy.

'I say so. Now kiss me once more, and go home to Ruth.'

He did as she said, and was relieved to be leaving before Wally and Mary arrived.

In the car, driving home, Nim pondered the complexities of his personal life. By comparison, the intricate conundrums of Golden State Power & Light seemed simple and preferable. At the top of his own immediate problem list were Ruth, their drifting-in-circles marriage, and now Ardythe. Then there were other women he had had affairs with from time to time, including a couple of recent ones still simmering. Those kinds of involvements seemed to happen to Nim without his seeking them. Or was he deluding himself there? Did he, in fact, search out entanglements, rationalizing later that they simply happened? Either way, for almost as long as he could remember, there had been no lack of sexual opportunities.

After his marriage to Ruth fifteen years ago, he had resolutely stayed a one-woman man – for about four years. Then an opportunity for extracurricular sex occurred, and he hadn't fought it.

Afterwards there had been still more opportunities – some the usual one-night stands, others that lasted enthusiastically for a while, then faded like bright stars dimming before extinction. At first Nim assumed he could keep his sexual philandering a secret from Ruth – the nature of his work with its heavy demands of time, plus irregular hours, helped make that possible. Probably it even worked for a while. Then common sense told him that Ruth, who was not only sensitive but shrewd, must realize what was happening. The extraordinary thing was that she never protested, simply seeming to accept. Illogically, Ruth's reaction – or, rather, the lack of it – galled him and still did. She *should* have minded, ought to have protested, perhaps shed angry tears. True, none of it might have made any difference, but Nim had asked himself : Wasn't his defection at least worth *that* much?

Something else Nim weighed from time to time was that news about his womanizing seemed to become known no matter how discreet he tried to be. There had been several examples of such leakages, the latest this afternoon. What was it Teresa Van Buren had said? *You've got a few things to learn about women, Nim – other than callisthenics in bed, and from rumours I hear, you're getting plenty of that.'* Obviously Teresa had more than rumours to go on or she would not have spoken so bluntly. And if Teresa knew, so did others in GSP & L.

Was Nim imperilling his own career? If so, was it worth it? Why did he do it, anyway? And was it for real or just a game?

'I'll be damned if I know,' Nim said aloud in the small closed car, and the remark seemed applicable to what he had been thinking about and a good deal more.

His own house, near the outskirts of the city, was silent when he arrived, with only a dim night-light in the downstairs hallway left burning. At Nim's urging, the Goldmans were a conservation-conscious family.

Upstairs he tiptoed into Leah's and Benjy's rooms. Both youngsters were sleeping soundly.

Ruth stirred as he came into their bedroom, and enquired sleepily, 'What time is it?'

He answered softly, 'A little past midnight.'

'How's Ardythe?'

'I'll tell you in the morning.'

The answer seemed satisfactory and Ruth returned to sleep.

Nim showered quickly, remembering that he should remove any traces of Ardythe's perfume, then climbed into his own twin bed. Moments later, surrendering to exhaustion from the pressures of the day, he was asleep himself.

6

'We are agreed, then,' J. Eric Humphrey said. His inquiring gaze swept over the nine men and two women seated with him around the conference room table. 'We are agreed we should accept Nim's planning report *in toto* and press at the highest level for immediate, urgent approval of the three projects – Tunipah coal-burning plant, Devil's Gate pumped storage, and opening the Fincastle geothermal field.'

As nods and murmured assent greeted the chairman's summation, Nim Goldman leaned back, for the moment relaxed. His presentation of future plans – the product of intense work by himself and many others – had been a gruelling one.

The group, GSP & L's management committee, included all officers reporting directly to the chairman. Officially, it rated second in authority to the Board of Directors. In fact, it was the real fount of policy decisions and power.

It was Monday afternoon and the meeting, which had carried over from the morning, had worked its way through a long agenda. A few around the table showed signs of weariness.

Five days had passed since the disastrous explosion at La Mission and the subsequent power failure. In the meantime there had been intensive studying of entrails – the cause and effect of what had happened, along with prognostications for the future. The inquisitions had continued late into every night and over the weekend. Also, since last Wednesday, because of cooler weather and some luck, no further blackouts had occurred. But one conclusion was inescapable. There would be other blackouts, far more serious, unless GSP & L began building more generating capacity soon.

'Soon' meant within the next year. Even then there could still be serious shortages ahead since a conventional fossil-fuelled power plant took five years to design and build, a nuclear plant six – preceded, in each case, by the four to six years it took to obtain the needed licences.

'As well as those three projects we've been talking about,' Oscar O'Brien, the utility's general counsel, said, 'I assume we'll still continue our nuclear licence applications.' O'Brien was a former government lawyer from Washington, a burly man, shaped like a bass fiddle, who smoked cigars continuously.

Across the table from him, Ray Paulsen, executive vice president of power supply, growled, 'We goddamn well better.'

Next to Paulsen, Nim Goldman doodled thoughtfully on a pad. He reflected: despite their mutual dislike, and disputes in many areas, the one thing he and Paulsen agreed on was a need for more power generation.

'Yes,' Eric Humphrey said, 'we shall keep our nuclear applications simmering. But we all know that since the Three Mile Island accident the chance of more nuclear plants being approved – for the next few years anyway – is slim.'

The chairman continued, 'Anticipating our decision here about the non-nuclear plants, I have already arranged a meeting with the Governor – in Sacramento, the day after tomorrow. I intend to urge him to bring pressure on all regulatory agencies to move swiftly. I shall also suggest, for each of the three projects, combined hearings before all regulatory bodies from whom we require approval, perhaps starting as early as next month.'

'It's never been done that way, Eric,' Stewart Ino, a senior vice president in charge of rates and valuation, objected. Ino was an old-timer at GSP & L; he had a chubby yeoman's face and with the addition of a ruff and velvet hat could have been a British beefeater. An expert on licensing procedures, he liked to follow them precisely. 'Separate hearings have always been the rule,' he added. 'To combine them would create complications.'

'Let the lousy bureaucrats worry about that,' Ray Paulsen told him. 'I'm for Eric's idea which would shove a live wire up their asses.'

'Three live wires,' someone said.

Paulsen grinned. 'Better still.'

Ino looked offended.

Ignoring the last exchange, Eric Humphrey observed, 'Let's

remember there are strong arguments in favour of exceptional action. Moreover, we shall never have a better time to press them. The power failure of last week showed clearly that a crisis can happen; therefore crisis methods are needed to counter it. Even in Sacramento I think they'll see that.'

'In Sacramento,' Oscar O'Brien said, 'all they see is politics, just as in Washington. And let's face it – the opponents of what we plan will use politics to the hilt, with Tunipah at the top of their hate list.'

There were reluctant murmurs of assent. Tunipah, as everyone around the table realized, could prove the most controversial of the three developments now being discussed. It was also, in several ways, the most vital of their plans.

Tunipah was a wilderness area near the California-Nevada border. It was neither inhabited – the nearest small town was forty miles distant – nor favoured by sportsmen or naturalists since it held little of interest for either. The region was difficult to get to and no roads, only a few trails, traversed it. For all these reasons Tunipah had been chosen carefully.

What Golden State Power & Light proposed to build at Tunipah was an enormous generating plant, capable of producing more than five million kilowatts of electricity – enough to supply six cities the size of San Francisco. The fuel to be used was coal. This would be transported by rail from Utah, seven hundred miles away, where coal was plentiful and relatively cheap. A rail link would be built – to the main line of the Western Pacific Railroad – at the same time as the plant.

Coal could be North America's answer to Arab oil. Coal deposits within the conterminous United States represent a third of the entire world's known supply and are more than enough to satisfy US energy needs for three centuries. Alaska is believed to have another two thousand years' supply. Admittedly, coal presented problems. Mining was one, air pollution another, though modern technologies were at work on both. At new electric utility plants in other states, smokestacks a thousand feet high, supplemented by electrostatic filters and scrubbers that removed sulphur from smokestack gases, were reducing pollution to acceptable levels. And at Tunipah, what pollution there was would be far removed from inhabited or recreation areas.

Something else Tunipah would do was to permit the closing

of some of GSP & L's older, oil-burning plants. This would further reduce dependence on imported oil and produce big cost savings, present and future.

Logic favoured the Tunipah project. But, as all public utilities had learned from experience, logic didn't rule, nor did the greater public good if a handful of determined objectors – no matter how warped or unqualified their judgements – decided otherwise. By the use of slow, procedural tactics applied with ruthless skill, a project like Tunipah could be so long delayed as to be, in reality, defeated. Those who consistently opposed any electric utility expansion made effective use of Parkinson's third law: *Delay is the deadliest form of denial.*

'Is there more discussion?' J. Eric Humphrey asked. Several of those around the conference table had begun stuffing papers into briefcases, assuming the meeting to be almost over.

'Yes,' Teresa Van Buren said. 'I'd like a nickel's worth.'

Heads turned towards the public relations vice president, her short, plump figure thrust forward to command attention. Her normally unruly hair was more or less tidy today, presumably in deference to the occasion, but she still wore one of her inevitable linen suits.

'Twisting the Governor's arm the way you plan, Eric, and stroking other egos around the state capital is okay,' she pronounced. 'I'm in favour of it. But it isn't enough, not nearly enough to achieve what we want, and here's the reason.'

Van Buren paused. Reaching down beside her seat, she produced two newspapers and spread them on the conference room table. 'This is this afternoon's *California Examiner* – an early edition I had sent in – and this one, this morning's *Chronicle-West*, which you've undoubtedly all seen. I've been through both papers carefully and there's not a word in either about last week's power outage. For one day, as we know, the subject was big news, the next day minor news; after that it disappeared. And what's true of the press is true of other media.'

'So what?' Ray Paulsen said. 'There's been other news. People lose interest.'

'They lose interest because no one keeps them interested. Out there' – Van Buren waved an arm in the general direction of the world beyond the conference room – 'out there the press and public think of an electric power shortage as a here-today-gone-tomorrow, short-term problem. Almost no one is considering the long-term effects of power shortages which *we* know are getting closer – drastically lower living standards, dislocation of industry, catastrophic unemployment. And nothing will change that outside, uninformed thinking unless we *make* it change.'

Sharlett Underhill, executive vice president of finance and the other woman at the table, asked, 'How do you *make* anybody think anything?'

'I'll answer that,' Nim Goldman said. He snapped down his pencil. 'One way is to start shouting the truth – the way things really are, not holding back – and to go on shouting loud and clear and often.'

Ray Paulsen said sardonically, 'In other words, you'd like to be on TV four times a week instead of twice?'

Nim ignored the interruption. He went on, 'We should, as company policy, keep on proclaiming what everyone at this table knows: that last week our peak load was twenty-two million kilowatts, and demand is growing by a million kilowatts a year. That, assuming the same growth rate, in three years we'll be short on reserves, in four years we'll have none. So how will we manage? The answer is: we won't. Any fool can see what's coming – three years from now, blackouts every time it's hot; and in six years, blackouts every summer day. We have *got* to get some new generators built and we have to tell the public the consequences of not building them.'

There was a silence which Van Buren broke. 'We all know every word of that is true, so why not say so? There's even an opportunity next week. Nim has been booked for Tuesday on *The Good Evening Show*, which has a big following.'

Paulsen grunted. 'Too bad I'll be out that night.'

'I'm not at all sure we should be that forthright,' Sharlett Underhill said. 'I need hardly remind everyone we have an application in process for a rate increase and we desperately need that extra revenue. I don't want to see our chances of getting it jeopardized.'

'Frankness is likely to improve our chances,' Van Buren said, 'not diminish them.'

The finance vice president shook her head. 'I'm not so sure. And something else I believe is that the kind of statements we're talking about, if made at all, should come from the chairman.'

'For the record,' Eric Humphrey put in mildly, 'I was asked to appear on *The Good Evening Show* and I deputed Nim. He seems to do that kind of thing quite well.'

'He'd do a whole lot better,' the PR vice president said, 'if we gave him *carte blanche* to issue some plain, ugly warnings instead of insisting on the "moderate line" we always do.'

'I'm still in favour of a moderate line.' This time the speaker was Fraser Fenton, who held the title of president, though his main responsibility was for the utility's gas operations. Fenton, thin, balding and ascetic, was another veteran.

'Not all of us,' he continued, 'accept your gloomy view, Tess, of what's ahead. I've been thirty-four years with this utility and I've seen problems come and go. I believe we'll get around the capacity shortage somehow . . .'

Nim Goldman interjected, 'How?'

'Let me finish,' Fenton said. 'Another point I want to make is about opposition. It's true that right now we encounter organized opposition to everything we try to do, whether it's build more plants, increase rates, or give stockholders a decent dividend. But I believe most, if not all of that – the opposition and consumerism – will pass. It's a fashion and a fad. Those involved will eventually become tired, and when that happens we'll go back to the way things used to be, when this utility and others did pretty much what they wanted. That's why I say we should continue taking a moderate line, and not stir up trouble and antagonism by alarming people needlessly.'

'I agree with all that,' Stewart Ino said.

Ray Paulsen added, 'Me, too.'

Nim's eyes met Teresa Van Buren's and he knew their thoughts were the same. Within the public utilities business, Fraser Fenton, Ino, Paulsen, and others like them represented a cadre of entrenched executives who had grown up in their jobs during easier times and refused to acknowledge that these were gone for ever. Mostly, such people attained their present eminence through seniority, never having been subject to the tough, sometimes cutthroat competition for advancement which was a norm in other industries. The personal security of the Fraser Fentons *et al* had become wrapped around them like a cocoon. The status quo was their holy grail. Predictably, they objected to anything they saw as rocking the boat.

There were reasons for this – often debated by Nim and other younger executives. One was the nature of a public utility – monopolistic, not subject to day-by-day competition in the market-place; this was why utilities like Golden State Power & Light sometimes resembled government bureaucracies. Secondly, utilities, through most of their history, had been in a strong seller's market, able to sell as much of their product as they could produce, the process helped along by abundant sources of cheap power. Only in recent years, as power sources became scarcer and more costly, had utility executives needed to face serious commercial problems and make hard, unpopular decisions. Nor, in older days, were they locked in combat with tough-minded, skilfully led opposition groups, including consumers and environmentalists.

It was these profound changes, the Nim Goldman types argued, which a majority of top level executives had failed to accept, or deal with realistically. (Walter Talbot, Nim remembered sadly, had been a notable exception.) The oldsters, for their part, regarded Nim and his kind as impatient, troublemaking upstarts and usually, since the older group comprised a majority, their point of view prevailed.

'I'll admit to being ambivalent,' J. Eric Humphrey told the group, 'on this question of should we, or shouldn't we, bore in harder with our public statements. My personal nature is against it, but at times I see the other side.' The chairman, smiling slightly, glanced at Nim. 'You were bristling just now. Anything to add?'

Nim hesitated. Then he said, 'Only this. When the serious blackouts begin – I mean the long-lasting and repeated blackouts a few years from now – we, the utilities, will be blamed, no matter what has, or hasn't, happened in the meantime. The press will crucify us. So will the politicians, doing their usual Pontius Pilate act. After that the public will blame us too, and say: Why didn't you warn us while there was still time? I agree with Teresa – that time is now.'

'We'll vote on it,' Eric Humphrey announced. 'A show of hands, please, for the harder approach we've just heard advocated.'

Three hands went up – Teresa Van Buren's, Nim's, and that of Oscar O'Brien, the general counsel.

'Against,' the chairman called.

This time the raised hands numbered eight.

Eric Humphrey nodded. 'I'll go with the majority, which means we continue what someone called our "moderate line".'

'And make goddamn sure,' Ray Paulsen cautioned Nim, 'you keep it moderate on those TV talk shows.'

Nim glared at Paulsen, but contained his anger, saying nothing.

As the meeting broke up, the participants divided into smaller segments – twos and threes – discussing their separate, special interests.

'We all need a few defeats,' Eric Humphrey told Nim cheerfully on the way out. 'A certain humbling from time to time is good.'

Nim avoided comment. Before today's meeting he had wondered if the old guard's *laissez-faire* viewpoint about public relations could be sustained after the events of last week. Now he had the answer. Nim wished, too, that the chairman had supported him. He knew that if the subject had been one on which Humphrey held strong views they would have prevailed, regardless of any vote.

'Come in,' the chairman said as they neared their adjoining offices down the hallway from the conference room. 'There's something I want you to handle.'

The chairman's office suite, while more spacious than others on the senior management floor, still conformed to a GSP & L policy of being relatively spartan. This was to impress on visitors that shareholders' and customers' money was spent on essentials, not frills. Nim, following custom, went to a lounge area containing several comfortable chairs. Eric Humphrey, after crossing to his desk to pick up a file, joined him.

Though it was bright daylight outside and windows of the suite commanded a view across the city, all blinds were drawn, with artificial lighting on. The chairman always evaded questions about why he worked this way, though one theory held that, even after thirty years, he missed the view of his native Boston and would accept no substitutes.

'I presume you've seen the latest report in here.' Humphrey indicated the file which was labelled:

PROPERTY PROTECTION DEPARTMENT
Subject: Theft of Power

'Yes, I have.'

'Obviously the situation's getting worse. I know in some ways it's a pinprick, but it makes me damned angry.'

'A twelve-million-dollar loss per year is a whopping pinprick,' Nim observed.

The report they were speaking of, by a department head named Harry London, described ways in which stealing of electric power and gas had become epidemic. The method of theft was through tampering with meters – usually by individuals, though there were indications that some professional service firms were involved.

Eric Humphrey mused, 'The twelve million figure is an estimate. It could be less, or perhaps a whole lot more.'

'The estimate is conservative,' Nim assured him. 'Walter Talbot believed that too. If you recall, the chief pointed out there was a two per cent gap last year between electric power we produced and the amount we were able to account for – billings to customers, company use, line losses, et cetera.'

It was the late chief engineer who had first sounded the alarm within GSP & L about theft of service. He, also, prepared a report – an early and thorough one which urged creation of a Property Protection Department. The advice was acted on. It was one more area, Nim thought, in which the chief's contribution would be missed.

'Yes, I do recall,' Humphrey said. 'That's an enormous amount of unaccounted-for electricity.'

'And the percentage is four times higher than two years ago.'

The chairman drummed fingers on his chair arm. 'Apparently the same is true with gas. And we can't just sit back and let it happen.'

'We've been lucky for a long time,' Nim pointed out. 'Power theft has been a worry in the East and Midwest far longer than it has been here. In New York last year Con Edison lost seventeen million dollars that way. Chicago – Commonwealth Edison – which sells less electricity than we do and no gas, set their loss at five to six million. It's the same in New Orleans, Florida, New Jersey ...'

Humphrey interrupted impatiently, 'I know all that.' He considered, then pronounced, 'All right, we'll intensify our own measures, if necessary increasing our budget for investigation. Regard this as your own over-all assignment, representing me.

Tell Harry London that. And emphasize I'm taking a personal interest in his department, and I expect to see results.'

7

'Some people around here have the misguided notion that stealing power is something new,' Harry London declared. 'Well, it isn't. Would you be surprised if I told you there was a recorded case in California over a century ago?' He spoke in the manner of a schoolmaster addressing a class, even though he had an audience of one – Nim Goldman.

'Most things don't surprise me; that does,' Nim said.

London nodded. 'Then get a load of this one.'

He was a short, craggy man with crisp speech which bordered on the pedantic when he set out to explain any subject, as he was doing now. A former master sergeant of Marines, with a Silver Star for gallantry in action, he had later been a Los Angeles police detective, then joined Golden State Power & Light five years ago as assistant chief of security. For the past six months Harry London had headed a new department – Property Protection – specially set up to deal with thefts of power, and during that time he and Nim had become good friends. The two men were in the department's makeshift quarters now – in London's office, one of a series of cramped glass cubicles.

'It happened in 1867 in Vallejo,' London said. 'The San Francisco Gas Company set up a plant there and the man in charge was an M. P. Young. One of Vallejo's hotels was owned by a guy named John Lee. Well, this Lee was caught cheating on his gas bills. What he'd done was put a bypass around his meter.'

'I'll be damned! That long ago?'

'Wait! That isn't the half of it. The gas company man, Young, tried to collect money from John Lee to pay for the gas which had been stolen. That made Lee so mad he shot Young and was later charged with assault and attempted murder.'

Nim said sceptically, 'Is all that true?'

'It's in California history books,' London insisted. 'You can look it up the way I did.'

'Never mind. Let's stick to here and now.'

'You read my report?'

'Yes. So did the chairman.' Nim repeated J. Eric Humphrey's decision about intensified action and his demand for results.

London nodded. 'You'll get results. Maybe as early as this week.'

'You mean Brookside?'

'Exactly.'

Brookside, a suburban community some twenty miles from the city centre, had been mentioned in the Property Protection Department report. A pattern of power theft cases had been discovered there and now a more thorough investigation was planned.

'D-day in Brookside,' Harry London added, 'is the day after tomorrow.'

'That's Thursday. I hadn't expected you could set things up so fast.'

The report had indicated, without specifying when, that a 'raid' on Brookside was planned. It would be spearheaded by the Property Protection staff, comprising London, his immediate deputy Art Romeo, and three assistants. They were to be supported by a contingent of other GSP & L employees – thirty specially trained meter readers, borrowed from Customer Service, plus a half-dozen service engineers and two photographers who would record any evidence on film.

The entire force would assemble downtown and be conveyed to Brookside by chartered bus. Accompanying them would be a radio van, to be used as the communications centre. Walkie-talkies would be issued to key people. A fleet of small vehicles would provide local shuttle service.

During the preceding day – 'D-day minus one' – the meter readers and engineers would be briefed on what was expected of them, though their actual destination would be kept secret.

On arrival at Brookside on D-day, the meter readers would begin house-to-house and business-to-business checks of electric and gas meters, searching for signs of tampering. They would also go to specific buildings, selected because of known theft patterns. Supermarkets, for example, were always prime suspects because electricity was their second largest operating cost (labour was the first) and many such businesses had cheated in the past. Thus all supermarkets in the area would be checked. As and when anything suspicious was located, the service engineers, backed up by Harry London's Property Protection men, would move in.

'The quicker you put something like this together, the less danger there is of leaks.' London grinned. 'In the Marines there were bigger jobs we did a whole lot faster.'

'Okay,' Nim said, 'I was just a dogface. But I'd like to be in on this operation.'

Although Nim's own military service had been brief, it gave him something of a common bond with Harry London. Immediately after college Nim was drafted and sent to Korea. There, a month after arrival and while his platoon was probing the enemy from an advanced position, they were strafed and bombed by American planes. (Afterwards the ghastly error was described in military double-talk as 'friendly fire.') Four US infantrymen were killed, others injured, including Nim, who sustained a perforated eardrum which became infected, leaving him permanently deaf on the left side. Soon after, he was sent home and quietly given a medical discharge, the Korean incident hushed up. Nowadays, most of Nim's colleagues and friends were aware they should sit on his right during conversations – the side of his good ear. But only a few knew exactly why. Harry London was one of the few.

'Be my guest on Thursday,' London said.

They arranged a rendezvous.

Afterwards they talked about the sabotage at La Mission which had killed Walter Talbot and the others. Although Harry London was not involved directly in the investigation, he and the utility's chief security officer were after-hours drinking cronies and exchanged confidences; also London's background as a police detective had given him contacts with law enforcement agencies which he kept operative. 'The county sheriff is working with the FBI and our own city police,' he informed Nim. 'So far all leads have run up against a brick wall. The FBI, which does most processing of evidence in this kind of case, believe they're looking for a new batch of kooks without police records, which makes everything harder.'

'How about the man in Salvation Army uniform?'

'That's being worked on, but there's a hundred ways they could have got the uniform, most not traceable. Of course, if they pull the same dodge again, that's something else. A lot of people will be alert and waiting.'

'You think they might?'

London shrugged. 'They're fanatics. Which makes them crazy-smart, brilliant in some ways, stupid in others. You never can tell. Often it just takes time. If I hear any rumbles I'll let you know.'

'Thanks.'

What he had just heard, Nim realized, was in essence what he had told Ardythe last Wednesday night. It reminded him that he should call Ardythe and perhaps go to her, soon. Nim had seen her once since Wednesday – briefly at Walter's funeral on Saturday morning, which many from GSP & L had attended. It had been, to Nim, a depressingly ritualistic occasion, supervised by an unctuous undertaker whom Walter Talbot would have detested. Nim and Ardythe had exchanged a few stilted words, but that was all.

Now he wondered: ought he to allow a 'decent' interval before telephoning Ardythe? Or was it hypocritical, at this stage, for him to consider decency at all?

He told Harry London, 'I'll see you on D-day.'

8

It would be another scorching day in that long, hot summer. That much was evident, even at 9am when Nim reached Brookside.

The D-day force had arrived an hour earlier. Its communications centre was set up on the parking lot of a conveniently central shopping plaza where a half-dozen of the utility's vehicles were clustered, identifiable by their distinctive orange and white colouring and the familiar GSP & L logo. Already the thirty meter readers had been driven to dispersal points. They were mostly young men, among them some college students working during the summer, and each was in possession of a batch of cards showing addresses where meters and related equipment were to be inspected. The cards were from a special computer printout last night. Normally the meter readers' job was simply to read numbers and report them; today they would ignore the numbers and search only for signs of power theft.

Harry London, emerging from the communications van, met Nim as he arrived. London appeared perky and cheerful. He wore a short-sleeved, military-style shirt and smartly creased tan slacks; his shoes were brightly shined. Nim removed his own suit coat and tossed it back into his Fiat. The sun had begun to bake the parking lot, sending heat waves upwards.

'We're getting results already,' London said. 'Five clear fraud cases in the first hour. Now our service guys are checking out three more.'

Nim asked, 'The first five – are they business or residential?'

'Four residential, one business, and that's a lulu. The guy's been stealing us blind, gas and electric both. Do you want to see?'

'Sure.'

London called into the communications van, 'I'll be in my car, with Mr Goldman. We're going to incident number four.'

As they drove away, he told Nim, 'I've already got two feelings. One, what we'll be seeing today is the tip of an iceberg. Two, in some cases we're up against professionals, maybe an organized ring.'

'Why do you think so?'

'Let me answer that after you've seen what I'm going to show you.'

'Okay.' Nim settled back, inspecting Brookside as they moved through it.

It was an affluent suburb, typical of many which mushroomed in the late 1950s and early sixties. Before then it was farmland; now the farms were gone, replaced by housing developments and businesses serving them. There was – at least, outwardly – no poverty in Brookside. Even small tract houses, in regimented rows, appeared well cared for, their handkerchief lawns manicured, paintwork fresh. Beyond this modest housing were several square miles of larger homes, including palatial mansions with three-car garages and separate service driveways. The community's stores, some in attractive tree-lined malls, displayed quality merchandise which reflected the area's prosperity. To Nim it seemed an unlikely locale for thefts of power.

As if reading his mind, Harry London offered, 'Things ain't always what they seem.' He turned the car away from the shopping area towards a gasoline garage complex which included pumps and a tunnel-type car wash. London stopped at the office and got out. Nim followed.

A GSP & L service truck was also parked. 'We've called for one of our photographers,' London said. 'Meanwhile the service guy is guarding the evidence.'

A man in grey coveralls walked towards them, wiping his hands on a rag. He had a spindly body, a fox-like face, and appeared worried. 'Listen,' he said, 'like I told you already, I don't know nothing about no . . .'

'Yes, sir, so you did.' London turned to Nim. 'This is Mr Jackson. He gave us permission to enter his premises to inspect the meters.'

'Now I'm not so sure I should've,' Jackson grumbled. 'Anyways I'm just the lessee here. It's another outfit owns the building.'

'But you own the business,' London said. 'And the gas and electric accounts are in your name. Right?'

'The way things are, the bank owns the goddamn business.'

'But the bank didn't interfere with your gas and electric meters.'

'I'm tellin' the truth.' The garageman's hands clutched the rag more tightly. 'I dunno who done it.'

'Yes, sir. Do you mind if we go in?'

The garageman scowled but didn't stop them.

London preceded Nim into the station office, then to a small room beyond, clearly used for storage. On the far wall were switches, circuit breakers, and meters for gas and electricity. A young man in GSP & L service uniform looked up as they came in. He said casually, 'Hi!'

Harry London introduced Nim, then instructed, 'Tell Mr Goldman what you found.'

'Well, the electric meter had the seal broken and was put in the way it is now – upside down.'

'Which makes the meter run backwards or stop,' London added.

Nim nodded, well aware of that simple but effective way to get free power. First, the seal on a meter was pried open carefully. After that, the meter – which was simply plugged in to slots behind it – could be lifted out, inverted, and replaced. From then on, as electricity was consumed, the meter would either reverse itself or stop entirely – if the first, the record of consumption would diminish instead of increasing as it should. Later – probably a few days before a power company meter reader was expected – the meter would be restored to normal functioning, with the disturbance of the seal carefully concealed.

Several power companies which had suffered this kind of theft countered it nowadays by installing newer-type meters which operated correctly whether upside down or not. Another prevention method was through elaborate locking rings which made meters non-removable, except with special keys. However, other ingenious ways of power theft existed; also there were still millions of older-type meters in use that could not accommodate locking rings, and they would cost a fortune to replace. Thus, through sheer numbers, plus the impossibility of inspecting all meters regularly, the cheaters held an advantage.

'The job on gas was fancier,' the serviceman said. He moved to a gas meter nearby and knelt beside it. 'Take a look here.'

Nim watched as, with one hand, the serviceman traced a pipe which emerged from a wall, then connected to the meter several feet away. 'This is the gas line coming in from outside.'

'From the street,' Harry London added. 'From the company main.'

Nim nodded.

'Over here' – the serviceman's hand moved to the far side of the meter – 'is a line to the customer's outlets. They use gas here for a big water heater, hot-air car dryers and for the stove and heater in an apartment upstairs. Every month that's a lot of gas. Now look at this – closely.' This time, using both hands, he fingered what appeared to be pipe joints where the two pipes he had pointed to disappeared into the wall. Around each the cement had been loosened, some of it now in a small pile on the floor.

'I did that,' the serviceman volunteered, 'to get a better look, and what you can see now is that those aren't ordinary joints. They're T-joints, connected to each other by another pipe, buried out of sight inside the wall.'

'An old-fashioned cheater's bypass,' London said, 'though this is the neatest one I've seen. What happens is that most of the gas used doesn't pass through the meter the way it should, but goes directly from the street to the appliances.'

'There's enough still goes through the meter to keep it operating,' the young serviceman explained. 'But gas flows where there's least resistance. There's some resistance in the meter, so most gas goes through that extra pipe – the freebie route.'

'Not any more,' London pronounced.

A pert young woman carrying cameras and equipment came in from outside. She inquired cheerfully, 'Somebody here want pictures?'

'Sure do.' London indicated the gas meter. 'That set-up first.' He told Nim, 'When we get a shot the way it is, we'll chip out the rest of the cement and expose the illegal pipe.'

The fox-faced garageman had been hovering in the rear. He protested, 'Hey, you guys can't break up no wall. This's my place.'

'I'll remind you, Mr Jackson, you gave us permission to come in and check on our company's equipment. But if you want to review your rights, and ours, I suggest you call your lawyer. I think you'll need one, anyway.'

'I don't need no lawyer.'

'That will be up to you, sir.'

'Mr Jackson,' Nim said, 'don't you realize the seriousness of all this? Tampering with meters is a criminal offence, and the photos we are taking can be evidence.'

'Oh, there'll be criminal prosecution all right,' London said, as if on cue. 'Though I will say that if Mr Jackson cooperates in two ways it might work out in his favour.'

The garageman looked at them suspiciously. 'What ways?'

As they talked, the photographer clicked away, shooting flash pictures of the gas meter, then moving to the electric one. The serviceman began loosening more cement, exposing more of the concealed pipe within the wall.

'The first thing you have to do,' London told Jackson, 'is pay for what you owe and what you stole. Since I was here the first time, I've been in touch with our Billing Department. Comparing recent bills with what your gas and electric charges used to be, they've come up with five thousand dollars owing. That includes a service charge for what we're doing today.'

The garageman paled; his mouth worked nervously. 'Jesus! It can't be that much. Why, it's only been . . .' He stopped.

'Yes?' Nim prompted. 'How long has it been since you began tampering with the meters?'

'If Mr Jackson tells us that,' London joined in, 'maybe he'd tell us who did the job on the gas meter. That's the second thing we'd look on as cooperation.'

The serviceman called over his shoulder, 'I'll tell you one thing for sure. Whoever did it was no amateur.'

London glanced at Nim. 'Remember what I told you? A lot of what we're seeing is professional work.' He returned to Jackson. 'How about that, sir? Feel like telling us who did it?'

The garageman scowled, but didn't answer.

London told him, 'When we've finished here, Mr Jackson, we'll be disconnecting your gas and electricity. They'll stay disconnected until the amount owing is paid.'

Jackson spluttered, 'Then how the hell do I run my business?'

'If it comes to that,' London retorted, 'how would we run ours if every customer was a cheat like you?' He asked Nim, 'Seen enough?'

'Too much,' Nim said. 'Let's go.'

Outside, London said, 'Ten will get you one, he's in hock too deep to pay what's owing. Doubt if he'll tell us who did the work either.'

As they got into the car, Nim asked, 'Can we prosecute and make it stick?'

The ex-policeman shook his head. 'I'd like to try, and we might even get a conviction. More likely, though, a court would insist we prove either that Jackson did the meter rigging, or knew about it. No way we can.'

'So in some ways it's a lost cause.'

'Some ways, maybe; not all. Word will get around; it probably has already, and that will scare a lot of other would-be Jacksons. Also remember, we've spread our net wide today. There'll be a lot more cheaters in it before sundown.'

'But only from Brookside.' Nim considered gloomily the enormous area which GSP & L served; within it Brookside was a single peanut in huge plantation.

A few minutes later they were back at the communications centre in the shopping plaza parking lot.

As Harry London had forecast, Brookside's D-day caught many meter-tampering offenders. By noon there were more than forty cases, either proved or suspected; it seemed likely there would be at least as many more during the afternoon. Some supermarkets were included in the bag; an entire local chain had been raided, with illegal installations found in five out of eight stores.

Nim stayed close to Harry London, observing, visiting the scene of some of the more interesting, ingenious violations.

During the late morning they had gone together to one of the trim tract houses Nim noted earlier. Two GSP & L vehicles were parked outside. One of the Property Protection staffers, a serviceman, and the same photographer as before were clustered around an exterior electric meter near the side door.

'Nobody's at home,' London said in explanation, 'but downtown they checked on the guy who lives here, and it seems he's a tool-and-die maker. It figures. Take a look at this.' As the others moved aside, London pointed to a tiny hole in the glass cover of the meter. A small piece of stiff wire protruded through it. Inside the meter the wire extended to a central metal disc which normally revolved as electricity was consumed.

'That wire, which shouldn't be there, stops the disc from turning,' London said.

Nim nodded his understanding. 'So the meter doesn't record, even though current goes on flowing.'

'Right. But stopping the disc does no harm, so when the wire's removed, everything's back the way it should be.'

'Except for that little hole.'

'You'd never notice it,' the serviceman behind them said, 'unless you were looking hard. My guess is, the guy used a jeweller's drill to make the hole, which is why the glass didn't break. Damn clever.'

'He won't feel so clever when he gets his next bill,' London said. 'Besides which, we'll watch the house tonight. More than likely the neighbours will tell about us being here, which will make him nervous and he'll want to take out that wire. When

60

he does, and if we catch him at it, we can make a prosecution stick.'

They left while the photographer was taking close-ups of the incriminating hole and wire.

At the communications centre, reports of other discoveries continued to flow in. An even more ingenious power thief had penetrated the heart of his electric meter, apparently filing off several teeth from a shaft gear which turned the meter recording disc. This had the effect of slowing the disc and reducing recorded consumption by approximately half. The downtown Billing Department, searching their records, estimated the cheating had gone on for three years, undetected.

In another instance a customer had adroitly switched meters. Somehow he had obtained an extra electric meter – Harry London suspected it was stolen – and substituted it for the regular meter supplied by GSP & L. Obviously the customer left his 'private' meter in place for a portion of each billing period, during which any electricity used was 'free'.

Though gas meters were considered more difficult to tamper with, this had not deterred some ambitious freeloaders. As London put it, 'Disconnecting or connecting a gas meter takes some plumbing skill but not much. A do-it-yourselfer can catch on fast.'

One such do-it-yourselfer, a meter reader found, had removed his gas meter entirely, filling the gap with a length of rubber hose. It was a dangerous theft method, but effective. Presumably the meter was left disconnected for part of each month, then replaced near the time a regular meter reading was expected.

Another offender – a businessman owning several adjacent stores which he leased to others – had acted similarly, except his gas meter was reversed, with its face turned towards the wall, causing it to run backwards. It was here the only violent incident of the day erupted. The businessman, enraged at being discovered, attacked the company serviceman with a pipe wrench and beat him badly. The serviceman was later taken to the hospital with a broken arm and nose, the businessman to jail where he faced assault and other charges.

One facet of the many cases being uncovered puzzled Nim. He told Harry London, 'I thought our billing computers were programmed to signal warnings of abrupt changes in any customer's consumption.'

'They are, and they do,' London acknowledged. 'Trouble is, people are getting wise to computers, learning to outwit them. It isn't hard. If you steal power and have the sense to reduce your bills gradually – a little the first month, then a little more every month after that, instead of a big reduction all at once – a computer will never pick it up.'

'Any way you look at it, we're on the losing side.'

'Maybe right now. But that will change.'

Nim was less sure.

Perhaps the most bizarre episode occurred at mid-afternoon when London received a message at the communications centre, calling him to an address a mile or so away.

The house, they saw on arrival, was large and modern; it had a landscaped garden and a long curved drive in which a shiny Mercedes was parked. The ubiquitous orange and white GSP & L vehicles were assembled on the road outside.

The same young serviceman who had been at the garage complex this morning approached London's car as it pulled up. 'Problems,' he announced. 'Need some help.'

'What kind of problems?'

One of the Property Protection staffers, who had joined them, said, 'The woman inside is threatening to turn a dog loose on us. It's a big German Shepherd. She says her husband's a doctor, a big wheel in the community, and they'll sue the company if we cause them any trouble.'

'What brought you here?'

The serviceman answered. 'One of the meter readers – a sharp college kid – reported a suspicious wire. He was right. I took a look behind the electric meter, and the pot strap's been dropped, with two wires bridging it. I traced the wires to a switch in the garage – there was no one around and the garage door was open. That's when the woman showed up with the dog.'

Nim looked puzzled. London ordered, 'Explain to Mr Goldman.'

'At the back of some types of meter there's a "potential strap",' the serviceman said. 'If it's disconnected – "dropped" – it breaks a circuit so the meter stops registering. But put a switch across, in place of the pot strap, and the meter can be turned on and off whenever you want.'

'And that's been done here?'

'Sure has.'

Nim cautioned, 'You're absolutely certain?'

'I'll swear to it.'

The Property Protection man added, 'I saw it, too. There isn't any doubt.' He consulted a notebook. 'The customer's name is Edgecombe.'

'Okay,' London said, 'to hell with the dog! Call for a photog, and let's try to get evidence.'

They waited while the serviceman used a radio transmitter in his truck, then Harry London led the small procession up the driveway. As they neared the house, a tall, handsome woman, probably in her forties, emerged through the front door. She was wearing blue linen slacks and a matching silk shirt; long, dark brown hair was tied back with a scarf. Beside her was a German Shepherd, growling and straining on a leash which the woman held.

She announced coldly, 'I warned you men that if you continue trespassing I'll release this dog and you can take the consequences. Now get off this property!'

'Madam,' London said firmly, 'I caution you to hang on to that dog or tie it up. I'm a security officer for Golden State Power & Light' – he produced a badge – 'and this is Mr Goldman, a vice president of the company.'

'Vice presidents don't impress me,' the woman snapped. 'My husband knows the president of your company well, *and* the chairman.'

'In that case,' Nim told her, 'I'm sure he'll appreciate that everyone here today is simply doing his job. You are Mrs Edgecombe?'

She answered haughtily, 'Yes.'

'Our Service Department has reported you have an illegal installation across your electric meter.'

'If there is, we know nothing about it. My husband's an important orthopaedic surgeon, and he's operating today or I'd call him to deal with your impertinence now.'

For all the bravado, Nim thought, there was a hint of nervousness in the woman's eyes and voice. London caught it, too. 'Mrs Edgecombe,' he said, 'we want to take photographs of the electric meter and some wires behind it; they lead to a switch in your garage. We'd appreciate it if you'd give us permission.'

'And if I won't?'

'Then we'll seek a court order. But I should point out in that case everything will become a matter of public record.'

The woman hesitated and Nim wondered if she realized Harry London was largely bluffing. By the time a court order was obtained the evidence could have been destroyed. But the exchange had flustered her. 'That won't be necessary,' she conceded. 'Very well, do what you must, but be quick about it.'

'Just one other thing, madam,' London said. 'When we're finished here, your electricity will be disconnected until the arrears, which our Billing Department will estimate, are paid.'

'That's ridiculous! My husband will have plenty to say about *that*.' Mrs Edgecombe turned away, fastening the dog's leash to a steel ring in the wall. Nim observed that her hands were trembling.

'Why do they do it – people like that?' Nim posed the question softly, asking it of himself as much as Harry London. They were in London's car, headed once more for the shopping plaza where Nim would retrieve his own car, then drive downtown. He had seen more than enough of Brookside, he decided, and enough of power thievery to grasp truly, for the first time, the size and hydra-headed nature of the beast.

'There's lots of reasons why they do it,' London answered. 'Where we've just been, and at the other places, too. For one thing, people talk. They like to boast about how smart they are, beating a big outfit like Golden State Power. And while they're talking, others listen, then do the same thing later.'

'You think that explains epidemics like we've seen today?'

'It's some pieces in the puzzle.'

'And the rest?'

'Some of it's crooked tradesmen – the ones I really want to catch. They put the word around that they'll do the meter fixing – at a price. It all sounds easy, and people go along.'

Nim said doubtfully, 'That still doesn't explain that last place. The wealthy doctor – an orthopaedic surgeon, one of the highest paid specialties. And you saw his wife, the house. *Why?*'

'I'll tell you something I learned as a cop,' London said. 'Don't let appearances fool you. Plenty of people with big incomes and flashy houses are deep in debt, struggling to stay afloat, to save a buck wherever they can, and not too fussy about how. I'll bet the same thing's true of this whole place, Brookside. And look at it this way : not so long ago utility bills didn't amount to much; but now bills are big and getting bigger, so some who wouldn't cheat before, because it wasn't worth it, have changed their minds. The stakes are higher; they'll take the risk.'

Nim nodded agreement, adding, 'And most public utilities are so huge and impersonal, people don't equate theft of power with other kinds of stealing. They're not as critical – the way they would be about burglary or purse snatching.'

'I've done a lot of thinking about that part of it. I believe the whole thing's bigger.' London stopped the car while waiting for a traffic light to change. When they were moving again he continued, 'The way I see it, most people have decided the system stinks because our politicians are corrupt, in one way or another, so why should ordinary Joes punish themselves by always being honest? Okay, they say, one bunch got flushed out with Watergate, but the new people, who were so damned righteous before they got elected, are doing the same crooked things – political payoffs and worse – now that they're in power.'

'That's a pretty depressing viewpoint.'

'Sure it is,' London said. 'But it explains a lot that's happening, and not just what we've seen today. I mean the crime explosion, all the way from big crime down to petty larceny. And I'll tell you something else : there are days – this is one – when I wish I was back in the Marines where everything seemed simpler and cleaner.'

'It wouldn't now.'

London sighed. 'Maybe.'

'You and your people did a good job today,' Nim said.

'We're in a war.' Harry London pushed aside his seriousness and grinned. 'Tell your boss – the commander-in-chief – we won a skirmish, and we'll win him some more.'

9

'At the risk of inflating your ego,' Ruth Goldman said across the breakfast table, 'I'll tell you you were pretty good on TV last night. More coffee?'

'Yes, please.' Nim passed his cup. 'And thanks.'

Ruth lifted the percolator and poured; as always, her movements were easy, graceful and efficient. She had on an emerald green housecoat in vivid contrast to her neatly combed black hair, and her small, firm breasts were attractively visible as she leaned forward; when Nim and Ruth were courting he had referred to them fondly as 'half-pint specials'. At this moment her face had the merest trace of make-up, exactly the right amount, complementing a milk-and-roses complexion. No matter how early it was, Ruth always looked naturally impeccable. Nim, who had seen many other women in their morning-after *déshabillé*, supposed he should be grateful.

It was Wednesday. Almost a week had passed since D-day at Brookside. Because he had been unusually tired – a result of long work hours and pressure over several weeks, culminating in last evening's session in a hot TV studio under lights – Nim had slept late this morning – late for him – until 8:30. Leah and Benjy had left for an all-day recreation programme before he came down, and now he was having a leisurely breakfast with Ruth, something which happened rarely. Nim had already telephoned his office to say he would not be at work until midmorning.

'Leah stayed up to watch *The Good Evening Show*,' Ruth said. 'Benjy wanted to, but fell asleep. Children aren't apt to say so, but they're both quite proud of you, you know. In fact they idolize you. Whatever you say, it's as if it came from God.'

'I like this coffee,' Nim said. 'Is it a new brand?'

Ruth shook her head. 'It's because you're not drinking it on the run. Did you hear what I said about Leah and Benjy?'

'Yes, and I was thinking about it. I'm proud of the kids too.' He chuckled. 'Is this my day for compliments?'

'If you're wondering if I want something from you, I don't.'

Except I'd like us to have breakfast this way more often.'

He said, 'I'll work on it.' He wondered if Ruth was being especially agreeable because, like himself, she sensed the gap which had been growing between them of late – the gap created by his own indifference and, more recently, by Ruth's mysterious pursuit of some private interest, whatever that might be. Nim tried to remember, but couldn't, when they had last made love. Why was it, he speculated, that a man could lose sexual interest in his own attractive wife, yet desire other women? He supposed the answer was familiarity, along with an urge for fresh territory, new conquests. Just the same, he thought guiltily, he should do something about sex with Ruth. Perhaps tonight.

'There were a couple of times on that TV show when you looked angry, ready to blow,' she said.

'But I didn't. I remembered the stupid rules.' It wasn't necessary to explain the management committee's 'moderate line' decision. He had told Ruth about it the same day it happened and she was sympathetic.

'Birdsong was baiting you, wasn't he?'

'The son-of-a-bitch tried.' Nim scowled, remembering. 'It didn't work.'

Davey Birdsong, who headed an activist consumer group called 'power & light for people', had been on the TV talk show too. Birdsong had made caustic comments about Golden State Power & Light, ascribing the basest motives to everything the company did. He had implied that Nim's personal objectives were no better. He also attacked GSP & L's latest application for an increase in rates, on which a decision was due soon. Despite all these provocations, Nim had kept his cool, reluctantly staying within the guidelines he had been given.

'This morning's *Chronicle* says Birdsong's group, as well as the Sequoia Club, will oppose the plan to develop Tunipah.'

'Let me see.'

She passed the paper. 'It's on page seven.'

That was something else about Ruth. Somehow she managed to stay a jump ahead of most others in keeping herself informed. It was characteristic that, as well as preparing breakfast, she had already been through the *Chronicle-West*.

Nim riffled pages and found the item. It was brief and told

him no more than Ruth had done already. But it gave him the idea for a course of action which made him impatient to be at his desk. He gulped the rest of his coffee and stood up.

'Will you be home for dinner tonight?'

'I'll try to be.' As Ruth smiled gently, he remembered how many times he had said the same thing, then for some reason failed to show. Irrationally, as he had in his car the evening he had gone to Ardythe's, he wished that once in a while Ruth would be less patient. He asked her, 'Why don't you blow up occasionally? Get mad?'

'Would it make any difference?'

He shrugged, not knowing what to make of her response, nor how to answer.

'Oh, there is one thing. Mother phoned yesterday. She and Dad would like us to go over for dinner a week from Friday and take Leah and Benjy.'

Inwardly Nim groaned. Going to the home of the Neubergers, Ruth's parents, was like entering a synagogue; they proclaimed their Jewishness in myriad ways. The food was always announced pointedly as kosher; there were reminders that the Neubergers kept two separate sets of utensils and crockery, one each for flesh and dairy food. There would be a prayer over bread and wine before dinner as well as a ceremony over washing hands. After dinner would be solemn prayers which the Neubergers, in Eastern European tradition, referred to as 'benching'. If there were meat at table, Leah and Benjy would not be permitted to drink milk, as they liked to do at home. Then there would be the not-so-subtle pressures, the wondering aloud why Nim and Ruth failed to observe the Sabbath and holy days; glowing descriptions of bar mitzvahs the Neubergers had attended, along with the implication that, of course, Benjy would attend a Hebrew school so his bar mitzvah would take place when he reach thirteen. And later at home, because the children were the ages they were, and curious, there would be questions for Nim to answer, questions he wasn't ready for because of the ambivalence within himself.

Ruth invariably kept quiet at such times, though he wondered occasionally if her silence wasn't really an alliance with her parents against him. Fifteen years ago, when Ruth and Nim were married, Ruth made clear she didn't care one way or the other about Jewish observances; it was an obvious reaction to the Orthodox strictness of her home. But had she changed? Was Ruth, beneath the surface, a traditional Jewish mother, wanting for Leah and Benjy all the trappings her parents' faith demanded? He recalled what she had said a few minutes ago about himself and the children. *In fact they idolize you. Whatever you say, it's as if it came from God.* Were the words an artful reminder of his own Jewish responsibility, a silken nudge towards religion? Nim had never made the mistake of taking Ruth's gentleness at its face value; beneath it, he realized, was as much real strength as any person could have.

But apart from all that, Nim knew there was no valid reason not to go to Ruth's parents, as she asked. It didn't happen often. And Ruth demanded very little of him, ever.

'Okay,' he said. 'Next week's pretty clear. When I get to the office I'll make sure about Friday and phone you.'

Ruth hesitated, then said, 'Don't bother doing that. Just tell me tonight.'

'Why?'

Again a second's hesitation. 'I'm leaving right after you've gone. I'll be out all day.'

'What's happening? Where are you going?'

'Oh, here and there.' She laughed. 'Do you tell *me* everywhere you go?'

So there it was again. The mystery. Nim felt a stab of jealousy against the unknown, then rationalized: Ruth had a point. As she had reminded him, there was plenty he didn't tell *her*.

'Have a good day,' he said. 'I'll see you this evening.'

In the hallway, he put his arms around her and they kissed. Her lips were soft; her figure beneath the housecoat felt good. *What a damn fool I am*, he thought. Yes, definitely, sex tonight.

10

Despite his haste in leaving home, Nim drove downtown at a leisurely pace, avoiding the freeway and using quiet streets. He

69

employed the time to think about the Sequoia Club, mentioned in this morning's *Chronicle-West*.

Though it was an organization which frequently opposed the programmes of GSP & L, and sometimes thwarted them, Nim admired the Sequoia Club. His reasoning was simple. History showed that when giant industrial concerns like Golden State Power & Light were left to their own devices, they paid little or no heed to protecting the environment. Therefore a responsible restraining force was needed. The Sequoia Club filled that role.

The California-based club had achieved a national reputation for skill and dedication in fights to preserve what remained of the natural unspoiled beauty of America. Almost always its methods were ethical, its arguments judicious and sound. True, the club had critics, but few failed to accord it respect. One reason was the Sequoia Club's leadership, which, through its eighty years of existence, had been of the highest calibre, a tradition which the incumbent chairman – a former atomic scientist, Laura Bo Carmichael – was continuing. Mrs Carmichael was able, internationally respected and, incidentally, a friend of Nim's.

He was thinking about her as he drove.

What he would do, he decided, was make a direct personal appeal to Laura Bo Carmichael concerning Tunipah and the other two power plants which Golden State Power proposed to build. Perhaps, if he argued the urgent need convincingly, the Sequoia Club might not oppose the projects or at least would be moderate in opposition. He must arrange a meeting as soon as possible. Preferably today.

Nim had been driving automatically, paying little attention to street names. Now he noticed, at an arterial stop, that he was at the intersection of Lakewood and Balboa. It reminded him of something. What?

Suddenly he remembered. The day of the explosion and power failure two weeks ago, the chief dispatcher had produced a map showing life-sustaining equipment in use in private homes. Coloured circles on the map denoted kidney dialysis machines, oxygen generating units, iron lungs and similar apparatus. At Lakewood and Balboa a red circle had warned of a person dependent on an iron lung or some other kind of powered respirator. The equipment was in an apartment building. For some reason the memory had stayed with Nim; so had the user's name – Sloan. At the time, he recalled, he had looked at the small red circle and wondered what Sloan was like.

There was only one apartment house at the intersection – an eight-storey, white stucco building, modest in design but, from its outward appearance, well maintained. Nim's car was along-side it now. A small forecourt contained several parking spaces, two unoccupied. On impulse, Nim turned in, wheeling the Fiat into one of the empty places. He got out and approached the apartment house entrance.

Above a series of mailboxes was a score of names, among them *K. Sloan*. Nim pressed a button beside the name.

Moments later the front door opened. A wizened old man appeared, wearing baggy trousers and a windbreaker. He looked like an ancient squirrel as he peered at Nim through thick lenses. 'You ring Sloan?'

'Yes, I did.'

'I'm the janitor. Rings down my place, too.'

'Can I see Mr Sloan?'

'Ain't no Mr Sloan.'

'Oh.' Nim pointed to the mailbox. 'Is it Mrs Sloan, then? Or Miss?' Unaccountably he had assumed Sloan to be a man.

'Miss Sloan. Karen. Who're you?'

'Goldman.' Nim showed a GSP & L identification card. 'Am I correct in believing Miss Sloan is an invalid?'

'You could be. Except she don't like being called that.'

'How should I describe her, then?'

'Disabled. She's a quadriplegic. Know the difference between that and para?'

'I think so. A paraplegic is paralysed from the waist down, a quadriplegic through the whole body.'

'That's our Karen,' the old man said. 'Been that way since she was fifteen. You want to see her?'

'Do you know if it's convenient?'

'Soon find out.' The janitor opened the front door wider. 'Come in. This way.'

A small lobby matched the building's exterior; it was simple and clean. The old man led the way to an elevator, motioned Nim inside, then followed. As they ascended he volunteered, 'Place ain't the Ritz. But we try to keep her shipshape.'

'That shows,' Nim said. The interior brass of the elevator gleamed and its machinery hummed smoothly.

They got out on the sixth floor. The janitor led the way and stopped before a door while he selected a key from a large bunch. He opened the door, knocked, then called out, 'It's Jiminy. Brung a visitor for Karen.'

'Come in,' a new voice said, and Nim found himself facing a short, sturdy woman with a dark skin and Hispanic features. She wore a pink nylon smock similar to a nurse's uniform.

'You selling something?' The question was asked cheerfully, without hostility.

'No. I was just passing and . . .'

'Never mind. Miss Sloan likes visitors.'

They were in a small, bright vestibule which opened onto a kitchen on one side and what appeared to be a living room on the other. In the kitchen, cheerful yellows and whites predominated; in the living room the decor was yellow and green. Part of the living room was out of sight and from it a pleasant voice called, 'Come in – whoever you are.'

'Leave you now,' the janitor said from behind Nim. 'Got things to do.'

As the outer door closed, Nim stepped inside the living room.

'Hello,' the same voice said. 'What do you know that's new and exciting?'

Long afterwards, and through the months ahead when fateful events unfolded like succeeding tableaux of a drama, Nim would remember this moment – the first in which he ever saw Karen Sloan – in sharply vivid detail.

She was a mature woman, but appeared young and was extraordinarily beautiful. Nim guessed her age as thirty-six; later he would learn she was three years older. Her face was long with perfectly proportioned features – full, sensuous lips, now opened in a smile, wide blue eyes appraising Nim with frankness, and a pert nose, suggesting mischief. Her skin was flawless and seemed opalescent. Long blonde hair framed Karen Sloan's face; parted in the middle, it fell to her shoulders, with golden highlights glinting in a shaft of sunlight. Her hands were on a padded lapboard, the fingers long, nails manicured and shining. She wore an attractive light blue dress.

And she was in a wheelchair. A bulge in her dress showed that a respirator was beneath it, breathing for her. A tube, emerging below the dress hemline, was connected to a suitcase-like device secured to the rear of the chair. The respirator mechanism emitted a steady hum along with a hiss of air, inward and out, at the normal pace of breathing. The chair's electric components were connected by a cord to a wall power outlet.

'Hello, Miss Sloan,' Nim said. 'I'm the electric man.'

The smile widened. 'Do you work on batteries or are you plugged in too?'

Nim grinned in response, a trifle sheepishly, and uncharacteristically he had a moment's nervousness. He wasn't sure what he had expected but, whatever it was, this exquisite woman before him was completely different. He said, 'I'll explain.'

'Please do. And won't you sit down?'

'Thank you.' He chose a soft armchair. Karen Sloan moved her head slightly, putting her mouth to a plastic tube extending on a gooseneck. She blew softly into the tube and at once her wheelchair swung around so she was facing him directly.

'Hey!' he said. 'That's a neat trick.'

'I can do lots more. If I sip instead of blow, the chair moves backwards.' She showed him while he watched, fascinated.

'I'd never seen that,' he told her. 'I'm amazed.'

'My head is the only part of me I can move.' Karen said it matter-of-factly, as if speaking of a minor inconvenience. 'So one learns to do some necessary things in unusual ways. But we got sidetracked; you were going to tell me something. Please go on.'

'I started to explain why I came,' Nim said. 'It all began two weeks ago, the day we had the power failure. I saw you as a small red circle on a map.'

'Me – on a map?'

He told her about the Energy Control Center and GSP & L's watchfulness over special power users, like hospitals and private homes with life-sustaining equipment. 'To be honest,' he said, 'I was curious. That's why I dropped in today.'

'That's nice,' Karen said. 'To be thought about, I mean. I do remember that day – well.'

'When the power went off, how did you feel?'

'A little frightened, I suppose. Suddenly my reading light went off and other electrical things stopped. Not the respirator, though. That switches over to battery right away.'

The battery, Nim observed, was a twelve-volt type, as used in automobiles. It rested on a tray, also fixed to the wheelchair at the rear, below the respirator mechanism.

'What you always wonder,' Karen said, 'is how long the power will be off, and how long the battery will last.'

'It ought to be good for several hours.'

'Six and a half when fully charged – that's if I use the respirator only, without moving the chair. But when I go out shopping or visiting, as happens most days, I use the battery a lot and it gets run down.'

'So if a power cut happened, then . . .'

She finished the sentence for him. 'Josie – that's who you met coming in – would have to do something quickly.' Karen added knowledgeably, 'The respirator draws fifteen amps, the wheelchair – when it's in motion – another twenty.'

'You've learned a lot about the equipment.'

'If your life depended on it, wouldn't you?'

'Yes, I expect I would.' He asked her, 'Are you ever alone?'

'Never. Josie is with me most of the time, then two other people come in to relieve her. Also, Jiminy, the janitor, is very good. He helps with callers, the way he did with you.' Karen smiled. 'He doesn't let people in unless he's sure they're okay. You passed his test.'

They went on chatting easily, as if they had known each other a long time.

Karen, Nim learned, had been stricken with poliomyelitis just one year before the Salk vaccine went into widespread use in North America and, with Sabin vaccine a few years later, wiped polio from the landscape. 'My bug bit too soon,' Karen said. 'I didn't get under the wire.'

Nim was moved by the simple statement. He asked, 'Do you think about that one year much?'

'I used to – a lot. For a while I cried over that one-year difference. I'd ask: Why did *I* have to be one of the last few? And I'd think: If only the vaccine had come just a little sooner, everything would have been different. I'd have walked, danced, been able to write, use my hands . . .'

She stopped, and in the silence Nim could hear the ticking of a clock and the soft purr of Karen's respirator. After a moment she went on, 'Then I got to telling myself: wishing won't change anything. What happened, happened. It can't be undone, ever.

So I started making the best of what there was, living a day at a time, and when you do that, if something unexpected happens, you're grateful. Today *you* came.' She switched on her radiant smile. 'I don't even know your name.'

When he told her, she asked, 'Is Nim for Nimrod?'

'Yes.'

'Isn't there something in the Bible . . . ?'

'In Genesis.' Nim quoted, *'Cush also begat Nimrod who was the first man of might on earth. He was a mighty hunter by the grace of the Lord.'* He remembered hearing the words from his grandfather, Rabbi Goldman. The old man had chosen his grandson's name – one of the few concessions to the past that Nim's father, Isaac, had allowed.

'Are *you* a hunter, Nim?'

On the point of answering negatively, he remembered what Teresa Van Buren had said not long ago: *'You're a hunter of women, aren't you?'* Perhaps, he thought, if circumstances had been different, he would have hunted this beautiful woman, Karen. Selfishly he, too, felt sad about that year-too-late vaccine.

He shook his head. 'I'm no hunter.'

Later, Karen told him that for twelve years she had been cared for in hospitals, much of that time in an old-fashioned iron lung. Then, more modern, portable equipment was developed, making it possible for patients like herself to live away from institutions. At first she had gone back to live with her parents, but that hadn't worked. 'It was too much of a strain on all of us.' Then she moved to this apartment where she had been for nearly eleven years.

'There are government allowances which pay the costs. Sometimes it's tight financially, but mostly I manage.' Her father had a small plumbing business and her mother was a salesclerk in a department store, she explained. At the moment they were trying to accumulate money to buy Karen a small van which would increase her mobility. The van, which Josie or someone from Karen's family would drive, would be adapted to contain the wheelchair.

Although Karen could do almost nothing for herself, and had to be washed, fed, and put to bed by someone else, she told Nim she had learned to paint, holding a brush in her mouth. 'And I can use a typewriter,' she told him. 'It's electric and I work it with a stick in my teeth. Sometimes I write poetry. Would you like me to send you some?'

'Yes, please. I'd like that.' He got up to go and was amazed to discover he had been with Karen more than an hour.

She asked him, 'Will you come again?'

'If you'd like me to.'

'Of course I would – Nimrod.' Once more the warm, bewitching smile. 'I'd like to have you as a friend.'

Josie showed him out.

The image of Karen, her breathtaking beauty, warm smile and gentle voice, stayed with Nim through the remainder of the drive downtown. He had, he thought, never met anyone quite like her. He was still thinking of her as he left his car in the parking garage of Golden State Power & Light's headquarters building, three floors down from street level.

An express elevator, accessible only with a key, operated from the parking garage to the senior executive offices on the twenty-second floor. Nim used his key – a status symbol at GSP & L – and rode up alone. On the way, he remembered his decision to make a personal appeal to the Sequoia Club chairman.

His secretary, Victoria Davis, a young, competent black woman, looked up as he entered his two-room office. 'Hi, Vicki,' he said. 'Is there much in the mail?'

'Nothing that's urgent. There are some messages, though – including several saying you were good on TV last night. I thought so, too.'

'Thanks.' He grinned. 'Welcome to my fan club.'

'Oh, there's a "private and confidential" on your desk; it just came. And I have some things for you to sign.' She followed him into his inner office. At the same moment a dull, heavy thud occurred some distance away. A water carafe and drinking glasses rattled; so did the window which overlooked an interior courtyard.

Nim halted, listening. 'What's that?'

'I've no idea. There was the same kind of noise a few minutes ago. Just before you got here.'

Nim shrugged. It could be anything from an earthquake tremor to the effect of some heavy construction going on nearby. At his desk he riffled through the messages and glanced at the

76

envelope which Vicki had referred to, marked 'private and confidential'. It was a buff manila envelope with a dab of sealing wax on the back. Absently he began to open it.

'Vicki, before we do anything else, see if you can get Mrs Carmichael on the phone.'

'At the Sequoia Club?'

'Right.'

She put the papers she was carrying in a tray marked 'signature' and turned to go. As she did, the outer office door flew open and Harry London raced in. His hair was disordered, his face red from exertion.

London saw Nim.

'No!' he screamed. 'No!'

As Nim stood still in bewilderment, London flew across the room and hurled himself across the desk. He seized the manila envelope and put it down.

'Out of here! Fast! All of us!'

London grabbed Nim's arm and pulled, at the same time pushing Victoria Davis roughly ahead. They went through the outer office to the corridor outside, London pausing only long enough to slam both doors behind them.

Nim began an angry protest. 'What the hell . . .'

He didn't finish. From the inner office came the boom of an explosion. The corridor walls shook. A framed picture nearby fell to the floor, its glass shattering.

A second later another thud, like the earlier one Nim had heard but this time louder and clearly an explosion, came from somewhere beneath their feet. It was unmistakably within the building. Down the corridor, figures were running out of other doors.

'Oh Christ!' Harry London said. His voice was despairing.

Nim exclaimed urgently, 'Dammit! *What is it?*'

Now they could hear excited shouting, telephones ringing stridently, the sound of approaching sirens in the street below.

'Letter bombs,' London said. 'They're not big, but enough to kill anybody close. That last one was the fourth. Fraser Fenton's dead, others injured. Everyone in the building's being warned, and if you feel like praying, ask that there aren't any more.'

11

With a short stub of pencil, Georgos Winslow Archambault (Yale, class of '72) wrote in his journal :

Yesterday, a successful foray against the fascist-capitalistic forces of oppression!

An enemy leader – Fenton, president of Golden State Piss & Lickspittle – is dead. Good riddance!

In the honoured name of Friends of Freedom, the headquarters bastion of the ruthless exploiters of the people's energy resources was successfully attacked. Out of ten F-of-F weapons directed at target, five scored direct hits. Not bad!

The true score of hits may be even greater since the establishment-muzzled press has, as usual, minimized this important people's victory . . .

Georgos repositioned the pencil stub. Even though it was uncomfortable, he invariably wrote with a stub, having once read that Mohandas K. Gandhi did so, holding that to discard a partially used pencil would be to denigrate the humble labour which created it.

Gandhi was one of Georgos Archambault's heroes, as were Lenin, Marx, Engels, Mao Tse-tung, Renato Curcio, Che Guevara, Fidel Castro, Cesar Chavez and assorted others. (The anomaly that Mohandas Gandhi was an apostle of non-violence seemed not to bother him.)

Georgos went on writing.

. . . Furthermore, the capitalist-bootlicking press today sanctimoniously deplored the death and injury of what it labelled 'innocent victims'. How naïvely ridiculous!

In any war, so-called 'innocents' are inevitably killed and maimed, and the larger the war, the larger the number of 'innocent' casualties. When belligerents are the misnamed 'great powers' – as in World Wars I and II and the despicable Viet Nam aggression by Amerika – such 'innocents' are slaughtered in their thousands, like cattle, and who objects? No one! Certainly not the dollar-worshipping press-Führers and their know-nothing, toadying writers.

A just, social war, like that now being waged by Friends of
Freedom, is no different – except that casualties are fewer . . .
Even at Yale, in written papers, Georgos had had the reputation
among his professors of belabouring a point, spreading adjec-
tives like buckshot. But then English had not been his major – it
was physics – and later he parlayed that degree into a doctorate
in chemistry. Later still, the chemistry knowledge proved useful
when he studied explosives – among other things – in Cuba.
And all along the way his interests narrowed, as did his personal views on life and politics.

The journal entry continued :

. . . Even the enemy press – which obediently exaggerates such
matters rather than minimizes them – admits there were only
two deaths and three major injuries. One of the dead was the
senior management criminal, Fenton, the other a pig security
guard – no loss! The rest were minor lackeys – typists, clerks, &c.
– who should be grateful for their martyrdom in a noble cause.

So much for the propaganda nonsense about 'innocent
victims'! . . .

Georgos paused, his thin, ascetic face mirroring an intensity of
thought. As always, he took considerable pains over his journal,
believing that one day it would be an important historical document, ranking alongside such works as *Das Kapital* and *Quota-*
tions from Chairman Mao Tse-tung.

He began a new train of thought.

. . . The demands of Friends of Freedom will be announced in a
war communiqué today. They are:

– Free supply of electricity and gas for one year to the
unemployed, those on welfare, and old people. At the end of a
year the matter will be reviewed again by Friends of Freedom.

An immediate 25 per cent reduction in charges for electric
power and gas supplied to small homes and apartments.

– All nuclear plants to be closed and dismantled immediately.
A permanent ban on any future nuclear development.

Failure to accept and obey these demands will result in a
stepped-up programme of attacks . . .

That would do for starters. And the threat of intensified action
was a real one. Georgos glanced around the crowded, cluttered
basement workroom in which he was writing. The supplies of
gunpowder, fuses, blasting caps, pipe casings, glycerine, acids

and other chemicals were ample. And he, as well as the three other freedom fighters who accepted his leadership, knew how to use them. He smiled, remembering the ingenious device which had gone into yesterday's letter bombs. A small plastic cylinder contained high explosive tetryl with a tiny detonator. Poised over the detonator was a spring-loaded firing pin and opening the envelope released the firing pin, which hit the detonator. Simple but deadly. The charge of tetryl was enough to blow the letter opener's head off, or a body wide open.

... Obviously our demands are awaited because already the press and its docile ally television have begun echoing the Golden State Piss & Lickspittle line that no policies will be changed 'as a result of terrorism'.

Garbage! Empty-headed stupidity! Of course terrorism will cause changes. It always has, and always will. History abounds with examples ...

Georgos considered some of the examples drilled into him during the Cuban revolutionary training. That was a couple of years after getting his doctorate, and in between the two he had been increasingly consumed by hatred for what he saw as the decadent, tyrannical country of his birth. He contemptuously spelled it *Amerika.*

His general disenchantment had not been helped by news that his father, a wealthy New York playboy, had gone through his eighth divorce and remarriage, and that Georgos' mother, an internationally adored Greek movie actress, was again between husbands, having shed her sixth. Georgos loathed both his parents and what they represented, even though he had not seen either since he was nine years old nor, in the intervening twenty years, had he heard from them directly. His costs of living and schooling, including the fees at Yale, were paid impersonally through an Athens law firm.

So terrorism wouldn't change anything, eh?

... Terrorism is an instrument of social war. It permits a few enlightened individuals (such as Friends of Freedom) to weaken the iron grip and will of reactionary forces which hold, and abuse, power.

Terrorism began the successful Russian Revolution.

The Irish and Israeli republics owe their existence to terrorism. IRA terrorism in the first World War led to an independent Eire. Irgun terrorism in Palestine forced the British to give up their

80

Mandate so the Jews could establish Israel.

Algeria won independence from France through terrorism.

The PLO, now represented at international conferences and the UN, used terrorism to gain worldwide attention.

Even more world attention has been achieved by terrorism of the Italian Red Brigade . . .

Georgos Winslow Archambault stopped. Writing tired him. Also, he realized, he was drifting out of the revolutionary jargon which (he had also learned in Cuba) was important, both as a psychological weapon and an emotional outlet. But it was sometimes hard to sustain.

He stood up, stretched and yawned. He had a good, lithe body and kept himself fit with a rigid daily exercise schedule. Glancing in a small, cracked wall mirror he fingered his bushy but trim moustache. He had grown it immediately after the attack on the La Mission generating plant when he had posed as a Salvation Army officer. According to news reports the following day, a plant security guard had described him as clean-shaven, so the moustache might at least confuse identification, if it ever came to that. The Salvation Army uniform had, of course, been destroyed long since.

The memory of the La Mission success pleased Georgos, and he chuckled.

One thing he had not done, either before or after La Mission, was grow a beard. That would be like a signature. People expected revolutionaries to be bearded and unkempt; Georgos was careful to be precisely the reverse. Whenever he left the modest East Side house he had rented he could be mistaken for a stockbroker or banker. Not that that was difficult for him since he was fastidious by nature and dressed well. The money which the Athens lawyer still paid regularly into a Chicago bank account helped with that, though the amount was less than it used to be, and Georgos needed considerably more cash to finance the future plans of Friends of Freedom. Fortunately he was already getting some outside help; now the amount from that source would have to be increased.

Only one factor contradicted the cultivated bourgeois image – Georgos' hands. In the early days of his interest in chemicals, and then explosives, he had been careless and worked without protective gloves. As a result his hands were scarred and discoloured. He was more careful now but the damage was done.

He had considered seeking skin grafts, but the risks seemed high. The best he could do, when away from the house, was keep his hands out of sight as much as possible.

The agreeable odour of lunch – stuffed bell peppers – drifted down to him from above. His woman, Yvette, was an accomplished cook who knew what Georgos liked and tried to please him. She was also in awe of his learning, having had a minimum of schooling herself.

He shared Yvette with the three other young freedom fighters who lived in the house – Wayde, a scholar like Georgos and a disciple of Marx and Engels; Ute, an American Indian who nursed a burning hatred of the institutions which eclipsed his people's nationhood; and Felix, a product of Detroit's inner city ghetto, whose philosophy was to burn, kill or otherwise destroy everything alien to his own bitter experience since birth.

But, for all the sharing with the others, Georgos had a proprietorial feeling, bordering on affection, for Yvette. At the same time, he despised himself for his own failure in an aspect of the *Revolutionary Catechism* (attributed to the nineteenth-century Russians, Bakunin and Nechayev), which read in part:

... The revolutionary is a lost man; he has no interests of his own, no feelings, no habits, no belongings ... Everything in him is absorbed by a single, exclusive interest, one thought, one passion – the revolution ... He has broken every tie with the civil order, with the educated world and all laws, conventions and ... with the ethics of this world.

All the tender feelings of family life, of friendship, love, gratitude and even honour must be stilled in him ... Day and night he must have one single thought, one single purpose: merciless destruction ...

The character of the true revolutionary has no place for any romanticism, sentimentality, enthusiasm or seduction ... Always and everywhere he must become not what his own inclination would have him become, but what the general interest of the revolution demands.

Georgos closed his journal, reminding himself that the war communiqué, with its just demands, must arrive at one of the city's radio stations later today.

As usual, it would be left in a safe location, then the radio station advised by phone. The radio idiots would fall all over themselves to pick it up.

The communiqué, Georgos thought with satisfaction, would make a lively item on the evening news.

12

'First of all,' Laura Bo Carmichael said when they had ordered drinks – a martini for her, a bloody mary for Nim Goldman – 'I'd like to say how sorry I am about your president, Mr Fenton. I didn't know him, but what happened was shameful and tragic. I hope the people responsible are found and punished.'

The Sequoia Club chairman was a slender, svelte woman in her late sixties with a normally brisk manner and alert, penetrating eyes. She dressed severely, wore flat-heeled shoes, and had her hair cropped short, as if to exorcise her femininity. Perhaps, Nim thought, it was because, as an early atomic scientist, Laura Bo Carmichael had competed in a field which, at the time, was dominated by men.

They were in the elegant Squire Room of the Fairhill Hotel, where they had met for lunch at Nim's suggestion. It was a week and a half later than he had intended, but the turmoil which followed the latest bombing at GSP & L had kept him occupied. Elaborate security measures, which Nim had shared in planning, were now in force at the giant utility's headquarters. More work had also come his way as a result of the critical need for a rate increase, now being considered by the Public Utilities Commission.

Acknowledging the remark about Fraser Fenton, he admitted, 'It was a shock, particularly after the earlier deaths at La Mission. I guess we're all running scared right now.'

And it was true, he thought. The company's senior executives, from the chairman down, were insisting on low profiles. They did not want to be in the news and thereby expose themselves to terrorist attention. J. Eric Humphrey had given orders that his name was no longer to be used in company announcements or news releases, nor would he be available to the press, except possibly for off-the-record sessions. His home address had been withdrawn from all company records and was now a guarded secret – as much as anything of that kind could be. Most senior executives already had unlisted home phone numbers. The chairman and senior officers would have bodyguards during any activity where they might be considered targets – including weekend golf games.

Nim was to be the exception.

His assistant, the chairman had made clear, would continue to be GSP & L's policy spokesman, Nim's public appearances, if anything, increasing. It put him, Nim thought wryly, squarely on the firing line. Or, more precisely, the bombing line.

The chairman had also, quietly, increased Nim's salary. Hazardous duty pay, Nim thought, even though the raise was overdue.

'Although Fraser was our president,' he explained to Laura Bo, 'he was not the chief executive officer and, in some ways, wasn't in the mainstream of command. He was also five months from retirement.'

'That makes it even sadder. How about the others?'

'One of the injured died this morning. A woman secretary.' Nim had known her slightly. She was in the treasurer's department and had authority to open all mail, even that marked 'private and confidential'. The privilege had cost her her life and saved that of her boss, Sharlett Underhill, to whom the booby-trapped envelope was addressed. Two of the five bombs which exploded had injured several people who were nearby; an eighteen-year-old billing clerk had lost both hands.

A waiter brought their drinks and Laura Bo instructed him, 'These are to be on separate checks. *And* the lunch.'

'Don't worry,' Nim said, amused. 'I won't suborn you with my company expense account.'

'You couldn't if you tried. However, on principle, I won't take *anything* from someone who might want to influence the Sequoia Club.'

'Any influencing I try will be out in the open. I simply thought that over a meal was a good way to talk.'

'I'll listen to you any time, Nim, and I'm happy to have lunch. But I'll still pay for my own.'

They had first met, years before, when Nim was a senior at

Stanford and Laura Bo was a visiting lecturer. She had been impressed by his penetrating questions, he by her willingness to address them frankly. They had kept in touch and, even though they were adversaries at times, respected each other and stayed good friends.

Nim sipped his bloody mary. 'It's about Tunipah mostly. But also our plans for Devil's Gate and Fincastle.'

'I rather thought it would be. It might save time if I told you the Sequoia Club intends to oppose them all.'

Nim nodded. The statement did not surprise him. He thought for a moment, then chose his words carefully.

'What I'd like you to consider, Laura, is not just Golden State Power & Light, or the Sequoia Club, or even the environment, but a whole wider spectrum. You could call it "basic civilized values", or "the life we lead", or maybe – more accurately – "minimum expectations".'

'Actually, I think about those things a good deal.'

'Most of us do, but lately not enough – or realistically. Because everything under all those headings is in peril. Not just in part, not a few bits and pieces of life as we know it, but everything. Our entire system is in danger of coming apart, of breaking up.'

'That isn't a new argument, Nim. I usually hear it in conjunction with a line like, "If this particular application – to build a polluting this or that, exactly where and how we want it – is not approved by tomorrow at the latest, then disaster will be swift and sure."'

Nim shook his head. 'You're playing dialectics with me, Laura. Sure, what you just said is stated or implied sometimes; at Golden State we've been guilty of it ourselves. But what I'm speaking of now is overall – and not posturing, but reality.'

Their waiter reappeared and presented two ornate menus with a flourish. Laura Bo ignored hers. 'An avocado and grapefruit salad with a glass of skim milk.'

Nim handed back his own menu. 'I'll have the same.'

The waiter went away looking disappointed.

'What seems impossible for more than a handful of people to grasp,' Nim continued, 'is the *total* effect when you add together all the resource changes and calamities – natural plus political – which have happened, virtually at once.'

'I follow the news, too.' Laura Bo smiled. 'Could it be I've missed something?'

'Probably not. But have you done the addition?'

'I think so. But give me your version.'

'Okay. Number One. North America is running out of natural gas. Oh, there'll be some temporary surpluses for a while, and we'll have inflows from Canada, and maybe Mexico, to ease our own depletion over the next ten years. But for large-scale unlimited use we're at the end of the line, except for gasification of our coal reserves, and stupidity in Washington has slowed *that* to a walk. Do you agree?'

'Of course. And the reason we're running out of natural gas is because the big utility companies – yours and others – put profits ahead of conservation and squandered a resource which could have lasted half a century more.'

Nim grimaced. 'We responded to public demand, but never mind. I'm talking hard facts, and *how* all that natural gas got used is history. It can't be undone.' On his fingers he ticked off a second point. 'Now, oil. There are still big supplies untapped, but the way oil is being guzzled, the world could be scraping the bottom of its wells by the turn of the century – *which isn't far away*. Coupled with that, all industrialized free world nations are dependent more and more on imported oil, which leaves us open, any damn day the Arabs want to kick us in the ass, to political and economic blackmail.'

He stopped, then added, 'Of course, we should be liquefying coal, just as the Germans did in World War II. But the politicians in Washington can get more votes by holding televised hearings where they vilify the oil companies.'

'You have a certain glib persuasiveness, Nim. Have you ever thought of running for office?'

'Should I try at the Sequoia Club?'

'Perhaps not.'

'All right,' he said, 'so much for natural gas and oil. Next, consider nuclear power.'

'Must we?'

He stopped, regarding her curiously. At the mention of 'nuclear', Laura Bo's face had tightened. It always did. In California and elsewhere she was an impassioned foe of nuclear power plants, her opinions listened to respectfully because of her association with the World War II Manhattan Project, which produced the first atomic bombs.

Nim said, without looking at her, 'That word is still like a dagger in the heart to you, isn't it?'

Their lunch had arrived, and she paused until the waiter had gone before replying.

'I imagine you know by now that I still see the mushroom cloud.'

'Yes,' he said gently. 'I know, and I think I understand.'

'I doubt that. You were so young, you don't remember. You weren't involved, as I was.'

Though her words were controlled, the agony of years still seethed beneath them. Laura Bo had been a young scientist who came to the atomic-bomb project in the last six months before Hiroshima. At the time she had wanted desperately to be a part of history, but after the first bomb – code name: *Little Boy* – had been dropped, she was horrified and sickened. What gave her greatest guilt, however, was that she had not protested, after Hiroshima, the dropping of the second bomb – code name: *Fat Man* – on Nagasaki. True, there had been only three days between the two. Equally true, no protest she might have made would have stayed the Nagasaki bomb and saved the eighty thousand souls who died there or were mutilated, merely – as many believed – to satisfy military and scientific curiosity. But she had *not* protested, to anyone, and thus her guilt was unalloyed.

She said, thinking aloud, 'They didn't need the second bomb, you know. It was totally unnecessary. The Japanese were going to surrender because of Hiroshima. But *Fat Man* was a different design from *Little Boy*, and those responsible wanted to try it out, to learn if it would work. It did.'

'It's all a long time ago,' Nim said. 'And the question has to be asked : should what happened then be a factor in building nuclear plants today?'

Laura Bo said with finality, 'To me the two things are inseparable.'

Nim shrugged. He suspected the Sequoia Club chairman was not the only anti-nuclear lobbyist expiating personal or collective guilts. But true or false, it made little difference now.

'There is also,' Lauro Bo added, 'the matter of the accident at

Three Mile Island. I trust you are not forgetting that.'

'No,' Nim said, 'no one will forget it – on our side as well as yours. But I'd remind you that disaster *was* averted there, that there have been corrections, and the lessons learned have been applied to other nuclear plants.'

'That, of course, is the soporific line we were fed *before* Three Mile Island happened.'

Nim sighed. 'It's true. No reasonable person can deny it.' He went on, 'But even without Three Mile Island, you and your people had already won the nuclear battle. You won because, while you were protesting, and using legal ruses to delay development and operating experience, you forced the cost of nuclear plants so high, and made the outcome of any nuclear proposal so indefinite, that most utilities simply can't commit themselves any more. They can't take a chance of waiting five to ten years, spending tens of millions in preliminaries, and then being turned down.'

Nim paused, then added, 'Therefore at every point in planning we need an escape hatch, a clear alternative route to go. That's coal.'

Laura Bo Carmichael picked at her salad.

'Coal and air pollution go together,' she said. 'Any coal-burning plant must be sited with extreme care.'

'Which is why we chose Tunipah.'

'There are ecological reasons why that choice is wrong.'

'Will you tell me what they are?'

'Certain species of plants and wildlife are found almost nowhere else but in the Tunipah area. What you're proposing would endanger them.'

Nim asked, 'Is one of the endangered plant species the Furbish lousewort?'

'Yes.'

He sighed. Rumours about Furbish lousewort – a wild snapdragon – had already reached GSP & L. The flower was rare and once believed extinct, but recently new growths had been discovered. One, in Maine, had been used by environmentalists to halt a $600 million hydroelectric project already in progress.

'You know, of course,' Nim said, 'that botanists admit the Furbish lousewort has no ecological value and isn't even pretty?'

Laura Bo smiled. 'Perhaps, for the public hearings, we'll find a botanist who takes an opposite view. Then there's the other Tunipah inhabitant to be considered – the Microdipodops.'

Nim asked, 'What in hell is that?'

'It's sometimes known as a kangaroo mouse.'

'Oh, my God!' Before their meeting Nim had cautioned himself to stay cool, but found his resolve slipping. 'You'd let a mouse, or mice, prohibit a project which will benefit millions of people?'

'I expect,' Laura Bo said calmly, 'those relative benefits are something we'll be discussing in the months ahead.'

'You're damn right we will! And I suppose you'll have the same kind of objections to the Fincastle geothermal plant and Devil's Gate pumped storage, both of which are the *cleanest* type of operation known to man or nature.'

'You can't expect me, Nim, to give away all our reasons for opposition. But I assure you we will have persuasive arguments against both.'

Impetuously Nim called to a passing waiter, 'Another bloody mary!' He motioned to Laura Bo's empty martini glass, but she shook her head.

'Let me ask you something.' Nim kept his voice controlled, annoyed at himself for revealing his anger a moment ago, 'Where would *you* locate any of those plants?'

'That's really not my problem. It's yours.'

'But wouldn't you – or, rather, the Sequoia Club – oppose *anything* we proposed, no matter where we suggested putting it?'

Laura Bo didn't answer, though her mouth tightened.

'There's another factor I left out,' Nim said. 'Weather. Climate patterns are changing world wide, making the energy outlook – especially electrical energy – worse. Meteorologists say we're facing twenty years of colder weather and regional droughts. We've already seen the effect of both in the mid-seventies.'

There was a silence between them, punctuated by the restaurant sounds and a hum of voices from other tables. Then Laura Bo Carmichael said, 'Let me be clear about something. Exactly why did you ask me here today?'

'To appeal to you – and the Sequoia Club – to look at the big picture, and then to moderate your opposition.'

'Has it occurred to you that you and I are looking at two *different* big pictures?'

'If we are, we shouldn't be,' Nim said. 'We're living in the same world.'

He persisted, 'Let me come back to where I started. If we – Golden State Power – are blocked in *everything*, the result can only be catastrophic in ten years or less. Daily blackouts, long ones, will be a norm. That means industry dislocation and massive unemployment, maybe as high as fifty per cent. Cities will be in chaos. Few people realize how much we live by electricity, though they will – when they're deprived of electric power in a big way. Out in the country there'll be crop failures because of limited irrigation, resulting in food shortages, with prices going through the roof. I tell you, people will lack the means to live; they'll go hungry, there will be a bigger impact on America than the Civil War. It will make the 1930s depression look like a tea party. *It isn't imagination, Laura.* Not any of it. It's hard, cold fact. Don't you and your people care?'

Nim gulped at his bloody mary, which had arrived while he was talking.

'All right,' Laura Bo said, her voice was harder, less friendly than when they started. 'I've sat here through all you've had to say. Now it's my turn, and you listen carefully.' She pushed her plate away, only half of the salad eaten.

'All your thinking, Nim, and that of others like you is nearterm. Environmentalists, including the Sequoia Club, are looking at the long-range future. And what we intend to halt, *by any means*, is three centuries of spoliation of this earth.'

He interjected, 'In some ways you've already done that.'

'Nonsense! We've scarcely made a dent, and even the little we've achieved will be undone if we let ourselves be seduced by voices of expediency. Voices like yours.'

'All that I'm pleading for is moderation.'

'What you call moderation I see as a step backwards. And taking it won't preserve a habitable world.'

Nim said scornfully, not bothering to conceal his feelings any more, 'How habitable do you think the kind of world will be which I just described – with less and less electric power?'

'It might surprise all of us by being better than you think,' Laura Bo answered calmly. 'More important, we'd be moving the way civilization should – towards less waste, less opulence, a lot less greed, and a less materialistic standard of living which would be a good thing for us all.'

She paused, as if weighing her words, then continued, 'We've lived so long here with the notion that expansion is good, that bigger is better and more is mightier, that people are brainwashed into believing it's true. So they worship "gross national product" and "full employment", overlooking the fact that both are suffocating and poisoning us. In what was once "America the Beautiful" we've created an ugly, filthy concrete wasteland, belching ashes and acids into what used to be clean air, all the while destroying natural life – human, animal and vegetable. We've turned sparkling rivers into stinking sewers, glorious lakes into garbage dumps; now, along with the rest of the world, we're fouling the seas with chemical and oil. All of it happens a little at a time. Then, when the spoilage is pointed out, your kind of people pleads for "moderation" because, you say, "This time around we won't kill *many* fish", or "We won't *poison* much vegetation", or, "We'll only destroy a *little* more beauty". Well, some of us have seen it happen too long and too often to believe that canard any more. So what we've done is dedicate ourselves to saving something of what's left. Because we think there *are* things in this world more important than GNP and full employment, and one of them is preserving some cleanliness and beauty, plus holding back a share of natural resources for generations not yet born, instead of squandering everything here and now. And those are the reasons the Sequoia Club will fight Tunipah, *and* your Devil's Gate pumped storage plant, *and* Fincastle geothermal. And I'll tell you something else – I think we'll win.'

'I agree with some of what you've said,' Nim acknowledged. 'You know I do, because we've talked about it before. But the mistake you make is to stomp on every opinion that's different from yours, and set yourself up as God, Jesus, Mohammed, Buddha, rolled up into one. Laura, you're part of a tiny group which knows what's best for everyone – or thinks it does – and you're prepared to ignore practicalities and damn the rest of us while you have your way like spoiled children. In the end, you may destroy us all.'

Laura Bo Carmichael said coldly, 'I don't believe we have anything more to say to each other.' She beckoned their waiter. 'Please bring our separate checks.'

13

Ardythe Talbot led the way into her living room.

'I thought you'd never call,' she said. 'If you hadn't, in a day or two I was going to call *you*.'

'We've had more trouble and I'm afraid it kept me busy,' Nim told her. 'I suppose you heard about it.'

It was early evening. Nim had driven to Ardythe's – as he put it to himself, 'on the way home'. This afternoon, depressed by his meeting with Laura Bo Carmichael and blaming himself for the antagonism with which it ended, he had telephoned Ardythe on impulse. Predictably, she was warm and friendly. 'I've been feeling lonely,' she confided, 'and I'd love to see you. *Please* come out after work and have a drink.'

But when he arrived a few minutes ago it was clear that what Ardythe had in mind was more than a drink. She had greeted him with an embrace and kiss which left no doubt of her intentions. Nim wasn't averse to what seemed likely to follow, but for a while over drinks they settled for conversation.

'Yes, I did hear what happened,' Ardythe said. 'Has the whole world gone mad?'

'I guess it always has been. When it's close to home you notice it more.'

Today, Nim thought, Ardythe seemed greatly improved from the grim day nearly a month ago when she learned of Walter's death. Then, and at the funeral – which was the last time she and Nim had seen each other – she seemed drawn and old. In the meantime, clearly, Ardythe's vitality and attractiveness had returned. Her face, arms and legs were tanned, and the shapely outline of her body beneath a snug print dress reminded him again of the excitement they aroused in each other last time he was here. Nim remembered, years ago, coming across a book called *In Praise of Older Women*. Though he recalled little more about it than the title, he had a notion now of what the author must have had in mind.

'Walter always believed,' Ardythe said, 'that everything that happens in the world – wars, bombings, pollution, all the rest –

are a necessary part of the balance of nature. Did he ever talk to you about that?'

Nim shook his head. Though he and the dead chief engineer had been friends, their talk was usually practical, seldom philosophic.

'Usually Walter kept that kind of thinking to himself,' Ardythe said. 'He'd tell me, though. He used to say, "People think human beings have control over the present and future, but we really don't." And: "Man's apparent free will is a delusion; human perversity is just one more instrument of the balance of nature." Walter believed even war and disease have a purpose in nature – to thin out populations which the earth can't support. "Humans," he once said, "are like lemmings who over-multiply, then rush over a cliff to kill themselves – except that humans do it more elaborately." '

Nim was startled. Though Ardythe's words were not in Walter Talbot's broad Scots accent, just the same Nim could hear an uncanny echo of Walter, who, when alive, expressed himself in just that thoughtful, half-sardonic way. How strange, too, that Walter should have stripped his mind bare for Ardythe, whom Nim had never regarded as a deep thinker. Or was it strange at all? Perhaps, Nim reasoned, he was learning about a mental intimacy of marriage which he himself had never known.

He wondered how Laura Bo Carmichael would react to Walter's conviction that environmental pollution was a needed part of nature's balance, a facet of some dimly perceived master plan. Then remembering his own spiritual questing recently, he asked Ardythe, 'Did Walter equate the balance of nature with God?'

'No. He always maintained that that was too easy, too elementary. He said God was "man-created, a straw grasped at by small minds afraid of darkness . . ." ' Ardythe's voice trailed off. Suddenly Nim saw tears course down her face.

She wiped them away. 'This is the time of day I miss Walter most. It's the time we would talk.'

For a moment there was an awkwardness between them, then Ardythe said firmly, 'No, I won't let myself go on being depressed.' She had been sitting near Nim and now moved closer. He became aware of her perfume, the same perfume which so aroused him the last time he was here. She said softly, with a smile, 'I think all that talk of nature has affected me.' Then, as they reached for each other, 'Make love to me, Nim! I need you more than ever.'

His arms around her tightened as they kissed fiercely. Ardythe's lips were moist and giving and she sighed with pleasure as their hands explored each other, both remembering the time before. Nim's own desire, never far below the surface, surged urgently so that he cautioned with a whisper, 'Let's slow down! Wait!'

She whispered back, 'We can go to my bedroom. It will be better.' He felt her stir; she stood up. So did Nim.

Still close, they ascended the stairs. Except for the sound of their movements, the house was silent. Ardythe's bedroom was at the end of a short landing and the door was open. Inside, Nim saw, the coverlet and top sheet were already folded back. Ardythe had clearly made her plans before he got there. He remembered, from a conversation long ago, that Ardythe and Walter had occupied separate bedrooms. Though no longer troubled by the inhibitions of a month ago, Nim was glad they would not be in Walter's bed.

He helped Ardythe off with the tight-fitting dress he had admired and shed his own clothes quickly. They sank together on to the bed, which was soft and cool. 'You were right,' he murmured happily, 'it *is* better here.' Then impatience conquered them. As he entered her, she thrust her body forward and cried aloud with joy.

Minutes later, passion expended, they lay contented and entwined. Nim reflected on something he had once heard; that the sex act left some men drained and depressed, wondering why they had gone to all the trouble which preceded it. But it never happened that way to Nim. Once more, as always, he felt uplifted and renewed.

Ardythe said softly, 'You're a sweet, tender man. Is there any way you can stay the night?'

He shook his head. 'Not this time.'

'I suppose I shouldn't have asked.' She traced a finger down his face, following the lines around his mouth. 'I promise I won't be greedy, Nim, or bother you. Just come sometimes, when you can.'

He promised he would, though wondering how to manage it amid the pressures and complications which grew in number daily.

While they were dressing, Ardythe said, 'I've been going through Walter's papers and there are some I'd like to turn over to you. Things he brought home from the office. They ought to go back.'

'Sure, I'll take them,' Nim agreed.

Ardythe showed him where the papers were – in three large cardboard cartons in what had been Walter's den. Nim opened two of the cartons and found the contents to consist of filed reports and letters. He rifled through a few while Ardythe was in the kitchen making coffee; he had declined another drink.

The papers appeared to concern matters in which Walter Talbot had taken a special personal interest. A good many were several years old and no longer relevant. One series of files contained copies of Walter's original report on theft of service and correspondence afterwards. At the time, Nim remembered, the report attracted wide attention in the utility industry and was circulated far beyond GSP & L. As a result, Walter had taken on the coloration of an expert. There had even been a court case in the East in which he appeared as an expert witness, part of his report being admitted into evidence. Later, the case had gone to higher courts, Walter's report along with it. Nim had forgottten the eventual outcome; not that it mattered now, he thought.

He glanced through more correspondence, then replaced the files and closed the cartons. After that he carried them out to the hallway so he would remember to take them with him to his car.

14

The earth underfoot vibrated. A great roaring, like a covey of jet aeroplanes taking off together, shattered the near-silence and a fat plume of steam shot violently skyward. Instinctively, those in the small group standing on a knoll pressed hands over their ears in self-protection. A few appeared frightened.

Teresa Van Buren, uncovering her own ears momentarily,

waved her arms and shouted, urging a return to the chartered bus in which the group arrived. No one heard the shouts but the message was clear. The twenty or so men and women moved hastily towards the bus parked fifty yards away.

Inside the air-conditioned vehicle, with doors closed tightly, the noise from outside was less intense.

'Jesus H. Christ!' one of the men protested. 'That was a lousy trick to pull, and if I've lost my hearing I'll sue the goddamned utility.'

Teresa Van Buren asked him, 'What did you say?'

'I said if I've frigging well gone deaf . . .'

'I know,' she interrupted, 'I heard you the first time. Just wanted to make sure you hadn't.'

Some of the others laughed.

'I swear to you,' the GSP & L public relations director told the group of reporters on the press tour, 'I had no idea that was going to happen. The way it worked out, we just got lucky. Because, folks, what you had the privilege of seeing was a new geothermal well come in.'

She said it with the enthusiasm of a wildcatter who had just brought in a Texas gusher.

Through windows of the still stationary bus, they looked back at the drill rig they had been watching when the unscheduled eruption occurred. In appearance it was the same kind of tower-topped mechanism used in an oil field; it could, in fact, be moved and converted to oil exploration at any time. Like Teresa Van Buren, the hard-hatted crew clustered around the rig was beaming.

Not far away were other geothermal well-heads, their natural pressurized steam deflected into huge insulated pipes. An above-ground network of the pipes, covering several square miles like a plumber's nightmare, conveyed the steam to turbine generators in a dozen separate buildings, severe and square, perched on ridges and in gullies. Combined output of the generators was, at this moment, better than seven hundred thousand kilowatts, more than enough electricity to sustain a major city. The new well would supplement this power.

Within the bus, Van Buren regarded a TV cameraman who was busy switching film containers. 'Did you get pictures when it happened?'

'Damn right!' Unlike the reporter who had complained – a

minor league stringer for some small-town papers – the TV man looked pleased. He finished his film changing. 'Ask the driver to open the door, Tess. I want a shot from another angle.'

As he went out, a smell of hydrogen sulphide – like rotten eggs – wafted in.

'Migawd, it stinks!' Nancy Molineaux of the *California Examiner* wrinkled her delicate nose.

'At European health spas,' a middle-aged *Los Angeles Times* writer told her, 'you'd have to *pay* to breathe that stuff.'

'And if you decide to print that,' Van Buren assured the *LA Times* man, 'we'll carve it on stone and salute it twice a day.'

The press party had travelled from the city, starting early this morning, and was now in the rugged mountains of California's Sevilla County, site of Golden State Power's existing geothermal generating plants. Later they would move on to neighbouring Fincastle Valley, where the utility hoped to create a further geothermal power complex. Tomorrow, the same group would visit a hydroelectric plant and the intended site of another.

Both proposed developments were soon to be the subject of public hearings. The two-day excursion was intended as a media preview.

'I'll tell you something about that smell,' the PR director continued. 'The hydrogen sulphide in the steam is only present in small amounts, not enough to be toxic. But we get complaints – mostly from real estate people who want to sell land in these mountains for resort development. Well, the smell was always here because steam filtered up through the ground, even before we harnessed it to generate electricity. What's more, old-timers say the smell isn't any worse now than it was originally.'

'Can you prove that?' a reporter from the *San Jose Mercury* asked.

Van Buren shook her head. 'Unfortunately no one had the foresight to take air samples before drilling began. So we can never compare the "before" and "after", and we're stuck with the critics.'

'Who are probably right,' *San Jose Mercury* said sardonically. 'Everybody knows a big outfit like Golden State Power bends the truth now and then.'

'I'll take that as a joke,' the PR director responded. 'But one thing *is* true. We try to meet our critics halfway.'

A new voice said sceptically, 'Give one example.'

'There's one right here. It has to do with the smell. Because of the objections I told you about, we located two recently built power plants on ridges. There are strong air currents there which dissipate all odours quickly.'

'So what happened?' Nancy Molineaux asked.

'There have been even more complaints than before – from environmentalists who say we've ruined the skyline.'

There was mild laughter and one or two people wrote in note-books.

'We had another no-win situation,' Van Buren said. 'GSP & L made a film about our geothermal generating system. When we started, the script had a scene showing how a hunter named William Elliott discovered this place in 1847. He shot a grizzly bear, then looked up from his rifle sights and saw steam gushing from the ground. Well, some wildlife people read the script and said we ought not to show a grizzly being killed because bears are now protected here. So . . . the script was rewritten. In the film the hunter misses. The bear gets away.'

A radio reporter with a tape machine going asked, 'What's wrong with that?'

'The descendants of William Elliott threatened to sue us. They said their ancestor was a famous hunter and a crack shot. He wouldn't have missed the grizzly; he'd have shot it. Therefore the film maligned his reputation – and the family's.'

'I remember that,' the *LA Times* man said.

Van Buren added: 'The point I'm making is: in advance of anything we do – as a public utility – we can be certain we'll be kicked in the butt from one direction or the other, sometimes both.'

'Would you prefer us to weep now?' Nancy Molineaux enquired. 'Or later?'

The TV cameraman rapped on the bus door and was readmitted.

'If everyone's ready we'll move on to lunch,' Van Buren said. She motioned to the bus driver. 'Let's go.'

A feature writer from *New West* magazine asked her, 'Any booze, Tess?'

'Maybe. If everyone agrees it's off the record.' As she looked around enquiringly there were calls of 'Okay', 'Off the record', and 'That's a deal'.

'In that case – yes, drinks before lunch.'

Two or three in the bus gave a ragged cheer.

Behind the exchange was a piece of recent history.

Two years earlier GSP & L had been generous in supplying food and liquor during a similar press tour. The press representatives had eaten and imbibed with gusto, then, in published reports, some had sniped at GSP & L for extravagant entertaining at a time of rising utility bills. As a result, food supplied to the press nowadays was deliberately modest and, unless an off-the-record pledge was given, liquor was withheld.

The stratagem worked. Whatever else the press criticized, they now kept silent about their own care and feeding.

The bus travelled about a mile within the geothermal field's rugged terrain, over narrow roads, uneven in places, winding between wellheads, generator buildings and the ever-present maze of hissing, steaming pipes. There were few other vehicles. Because of danger from scalding steam, the public was banned from the area and all visitors escorted.

At one point the bus passed a huge switching and transformer yard. From here, high voltage transmission lines on towers carried power across the mountains to a pair of sub-stations forty miles away, where it was funnelled into the backbone of the Golden State Power & Light electric system.

On a small, asphalted plateau were several house trailers which served as offices, as well as living quarters, for on-site crews. The bus halted beside them. Teresa Van Buren led the way into one trailer where places had been set on trestle tables. Inside she told a white-coated kitchen helper, 'Okay, open the tiger cage.' He produced a key and unlocked a wall cabinet to reveal liquor, wine, and mixes. A moment later a bucket of ice was brought in and the PR director told the others, 'Everybody help yourselves.'

Most were on their second drink when the sound of an aircraft engine overhead became audible, then grew quickly in volume. From the trailer's windows several people watched a small helicopter descending. It was painted in GSP & L's orange and white and bore the company insignia. It alighted immediately outside and the rotors slowed and stopped. A door at the front of the fuselage opened. Nim Goldman clambered out.

Moments later Nim joined the group inside the trailer. Teresa Van Buren announced, 'I think most of you know Mr Goldman. He's here to answer questions.'

'I'll put the first question,' a TV correspondent said cheerfully. 'Can I mix you a drink?'

Nim grinned. 'Thanks. A vodka and tonic.'

'My, my!' Nancy Molineaux observed. 'Aren't you the important one, to come by helicopter when the rest of us rated a bus!'

Nim regarded the young, attractive black woman cagily. He remembered their previous encounter and clash; also Teresa Van Buren's assessment of Ms Molineaux as an outstanding newspaperwoman. Nim still thought she was a bitch.

'If it's of any interest,' he said, 'I had some other work to do this morning, which is why I left later than you and came the way I did.'

Nancy Molineaux was not deterred. 'Do all the utility executives use helicopters when they feel like it?'

'Nancy,' Van Buren said sharply, 'you know damn well they don't.'

'Our company,' Nim volunteered, 'owns and operates a half-dozen small aircraft, including two helicopters. Mainly they are used for patrolling transmission lines, checking mountain snow levels, conveying urgent supplies, and in other emergencies. Occasionally – very occasionally – one will convey a company executive if the reason is important. I was *told* this session was.'

'Are you implying that now you're not so sure?'

'Since you ask, Miss Molineaux,' Nim said coldly, 'I'll admit to having doubts.'

'Hey, knock it off, Nancy!' a voice called from the rear. 'The rest of us are not interested in this.'

Ms Molineaux wheeled on her colleagues. 'Well, I *am*. I'm concerned about how the public's money is squandered, and if you aren't, you should be.'

'The purpose of being here,' Van Buren reminded them all, 'is to view our geothermal operations and talk about . . .'

'No!' Ms Molineaux interrupted. 'That's *your* purpose. The press decides its own purposes, which may include some of yours, but also anything else we happen to see or hear and choose to write about.'

'She's right, of course.' The comment came from a mild-mannered man in rimless glasses, representing the *Sacramento Bee*.

'Tess,' Nim told Van Buren as he sipped his vodka and tonic, 'I just decided I prefer my job to yours.'

Several people laughed as the PR director shrugged.

'If all the horseshit's finished,' Nancy Molineaux said, 'I'd like to know the purchase price of that fancy eggbeater outside, and how much an hour it costs to operate.'

'I'll enquire,' Van Buren told her, 'and if the figures are available, and if we decide to make them public, I'll make an announcement tomorrow. On the other hand, if we decide it's internal company business, and none of yours, I'll report *that*.'

'In which case,' Ms Molineaux said, unperturbed, 'I'll find out some other way.'

Food had been brought in while they talked – a capacious platter of hot meat pies and, in large eathenware dishes, mashed potatoes and zucchini. Two china jugs held steaming gravy.

'Pile in!' Teresa Van Buren commanded. 'It's bunkhouse food, but good for gourmands.'

As the group began helping itself, appetites sharpened by the mountain air, the tensions of a moment earlier eased. When the first course was eaten, a half-dozen freshly baked apple pies appeared, accompanied by a gallon of ice-cream and several pots of strong coffee.

'I'm sated,' *Los Angeles Times* announced at length. He leaned back from the table, patted his belly and sighed. 'Better talk some shop, Tess, while we're still awake.'

The TV man who had mixed Nim's drink now asked him, 'How many years are these geysers good for?'

Nim, who had eaten sparingly, took a final sip of black, unsweetened coffee, then pushed his cup away. 'I'll answer that, but let's clear up something first. What we're sitting over are fumaroles, not geysers. Geysers send up boiling water with steam; fumaroles, steam only – much better for driving turbines. As to how long the steam will last, the truth is: no one knows. We can only guess.'

'So guess,' Nancy Molineaux said.

'Thirty years minimum. Maybe twice that. Maybe more.'

New West said, 'Tell us what the hell's going on down there in that crazy teakettle.'

Nim nodded. 'The earth was once a molten mass – gaseous and liquid. When it cooled, a crust formed, which is why we're living here and now and not frying. Down inside, though – twenty miles down – it's as damned hot as ever and that residual heat sends up steam through thin places in the crust. Like here.'

Sacramento Bee asked, 'How thin is thin?'

'We're probably five miles above the hot mass now. In that five miles are surface fractures where the bulk of the steam has collected. When we drill a well we try to hit such a fracture.'

'How many other places like this produce electricity?'

'Only a handful. The oldest geothermal generating plant is in Italy, near Florence. There's another in New Zealand at Wairakei, and others in Japan, Iceland, Russia. None is as big as California's.'

'There's a lot more potential, though,' Van Buren interjected. 'Especially in this country.'

Oakland Tribune asked, 'Just where?'

'Across the entire western United States,' Nim answered. 'From the Rocky Mountains to the Pacific.'

'It's also one of the cleanest, non-polluting, safest forms of energy,' Van Buren added. 'And – as costs go nowadays – cheap.'

'You two should do a soft-shoe routine,' Nancy Molineaux said. 'All right – two questions. Number one: Tess used the word "safe". But there have been accidents here. Right?'

All the reporters were now paying attention, most of them writing in notebooks or with tape recorders switched on.

'Right,' Nim conceded. 'There were two serious accidents, three years apart, each when well-heads blew. That is, the steam got out of control. One well we managed to cap. The other – "Old Desperado" it's known as – we never have entirely. There it is, over there.'

He crossed to a window of the trailer and pointed to a fenced-in area a quarter mile away. Inside the fence, steam rose sporadically at a dozen points through bubbling mud. Outside, large red signs warned: *Extreme Danger – Keep Away.* The others craned to see, then returned to their seats.

'When Old Desperado blew,' Nim said, 'for a mile around it was raining hot mud, with rocks cascading down like hail. It did a lot of damage. Muck settled on power lines and transformers, shorting everything, putting us out of action for a week. Fortunately, it happened at night when few people were at work and there were only two injuries, no deaths. The second blow-out, of another well, was less severe. No casualties.'

'Could Old Desperado ever blow again?' the stringer for small-town papers enquired.

'We believe not. But, like everything else to do with nature, there's no guarantee.'

'The point is,' Nancy Molineaux insisted, 'there *are* accidents.'

'Accidents happen everywhere,' Nim said tersely. 'The point Tess was making, correctly, is that the incidence is low. What's your second question?'

'It's this: assuming everything the two of you have said is true, why isn't geothermal more developed?'

'That's easy,' *New West* offered. 'They'll blame environmentalists.'

Nim countered sharply, 'Wrong! Okay, Golden State Power has had its differences with environmentalists, and will probably have more. But the reason geothermal resources haven't been developed faster is – politicians. Specifically, the US Congress.'

Van Buren shot Nim a warning look which he ignored.

'Hold it!' one of the TV correspondents said. 'I'd like some of this on film. If I make notes now, will you do it again outside?'

'Yes,' Nim agreed. 'I will.'

'Christ!' *Oakland Tribune* protested. 'Us *real* reporters will settle for once around. Let's cut the crap and get *on*!'

Nim nodded. 'Most of the land which should have been explored, long ago, for geothermal potential is federal government property.'

'In which states?' someone asked.

'Oregon, Idaho, Montana, Nevada, Utah, Colorado, Arizona, New Mexico. And *lots* more sites in California.'

Another voice urged, 'Keep going!' Heads were down, ballpoints racing.

'Well,' Nim said, 'it took a full ten years of Congressional donothing, double-talk and politics before legislation was passed which authorized geothermal leasing on public lands. After that were three more years of delay while environmental standards and regulations got written. And even now only a few leases have been granted, with ninety per cent of applications lost in bureaucratic limbo.'

'Would you say,' *San Jose Mercury* prompted, 'that during all this time our patriotic politicians were urging people to conserve power, pay higher fuel costs and taxes, and be less dependent on imported oil?'

Los Angeles Times growled, 'Let *him* say it. I want a direct quote.'

'You have one,' Nim acknowledged. 'I accept the words just used.'

Teresa Van Buren broke in firmly. 'That's enough! Let's talk about Fincastle Valley. We'll all be driving there as soon as we're finished here.'

Nim grinned. 'Tess tries to keep me out of trouble, not always succeeding. Incidentally, the helicopter's going back shortly; I'm staying with you through tomorrow. Okay – Fincastle.' He produced a map from a briefcase and pinned it to a bulletin board.

'Fincastle – you can see it on the map – is two valleys over to the east. It's unoccupied land and we *know* it's a geothermal area. Geologists have advised us there are spectacular possibilities – for perhaps twice the electric power being generated here. Public hearings on our Fincastle plans are, of course, to begin soon.'

Van Buren asked, 'May I . . . ?'

Nim stepped back and waited.

'Let's spell out something loud and clear,' the PR director told the group. 'In advance of the hearings we aren't trying to convert you, or to undercut the opposition. We simply want you to understand what's involved, and where. Thanks, Nim.'

'A piece of gut information,' Nim continued, 'about Fincastle – and also Devil's Gate which we'll visit tomorrow – is this : they represent a Niagara of Arab oil which America will *not* have to import. Right now our geothermal set-up saves ten million barrels of oil a year. We can triple that if . . .'

The briefing, with its information and cross-examination, leavened by badinage, rolled on.

15

The pale blue envelope bore a typewritten address which began :
NIMROD GOLDMAN, ESQUIRE – PERSONAL

A note from Nim's secretary, Vicki Davis, was clipped to the envelope. It read:

Mr London, himself, put this through the mailroom metal detector. He says it's okay for you to open.

Vicki's note was satisfactory on two counts. It meant that mail arriving at GSP & L headquarters and marked 'personal' (or 'private and confidential', as the recent letter bombs had been) was being handled warily. Also, a newly installed detection device was being used.

Something else Nim had become aware of: since the traumatic day on which Harry London had almost certainly saved the lives of Nim and Vicki Davis, London appeared to have appointed himself Nim's permanent protector. Vicki, who nowadays regarded the Property Protection Department head with something close to veneration, cooperated by sending him an advance daily schedule of Nim's appointments and movements. Nim had learned of the arrangement accidentally and was unsure whether to be grateful, irritated or amused.

In any case, he thought, he was a long way from Harry's surveillance now.

Nim, Teresa Van Buren, and the press party had spent last night here at a Golden State Power outpost – Devil's Gate Camp – having continued by bus from Fincastle Valley. It had been a four-hour journey, in part through the breathtaking beauty of Plumas National Forest.

The camp was thirty-five miles from the nearest town and sheltered in a rugged fold of mountains. It comprised a half-dozen company-owned houses for resident engineers, foremen and their families, a small school – now closed for summer vacation – and two motel-type bunkhouses, one for GSP & L employees, the second for visitors. High overhead were high voltage transmission lines on steel-gridded towers – a reminder of the small community's purpose.

The press party had been divided by sex, then housed four to a room in the visitors' quarters, which were plain but adequate. There had been mild grumbling about the four-in-a-room arrangement, one implication being that, given more privacy, some bed-hopping might have developed.

Nim had a room to himself over in the employees' bunkhouse. After dinner last night he stayed on for drinks with some of the reporters, joined a poker game for a couple of hours, then excused himself and turned in shortly before midnight. This morning he had awakened refreshed, and was now ready for breakfast, which would be in a few minutes, at 7:30am.

On a veranda outside the employees' bunkhouse, in the clear morning air, he examined the blue envelope, turning it over in his hand.

It had been brought by a company courier, travelling through the night like a modern Paul Revere and bearing company mail for Devil's Gate and other GSP & L frontiers. It was all part of an internal communications system, so the letter for Nim imposed no extra burden. Just the same, he thought sourly, if Nancy Molineaux learned about a personal letter routed that way, her bitchiness would have another workout. Fortunately she wouldn't.

The disagreeable reminder of the Molineaux woman had been prompted by Teresa Van Buren. In bringing Nim his letter a few minutes ago, Tess reported that she, too, had received one – containing information she had asked for yesterday about helicopter costs. Nim was shocked. He protested, 'You're actually going to help that trollop nail us to a board?'

'Calling her nasty names won't change anything,' Van Buren had said patiently, then added, 'Sometimes you big-wheel executives don't understand what public relations is all about.'

'If that's an example, you're damn right!'

'Look – we can't win 'em all. I'll admit Nancy got under my skin yesterday, but when I thought about it some more, I reasoned she's going to write about that helicopter whatever we do or say. Therefore she might as well have the correct figures because if she asks elsewhere, or someone guesses, for sure they'll be exaggerated. Another thing: I'm being honest with Nancy now, and she knows it. In future, when something else comes up, she'll trust me and maybe that time will be a lot more important.'

Nim said sarcastically, 'I can hardly wait for that acid-mouthed sourpuss to write something favourable.'

'See you at breakfast,' the PR director had said as she left. 'And do yourself a favour – simmer down.'

But he didn't. Now, still seething inwardly, he ripped open the blue envelope.

It contained a single sheet of paper, matching the blue envelope. At the top was printed: *From Karen Sloan.*

Suddenly he remembered. Karen had said *'Sometimes I write poetry. Would you like me to send you some?'* And he had answered yes.

The words were neatly typed.

Today I found a friend,
Or maybe he found me,
Or was it fate, chance, circumstance –
Predestination, by whatever name?
Were we like nanoid stars whose orbits,
Devised at time's beginning,
In due season
Intersect?
Though we will never know,
No matter! For instinct tells me
That our friendship, nurtured,
Will grow strong.

So much of him I like:
His quiet ways, warmth,
A gentle wit, and intellect,
An honest face, kind eyes, a ready smile.

'Friend' is not easily defined. And yet,
These things mean that to me
Concerning one whom, even now,
I hope to see again
And count the days and hours
Until a second meeting.

What else was it Karen had said that day in her apartment? *'I can use a typewriter. It's electric and I work it with a stick in my teeth.'*

With a flash of emotion Nim pictured her toiling – slowly, patiently – over the words he had just read, her teeth gripping the stick tightly, her blonde head – *the only part of her she could move* – repositioning itself after each laborious effort to touch a keyboard letter. He wondered how many drafts Karen had done before the letter-perfect final version she had sent him.

Unexpectedly, he realized, his mood had changed. The sourness of a moment earlier was gone, a warmth and gratitude replacing it.

On his way to join the press party at breakfast, Nim was surprised to meet Walter Talbot Jr. Nim had not seen Wally since the day of his father's funeral. Momentarily, Nim was embarrassed, remembering his recent visit to Ardythe, then rationalized that Wally and his mother led separate, independent lives.

Wally greeted him cheerfully. 'Hi, Nim! What brings you here?'

Nim told him about the two-day press briefing, then asked, 'And you?'

Wally glanced at the high voltage lines above them. 'Our helicopter patrol found broken insulators on one of the towers – probably a hunter using them for target practice. My crew will replace the whole string, working with the line hot. We hope to be finished this afternoon.'

While they talked, a third man joined them. Wally introduced him as Fred Wilkins, a company technician.

'Glad to meet you, Mr Goldman. I've heard of you. Seen you a lot on TV.' The newcomer was in his late twenties, had a shock of bright red hair and was healthily suntanned.

'As you can see from the look of him,' Wally said, 'Fred lives out here.'

Nim asked, 'Do you like the camp? Doesn't it get lonely?'

Wilkins shook his head emphatically. 'Not for me, sir, or the wife. Our kids love it, too.' He inhaled deeply. 'Breathe that air, man! A lot better'n you'll get in any city. And there's plenty of sunshine, all the fishing you need.'

Nim laughed. 'I might try it for a vacation.'

'Daddy!' a child's voice piped. 'Daddy, has the mailman come?'

As the trio turned their heads, a small boy ran towards them. He had a cheerful, freckled face and bright red hair, making his parentage unmistakable.

'Just the company mailman, son,' Fred Wilkins said. 'The post office van'll be another hour.' He explained to the others, 'Danny's excited because it's his birthday. He's hoping for some packages.'

'I'm eight,' the small boy volunteered; he looked strong and sturdy for his age. 'I had some presents already. But there might be more.'

'Happy birthday, Danny!' Nim and Wally said together.

Moments later they parted company, Nim continuing towards the visitors' bunkhouse.

16

In the tailrace tunnel's semi-darkness, above the mighty thunderous sound of confined rushing water, *Oakland Tribune* shouted, 'When I get through these two days I'm gonna ask for a quiet week on the obit desk.'

Several others nearby smiled but shook their heads, unable to hear the words for two reasons – the all-enveloping water sound and plugs of cotton-wool in their ears. Material for the plugs, which muffled the echoing tunnel noise a little, had been handed them outside by Teresa Van Buren. That was after the group scrambled down a steep rock stairway to where the tailrace of Devil's Gate 1 generating plant emptied boisterously into Pineridge River, twenty feet below.

As they fiddled with the earplugs, preparing to enter the tunnel, someone had called out, 'Hey Tess! Why you takin' us in by the back door?'

'It's the tradesmen's entrance,' she answered. 'Since when did you characters deserve better? Besides, you're always sounding off about needing colour for your stories. Here it is.'

'Colour? In *there?*' *Los Angeles Times* had said sceptically, peering forward into the blackness which was punctuated only by a few dim light bulbs. The tunnel was approximately circular, hewn out of solid rock, with the walls left rough and unfinished as at the time of excavation. The light bulbs were near the roof. Suspended halfway between them and the turbulent water was a narrow catwalk on which the visitors would walk. Ropes on either side of the catwalk could be grabbed as handholds.

Earlier, following breakfast, Nim Goldman had explained what they would be seeing – 'a hydro-electric plant that's completely underground, inside a mountain. Later we'll talk about the proposed Devil's Gate pumped storage plant which will also be underground – entirely out of sight.'

He continued, 'The tailrace, where we're going, is actually the *end* of the generating process. But it will give you an idea of the kind of forces we're dealing with. The water you'll see has passed through the turbine blades after having been used to spin the turbines, and comes out in tremendous quantities.'

The massive flow had been evident outside the tunnel to some who had leaned over a metal guardrail above the river, watching the awesome torrent join the already angry maelstrom below.

'By God! I'd hate to fall in,' *KFSO Radio* observed. He asked Van Buren, 'Has anyone ever?'

'Once that we know of. A workman slipped from here. He was a strong swimmer, even had some medals we found out after, but the flow in the tailrace pulled him under. It was three weeks before the body came up.'

Instinctively, those nearest the guardrail took a step backward.

Something else Nim had told them in advance was that this particular tailrace was unique. 'The tunnel is a third of a mile long and was cut horizontally into the side of a mountain. While the tunnel was being built, and before any water was let in, there were points where two construction trucks could pass side by side.'

Nancy Molineaux had pointedly stifled a yawn. 'Shit! So you got a long, fat, wet cave. Is that *news?*'

'It doesn't have to be news. This entire two-day deal is for background,' Van Buren pointed out. 'That was explained to everyone beforehand, including your editors.'

'Did you say "background" or "craparound"? Ms Molineaux asked.

The others laughed.

'Never mind,' Nim said. 'I'd finished anyway.'

Some twenty minutes later, after a short bus ride, he had led the way into the tailrace tunnel.

The cool dampness was in contrast to the warm, sunny day outside. As the group moved forward in single file, only a few feet above the foam-flecked water rushing beneath them, the circle of daylight behind receded to a pinpoint. Ahead, the few dim light bulbs seemed to stretch into limitless distance. Now and then someone would pause to look down, all the while clinging tightly to the guide ropes.

At length, the end of the tunnel and a vertical steel ladder came in sight. At the same time a new sound intruded – a hum of generators, growing to a mighty roar as the ladder was reached. Nim motioned upwards and ascended first, the others following.

They passed through an open trapdoor into a lower generating chamber, then, by way of a circular staircase, to a brightly lighted control room two floors above. Here, to general relief, the noise level was diminished, only a faint hum penetrating the insulated walls.

A wide, plate glass window provided a view of two huge generators, both in operation, immediately below.

In the control room a solitary technician was writing in a logbook as he studied an array of dials, coloured lights and graphic pen recorders which occupied one wall. Hearing the group enter, he turned. Even before that, Nim recognized him from his shock of red hair.

'Hullo, Fred Wilkins.'

'Hi, Mr Goldman!' The technician offered a brief 'good morning' to the visitors, then continued writing.

'Where we are standing,' Nim announced, 'is five hundred feet underground. This plant was built by sinking a shaft from above, the way you would for a mine. There's an elevator goes from here to the surface and, in another shaft, high voltage transmission lines.'

'Not many people working here,' *Sacramento Bee* commented. He was looking through the window at the generator floor where no one was in sight.

The technician closed his logbook and grinned. 'In a couple of minutes you won't see *any*.'

'This is an automated generating plant,' Nim explained. 'Mr Wilkins here comes in to make a routine check' – he queried the technician – 'how often?'

'Just once a day, sir.'

'Otherwise,' Nim continued, 'the place stays tightly locked and unattended, except for occasional maintenance or if something goes wrong.'

Los Angeles Times asked, 'How about starting up and shutting down?'

'It's done from the control centre a hundred and fifty miles away. Most new hydro-electric plants are designed this way. They're efficient, and there's a big saving in labour costs.'

'When something *is* wrong, and there's a panic,' *New West* enquired, 'what then?'

'Whichever generator is affected – or even both – will send a warning to control, then shut down automatically until a service

111

crew gets here.'

'It's *this* kind of generating plant,' Teresa Van Buren interjected, 'that Devil's Gate 2, the proposed pumped storage plant, will be – removed from view so it won't mar the landscape, also non-polluting and economic.'

Nancy Molineaux spoke for the first time since coming in. 'There's one teensy item you left out of that snow job, Tess. The goddamn great reservoir that would have to be built and the natural land which would be flooded.'

'A lake in these mountains, which is what it will be, is every bit as natural as dry wilderness,' the PR director retorted. 'What's more, it will provide fishing . . .'

Nim said gently, 'Let me, Tess.' He was determined, today, not to let Nancy Molineaux or anyone else ruffle him.

'Miss Molineaux is right,' he told the group, 'to the extent that a reservoir is needed. It will be a mile from here, high above us and visible only from aeroplanes or to nature lovers willing to make a long, hard climb. In building it we'll observe every environmental safeguard . . .'

'The Sequoia Club doesn't think so,' a male TV reporter interrupted. 'Why?'

Nim shrugged. 'I have no idea. I guess we'll find out at the public hearing.'

'Okay,' the TV man said. 'Carry on with your propaganda spiel.'

Remembering his resolve, Nim curbed a sharp reply. With media people, he thought, it was so often an uphill battle, a fight against disbelief no matter how straightforward anyone involved with industry and business tried to be. Only radical crusaders, and never mind how misinformed, seemed to have their viewpoints quoted verbatim, without question.

Patiently, he explained pumped storage – 'the only known method of hoarding large quantities of electricity for use later at times of peak demand. In a way, you could think of Devil's Gate 2 as an enormous storage battery.'

There would be two levels of water, Nim continued – the new reservoir and Pineridge River, far below. Connecting the two levels would be massive underground pipes – or penstocks and tailrace tunnels.

The generating plant would be between the reservoir and

river, the penstocks ending at the plant, where the tailrace tunnels start.

'When the plant is producing electricity,' Nim said, 'water from the reservoir will flow downwards, drive the turbines, then discharge into the river *beneath* the river surface.'

But at other times the system would operate *the opposite way around*. When electrical demands everywhere were light – mostly during the night – no electricity would be produced by Devil's Gate 2. Instead, water would be pumped upwards from the river – some three hundred million gallons an hour – to replenish the reservoir, ready for next day.

'At night we have great quantities of spare electric power elsewhere in the GSP & L system. We'd simply use some of it to operate the pumps.'

Nat West said, 'Con Edison in New York has been trying to build a plant like that for twenty years. Storm King, they call it. But ecologists and lots of others are against it.'

'There are also responsible people who are *for* it,' Nim said. 'Unfortunately nobody is listening.'

He described one demand of the Federal Power Commission – proof that Storm King would not disturb fish life in the Hudson River. After several years of study the answer was: there would be a reduction of only four to six per cent in the adult fish population.

'Despite that,' Nim concluded, 'Con Edison still doesn't have approval, and some day the people of New York will wake up to regret it.'

'That's your opinion,' Nancy Molineaux said.

'Naturally it's an opinion. Don't *you* have opinions, Miss Molineaux?'

Los Angeles Times said, 'Of course she doesn't. You know how totally unprejudiced we servants of the truth are.'

Nim grinned. 'I'd noticed.'

The black woman's features tightened, but she made no comment.

A moment earlier, when speaking about Hudson River fish, Nim had been tempted to quote Charles Luce, Con Edison's chairman, who once declared in a public moment of exasperation, '*There comes a point where human environment must prevail over fish habitat. I think in New York we've reached it!*'

But caution prevailed. The remark had got Chuck Luce into trouble and produced a storm of abuse from ecologists and others. Why join him?

Besides, Nim thought, he already had public image problems himself over that damned helicopter. It was coming this afternoon to Devil's Gate to return him to the city where urgent work was piled up on his desk. He had made sure, though, that the chopper would not arrive until after the press contingent had departed by bus.

Meanwhile, disliking this chore and relieved that it would end soon, he continued fielding questions.

At 2pm at Devil's Gate Camp the last few stragglers were climbing aboard the press bus, which had its motor running and was ready to leave. The group had lunched; their journey back to the city would take four hours. Fifty yards away, Teresa Van Buren, who was also going on the bus, told Nim, 'Thanks for all you did, even though you hated some of it.'

He said with a smile, 'I get paid to do a few things, now and then, that I'd rather not. Was anything accomplished, do you . . . ?'

Nim stopped, not certain why, except for a sudden chilling instinct that something was wrong in the scene around him, something out of place. They were standing roughly where he had been this morning when he paused en route to breakfast; the weather was still beautiful – clear sunshine highlighting a profusion of trees and wild flowers, with a breeze stirring the fragrant mountain air. Both bunkhouses were visible, the bus in front of one, a couple of off-duty employees sunning themselves on a balcony of the other. In the opposite direction, over by the staff houses, a group of children was playing; a few minutes earlier Nim had noticed among them the red headed boy Danny, whom he had spoken to this morning. The boy was flying a kite, perhaps a birthday present, though at the moment both boy and kite had disappeared from view. Nim's gaze moved on to a GSP & L heavy-duty service truck and a cluster of men in work gear. Among them he caught a glimpse of the trim, bearded figure of Wally Talbot Jr. Presumably Wally was with the transmission line crew he had mentioned earlier. On the road leading into camp a small blue tradesman's van appeared.

Someone at the bus called over impatiently, 'Tess, let's go!'

Van Buren said curiously, 'Nim, what is it?'

'I'm not sure. I . . .'

An urgent, frantic shout cut across the camp clearing and all other sounds.

'Danny! Danny! *Don't move! Stay where you are!*'

Heads turned – Nim's and Van Buren's simultaneously – seeking the source of the voice.

Another shout, this time close to a scream. '*Danny! Do you hear me?*'

'Over there.' Van Buren pointed to a steep path, partially hidden by trees, on the camp's far side. A red-haired man – the technician, Fred Wilkins, was racing down it, shouting as he ran.

'*Danny! Do what I tell you! Stop! Don't move!*'

Now the children had stopped playing. Bewildered, they turned together in the direction where the shouting was aimed. Nim did the same.

'*Danny! Don't go any further! I'm coming for you! Keep still!*'

'Oh Christ!' Nim breathed.

Now he could see.

High overhead, on one of the towers carrying high voltage lines across the camp, the small boy, Danny Wilkins, was ascending. Clinging tightly to a steel support member more than halfway from the tower base, he was clambering upwards, slowly, steadily. His objective was visible above him – the kite he had been flying, now entangled in a transmission line atop the tower. A flash of sunlight showed Nim what moments earlier he had seen, so swiftly and briefly that it barely registered – the reflection from a slim aluminium pole the boy was clutching, a pole with a hook at one end. Clearly, Danny planned to use it to retrieve the kite. His small face was set determinedly as his sturdy body moved higher, and either he failed to hear his father's shouts or was ignoring them.

Nim and others began running hard towards the tower, but with a sense of helplessness as the small boy continued climbing steadily towards the high voltage lines. *Five hundred thousand volts.*

Fred Wilkins, still some distance away, was forcing himself to even greater speed, his face despairing.

Nim joined the shouting. '*Danny! The wires are dangerous!*'

115

Don't move! Stay there!'

This time the boy paused and glanced down. Then he looked up again at the kite and continued climbing, though more slowly, the aluminium pole extended out in front. He was now only a few feet from the nearest power line.

Then Nim saw that a new figure, nearer to the tower than anyone else, had sprung into action. Wally Talbot. Shooting forwards, his stride long, feet barely seeming to touch the ground, Wally was racing like an Olympic sprinter.

The press reporters were scrambling from the bus.

The tower, like others in the camp area, was surrounded by a protective chain link fence. Later it would be learned that Danny had surmounted the fence by climbing a tree and dropping from a low branch. Now Wally Talbot reached the fence and leaped. With what seemed a superhuman effort he grabbed the top and scrambled over. As he landed inside it could be seen that one of his hands was cut and bleeding. Then he was on the tower and climbing fast.

Breathlessly, tensely, the hastily assembled group of spectators, reporters and others watched from below. While they did, a trio of workmen from Wally's transmission line crew arrived and, after trying several keys, unlocked a gate in the chain link fence. Once inside the enclosure they, too, began climbing the tower. But Wally was far ahead, rapidly closing the distance between himself and the small redheaded boy.

Fred Wilkins had reached the base of the tower; he was winded and trembling. Briefly he moved as if to climb also, but someone restrained him.

All eyes were focused on the two figures nearest the top – Danny Wilkins, only a foot or two from the transmission lines, and Wally Talbot, now close behind.

Then it happened – so swiftly that those watching could not agree afterwards on the succession of events or even precisely what they were.

In what seemed a single moment, Danny – perched, it seemed, within inches of an insulator which separated the tower from a transmission line conductor – reached out with the aluminium pole in an attempt to snare the kite. Simultaneously, from just below and slightly to one side, Wally Talbot grabbed at the boy and pulled and held him. A pulsebeat later both appeared to slip, the boy sliding downwards, clinging to a girder, and Wally losing his grasp. At the same time, Wally, perhaps instinctively to maintain a precarious balance, seized the metal pole as Danny released it. The pole swung in an arc. Instantly a great ball of crackling orange light erupted, the pole disappeared, and Wally Talbot was enveloped in a corona of transparent flame. Then, with equal suddenness, the flame was gone and Wally's body sagged limply, motionless, across a tower support.

Miraculously, neither fell. Seconds later two of Wally Talbot's crew reached his body and began easing it down. The third man pinned Danny Wilkins to a girder and held him there while the others descended. The boy was apparently unhurt; he was sobbing and the sound could be heard below.

Then, somewhere on the other side of the camp, a siren began sounding short, sharp blasts.

17

The cocktail bar pianist switched nostalgically from 'Hello, Young Lovers!' to 'Whatever Will Be, Will Be'.

'If he plays many more of those oldies,' Harry London said, 'I'm gonna start crying in my beer. Another vodka, pal?'

'Why the hell not? Make it a double.' Nim, who had been hearing the music too, now listened to himself objectively. His speech was slurring at the edges, he observed, which figured. He had already had too much to drink, and knew it, but found himself not caring. Groping in a pocket, he took out his car keys and pushed them across the small, black-topped table. 'Take care of these. See that I get a taxi home.'

London pocketed the keys. 'Sure thing. You can stay at my place overnight, if you want.'

'No thanks, Harry.' Soon, when the liquor had dulled his perceptions further, Nim intended to go home, in fact wanted to. He wasn't worried about appearing there drunk – at least, not tonight. Leah and Benjy would be asleep and wouldn't see him. And Ruth, with her compassion and sympathy, would be forgiving.

'Testing, testing,' Nim said. He had wanted to hear his voice again before using it. Now, satisfied with his coherence, he told Harry, 'Y'know what I think? I think Wally'd be better off dead.'

London took a swig of beer before answering. 'Maybe Wally won't see it that way. Okay, so he got burned bad and lost his pecker. But there's other . . .'

Nim's voice rose. 'For Chrissakes, Harry! Do you *understand* what you're saying?'

'Take it easy,' London cautioned. Others in the bar had glanced their way. He added quietly, 'Sure, I understand.'

'In time . . .' Nim leaned across the table, balancing his words the way a conjurer might stand a plate on edge. 'In time the burns will heal. They'll do skin grafts. But you can't order a new penis from the Sears catalogue.'

'It's true. Can't deny it.' London shook his head sadly. 'That poor benighted bastard!'

The cocktail pianist was now into 'Lara's Theme' and Harry London wiped away a tear.

'Twenty-eight!' Nim said. 'That's how old he is. For God's sake, *twenty-eight*! Why, any normal man that age has still got ahead of him a lifetime of . . .'

London said curtly, '*I* don't need a diagram.' He finished his beer and motioned a waiter for another. 'One thing you gotta remember, Nim. Not every guy's an all-star cocksman like you. With you, if you lost out the way Wally has, I could understand it being the end of the road, or you thinking it was.' He asked curiously, 'You ever kept score? Maybe you could get in *The Guinness Book of Records*.'

'There's a Belgian writer,' Nim said, his thoughts for the moment diverted, 'Georges Simenon, who says he made it with ten thousand different women. I'm not up to that many, or even near it.'

'Leave out the numbers, then. The point is, maybe his dong was never as all-fired important to Wally as yours is to you.'

Nim shook his head. 'I doubt it.' He remembered the times he had seen Wally Jr and his wife, Mary, together. Nim's finely

118

honed instincts told him the two of them had a good thing going sexually. He wondered sadly what might happen to their marriage.

The beer and double vodka arrived. 'When you're coming back,' Nim told the waiter, 'bring the same again.'

It was early evening. The bar they were in – The Ezy Duzzit, smallish and dark, with a sentimental pianist who was just easing into 'Moon River' – was not far from GSP & L headquarters. Nim and Harry London had walked over here at the end of their working day. The third day.

The past three days had been the worst short period of his life that Nim ever remembered.

On the first day, at Devil's Gate, the sense of stupefaction following the electrocution of Wally Talbot Jr had lasted only seconds. Then, while Wally was still being brought down from the tower, standard emergency procedures went into high gear.

In any big utility company, electrocutions are rare but inevitably they happen – usually several times a year. The cause is either momentary carelessness, nullifying costly and rigid safety precautions, or a 'thousandth chance' accident such as that which happened so swiftly while Nim and others watched.

Ironically, Golden State Power had an aggressive publicity programme, aimed at parents and children, warning of dangers when kites were flown near overhead power lines. The utility had expended thousands of dollars on posters and comic books devoted to the subject and distributed them to schools and other agencies.

As Fred Wilkins, the red-haired technician, was to disclose with anguish later, he knew of the warning programme. But Wilkins' wife, Danny's mother, didn't know. She tearfully admitted having a vague impression that she might have heard something of the kind, but had forgotten when or where, nor had the memory surfaced when the kite – a birthday present from grandparents – arrived with the morning mail and she helped Danny put it together. As for Danny's climbing the tower, he was described by those who knew him as 'a determined boy, and fearless'. The hooked aluminium rod he had carried aloft was a gaff his father used for occasional deep sea fishing; it was stored in a tool shed where the boy had seen it often.

None of that was known, of course, when a trained first-aid

team, alerted by the camp siren, rushed to administer help to Wally Talbot. He was unconscious, had been badly burned over large areas of his body, and breathing had stopped.

The aid team, led by a registered nurse who ran the camp's small medical clinic, competently began mouth-to-mouth breathing in conjunction with external cardiac compression. While the resuscitation continued, Wally was carried to the one-bed clinic. There, the nurse – taking radiophone instructions from a doctor in the city – used a closed-chest defibrillator in an attempt to restore normal heart action. The attempt succeeded. That, and the other measures, saved Wally's life.

By then a company helicopter was on the way to Devil's Gate – the same machine which was to have collected Nim. Wally, accompanied by the nurse, was flown directly to a hospital for more intensive treatment.

It was not until next day that his survival was assured and the detailed nature of his injuries made known.

On that second day, newspapers played the story big, its impact strengthened by eyewitness accounts from reporters on the scene. The morning *Chronicle-West* gave it front-page treatment with a headline:

ELECTROCUTED MAN IS HERO

By afternoon, though the immediacy had lessened, the *California Examiner* devoted half of page three to a Nancy Molineaux by-line story headed:

Sacrifices Self in Saving Child

The *Examiner* also ran a two-column cut of Wally Talbot Jr and another of young Danny Wilkins with one side of his face bandaged – the result of abrasions when the boy slid downwards near the top of the tower, the only injury he received.

TV and radio had carried bulletins the night before, but continued their coverage the following day.

Because of its human interest, the story drew statewide and some national attention.

At the city's Mount Eden Hospital, shortly after noon on that second day, an attending surgeon held an impromptu press conference in a corridor. Nim, who had visited the hospital earlier, had just returned and listened from the fringes.

'Mr Talbot's condition is critical but stable, and he is out of immediate danger,' the young surgeon, who looked like a rein-carnated Robert Kennedy, announced. 'He has severe burns over twenty-five per cent of his body and has suffered certain other injuries.'

'Could you be more specific, Doctor?' one of a dozen news reporters asked. What are the other injuries?'

The surgeon glanced at an older man beside him whom Nim knew to be the hospital administrator.

'Ladies and gentlemen of the press,' the administrator said, 'normally, out of respect for privacy, no additional information would be disclosed. In this instance, however, after discussion with the family, it has been decided to be open with the press – quite frankly, to put an end to speculation. Therefore the last question will be answered. But before it is, I plead with you – out of consideration for the patient and his family – to be discreet in what you write and speak. Thank you. Please continue, Doctor.'

'The effects of electrocution on the human body are always unpredictable,' the surgeon said. 'Often, death results when large charges of electricity pass through internal organs before escaping to ground. In the case of Mr Talbot this didn't happen, so to that extent he was fortunate. Instead the electricity passed over the upper surface of his body and exited – to ground through the metal tower – by the route of his penis.'

There were gasps, and a shocked silence during which no one seemed eager to ask the next question. Eventually an elderly male reporter did. 'And, Doctor, the condition of . . .'

'It was destroyed. By burning. Totally. Now, if you'll excuse me . . .'

The press group, unusually subdued, drifted away.

Nim had stayed on. He identified himself to the administrator and enquired about Wally Jr's family – Ardythe and Mary. Nim had not seen either since the accident, but knew he would have to meet both women soon.

Ardythe, Nim learned, was at the hospital under sedation. 'She went into shock,' the administrator said. 'I presume you know about her husband's death just a short time ago.'

Nim nodded.

'The younger Mrs Talbot is with her husband, but no other visitors are being allowed for the time being.'

While the administrator waited, Nim scribbled a note to Mary, telling her he was available if needed, and in any case would return to the hospital next day.

That night, as during the preceding one, Nim slept only fitfully, the scene at Devil's Gate Camp repeating itself in his mind again and again, like a recurring nightmare.

On the morning of the third day he saw Mary, then Ardythe.

Mary met him outside the hospital room where Wally was still under intensive care. 'Wally's conscious,' she said, 'but doesn't want to see anyone. Not yet.' Wally's wife looked pale and tired, but some of her normal businesslike manner still came through. 'Ardythe wants to see you, though. She knew you were coming.'

Nim said gently, 'I guess words aren't a lot of good, Mary. Just the same, I'm sorry.'

'We all are.' Mary led the way to a door a few yards distant and opened it. 'Here's Nim, Mother.' She told him, 'I'm going back to Wally. I'll leave you now.'

'Come in, Nim,' Ardythe said. She was dressed and resting on a bed, propped up by pillows. 'Isn't this ridiculous – for me to be in the hospital too?'

There was hysteria beneath her voice, he thought, and her cheeks were too flushed, her eyes showed an artificial brightness. Nim remembered what the administrator had said about shock and sedation, though Ardythe appeared not to be sedated now.

He began hesitantly, 'I wish I knew what to say . . .' Pausing, he bent to kiss her.

To his surprise, Ardythe stiffened and turned her head away. He ended by clumsily touching his lips to her cheek, which felt hot.

'No!' Ardythe remonstrated. 'Please . . . don't kiss me.'

Wondering if he had offended her in some way, finding it hard to gauge her mood, he moved a chair and sat beside the bed.

There was a silence, then she said, half musingly, 'They say Wally will live. Yesterday we didn't know, so at least today is that much better. But I suppose you know *how* he will live; I mean, what's happened to him.'

'Yes,' he said, 'I know.'

'Have you been thinking the way I have, Nim? About a *reason* for what happened?'

'Ardythe, I was there. I saw . . .'

122

'I don't mean that. I mean *why*.'

Bewildered, he shook his head.

'I've done a lot of thinking since yesterday, Nim. And I've decided that what seemed like an accident could be because of us – you and me.'

Still not understanding, he protested, 'Please. You're overwrought. It's a terrible shock, I know, especially coming so soon after Walter.'

'That's the point.' Ardythe's face and voice were tense. 'You and I were sinful, so *soon* after Walter died. I've a feeling I'm being punished, that Wally, Mary, the children, are all suffering because of me.'

For a moment he was reduced to shocked silence, then said vehemently, 'For God's sake, Ardythe, stop this! It's ridiculous!'

'Is it? Think about it when you're alone, the way I've been doing. And just now you said "for God's sake." You're a Jew, Nim. Doesn't your religion teach you to believe in God's anger and punishment?'

'Even if it does, I don't accept all that.'

'I didn't either,' Ardythe said mournfully. 'But now I'm wondering.'

'Look,' he said, searching desperately for words to change her thinking, 'sometimes life causes one family to suffer – the way it seems: firing at it with both barrels – while other families go untouched. It isn't logical, it isn't fair. But it happens. I can think of other instances; so can you.'

'How do we know those other instances weren't punishments also?'

'Because there's no way they could be. Because all of life is chance – the chances we make ourselves, by error or bad luck, including the bad luck of being in the wrong place at the wrong time. That's *all* it is, Ardythe, and it's madness to blame yourself, *in any way*, for what's happened to Wally.'

She answered dully. 'I want to believe you. But I can't. Leave me now, Nim. They're going to send me home this afternoon.'

Standing, he told her, 'I'll drive out soon.'

She shook her head. 'I'm not sure you should. But phone me.'

He bent to kiss her cheek, then remembering her wishes, abandoned the attempt and went out quietly.

His mind was in turmoil. Clearly, Ardythe needed psychiatric help, but if Nim himself suggested it to Mary or anyone else, he would have to explain why – in detail. Even under the seal of medical confidence, he couldn't see himself doing that. At least, not yet.

The grief about Wally, Ardythe, and his own dilemma stayed with him through the day, refusing to be pushed away.

As if that wasn't enough, Nim was pilloried that afternoon in the *California Examiner*.

He had wondered if, in view of the emergency employment of a helicopter to airlift Wally out of Devil's Gate Camp, Nancy Molineaux might abandon her intention to write about the helicopter's other uses.

She hadn't.

Her story was in a box facing the editorial page.

The Captains and the Kings
. . . and GSP & L's Mr Goldman

Ever wonder what it would be like to have a private helicopter whisk you wherever you wanted while you sat back and relaxed ?

Most of us will never experience that exotic pleasure.

Those who do fall into certain catagories – the President of the United States, the British Royal Family, the late Howard Hughes, occasionally the Pope, and, oh yes, certain favoured executives of your friendly public utility, Golden State Power & Light. For example – Mr Nimrod Goldman.

Why Goldman ?, you might ask.

Well, it seems that Mr Goldman, who is a GSP & L vice president, is too important to ride on a bus, even though one – privately chartered by Golden State Power – was going his way the other day and had plenty of spare seats. Instead he chose a helicopter which . . .

There was more, along with a picture of a GSP & L helicopter and an unflattering portrait of Nim which, he suspected, Ms Molineaux chose from the newspaper's files.

Especially damaging was a paragraph which read:

Electric and gas consumers, already beset by high utility bills, and who have been told that rates must soon go up again, may wonder about the way their money is being spent by GSP & L, a quasi-public company. Perhaps if executives like Nimrod Goldman were willing to travel – like the rest of us – less glamorously, the resultant savings, along with other economies, could help to hold down those persistent rate increases.

In mid-afternoon Nim folded the newspaper and flagged the article, then gave it to J. Eric Humphrey's secretary. 'Tell the chairman I figured he'd see this anyway, so he might as well get it from me.'

Minutes later Humphrey strode into Nim's office and tossed the paper down. He was angrier than Nim had ever seen him and, uncharacteristically, raised his voice. 'In God's name what were you thinking of to get us into this mess? Don't you *know* the Public Utilities Commission is considering our application for a rate increase, and will hand down a decision in the next few days? This is just the kind of thing to raise a public clamour which could make them cut our throats.'

Nim released some irritability of his own. 'Of course I know that.' He motioned to the newspaper. 'I'm as upset about this as you are. But that damn woman reporter had her scalping knife out. If she hadn't picked the helicopter, it would have been something else.'

'Not necessarily; not if she hadn't found anything. By using the helicopter indiscreetly as you did, you dumped an opportunity in her lap.'

On the point of snapping back, Nim decided to keep quiet. Taking blame unfairly, he supposed, could be considered part of an assistant's job. Only two weeks earlier the chairman had told his senior aides at an informal meeting, 'If you can save yourself half a day's travel, and do your job faster and more efficiently, use a company helicopter because it's cheaper in the long run. I realize we need those aircraft for transmission line patrols and emergencies, but when they're not in use that way, it costs very little more to have them in the air than it does to keep them on the ground.'

Something else Eric Humphrey had presumably forgotten was asking Nim to take on the two-day press briefing *and* to represent him at an important Chamber of Commerce meeting the morning of the first day of the press tour. There was no way Nim could have done both without using the helicopter. However, Humphrey was a fair man and would probably remember later. Even if he failed to, Nim reasoned, it didn't much matter.

But that three-day combination of events had left him exhausted and melancholy. Thus, when Harry London, who knew some – though not all – of the reasons behind Nim's depression, had dropped in to suggest some drinking after work, Nim accepted promptly.

Now he felt the liquor taking hold and, while he wasn't any

happier, an increasing numbness was somehow comforting. In a corner of his brain still functioning with clarity, Nim despised himself for what he was doing, and the implied weakness. Then he reminded himself it didn't happen often – he couldn't remember the last time he had had too much to drink – and maybe just letting yourself go once in a while, saying *to hell with everything*, could be therapeutic.

'Let me ask you something, Harry,' Nim said thickly. 'You a religious man? Do you believe in God?'

Once more London drank deeply, then used a handkerchief to wipe beer foam from his lips. 'No to the first. About the second, put it this way : I've never made a big deal about not believing.'

'How about personal guilt? You carry a lot of that around?' Nim was remembering Ardythe, who had asked : *'Doesn't your religion teach you to believe in God's anger and punishment?'* This afternoon he had dismissed the question. Since then, annoyingly, it had replayed itself in his mind several times.

'I guess everybody's got some guilts.' London seemed inclined to end his statement there, then changed his mind and added, 'I sometimes think about two guys in Korea, close buddies of mine. We were on a recce patrol near the Yalu River. Those two were further forward than the rest of us, then we were all pinned down by enemy fire. The two guys needed help to get back. I was a topkick, in charge, and should have led the rest of us right then, taking a chance to reach them. While I was still dithering, making up my mind, the gooks found them; a grenade blew them both to bits. That's a guilt I carry around; that and some others.'

He drank again, then said, 'You know what you're doing, pal? You're getting us both . . . what's that word?'

'Maudlin,' Nim said, having trouble pronouncing it.

'You got it ! . . . maudlin.' Harry London nodded solemnly as the cocktail bar pianist began playing 'As Time Goes By'.

Part Two

1

Davey Birdsong, who had been inspecting the Sequoia Club's impressive headquarters, inquired cheekily, 'Where's the chairman's private sauna? And after that I'd like to see your solid gold toilet seat.'

'We don't have either,' Lauro Bo Carmichael said, a trifle stiffly. She was not entirely at ease with the bearded, portly, jesting Birdsong, who, though a naturalized American for many years, still exhibited some of the rough outback manners of his native Australia. Laura Bo, who had met Birdsong a few times previously at outside meetings, equated him with the Jolly Swagman in 'Waltzing Matilda'.

Which was ridiculous, of course, and she knew it. Though Davey Birdsong seemed to make a point of sounding uncultured and dressed the same way – today he wore shabby, patched jeans and running shoes with string for laces – the Sequoia Club chairman was well aware he was a scholar of stature, holding a master's degree in sociology, as well as being a part-time lecturer at the University of California at Berkeley. He had also put together a coalition of consumer, church and left-wing political groups which called itself p & lfp – or, power & light for people. (The lower case initials were, in Birdsong's words, 'to emphasize we are not capitalists'.)

The declared aim of p & lfp was 'to fight the profit-bloated monster GSP & L on all fronts'. In various confrontations so far, p & lfp had opposed rate increases for electricity and gas, had fought licensing of a nuclear power plant, had objected to GSP & L public relations activities – 'ruthless propaganda unwillingly paid for by consumers', was how Birdsong and p & lfp described it – and had urged a compulsory takeover of the power company by municipalities. Now, Birdsong's movement was seeking to join forces with the prestigious Sequoia Club in opposing the latest GSP & L expansion plans. That proposal was to be reviewed at a meeting with top club officials, due to begin shortly.

'Geez, Laura baby,' Birdsong observed, his gaze still roaming the imposing panelled boardroom where they were talking, 'I guess it's real soul-inspiring to work in a ritzy layout like this. You should see my dump. Compared with what you got here it's a bum's nightmare.'

She told him, 'Our headquarters was deeded to us many years ago as part of a bequest. A condition was that we occupy the building; otherwise we would not receive the substantial income which accompanies it.' At certain moments – this was one of them – Laura Bo Carmichael found the stately Cable Hill mansion, which the Sequoia Club occupied, something of an embarrassment. It was once a millionaire's town house which still bespoke wealth, and personally she would have preferred simple quarters. To move, however, would have been financial madness. She added, 'I'd prefer you not call me "Laura baby".'

'I'll make a note of that.' Grinning, Birdsong produced a notebook, unclipped a ball-point pen and wrote something down.

Putting the notebook away, he regarded the slight, trim figure of Mrs Carmichael, then said reflectively, 'Bequests, eh? From dead donors. I guess that, and those big live donors, is what keeps the Sequoia Club so rich.'

'Rich is a relative word.' Laura Bo Carmichael wished the three of her colleagues who were to join her for this meeting would arrive. 'It's true our organization is fortunate in having national support, but we have substantial expenses.'

The big bearded man chuckled. 'Not so many, though, that you couldn't spread some of that bread around to other groups – doing your kind of work – which need it.'

'We'll see. But,' Mrs Carmichael said firmly, 'please don't assume we are so naïve that you can come here posing as a poor relation, because we know better.' She consulted some notes she had not intended to use until later. 'We know, for example, that your p & lfp has some twenty-five thousand members who pay three dollars a year each, collected by paid door-to-door canvassers, which adds up to $75,000. Out of that you pay yourself a salary of $20,000 a year, plus unknown expenses.'

'Fella hasta make a living.'

'A remarkably good one, I'd say.' Laura Bo continued reading. 'In addition there are your university lecture fees, another fixed salary from an activist training organization, and payment for articles you write, all of which is believed to bring your personal income as a protester to $60,000 a year.'

Davey Birdsong, whose smile had grown broader while he listened, seemed not in the least taken aback. He commented, 'A right nifty job of research.'

It was the Sequoia Club chairman's turn to smile. 'We do have an excellent research department here.' She folded the notes and put them away. 'None of the material I have quoted is for outside use, of course. It's merely to make you aware of *our* awareness that professional protesters like you have a good thing going. That mutual knowledge will save time when we get down to business.'

A door opened quietly and a neat, elderly man with iron-grey hair and rimless glasses entered the boardroom.

Laura Bo said, 'Mr Birdsong, I believe you know our manager-secretary, Mr Pritchett.'

Davey Birdsong put out a large, meaty hand. 'We met on the battlefield a time or two. Hiya, Pritchy!'

When his hand had been pumped vigorously the newcomer said drily, 'I hadn't considered environmental hearings to be battlefields, though I suppose they could be construed that way.'

'Damn right, Pritchy! And when *I* go into battle, especially against the people's enemy, Golden State Power, I fire every big gun and keep on firing. Tough 'n' tougher, that's the prescription. Oh, I'm not saying there isn't a place for your kind of opposition. There is! – you people bring a touch of class. I'm the one, though, who makes headlines and gets on TV news. By the way, did you kids see me on TV with that GSP & L prick, Goldman?'

'*The Good Evening Show*,' the manager-secretary acknowledged. 'Yes, I did. I thought you were colourful, though – to be objective – Goldman was shrewd in resisting your baiting.' Pritchett removed his glasses to polish them. 'Perhaps, as you say, there is a place for *your* kind of opposition to GSP & L. Possibly, even, we need each other.'

'Attaboy, Pritchy!'

'The correct pronunciation is Pritch*ett*. Or, if you prefer, you may call me Roderick.'

'I'll make a note of that, Roddy old man.' Grinning broadly at Laura Bo, Birdsong went through his notebook routine once more.

While they were talking two others had come in. Laura Bo Carmichael introduced them as Irwin Saunders and Mrs Priscilla Quinn, the remaining members of the Sequoia Club executive committee. Saunders was a balding, gravel-voiced lawyer who handled big-name divorce cases and was frequently in the news. Mrs Quinn, fashionably dressed and attractive in her late forties, was the wife of a wealthy banker and noted for her civic zeal, also for limiting her friendships to other wealthy or important people. She accepted Davey Birdsong's outstretched hand with reluctance, regarding him with a mixture of curiosity and distaste.

The chairman suggested, 'I think we might all be seated and get on with business.'

The five grouped themselves near one end of a long mahogany table, Laura Bo at the head.

'We are all concerned,' she said, 'about the recent proposals of Golden State Power & Light which the Sequoia Club has already decided would be harmful to the environment. We will actively oppose them at forthcoming hearings.'

Birdsong thumped the table loudly. 'And *I* say: three bloody cheers for the Sequoia mob!'

Irwin Saunders appeared amused. Mrs Quinn raised her eyebrows.

'What Mr Birdsong has suggested in connection with that opposition,' the chairman continued, 'are certain liaison arrangements between our organization and his. I'll ask him to describe them.'

Attention swung to Davey Birdsong. For a moment he eyed the other four amiably, one by one, then plunged into his presentation.

'The kind of opposition all of us are talking about is a war – with GSP & L the enemy. To regard the scene otherwise would be to court defeat. Therefore, just as in a war, an attack must be mounted on several fronts.'

Noticeably, Birdsong had shed his clown's veneer and the earlier breeziness of language. He proceeded, 'To carry the war simile a stage further – as well as doing combat on specific issues, no opportunity should be lost to snipe at GSP & L whenever such an opening occurs.'

'Really,' Mrs Quinn interjected. 'I'm aware you advised us it was a simile, but I find this talk of war distasteful. After all . . .'

The lawyer, Saunders, reached out to touch her arm. 'Priscilla, why not let him finish?'

She shrugged. 'Very well.'

'Causes are often lost, Mrs Quinn,' Birdsong declared, 'because of too much softness, an unwillingness to face the hard nub of reality.'

Saunders nodded. 'A valid point.'

'Let's get to specifics,' Pritchett, the manager-secretary, urged. 'Mr Birdsong, you referred to "several fronts". Precisely which?'

'Right!' Birdsong became businesslike again. 'Fronts one, two and three – the public hearings on the announced plans for Tunipah, Fincastle Valley and Devil's Gate. You people will fight on all of them. So will my gallant p & lfp.'

'As a matter of interest,' Laura Bo enquired, 'on what grounds will you oppose?'

'Not sure yet, but don't worry. Between now and then we'll think of something.'

Mrs Quinn seemed shocked. Irwin Saunders smiled.

'Then there are the rate hearings; that's front number four. Any time there's a proposal for increased utility rates, p & lfp will oppose them fiercely, as we did last time. With success, I might add.'

'What success?' Roderick Pritchett asked. 'So far as I know, a decision hasn't been announced.'

'You're right, it hasn't.' Birdsong smiled knowingly. 'But I have friends at the PUC, and I know what's coming out of there in two or three days – an announcement which will be a kick in the crotch to GSP & L.'

Pritchett asked curiously, 'Does the utility know yet?'

'I doubt it.'

Laura Bo Carmichael said, 'Let's get on.'

'The fifth front,' Birdsong said, 'and a mighty important one, is the annual meeting of Golden State Power & Light which takes place two and a half weeks from now. I have some plans for that, though I'd be glad if you didn't ask me too much about them.'

'You're implying,' Saunders said, 'that we'd be better off not knowing.'

'Exactly, counsellor.'

'Then what,' Laura Bo asked, 'is all this talk of liaison about?'

Birdsong grinned as he rubbed a thumb and two fingers together suggestively. 'This kind of liaison. Money.'

'I thought we'd get to that,' Pritchett said.

'Something else about our working together,' Birdsong told the Sequoia group. 'It would be better if it wasn't out in the open. It should be confidential, *entre nous*.'

'Then in what possible way,' Mrs Quinn asked, 'would the Sequoia Club benefit?'

Irwin Saunders said, 'I can answer that. The fact is, Priscilla, anything which damages the image of GSP & L, in *any* area, is likely to diminish their strength and success in others.' He smiled. 'It's a tactic which lawyers have been known to use.'

'Why do you need money?' Pritchett asked Birdsong. 'And what sum are we talking about?'

'We need it because p & lpf alone cannot afford all the preparation and people which are necessary if our combined opposition – on the table and under it – is to be effective.' Birdsong turned directly to the chairman. 'As you pointed out, we have resources of our own, but not nearly enough for a project of this size.' His glance returned to the others. 'The amount I'm suggesting the Sequoia Club contribute is fifty thousand dollars in two instalments.'

The manager-secretary removed his glasses and inspected them for clarity. 'You certainly don't think small.'

'No, and neither should you, considering what's at stake – in your case a possible major impact on the environment.'

'What bothers me in all of this,' Mrs Quinn observed, 'are certain implications of gutter fighting which I do not care for.'

Laura Bo Carmichael nodded. 'I have precisely the same feeling.'

Again it was the lawyer, Saunders, who interceded.

'Certain facts of life,' he told his colleagues, 'ought to be faced. In opposing these latest projects of Golden State Power – Tunipah, Fincastle, Devil's Gate – the Sequoia Club will present what we know to be reasoned arguments. However, remembering the climate of the times and misguided demands for more and more energy, reason and rationale are not certain to prevail. So what else do we do? I say we need another element – an ally that is more aggressive, more flamboyant, more calculated to excite

133

public attention which, in turn, will influence the regulators who are only politicians once removed. In my view Mr Birdsong and his whatever-he-calls-it group . . .'

'Power & light for people,' Birdsong interjected.

Saunders waved a hand as if the detail were unimportant. 'Both ahead of those hearings, and at them, he'll add that missing element we lack.'

'TV and the press love me,' Birdsong said. 'I give them a show, something to leaven and liven their stories. Because of that, anything I say gets printed and is put on the air.'

'That's true,' the manager-secretary affirmed. 'Even some outrageous statements of his have been used by the media while they've omitted our comments and those of GSP & L.'

The chairman asked him, 'Am I to assume you are in favour of what's proposed?'

'Yes, I am,' Pritchett said. 'There is one assurance, though, I'd like from Mr Birdsong, namely that whatever his group does, no violence or intimidation will be countenanced.'

The boardroom table quivered as Birdsong's hand slammed down. 'Assurance given! My group despises violence *of any kind*. We have issued statements saying so.'

'I'm glad to hear it,' Pritchett acknowledged, 'and the Sequoia Club, of course, shares that view. By the way, I presume everyone saw the report, in today's *Chronicle-West*, of more bombings at GSP & L.'

The others nodded. The report had described havoc at a GSP & L truck depot where more than two dozen vehicles were damaged or destroyed during the night – the result of a fire started by a bomb. Several days earlier a sub-station had been bombed, though damage was slight. In both instances the underground Friends of Freedom had claimed responsibility.

'Are there more questions for Mr Birdsong?' Laura Bo Carmichael asked.

There were several. They concerned the tactics to be employed against GSP & L – 'continual harassment on a broad public information front' was how Birdsong put it – and the use to which the Sequoia Club's money would be put.

At one point Roderick Pritchett ruminated aloud, 'I'm not sure it would be to our advantage to insist on a detailed accounting, but naturally we would require proof that our money was expended effectively.'

'Your proof would be in results,' Birdsong answered.

It was conceded that certain matters would have to be taken on trust.

At length Laura Bo Carmichael announced, 'Mr Birdsong, I'll ask you to leave us now so that the rest of us can discuss your proposal privately. One way or the other, we will be in touch with you soon.'

Davey Birdsong stood, beaming, his big body towering over the others. 'Well, cobbers all, it's been a privilege and pleasure. For now – so long!' As he went out there was an awareness that he had slipped – like putting on a garment – into his bluff public role.

When the boardroom door had closed behind Birdsong, Mrs Quinn spoke first and firmly. 'I don't like any of it. I dislike the man and all my instincts are against trusting him. I'm totally opposed to any linkage with his group.'

'I'm sorry to hear that,' Irwin Saunders said, 'because I believe his diversionary tactics are exactly what we need to beat these new GSP & L proposals, which is the important thing.'

'I must say, Mrs Quinn,' Pritchett remarked, 'I agree with Irwin's view.'

Priscilla Quinn shook her head decisively. 'Nothing any of you say will make me change my mind.'

The lawyer sighed. 'Priscilla, you're being altogether too prim and proper.'

'Possibly that's true.' Mrs Quinn's face flushed red. 'But I also have principles, something that disgusting man appears to lack.'

Laura Bo said sharply, 'No acrimony among ourselves, please!'

Pritchett interjected smoothly, 'May I remind everyone that this committee has authority to make a binding decision and, if it so decides, to expend the amount of money we've discussed.'

'Madam Chairman,' Saunders said, 'the way I count the voting so far is two in favour, one against, which leaves the swing vote up to you.'

'Yes,' Laura Bo acknowledged, 'I realize that, and I'll admit to some ambivalence.'

'In that case,' Saunders said, 'let me state some reasons why I think you should come to my view, and Roderick's.'

'And when you've finished,' Priscilla Quinn told him, 'I'll argue the opposite.'

For another twenty minutes the debate went back and forth.

Laura Bo Carmichael listened, making a contribution here and there, at the same time weighing mentally the way her vote should go. If she opposed cooperating with Birdsong there would be a 2–2 stalemate which would have the same effect as outright rejection. If she voted 'for', it would be a decisive 3–1.

Her inclination was to cast a 'no'. While seeing merit in Saunders' and Pritchett's pragmatism, Laura Bo's instincts about Davey Birdsong paralleled Priscilla Quinn's. The trouble was, she didn't particularly *want* to be linked with Priscilla Quinn – an undoubted snob, a society do-gooder forever in the social columns, married to old California money, and thus representing many things which Laura Bo abhorred.

Something else she was aware of: If she sided with Priscilla against the other two it would be a clear case of the women versus the men. Never mind that Laura Bo would not intend it that way and was capable of judging any issue irrespective of her sex, that was the way it would *look*. She could imagine Irwin Saunders, a male chauvinist, thinking: *the damn women stuck together*, even if not saying it aloud. Saunders had not been one of Laura Bo's supporters when she was a candidate for the Sequoia Club chairmanship; he had backed a male contender. Now Laura Bo, as the first woman to assume the club's highest office, wanted to show that she could fill that post as well and impartially as any man, perhaps a good deal better.

And yet . . . there was still her instinct that the Birdsong connection would be *wrong*.

'We're going in circles,' Saunders said. 'I suggest we take a final vote.'

Priscilla Quinn asserted, 'My vote remains "no".'

Saunders growled, 'Strongly – "yes".'

'Forgive me, Mrs Quinn,' Pritchett said. 'I vote "yes".'

The eyes of the other three were focused on Laura Bo. She hesitated, reviewing once more the implications and her doubts. Then she said decisively, 'I will vote "yes".'

'That does it!' Irwin Saunders said. He rubbed his hands together. 'Priscilla, why not be a good loser? Join the rest of us and make it unanimous.'

Tight-lipped, Mrs Quinn shook her head negatively. 'I think you will all regret that vote. I wish my dissent to be recorded.'

2

While the Sequoia Club committee continued its discussion in his absence, Davey Birdsong left the club's headquarters building humming a jaunty tune. He had not the least doubt what the outcome would be. The Quinn woman, he knew, would be against him; he was equally sure the other three – for individual reasons – would see the situation his way. The fifty thousand smackeroos was in the bag.

He retrieved his car – a beat-up Chevrolet – from a nearby parking lot and drove through the city's centre, then south-east for several miles. He stopped on a nondescript street where he had never been before but which was the sort of location where he could leave the car for several hours without its attracting attention. Birdsong locked the car, memorized the street name, then walked several blocks to a busier thoroughfare where, he had observed *en route*, several bus lines operated. He took the first westbound bus which came along.

On the way from the car he had donned a hat which he normally never wore and also put on horn-rimmed glasses which he didn't need. The two additions changed his appearance surprisingly, so that anyone used to seeing him on TV or elsewhere would almost certainly fail to recognize him now.

After riding in the bus for ten minutes, Birdsong got off and hailed a cruising taxi which he directed to drive northwards. Several times he glanced through the taxi's rear window, inspecting other traffic following. The inspections seemed to satisfy him and he ordered the taxi to stop and paid it off. A few minutes later he boarded another bus, this time going east. By now his journey since parking the car had assumed the approximate shape of a square.

As he left the second bus, Birdsong inspected the other passengers getting off, then began walking briskly, turning several corners and glancing back each time. After about five minutes of walking he stopped at a small row house, then ascended a half-dozen steps to a recessed front door. He depressed a bell push and stood where he could be seen from the other side of the door through a tiny one-way peephole. Almost at once the door opened and he went inside.

In the small dark hallway of the Friends of Freedom hideaway Georgos Archambault asked, 'Were you careful in coming here?'

Birdsong growled, 'Of course I was careful. I always am.' He said accusingly, 'You botched the sub-station job.'

'There were reasons,' Georgos said. 'Let's go below.' He led the way down a flight of cement stairs to the basement workroom with its usual clutter of explosives and accessories.

On a makeshift couch against one wall a girl lay stretched out. She appeared to be in her twenties. Her small round face, which in other circumstances might have been pretty, was waxen pale. Stringy blonde hair, in need of combing, spilled over a grubby pillow. Her right hand was heavily bandaged, the bandage stained brown where blood had seeped through and dried.

Birdsong exploded. 'Why is *she* here?'

'That's what I was going to explain,' Georgos said. 'She was helping me at the sub-station and a blasting cap went off. It took off two of her fingers and she was bleeding like a pig. It was dark; I wasn't sure if we'd been heard. I did the rest of the job in a big hurry.'

'And where you put the bomb was stupid and useless,' Birdsong said. 'A firecracker would have done as much damage.'

Georgos flushed. Before he could answer, the girl said, 'I ought to go to a hospital.'

'You can't and you won't.' Birdsong exhibited none of the affability which was his trademark. He told Georgos angrily, 'You know our arrangement. Get her out of here!'

Georgos motioned with his head and unhappily the girl got off the couch and went upstairs. He had made another mistake, Georgos knew, in allowing her to stay. The arrangement Birdsong had mentioned – a sensible precaution – was that only he and Georgos should meet face-to-face. Davey Birdsong's connection was unknown to the others in the underground group – Wayde, Ute and Felix – who either left the house or kept out of sight when a visit from the Friends of Freedom outside conduit – Birdsong – was expected. The real trouble was, Georgos realized, he had become soft about his woman, Yvette, which was not good. It had been the same way when the blasting cap went off; at that moment Georgos had been more concerned about Yvette's injuries than the job in hand, so that wanting to get her away safely was the real reason he had hurried – and botched.

When the girl had gone, Birdsong said, low-voiced, 'Just make damn sure – no hospital, no doctor. There'd be questions and she knows too much. If you have to, get rid of her. There are easy ways.'

'She'll be all right. Besides, she's useful.' Georgos was uncomfortable under Birdsong's scrutiny and changed the subject. 'The truck depot last night went well. You saw the reports?'

The big man nodded grudgingly. 'They should all go that way. There isn't time or money to waste on bummers.'

Georgos accepted the rebuke silently, though he didn't have to. He was the leader of Friends of Freedom. Davey Birdsong's role was secondary, as a link to the outside, particularly to those supporters of revolution – 'drawing room Marxists' – who favoured active anarchy but didn't want to share its risks. Yet Birdsong, by his nature, liked to appear dominant, and sometimes Georgos let him get away with it because of his usefulness, particularly the money he brought in.

Money was the reason right now for avoiding an argument; Georgos needed more since his earlier sources had abruptly dried up. His bitch of a mother, the Greek movie actress who had supplied him with a steady income for twenty years, had apparently hit hard times herself; she wasn't getting film parts any more because not even makeup could conceal the fact she was fifty, her young goddess looks gone for ever. That part Georgos was delighted about and hoped things would get progressively worse for her. If she were starving, he told himself, he wouldn't give her a stale biscuit. Just the same, a notification from the Athens lawyers – impersonal as usual – that no more payments would be made into his Chicago bank account had come at an awkward time.

Georgos' cash needs involved current costs and future plans. One project was to build a small nuclear bomb and explode it in or near the headquarters of Golden State Power & Light. Such a bomb, Georgos reasoned, would destroy the building, the exploiters and lackeys in it, and also much else around – a salutary lesson to the capitalist oppressors of the people. At the same time, Friends of Freedom would become an even more formidable force than now, to be treated with awe and respect.

The idea of creating an atomic bomb was ambitious and perhaps unrealistic – though not entirely. After all, a twenty-one-year-old Princeton student named John Phillips had already demonstrated in a much-publicized term paper that the 'how to' details were available in library reference materials to anyone having the patience to assemble them. Georgos Winslow Archambault, steeped in physics and chemistry, had obtained all the information he could about Phillips' research and had built up a file of his own, also using library data. One non-library item in the file was a ten-page handbook put out by California's Office of Emergency Services and directed to police agencies; it outlined ways of dealing with atomic bomb threats and that, too, had provided useful information. Georgos was now close, he believed, to creating a detailed working drawing. However, actual construction of a bomb would require fissionable material, which would have to be stolen, and that would take money – a lot, plus organization and luck. But it just *might* be done; stranger things had happened.

He told Birdsong, 'Since you've brought up time and money, we need some long green now.'

'You'll get it.' Birdsong permitted himself a wide smile, the first since coming in. 'And plenty. I found another money tree.'

3

Nim was shaving. It was shortly after 7am on a Thursday in late August.

Ruth had gone downstairs ten minutes earlier to prepare breakfast. Leah and Benjy were still sleeping. Now Ruth returned, appearing at the bathroom door with a copy of the *Chronicle-West*.

'I hate to start your day off badly,' she said, 'but I know you'll want to see this.'

'Thanks.' He put down his razor and took the newspaper with wet hands, scanning the front page. Below the fold was a single-column item:

GSP & L RATE HIKE DISALLOWED

Electricity and gas rates are not going up.

This was revealed yesterday afternoon by the California Public Utilities Commission in announcing its turndown of an application by Golden State Power & Light for a 13 per cent increase in gas and electric rates which would bring the giant utility another $580 million annual revenue.

'We do not see the need for an increase at this time,' the PUC stated in a decision arrived at by a 3 – 2 vote of the commissioners.

At public hearings GSP & L had argued that it needs more money to offset rising costs due to inflation and to raise capital for its construction program.

High officials of GSP & L were not available for comment, though a spokesman expressed regret and concern for the future energy situation in California. However, Davey Birdsong, leader of a consumers group – power & light for people – hailed the decision as . . .

Nim put the newspaper on the toilet tank beside him while he finished shaving; he had learned of the decision late yesterday so the report was confirmation. When he went downstairs Ruth had his breakfast ready – lamb kidneys with scrambled eggs – and she sat opposite him with a cup of coffee while he ate.

She asked, 'What does that commission decision really mean?'

He grimaced. 'It means that three people, who got jobs because of politics, have the right to tell big corporations like GSP & L and the phone company how to manage their affairs – and do.'

'Will it affect you?'

'Damn right it will! I'll have to revamp the construction programme; we'll cancel or slow down some projects and that will lead to layoffs. Even then there'll be a cash bind. Long faces this morning, especially Eric's.' Nim cut and speared a kidney. 'These are great. You do them better than anybody.'

Ruth hesitated, then said, 'Could you get your own breakfast for a while, do you think?'

Nim was startled. 'Sure, but why?'

'I may be going away.' In her quiet voice Ruth corrected herself. 'I *am* going away. For a week, perhaps longer.'

He put down his knife and fork, staring across the table. 'Why? Where?'

'Mother will have Leah and Benjy while I'm gone, and Mrs Blair will come in as usual to clean. So it will just mean your having dinner out, and I'm sure you can arrange that.'

Nim ignored the barb. He insisted, his voice rising, 'You didn't answer my question. Where are you going, and why?'

'There's no need for either of us to shout.' Beneath Ruth's composure he sensed an uncharacteristic hardness. 'I heard your question, but the way things are between us, I don't believe I should have to answer. Do you?'

Nim was silent, knowing precisely what Ruth meant: why should there be a double standard? If Nim chose to break the rules of marriage, have a succession of affairs, and stay out many evenings for his own diversions, why shouldn't Ruth exercise similar freedom, also without explanations?

On that basis, her declaration of equality – which it clearly was – seemed reasonable. Just the same, Nim felt a stab of jealousy because he now was sure Ruth was involved with another man. Originally he hadn't thought so; now he was convinced, and while he knew that give-and-take arrangements existed in some marriages, he found it hard to accept them in his own.

'We both know,' Ruth said, interrupting his thoughts, 'that for a long time you and I have only been going through the motions of being married. We haven't talked about it. But I think we should.' This time, despite an attempt at firmness, there was a tremor in her voice.

He asked, 'Do you want to talk now?'

Ruth shook her head. 'Perhaps when I come back.' She added, 'As soon as I work some things out, I'll let you know when I'm leaving.'

Nim said dully, 'All right.'

'You haven't finished your breakfast.'

He pushed the plate away. 'I don't feel like eating any more.'

Though the exchange with Ruth – jolting in its suddenness – preoccupied Nim during his drive downtown, activity at GSP & L headquarters quickly eclipsed personal thoughts.

The ruling of the Public Utilities Commission took priority over all other business.

All morning a procession of executives from the utility's financial and legal departments, their expressions serious, hastened in and out of the chairman's office. Their comings and goings marked a succession of conferences, each concerned with the essential question: without any increase whatever in the rates it could charge customers, how could GSP & L carry out its needed construction plans and stay solvent? The consensus: without some drastic and immediate cutback in expenses, it simply wasn't possible.

At one point J. Eric Humphrey paced the rug behind his desk and demanded rhetorically, 'Why is it that when the price of bread goes up because of inflation, or meat prices soar, or it costs more to get into a ball game or a movie – no one is ever surprised and it's all accepted? But when we point out, truthfully, that we can't produce electricity at our old rates because *our* costs have gone up too, nobody believes us.'

Oscar O'Brien, the general counsel, answered while he lit one of his inevitable cigars. 'They don't believe us because they've been conditioned not to – mostly by politicians trying to suck up to voters and looking for an easy target. Public utilities have always been one.'

The chairman snorted. 'Politicians! They disgust me! They invented inflation, created it, worsened it, keep it going as they build public debt – all so they can buy votes and hang on to their jobs. Yet those charlatans, those obscurers of the truth, blame inflation on everybody else – unions, business – anyone, anything, except themselves. If it weren't for politicians, we wouldn't be asking for a rate increase because we wouldn't need to.'

Sharlett Underhill, executive vice president of finance and the fourth person in the chairman's office, murmured, 'Amen!' Mrs Underhill, a tall brunette in her forties, capable, normally unruffled, today appeared harried. Which was understandable, Nim thought. Whatever financial decisions were made as a result of the PUC turndown, they would inevitably be harsh and Sharlett Underhill would have to implement them.

Eric Humphrey, who had stopped his pacing, asked, 'Does anyone have a theory about why *everything* we sought was rejected? Did we misjudge the profiles? Where was our strategy wrong?'

'I'm not sure our strategy *was* wrong,' O'Brien said. 'And we sure as hell studied the profiles, and acted on them.'

Behind the question and answer was a common practice of utility companies – but also a closely guarded secret.

Whenever a Public Utility Commissioner was appointed, companies which would be affected by the new commissioner's decisions began a detailed undercover study of the individual, including a psychiatric profile. The resultant material was pored over by experts in psychology who searched for prejudices to be guarded against or weaknesses to be exploited.

Later an executive of the utility would attempt to strike up a friendship in the course of which the commissioner would be entertained at the executive's home, invited to play golf, share hard-to-get seats at sports events, or taken trout fishing at a Sierra hideaway. The entertainment was always pleasant, private, and discreet, but never lavish. During casual conversations some discussion might occur about the utility's affairs, but no direct favours were asked; the influence was more subtle. Often the tactic worked in a utility's favour. Occasionally it didn't.

'We knew two of the commissioners would vote against us anyway,' the lawyer said, 'and we knew for sure that two of the other three were in our corner. So that left Cy Reid's as the swing vote. We'd worked on Reid, we thought he'd see things our way, but we were wrong.'

Nim knew about Commissioner Cyril Reid. He was a PhD economist and former university lecturer whose practical business experience was nil. But Reid had worked closely with California's incumbent Governor through two election campaigns and insiders now believed that when the Governor moved from Sacramento to the White House, as he hoped to, Cy Reid would go with him as chief of staff.

According to a confidential file which Nim had read, Commissioner Reid was once an ardent believer in Keynesian economics, but had recanted, now accepting that the deficit spending doctrines of John Maynard Keynes had led to economic disaster worldwide. A recent report from a senior vice president of GSP & L, Stewart Ino, who had cultivated Reid, declared that the commissioner had 'faced up to the realities of income statements and balance sheets, including those of public utilities'. But perhaps, Nim thought, Cy Reid the politician had been laughing at them all along, and was doing so right now.

'During the pendency of the case,' the chairman persisted, 'surely there were backstage discussions with commission staff? Weren't compromises reached?'

Sharlett Underhill answered, 'The answer to both questions is yes.'

'Then if compromises were agreed on, what happened to them?'

Mrs Underhill shrugged. 'Nothing done behind scenes is binding. Three of the commissioners, including Reid, ignored recommendations of their staff.'

Something else most people never knew about, Nim thought, were negotiations which proceeded, out of sight, during and after public hearings.

Utilities like GSP & L, when seeking more revenue through a rate increase, often asked more than was needed and more than they expected to get. What followed was a ritualistic dance in which PUC commissioners joined. The commissioners *lopped off* some of what was asked, thus appearing to be vigilant in their public duty. The utility, though seemingly rebuffed, in fact got what it wanted, or thereabouts.

Essential details were worked out by the commission's staff during off-the-record talks with other staff from the public utility. Nim had once attended such a session in a small, closed room and heard a PUC staffer ask, 'Now how big an increase do you people *really* need? Never mind the public hearings bullshit. Just tell us, and we'll tell *you* how far we can go.' Frankness on both sides had followed, with the outcome settled privately in much less time than was occupied in public hearings.

On the whole, the system was reasonable and it worked. But this time, obviously, it hadn't.

Aware that the chairman was still seething, Nim said cautiously, 'It doesn't look as if inquests, at this moment, will do a lot of good.'

Humphrey sighed. 'You're right.' He addressed the finance vice president. 'Sharlett, financially speaking, how do we get through next year?'

'The options are limited,' Mrs Underhill said, 'but I'll go over them.' She spread out several sheets of complex calculations.

The discussions continued through most of the day, with still more staff members summoned to the chairman's office, their input sought. But in the end it became evident there were two choices only. One was to cut back on all planned construction, curtail maintenance and reduce customer service. The other was to cease paying dividends to shareholders. It was affirmed that the first was unthinkable, the second could be disastrous because it would send GSP & L's stock plummeting and place the company's future in jeopardy. However, it was also agreed that no other courses of action were possible.

Late in the afternoon, J. Eric Humphrey, visibly tired and downcast, pronounced the verdict which the small top-level coterie had known from the beginning to be inevitable. 'Management will recommend to the board of directors that payment of all dividends on the company's common stock be suspended immediately and indefinitely.'

It was a historic decision.

Since the formation of Golden State Power & Light three quarters of a century earlier when its predecessor company was combined with several others to become a single entity, the corporation had been a model of financial rectitude. Never in the ensuing years had it failed to meet its obligations or to pay a dividend on its stock. As a result, GSP & L was known among investors large and small as 'old faithful' and 'the widows' and orphans' friend'. Retirees in California and elsewhere put their life savings confidently into GSP & L shares, relying on regular dividends as their means of support. Cautious trustees of other people's money did the same. Thus the omission of dividends would have widespread effect, not only in lost income but in reduction of capital when the value of the shares dropped, as was bound to happen.

Shortly before the chairman's anguished pronouncement, the original morning quartet had reassembled – Eric Humphrey, Oscar O'Brien, Sharlett Underhill, and Nim – plus Teresa Van Buren. The PR head had been called in because of the major public impact the decision would soon have.

A regular board of directors meeting was already scheduled for 10am next Monday, and the directors' finance committee would meet a half hour earlier. Presumably at both sessions the management decision would be confirmed, after which an immediate public statement would be made. Meanwhile, precautions were necessary to guard against informational leaks which might trigger speculative trading in the company's stock.

'Outside this room,' Sharlett Underhill now reminded the others, 'there must be no whisper of what is intended until that official statement. Also, as financial officer, I must caution everyone that because of the inside information the five of us possess, any personal trading in the company's shares, prior to Monday's announcement, would be a criminal offence under Securities and Exchange Commission laws.'

In an attempt at lightness, Nim said, 'Okay, Sharlett, we won't sell short and make our fortunes.' But no one laughed.

'I presume,' Teresa Van Buren observed, 'that everyone has remembered the annual meeting is in two weeks. We're going to face a lot of angry shareholders.'

'Angry!' O'Brien grunted; he was relighting his cigar, which had gone out. 'They'll all be foaming at the mouth and that meeting will need a riot squad to handle it.'

'Handling it will be my job,' J. Eric Humphrey said; for the first time in several hours the chairman smiled. 'I've been wondering, though, if I shouldn't wear a bulletproof vest.'

4

Twice since receiving Karen Sloan's letter at Devil's Gate Camp, Nim had talked to her on the telephone. He promised to visit her again when he could.

But the letter had arrived on the day that was marred by Wally Talbot's tragic accident and, since then, other events had crowded in, so Nim's intended visit was postponed. He still hadn't made it. Karen had remembered *him*, however – with another letter.

He was reading it now, in his office, in a moment of quietness.

Across the top of Karen's elegant blue stationery she had typed in capitals:

I WAS SAD WHEN YOU TOLD ME OF YOUR FRIEND'S ACCIDENT
AND WHEN I READ ABOUT HIS INJURIES

Below was still more of her immaculate stick-in-mouth typing.

Tell him from one who knows:

A sputtering candlewick
Though burning dimly
Is brighter by far
Than cimmerian blackness.
For life,
On whatever terms,
Outranks oblivion.

Yes! – the 'if onlys' do persist for ever
As hovering, wraithlike, used-up wishes,
Their afterburners spent:
'If only' this or that
On such and such a day
Had varied by an hour or an inch;
Or something neglected had been done
Or something done had been neglected!
Then 'perhaps' the *other* might have been,
And other others . . . to infinity.
For 'perhaps' and 'if only' are first cousins
Addicted to survival in our minds.

Accept them,
And all else.

For what seemed a long time Nim sat still and silent, reading and
rereading Karen's words. At length he became aware that his
telephone was buzzing and realized it had done so twice before.

As he picked it up his secretary's voice said brightly, 'Did I
wake you?'

'Yes, in a way.'

'Mr London would like to see you,' Vicki said. 'He can come
now if you're free.'

'Tell him okay.'

Nim put the sheet of blue stationery away in a desk drawer
where he kept private papers. When the right moment came he
would show it to Wally Talbot. The thought reminded him that
he had not spoken to Ardythe since their unsatisfactory encounter at the hospital, but he decided he would leave that problem
on the shelf for the time being.

The door of Nim's office opened. 'Here's Mr London,' Vicki
announced.

'Come in, Harry.' Nim was aware that the Property Protection head had been dropping in more frequently of late, some-

times with a work-related purpose, more often without. But Nim had no objection. He enjoyed their growing friendship and exchange of views.

'Just read about that no-dividend deal,' London said, settling into a chair. 'Thought you could stand a bit of good news for a change.'

Announcement of the dividend's cancellation, reluctantly agreed to by the board of directors, had made big news yesterday afternoon and today. Reaction in the financial world had been one of incredulity and stockholder protests were already flooding in. On the New York and Pacific stock exchanges, panic selling, after a four-hour trading suspension, had depressed GSP & L stock a devastating nine dollars a share, or a third of its pre-announcement value.

Nim asked, 'Which good news?'

'Remember D-day in Brookside?'

'Of course.'

'We just got four court convictions.'

Nim ran his mind over the meter-tampering incidents he had seen personally that day. 'Which ones?'

'The guy with the gas station and car wash was one. He might have got away with it, but his lawyer made the mistake of putting him on the witness stand. While he was cross-examined he tripped himself up a half-dozen times. Another was the tool-and-die maker. Remember that?'

'Yes.' Nim recalled the small tract house where no one was at home but which London had put under surveillance. As the investigators hoped, neighbours reported the GSP & L activity and the man had been caught trying to remove the illegal wire device from his meter.

'In both those cases,' London said, 'and two others you didn't see, the court handed down five-hundred-dollar fines.'

'What about the doctor – the one with the bridging wires and switch behind his meter?'

'And the haughty wife with the dog?'

'Right.'

'We didn't prosecute. That woman said they had important friends, and so they did. Pulled every string, including some inside this company. Even then we might have gone to court, except our legal department wasn't sure they could *prove* the doctor knew about the switch and meter. Or so I was told.'

Nim said sceptically, 'Sounds like the old story – there are two kinds of justice, depending on who you are and whom you know.'

'That happens,' London agreed. 'Saw plenty of it when I was a cop. Just the same, that doctor paid up all the money owing, and we're collecting from a lot of others, including some more we're prosecuting where there's strong evidence.' He added, 'I got some other news, too.'

'Such as?'

'All along I've said that in a lot of these theft cases we're dealing with professionals – people who know how to do good work, then cover it up so our own company guys have trouble finding it. Also I thought the professionals might be working in groups, even a single big group. Remember?'

Nim nodded, trying not to be impatient, letting Harry London get to the point in his own didactic way.

'Well, we got a break. My deputy, Art Romeo, had a tip-off about a big office building downtown where current transformers have been tampered with and the gas system, which heats the whole building, has a massive illegal shunt. He did some checking and found it's all true. Since then I've been in there myself – Art recruited a janitor who's working with us; we're paying him to keep watch. I'm telling you, Nim, this is big-time, and the job's the slickest I've seen. Without the tip-off Art got, we might never have found it.'

'Where did he get the tip?' Nim had met Art Romeo. He was a shifty little man who looked like a thief himself.

'Let me tell you something,' Harry London said. 'Never ask a cop that question – or a Property Protection agent either. A tipster sometimes has a grudge, mostly he wants money, but either way he has to be protected. You don't do that by telling a lot of other people his name. *I* didn't ask Art.'

'Okay,' Nim conceded. 'But if you know the illegal installation is there, why aren't we moving on it right away?'

'Because then we'd seal up one rathole and close off access to a lot of others. Let me tell you some of the things we've found out.'

Nim said drily, 'I was hoping you would.'

'The outfit that owns that office building is called Zaco Properties,' London said. 'Zaco has other buildings – apartments, offices, some stores they lease to supermarkets. And we figure what they've done in one place they'll try in others, maybe have already. Checking out those other places, without it being known, is what Art Romeo is working on now. I've pulled him off everything else.'

'You said you're paying the janitor in the first building to keep watch. What for?'

'When an operation is that big – even stealing – there has to be a check up occasionally and adjustments.'

'In other words,' Nim said, 'whoever bypassed those meters is likely to come back?'

'Right. And when they do, the janitor will tell us. He's an old-timer who sees most of what goes on. He's already talked a lot; doesn't like the people he works for; it seems they did him dirt somehow. He says the original work was done by four men who came well organized for it, on three occasions, in two well-equipped trucks. What I want are licence numbers of one or both of those trucks, a better description of the men.'

It was obvious, Nim thought, that the janitor had been the original informant, but he kept the conclusion to himself. 'Assuming you get all or most of the evidence you need,' he said, 'what then?'

'We bring in the District Attorney's office and the city police. I know who to contact in both places, and who's reliable and will move fast. Not yet, though. The fewer people who know what we've uncovered, the better.'

'All right,' Nim acknowledged. 'It all sounds promising, but remember two things. Number one, warn your man Romeo to be careful. If this operation is as big as you say, it can also be dangerous. The other is – keep me informed of everything that happens.'

The Property Protection head gave a wide, cheerful grin. 'Yessir!'

Nim had the feeling that Harry London was restraining himself from snapping off a smart salute.

5

Traditionally, the annual meeting of Golden State Power & Light shareholders was a sedate, even dull, proceeding. Only two hundred or so of the company's more than 540,000 shareholders normally attended; most ignored it. All that the absentees cared about, it seemed, were their regular quarterly dividends, until now as predictable and reliable as each year's four seasons.

But not any more.

At 12 noon, two hours before the annual meeting was due to begin, a trickle of shareholders began presenting credentials and entering the ballroom of the St Charles Hotel where seating – to allow for all possible contingencies – had been provided for about two thousand. By 12:15 the trickle had become a flow. At 12:30 it was a flood tide.

Among those arriving, more than half were elderly people, some walking with the aid of sticks, a few on crutches, a half-dozen in wheelchairs. A majority was not well dressed. A large number had brought coffee in thermos bottles and sandwiches on which they lunched while waiting.

The mood of most arrivals was clearly evident; it varied between resentment and anger. Most were barely polite to GSP & L staff whose job was to check identifications before allowing admittance to the hall. Some shareholders, delayed in the process, became belligerent.

By 1pm, with an hour still to go, all two thousand seats were filled, leaving standing room only, and the influx of arrivals had become even heavier. The ballroom now presented a babel of noise as countless conversations and group discussions proceeded, some heatedly, with participants raising voices. Occasionally, words and phrases were audible above the rest.

'. . . said it was a safe stock, so we put in our savings and . . .'

'. . . lousy, incompetent management . . .'

'. . . all very well for you, I told the guy who came to read the meter, but what am I supposed to *live* on – air?'

'. . . bills are high enough, so why *not* pay a dividend to those who . . .'

'. . . bunch of fat cats in the boardroom; what do *they* care?'

'. . . after all, if we sat here and simply refused to leave until . . .'

'String the bastards up, I say; they'd soon enough change their . . .'

The variations and permutations were endless, though a single theme persisted : GSP & L management was the enemy.

A press table near the front of the hall was already partially occupied and two reporters were moving around in search of human interest vignettes. A grey-haired woman in a light green trouser-suit was being interviewed. She had spent four days travelling by bus from Tampa, Florida, 'because the bus is cheapest and I don't have much money left, especially now.' She described how five years ago she quit working as a salesclerk, moved into a retirement home and, with her modest life savings, bought GSP & L stock. 'I was told it was as safe as a bank. Now my income has stopped, so I have to move out of the home and I don't know where I'll go.' Of her journey to California : 'I couldn't afford to come but I couldn't afford to stay away. I had to know why these people here are doing this awful thing to me.' As words tumbled out emotionally, a wire service photographer shot close-ups of her anguish which tomorrow would be displayed in newspapers across the country.

Only still photographers were being allowed inside the meeting hall. Two TV crews, encamped in the hotel lobby, had protested their exclusion to Teresa Van Buren. She told them, 'It was decided that if we let television cameras in it would turn the annual meeting into a circus.'

A TV technician grumbled, 'From the looks of things, it's already a circus.'

It was Van Buren who was first to signal an alarm when it became evident, soon after 12:30, that the space and seating reserved would be totally inadequate. A hastily called conference then took place between GSP & L and hotel officials. It was agreed to open another hall, about half the size of the ballroom, where an overflow crowd of fifteen hundred could be accommodated, proceedings in the main hall to be transmitted there by a public address system. Soon, a squad of hotel employees was setting up chairs in the extra room.

But fresh arrivals quickly objected. 'Nuts to that! I'm not sittting in some second-class outhouse,' a heavy-set, red-faced

153

woman insisted loudly. 'I'm a stockholder with a right to be at the annual meeting and that's *where* I'll be.' With one beefy hand she shoved aside an elderly security guard; the other she used to unfasten a roped-off area, then marched into the already crowded ballroom. Several others pushed past the guard and followed her. He shrugged helplessly, then replaced the rope and tried to direct still more people to the overflow accommodation.

A thin, serious-faced man appealed to Teresa Van Buren. 'This is ridiculous. I've flown here from New York and I've questions to ask at the meeting.'

'There will be microphones in the second hall,' she assured him, 'and questions from there will be heard and answered in both halls.'

The man looked disgustedly at the milling throng. 'Most of these people are just small stockholders. I represent ten thousand shares.'

A voice behind said, 'I got twenty, mister, but my rights are as good as yours.'

Eventually both were persuaded to go to the smaller hall.

'He was right about small stockholders,' Van Buren observed to Sharlett Underhill, who had joined her briefly in the hotel foyer.

The finance vice president nodded. 'A lot of the people here own ten shares or less. Very few have more than a hundred.'

Nancy Molineaux of the *California Examiner* had also been observing the influx. She was standing near the other two women.

'You hear that?' Van Buren asked her. 'It refutes the charges that we're a huge, monolithic company. These people you're seeing are the ones who own it.'

Ms Molineaux said sceptically, 'There are plenty of big, wealthy shareholders, too.'

'Not as many as you'd think,' Sharlett Underhill interjected. 'More than fifty per cent of our shareholders are small investors with a hundred shares or less. And our largest single stockholder is a trust which holds stock for company employees – it has eight per cent of the shares. You'll find the same thing true of other public utilities.'

The reporter seemed unimpressed.

'I haven't seen you, Nancy,' Teresa Van Buren said, 'since you wrote that rotten, unfair piece about Nim Goldman. Did you really have to do that? Nim's a nice, hard-working guy.'

Nancy Molineaux smiled slightly; her voice affected surprise. 'You didn't like that? My editor thought it was great.' Unperturbed, she continued surveying the hotel foyer, then observed, 'Golden State Power doesn't seem able to do *anything* right. A lot of people here are as unhappy about their utility bills as about their dividends.'

Van Buren followed the reporter's gaze to where a small crowd surrounded an accounts service desk. Knowing that many shareholders were also its customers, GSP & L set up the desk at annual meetings so that any queries about gas and electric charges could be dealt with on the spot. Behind the desk a trio of clerks was handling complaints while a lengthening line waited. A woman's voice protested, 'I don't care what you say, that bill *can't* be right. I'm living alone, not using any more power than I did two years ago, but the charge is double.' Consulting a video display connected to billing computers, a young male clerk continued explaining the bill's details. The woman remained unmollified.

'Sometimes,' Van Buren told Nancy Molineaux, 'the same people want lower rates *and* a bigger dividend. It's hard to explain why you can't have both.'

Without commenting, the reporter moved on.

At 1:40, twenty minutes before the meeting would begin, there was standing room only in the second hall and new arrivals were still appearing.

'I'm worried as hell,' Harry London confided to Nim Goldman. The two were midway between the ballroom and overflow room where the din from both made it hard to hear each other.

London and several of his staff had been 'borrowed' for the occasion to beef up GSP & L's regular security force. Nim had been sent, a few minutes ago, by J. Eric Humphrey to make a personal appraisal of the scene.

The chairman, who usually mingled informally with stockholders before the annual meeting, had been advised by the chief security officer not to do so today because of the hostile crowd. At this moment Humphrey was closeted behind scenes with senior officers and directors who would join him on the ballroom platform at 2pm.

'I'm worried,' London repeated, 'because I think we'll see some violence before all this is through. Have you been outside?'

Nim shook his head, then, as the other motioned, followed him towards the hotel's outer lobby and the street. They emerged through a side door and walked around the building to the front.

The St Charles Hotel had a forecourt which normally accommodated hotel traffic – taxis, private cars and buses. But now all traffic movement was prevented by a crowd of several hundred placard-waving, shouting demonstrators. A narrow entryway for pedestrians was being kept open by city police officers who were also restraining demonstrators from advancing further.

The TV crews which had been refused admittance to the stockholders' meeting had come outside to film the action.

Some signs being held aloft read:

Support
power & light
for people

The People Demand
Lower Gas/Electric
Rates

Kill the Capitalist
Monster
GSP & L

p & lfp
Urges
Public Ownership
Of GSP & L

Put People
Ahead of Profits

Groups of GSP & L stockholders, still arriving and moving through the police lines, read the signs indignantly. A small, casually dressed, balding man with a hearing aid stopped to cry angrily at the demonstrators, 'I'm just as much "people" as you are; and I worked hard all my life to buy a few shares . . .'

A pale, bespectacled youth in a Stanford University sweatshirt jeered, 'Get stuffed, you greedy capitalist!'

Another among the arrivals – a youngish, attractive woman – retorted, 'Maybe if some of you worked harder and saved a little . . .'

She was drowned out by a chorus of 'Screw the profiteers!' and 'Power belongs to the people!'

The woman advanced on the shouters, a fist raised. 'Listen, you bums! I'm no profiteer. I'm a worker, in a union, and . . .'

'Profiteer!' . . . 'Bloodsucking capitalist!' . . . One of the waving signs descended near the woman's head. A police sergeant stepped forward, shoved the sign away and hurried the woman, along with the man with the hearing aid, into the hotel. The shouts and jeering followed them. Once more the demonstrators surged forward; again the police held firm.

The TV crews had now been joined by reporters from other media – among them, Nim saw, Nancy Molineaux. But he had no wish to meet her.

Harry London observed quietly, 'You see your friend Birdsong over there, masterminding this?'

'No friend of mine,' Nim said. 'But yes, I see him.'

The bulky, bearded figure of Davey Birdsong – a broad smile on his face as usual – was visible at the demonstration's rear. As the two watched, Birdsong raised a walkie-talkie radio to his lips.

'He's probably talking to someone inside,' London said, 'He's already been in and out twice; he has one share of stock in his name. I checked.'

'One share is enough,' Nim pointed out. 'It gives anyone a right to be at the annual meeting.'

'I know. And probably some more of his people have the same. They've something else planned. I'm sure of it.'

Nim and London returned inside the hotel unnoticed. Outside, the demonstrators seemed noisier than before.

In a small private meeting room off a corridor behind the ballroom stage, J. Eric Humphrey paced restlessly, still reviewing the speech he would shortly make. Over the past three days a dozen drafts had been typed and retyped, the latest an hour ago. Even now, as he moved, silently mouthing words and turning pages, he would pause occasionally to pencil in a change.

Out of deference to the chairman's concentration, the others present – Sharlett Underhill, Oscar O'Brien, Stewart Ino, Ray Paulsen, a half-dozen directors – had fallen silent, one or two of the directors mixing drinks at a portable bar.

Heads turned as an outside door opened. It framed a security guard and, behind him, Nim, who came in, closing the door.

Humphrey put down the pages of his speech. 'Well?'

'It's a mob scene out there.' Nim described tersely his observations in the ballroom, overflow hall and outside the hotel.

A director enquired nervously, 'Is there any way we can postpone the meeting?'

Oscar O'Brien shook his head decisively. 'Out of the question. It's been called legally. It must go on.'

'Besides,' Nim added, 'if you did there'd be a riot.'

The same director said, 'We may have that anyway.'

The chairman crossed to the bar and poured himself a plain soda water, wishing it were a scotch but observing his own rule of no drinking by officers during working hours. He said testily, 'We knew in advance this was going to happen so any talk of postponement is pointless. We simply have to do the best we can.' As he sipped his soda : 'Those people out there have a right to be angry – at us, and about their dividends. I'd feel the same way myself. What *can* you tell people who put their money where they believed it was safe, and suddenly find it isn't after all?'

'You could try telling them the truth,' Sharlett Underhill said, her face flushing with emotion. 'The truth that there isn't *any* place in this country where the thrifty and hard-working can put their money with an assurance of preserving its value. Not in companies like ours any more; certainly not in savings accounts or bonds where the interest doesn't keep pace with government-provoked inflation. Not since those charlatans and crooks in Washington debased the dollar and keep right on doing it, grinning like idiots while they ruin us. They've given us a dishonest fiat paper currency, unbacked by anything but politicians' worthless promises. Our financial institutions are crumbling. Bank insurance – the FDIC – is a façade. Social Security is a bankrupt fraud; if it were a private concern those running it would be in jail. And good, decent, efficient companies like ours are pushed to the wall, forced into doing what we've done, and taking the blame unfairly.'

There were murmurs of approval, someone applauded, and the chairman said drily, 'Sharlett, maybe you should make the speech instead of me.' He added thoughtfully, 'Everything you say is true, of course. Unfortunately most citizens aren't ready to listen and accept the truth – not yet.'

'As a matter of interest, Sharlett,' Ray Paulsen asked, 'where do *you* keep your savings?'

The financial vice president snapped back, 'In Switzerland – one of the few countries where there's still financial sanity – and the Bahamas – in gold coins and Swiss francs, the only honest currencies left. If you haven't already, I advise the rest of you to do the same.'

Nim was looking at his watch. He went to the door and opened it. 'It's a minute to the hour. Time to go.'

'Now I know,' Eric Humphrey said as he led the way out, 'how the Christians felt when they had to face the lions.'

The management representatives and the directors filed quickly on to the platform, the chairman going directly to a podium with a lectern, the others to chairs on his right. As they did so the hubbub in the ballroom still briefly. Then, near the front, a few scattered voices shouted, 'Boo!' Instantly the cry was taken up until a cacophony of boos and catcalls thundered through the hall. On the podium J. Eric Humphrey stood impassively, waiting for the disapproving chorus to subside. When it lessened slightly he leaned forward to the microphone in front of him.

'Ladies and gentlemen, my opening remarks on the state of our company will be brief. I know that many of you are anxious to ask questions . . .'

His next words were drowned out in another uproar. Amid it were cries of 'You're damned right!' . . . 'Take questions now!' . . . 'Cut the horseshit!' . . . 'Talk dividend!'

When he could make himself heard again, Humphrey countered, 'I certainly do intend to talk about dividends but first there are some mattters which must . . .'

'Mr Chairman, Mr Chairman, on a point of order!'

A new, unseen voice was booming through the PA system. Simultaneously a red light glowed on the chairman's lectern, indicating that a microphone in the overflow room was being used.

Humphrey spoke loudly into his own mike. 'What is your point of order?'

'I object, Mr Chairman, to the manner in which . . .'

Humphrey interrupted. 'State your name, please.'

'My name is Homer F. Ingersoll. I am a lawyer and I hold

three hundred shares for myself, two hundred for a client.'

'What is your point of order, Mr Ingersoll?'

'I started to tell you, Mr Chairman. I object to the way in which inadequate, inefficient arrangements were made to hold this meeting, with the result that I and many others have been relegated, like second-class citizens, to another hall where we cannot properly participate . . .'

'But you *are* participating, Mr Ingersoll. I regret that the unexpectedly large attendance today . . .'

'I am raising a point of order, Mr Chairman, and I hadn't finished.'

As the booming voice cut in again, Humphrey said resignedly, 'Finish your point of order, but quickly, please.'

'You may not know it, Mr Chairman, but even this second hall is now jampacked and there are many stockholders outside who cannot get into either one. I am speaking on their behalf because they are being deprived of their legal rights.'

'No,' Humphrey acknowledged, 'I did not know it. I am genuinely sorry and I concede our preparations were inadequate.'

A woman in the ballroom stood up and cried, 'You should all resign! You can't even organize an annual meeting.'

Other voices echoed, 'Yes, resign! Resign!'

Eric Humphrey's lips tightened; for a moment, uncharacteristically, he appeared nervous. Then, with an obvious effort, he controlled himself and tried again. 'Today's attendance, as many of you know, is unprecedented.'

A strident voice: 'So was cutting off our dividends!'

'I can only tell you – I had intended to say this later but I'll state it now – that omission of our dividend was an action which I and my fellow directors took with great reluctance . . .'

The voice again: 'Did you try cutting your own fat salary?'

'. . . and with full awareness,' Humphrey persisted, 'of the unhappiness, indeed hardship, which . . .'

Several things then happened simultaneously.

A large, soft tomato, unerringly aimed, struck the chairman in the face. It burst, leaving a mess of pulp and juice which dripped down his face, suit and shirtfront.

As if on signal, a barrage of more tomatoes and several eggs followed, splattering the stage and the chairman's podium. Many in the ballroom audience jumped to their feet; a few were laughing but others, looking around them for the throwers, appeared shocked and disapproving. At the same time a new disturbance could be heard, with raised voices growing in volume, immediately outside.

Nim, also on his feet near the centre of the ballroom where he had gone when the management group occupied the platform, was searching for the source of the fusillade, ready to intervene if he could find it. Almost at once he saw Davey Birdsong. As he had been doing earlier, the p & lfp leader was speaking into a walkie-talkie; Nim guessed that he was giving orders. Nim tried to push his way towards Birdsong but found it impossible. By now the scene in the ballroom was one of total confusion.

Abruptly Nim found himself face to face with Nancy Molineaux. For an instant she betrayed uncertainty.

His anger flared. 'I suppose you're loving all of this so you can write about us as viciously as usual.'

'I just try to be factual, Goldman.' Her self-assurance returning, Ms Molineaux smiled. 'I do investigative reporting where I think it's needed.'

'Yeah, investigative, meaning one-sided, slanted!' Impulsively he pointed across the room to Davey Birdsong and his walkie-talkie. 'Why not investigate *him*?'

'Give me one good reason why I should.'

'I believe he's creating a disturbance here.'

'Do you *know* he is?'

Nim admitted, 'No.'

'Then let me tell *you* something. Whether he helped or not, this disturbance happened because a lot of people believe that Golden State Power & Light isn't being run the way it should be. Or don't you ever face reality?'

With a contemptuous glance at Nim, Nancy Molineaux moved away.

Then the noise outside increased still further and, adding to the ballroom shambles, a phalanx of newcomers pushed their way in. Behind them were still more people, among them bearers of anti-GSP & L signs and placards.

What had happened – as became clear later – was that a few individuals among those shareholders denied access to both halls had urged others to join them in using force to enter the ballroom. Together they had shoved aside temporary barriers and

161

overwhelmed the security guards and other GSP & L staff.

At virtually the same moment the crowd of demonstrators in the hotel forecourt had rushed the police lines and this time broken them. The demonstrators poured into the hotel, heading for the ballroom, where they reinforced the invading shareholders.

As Nim suspected but could not prove, Davey Birdsong orchestrated all movements, beginning with the tomato throwing, by issuing commands through the walkie-talkie. As well as arranging the forecourt demonstration, the p & lfp had infiltrated the shareholders' meeting by the simple – and legitimate – device of having a dozen of its members, including Birdsong, purchase single shares of GSP & L stock several months earlier.

In the ensuing turmoil only a few heard J. Eric Humphrey announce over the PA system, 'This meeting stands recessed. It will resume in approximately half an hour.'

6

In the living room of her apartment Karen bestowed on Nim the same radiant smile he remembered so well from their previous encounter. Then she said sympathetically, 'I know this week has been difficult for you. I read about your company's annual meeting and saw some of it on television.'

Instinctively Nim grimaced. The TV coverage had concentrated on riotous aspects, ignoring the complex issues aired during five hours of business – questions, discussion, voting on resolutions – which had followed the enforced recess. (To be fair, Nim acknowledged, the television cameras had only external film shots to work with; using hindsight, he realized it would have been better to have allowed them in.) During the half-hour recess, order was restored and the marathon business session ensued. At the end nothing had changed except that all participants were weary, but much that needed to be said had been brought into the open. To Nim's surprise next day the most comprehensive and balanced view of the proceedings had appeared in the *California Examiner* under Nancy Molineaux's by-line.

'If you don't mind,' he told Karen, 'our annual circus is something I'd like to blot out for a while.'

'Consider it blotted, Nimrod. *What* annual meeting? I never even heard of one.'

He laughed, then said, 'I enjoyed your poetry. Have you published any?'

She shook her head and he was reminded again, as she sat in the wheelchair opposite him, that it was the only part of her body she could move.

He had come here today partly because he felt the need to get away, even if briefly, from the turmoil of GSP & L. He had also wanted, very much, to see Karen Sloan, a desire now reinforced by her charm and remarkable beauty. The last was just as he remembered – the shining shoulder-length blonde hair, perfectly proportioned face, full lips and flawless, opalescent skin.

A touch whimsically, Nim speculated on whether he was falling in love. If so, it would involve a reversal, he thought. On plenty of occasions he had experienced sex without love. But with Karen it would be love without sex.

'I write poetry for pleasure,' Karen said. 'What I was working on when you came was a speech.'

He had already noticed the electric typewriter behind her. It contained a partially typed sheet. Other papers were spread out on a table alongside.

'A speech to whom? And about what?'

'It will be to a convention of lawyers. A State Bar group is working on a report about laws which apply to disabled persons – those in most states and other countries. There are some laws which work; others don't. I've made a study of them.'

'*You're* telling lawyers about the law?'

'Why not? Lawyers get cocooned in theory. They need someone practical to tell them what really happens under laws and regulations. That's why they've asked me; besides, I've done it before. Mostly I'll talk about para- and quadriplegics and also clear up some misconceptions.'

'What kind of misconceptions?'

From the adjoining room, while they talked, kitchen sounds were audible. When Nim had telephoned this morning, Karen invited him for lunch. Now, Josie, the aide-cum-housekeeper whom Nim had met on his previous visit, was preparing the meal.

'Before I answer that,' Karen said, 'my right leg is getting uncomfortable. Will you move it for me?'

He stood up and approached the wheelchair uncertainly. Karen's right leg was crossed over her left.

'Just arrange them the other way. Left over right, please.' She said it matter-of-factly and Nim reached out, suddenly aware that her nylon-covered legs were slim and attractive. And they were warm, momentarily exciting, to the touch.

'Thank you,' Karen acknowledged. 'You have gentle hands.' When he appeared surprised, she added, 'That's one of the misconceptions.'

'What is?'

'That all paralysed people are deprived of normal feeling. It's true that some can't feel anything any more, but post-polios like me *can* have all their sensory abilities intact. So although I can't move my limbs, I have as much physical sensation as anyone else. It's why a leg or arm can get uncomfortable or "fall asleep" and need its position changed, the way you did just now.'

He admitted, 'You're right. I guess I did think the way you said, subconsciously.'

'I know.' She smiled mischievously. 'But I could feel your hands on my legs and, if you want to know, I rather liked it.'

A sudden, startling thought occurred to him, then he dismissed it and said, 'Tell me another misconception.'

'That quadriplegics shouldn't be asked to talk about themselves. You'd be surprised how many people are reluctant or embarrassed to have any contact with us, some even frightened.'

'Does that happen often?'

'All the time. Last week my sister Cynthia took me to a restaurant for lunch. When the waiter came he wrote down Cynthia's order then, without looking at me, he asked, 'And what will *she* have?' Cynthia, bless her, said, "Why don't you ask her?" But even then, when I gave my order, he wouldn't look at me directly.'

Nim was silent, then he reached out, lifted Karen's hand and held it. 'I'm ashamed for all of us.'

164

'Don't be. You're making up for a lot of others, Nimrod.'

Releasing her hand, he said, 'The last time I was here you talked a little about your family.'

'I won't need to today because you're going to meet them – at least, my parents. I hope you don't mind but they're dropping in right after lunch. It's my mother's day off from work and my father is working on a plumbing job not far from here.'

Her parents, Karen explained, were originally from Austrian families and, in their teens during the mid-1930s, were brought to the United States as immigrants while war clouds gathered over Europe. In California they met, married, and had two children – Cynthia and Karen. The family name on the father's side had been Slonhauser, which was anglicized to Sloan during naturalization. Karen and Cynthia knew little of their Austrian heritage and were brought up as native American children.

'Then Cynthia is older than you?'

'Three years older and very beautiful. My big sister. I want you to meet her another day.'

The sounds from the kitchen stopped and Josie appeared, wheeling a loaded tea trolley. She set a small folding table in front of Nim and fitted a tray to Karen's wheelchair. From the cart she served lunch – cold salmon with a salad and warm French bread. Josie poured wine into two glasses – a chilled Louis Martini Pinot Chardonnay. 'I can't afford wine every day,' Karen said. 'But today is special – because you came back.'

Josie asked her, 'Shall I feed you or will Mr Goldman?'

'Nimrod,' Karen asked, 'would you like to?'

'Yes,' he said, 'though if I do anything wrong you'll have to tell me.'

'It's really not difficult. When I open my mouth you pop some food in. You'll just work twice as hard as you would feeding yourself.'

With a glance at Karen, and a knowing smile, Josie retreated to the kitchen.

'You see,' Karen said while their lunch proceeded, and after a sip of wine, 'you're very good. Will you wipe my lips, please?' He did so with a napkin as she tilted her face towards him.

Continuing to feed Karen, he thought: there was a strange sense of intimacy in what they were doing together, a sharing and closeness unique in his experience. It even had a kind of sensual quality.

Near the end of the meal, their awareness of each other heightened by the wine, she said, 'I've told you a lot about me. Now tell me more about you.'

He began casually, speaking of his background – boyhood, family, work, marriage to Ruth, his children Leah and Benjy. Then, prompted by questioning from Karen, he revealed his current doubts – about his religious heritage and whether it would be perpetuated through his children, where his own life was headed, the future – if any – of his marriage.

'That's enough,' he said at length. 'I didn't come here to bore you.'

Smiling, Karen shook her head. 'I don't believe you could ever do that, Nimrod. You're a complex man and complex people are the most interesting. Besides that, I like you more than anyone I've met in a long time.'

He told her, 'I have that feeling about you.'

A touch of red suffused Karen's face. 'Nimrod, would you like to kiss me?'

As he rose and crossed the few feet of space dividing them, he answered softly, 'I want to very much.'

Her lips were warm and loving; their kiss was lingering. Neither wanted to break away. Nim moved his arms, intending to draw Karen closer to him. Then from outside he heard the sharp note of a buzzer followed by a door opening and voices – Josie's and two others. Nim let his arms fall back. He moved away.

Karen whispered softly, 'Damn! What lousy timing!' Then she called, 'Come in!' and a moment later announced, 'Nimrod, I'd like you to meet my parents.'

An elderly, dignified man with a thatch of greying, curly hair and a weather-beaten face extended his hand. When he spoke his voice was deep and guttural, the Austrian origin still evident. 'I'm Luther Sloan, Mr Goldman. This is my wife Henrietta. Karen told us about you and we've seen you on TV.' The hand Nim accepted was a manual worker's, rough and calloused, but looking as if it were scrubbed frequently; the fingernails were clean. Though Luther Sloan wore coveralls with traces of the work he had just left, those also showed signs of care and had been neatly patched in several places.

Karen's mother shook hands. 'It's good of you, Mr Goldman,

to visit our daughter. I know she appreciates it. So do we.' She was a small, neat woman, modestly dressed, with her hair in an old-fashioned bun; she appeared to be older than her husband. Once, Nim thought, she was probably beautiful, which explained Karen's attractiveness, but now her face was aged, while her eyes betrayed strain and weariness. Nim guessed the signs of the last two had been there a long time.

'I'm here for one simple reason,' he assured her. 'I enjoy Karen's company.'

As Nim returned to his chair and the older Sloans sat down, Josie brought in a pot of coffee and four cups. Mrs Sloan poured and helped Karen with hers.

'Daddy,' Karen said, 'how's your business going?'

'Not as good as it might.' Luther Sloan sighed. 'Materials cost so much – more every day; you will know about that, Mr Goldman. So when I charge what it costs *me*, then add on labour, people think I'm cheating.'

'I do know,' Nim said. 'At Golden State Power we're accused of the same thing for identical reasons.'

'But yours is a big company with a broad back. Mine is just a small business. I employ three other people, Mr Goldman, and work myself, and some days I tell you it is scarcely worth the trouble. Especially with all the government forms – more all the time, and half the things I do not see why they need to know. I spend evenings and weekends filling those forms in, and nobody pays me for *that*.'

Henrietta Sloan reproved her husband, 'Luther, the whole world does not have to hear our problems.'

He shrugged. 'I was asked how business was. So I told the truth.'

'Anyway, Karen,' Henrietta said, 'none of that makes the slightest difference to you, or to our getting you a van. We have almost enough money for a down payment, then we will borrow the rest.'

'Mother,' Karen protested, 'I've said before, there isn't any urgency. I'm managing to get outdoors. Josie goes with me.'

'But not as often as you could, or as far as you'd like to go.' The mother's mouth set firmly. 'There *will* be a van. I promise you, dear. Soon.'

'I've been thinking about that too,' Nim said. 'Last time I was

167

here, Karen mentioned wanting a van which would hold the wheelchair, and which Josie could drive.'

Karen said firmly, 'Now will all of you stop worrying. Please!'

'I wasn't worrying. But I did remember that our company – GSP & L – often has small vans which are sold off after they've been used a year or two and are replaced by new ones. Many are still in good condition. If you like, I could ask one of our people to look out for something which could be a bargain.'

Luther Sloan brightened. 'That would be a large help. Of course, however good the van is, it will need adapting so the wheelchair can go in and be secure.'

'Maybe we can help with that as well,' Nim said. 'I don't know, but I'll find out.'

'We will give you our telephone number,' Henrietta told him. 'Then if there is news, you can call us.'

'Nimrod,' Karen said, 'you are truly dear and wonderful.'

They went on talking easily until, glancing at his watch, Nim was startled to see how much time had passed since he arrived. He announced, 'I have to go.'

'So do we,' Luther Sloan said. 'I am renewing some gas lines in an old building near here – for *your* gas, Mr Goldman – and the job must be completed today.'

'And in case you think I'm not busy,' Karen chimed in, 'I have a speech to finish.'

Her parents took their leave affectionately. Nim followed them out. Before going, he and Karen were alone briefly and he kissed her for the second time, intending to do so on her cheek, but she turned her head so their lips met. With a dazzling smile she whispered, 'Come again soon.'

The Sloans and Nim had the elevator to themselves going down; all three were briefly silent, each occupied with private thoughts. Then Henrietta said in a monotone. 'We try to do the best we can for Karen. Sometimes we wish it could be more.' The strain and weariness Nim observed earlier – perhaps nearer to a sense of defeat – were in her eyes again.

He said quietly, 'I don't believe Karen feels that way. From what she's told me, she appreciates your support and everything you've done for her.'

Henrietta shook her head emphatically, the bun of hair at her neck emphasizing the movement. 'Whatever we do is the *least* we can do. Even then it is a poor way to make up for what happened to Karen – because of what *we* did – long ago.'

Luther put a hand gently on his wife's arm. '*Liebchen,* we have been over it all, so many times. Do not do this to yourself. It does no good, only harm to you.'

She turned on him sharply. 'You think the same things. You *know* you do.'

Luther sighed, then abruptly queried Nim. 'Karen told you she contracted polio?'

He nodded. 'Yes.'

'Did she tell you how? And why?'

'No. Well, not exactly.'

Henrietta said, 'She doesn't, usually.'

They had reached the street floor and stepped from the elevator, pausing in the small, deserted lobby while Henrietta Sloan continued :

'Karen was fifteen, still in high school. She was a straight A student; she took part in school athletics. Everything ahead seemed good.'

'The point my wife is making,' Luther said, 'is that that summer we ourselves – the two of us – had arranged to go to Europe. It was with others from our Lutheran church – a religious pilgrimage to holy places. We had arranged, while we were gone, that Karen should go to summer camp. We told ourselves that some time in the country would be good for her; also, our daughter Cynthia had been to the same camp two years before.'

'The real truth is,' Henrietta said, 'we were thinking more of ourselves than Karen.'

Her husband went on as if he had not been interrupted. 'But Karen did not want to go to camp. There was a boy she was seeing; he was not leaving town. Karen wanted to stay at home for the summer and be near him. But Cynthia was already away; Karen would have been alone.'

'Karen argued and argued,' Henrietta said. 'She said being alone did not matter and, as to the boy, that we could trust her. She even talked about having a premonition that if she went as we wished something would go wrong. I have never forgotten that. I never will.'

His own experience gave Nim a sense of the scene being described: the Sloans as young parents, Karen barely out of childhood, and the strong and clashing wills – all three so different then from what they had become.

Once more Luther took up the narrative, speaking quickly as if wishing to have it done. 'The upshot was, we had a family fight – the two of us taking one side, Karen the other. We insisted she go to camp, and in the end she did. While she was there, and we were in Eurpoe, a polio outbreak happened. Karen was one of the victims.'

'If only she had stayed home,' Henrietta began, 'the way she wanted . . .'

Her husband interrupted. 'That's enough! I'm sure Mr Goldman has the picture.'

'Yes,' Nim said softly, 'I think I do.' He was remembering the verses Karen had written him after Wally Talbot Jr's electrocution.

'If only' this or that
On such and such a day
Had varied by an hour or an inch;
Or something neglected had been done
Or something done had been neglected!

He understood better now. Then, presuming something should be said but not sure what, he added, 'I don't see why you should go on blaming yourselves for circumstances . . .'

A glance from Luther and a 'Please, Mr Goldman,' silenced him. Nim realized what he should have known instinctively: There was nothing else to say; the arguments had been marshalled before, and emphatically rejected. There was no way, never had been, in which these two could be relieved of one iota of the burden they carried.

'Henrietta's right,' Luther said. 'I *do* think the same way she does. Both of us will take the guilt with us to our graves.'

His wife added, 'So you see what I mean when I say that whatever we do – including working to pay for a van for Karen – is really nothing.'

'It isn't nothing,' Nim said. 'Whatever else is true, it's a whole lot more than that.'

They walked from the apartment lobby to the street outside. Nim's car was parked a few yards away.

'Thank you for telling me what you did,' he said. 'I'll try to do something about the van, just as soon as I can.'

As Nim had come to expect, some verse from Karen arrived two days later.

When young
Did you ever run on sidewalks,
Playing the game
Of avoiding cracks?
Or, much later,
Straddle hairlines mentally
And strut vicarious tightropes,
Dreading, yet perversely courting,
Disaster from a fall?

'Disaster' did I say?
An aberrant word!
For there are other falls and penalties
Not wholly catastrophic,
But cushioned by largesse
Of joy and glory.
Falling in love is one.

Yet wisdom cautions:
A fall is a fall
With aftermaths of hurt and pain
Only delayed, not circumvented.

Tish, tosh!
Away with wisdom!
Hooray for crazy paving, tightropes, hairlines!
Right now, who's wise, or wants to be?
Not I.
Are you?

7

The subject was Tunipah.

'Talking to the Governor of this state about anything,' J. Eric Humphrey declared in his clipped Bostonian accent, 'has about the same effect as putting one's hand into a pail of water. As soon as you take the hand out, the water is exactly the way it was before, as if the hand had never been there.'

'Except,' Ray Paulsen pointed out, 'your hand would be wet.'

'Clammy,' the chairman corrected.

'I warned you,' Teresa Van Buren said. 'I warned you right after the blackout two months ago that public memory is short, that people – including politicians – would forget the power shortage and the reasons.'

'Memory isn't the Governor's problem,' Oscar O'Brien assured her. The general counsel had been with Eric Humphrey during recent sessions at the state capital, where proposals for new generating plants – including Tunipah – had been discussed. He went on. 'There's only one trouble with our Governor: he wants to be President of the United States. He wants it so bad, he can taste it.'

Nim Goldman said, 'Who knows? He might make a good president.'

'He might at that,' O'Brien conceded. 'In the meantime, though, California is rudderless, stuck with a head of state who won't take stands or hand down decisions. Not if they're likely to offend a single national voter.'

'Allowing for slight exaggeration,' Eric Humphrey said, 'that is the essence of our problem.'

'Furthermore,' O'Brien added, blowing cigar smoke, 'the same thing applies – for similar if different reasons – to every other public figure in Sacramento.'

The five of them were at Golden State Power & Light headquarters, in the chairman's office suite, seated informally in the lounge area.

In less than two weeks public hearings on the proposed coal-burning, high-capacity generating plant at Tunipah would begin. And while the project was vital to California – a viewpoint agreed to privately by the Governor, his aides and senior legislators – for political reasons none would lend public support to the Tunipah plan. The utility, despite strong opposition forces, must 'go it alone'.

Something else the Governor had rejected was GSP & L's plea that the several regulatory agencies which would be involved with licensing Tunipah should hold joint hearings because of urgency. Instead, regular procedures would take their course. It meant a long, exhausting series of submissions and arguments before four separate government bodies, each concerned with a differing aspect, though often overlapping.

Teresa Van Buren asked, 'Is the Governor, or anyone else, likely to have a change of heart?'

'Only if the bastards see an advantage to themselves,' Ray Paulsen growled. 'And they won't.' Paulsen had grown increasingly bitter of late about the frustrating delays in having plans approved. As the executive in charge of power supply, Paulsen would have the unpopular job of initiating power cuts when they became needed in the future.

'Ray's right,' O'Brien acknowledged. 'We all know how the Sacramento gang left us holding the bag on nuclear, admitting – off the record – the need for nuclear plants, but without the guts to say so out loud.'

'Well,' Eric Humphrey said incisively, 'whether we like that attitude or despise it, the same is true again. Now about the Tunipah hearings. I have some thoughts to share with you. I want our own participation in those hearings to be of the highest calibre. Our presentation must be factual, reasoned, calm and dignified. Under cross-examination the responses of all our representatives must be the same, with emphasis on courtesy and patience. As part of their tactics, the opposition will try to provoke us. We must resist that provocation and I want all our people briefed to that effect.'

'It will be done,' Oscar O'Brien said.

Ray Paulsen regarded Nim sombrely. 'Remember that applies to you.'

Nim grimaced. 'I'm already practising restraint, Ray – right now.'

Neither had forgotten their clash at the management meeting where Nim and Van Buren favoured a hard-line public airing of the utility's problems, Paulsen and a majority of others the reverse. Judging by the chairman's instructions, the 'moderate line' was still in effect.

'Do you still believe, Oscar,' Eric Humphrey asked, 'that it is necessary for me, personally, to appear at those hearings?'

O'Brien nodded. 'Absolutely yes.'

Behind the question, obviously, was Humphrey's wish to avoid public attention. During the past ten days there had been two more bombings at GSP & L installations, none causing major damage but a reminder of the continuing danger to the utility and its personnel. Only yesterday a warning, telephoned to a radio station, declared that 'more Golden State Piss & Lickspittle management criminals will shortly pay the people's penalty for their misdeeds.'

O'Brien added, 'I promise it will be a brief appearance, Eric, but we need you on the record.'

The chairman sighed. 'Very well.'

Nim thought with wry humour: as usual, the low-profile strategy would not apply to him. At the upcoming hearings Nim would appear as a key witness and, while others from the utility would testify on technical matters, Nim would present the broad sweep of the Tunipah project. Oscar O'Brien would lead the witnesses through interrogation.

Nim and O'Brien already had had several rehearsals in which Ray Paulsen shared.

During their work with O'Brien, Paulsen and Nim had suppressed their normal antagonism and at moments had come close to amiability.

Taking advantage of this, Nim raised with Paulsen the subject of a used van for Karen Sloan because transportation was a subordinate department under Power Supply.

To Nim's surprise, Paulsen was interested and helpful. Within forty-eight hours of their conversation, he had located a suitable van which would shortly be available for sale. More than that, Ray Paulsen was personally designing some modifications. They would facilitate loading Karen's wheelchair into the van and, once inside, locking it in place. Karen telephoned Nim to say that a GSP & L mechanic had visited her to measure her chair and check on electrical connections.

'One of the best things that's ever happened to me,' Karen told Nim during their phone talk, 'was your seeing that red circle on the map that day and afterwards coming here. Speaking of that, when are you coming again, dear Nimrod? Soon, I hope.' He had promised he would. Later, Nim had phoned Karen's parents, Luther and Henrietta, who were delighted about the van and were now arranging a bank loan to cover most of its cost.

Oscar O'Brien's voice brought Nim back to the present. 'I

presume all of you realize how long this entire process concerning Tunipah is likely to take.'

Paulsen said gloomily, 'Too damn long!'

Van Buren enquired, 'What's your best estimate, Oscar?'

'Assuming we are successful at the various sets of hearings, and allowing for delaying court actions subsequently, which our opponents are certain to resort to – I'd say six to seven years.' The general counsel shuffled papers. 'You may also be interested in costs. My department estimates that our own costs – just to seek the licence to build, and whether we win or lose – will be five and a half million dollars. Environmental studies will cost a few million more, and we won't have turned a spade until construction is fully licensed.'

'Let us make sure, Tess,' Eric Humphrey told the PR director, 'that that information becomes as widely known as possible.'

'I'll try,' Van Buren said. 'Though I can't guarantee that many outside this room will care.'

'They'll care when the lights go out,' Humphrey snapped. 'All right, I want to review progress, if any, on our other applications – Devil's Gate pumped storage and Fincastle geothermal.'

' "If any" is right,' O'Brien observed. He reported that so far only the earliest skirmishes through bureaucratic jungles had been accomplished. Countless others lay ahead. Meanwhile, massive opposition to Devil's Gate and Fincastle was growing . . .

Listening, Nim experienced a surge of anger at the cumbrous, inefficient system and the utility's own faintheartedness in failing to attack it strongly. Nim knew he would have trouble at the Tunipah hearings. Trouble in exercising restraint, difficulty in maintaining patience, a reluctance to curb his own harsh words which could speak the truth forthrightly.

8

J. Eric Humphrey sat red-faced and uncomfortable in the elevated, hard-backed witness chair. He had been there half a day – already several hours longer than the 'brief appearance' Oscar O'Brien had promised him.

Three feet away, in the courtroom-like setting, Davey Birdsong stood facing the witness and towering over him. Birdsong swayed slightly as he transferred his formidable weight from his heels to the balls of his feet, then back, forwards, back again. 'Since you must be hard of hearing, I'll repeat my question. How much do you get paid each year?'

Humphrey, who had hesitated when the question was first posed, glanced at O'Brien, seated at counsel's table. The lawyer gave the slightest of shrugs.

Tight-lipped, the GSP & L chairman answered, 'Two hundred and forty-five thousand dollars.'

Birdsong waved a hand airily. 'No, sport, you misunderstand me. I didn't ask the capitalization of Golden State Power & Light. I asked how much bread *you* earn.'

Humphrey, unamused, replied, 'That is the figure I gave.'

'I can hardly believe it!' Birdsong clapped a hand to his head in a theatrical gesture. 'I *didn't believe* that any one person *could* earn so much money.' He emitted a long, low whistle. 'Wow!'

From the audience in the warm, crowded hearing room came echoing whistles and other 'wows!' Someone called out, 'We consumers are the ones who pay it! Too damn much!' There was applause for the heckler and stomping on the floor.

On the bench above, looking down at witness, questioner and spectators, the presiding commissioner reached for a gavel. He tapped with it lightly and commanded, 'Order!' The commissioner, in his mid-thirties and with a pink, boyish face, had been appointed to his post a year ago after service in the ruling political party. He was an accountant by training and was rumoured to be a relative of the Governor.

As the commissioner spoke, O'Brien lumbered to his feet. 'Mr Chairman, is this harassment of my witness necessary?'

The commissioner regarded Birdsong, who was wearing his

uniform of shabby jeans, a multicoloured shirt open at the neck, and tennis shoes. In contrast, Humphrey, who ordered his three-piece suits from deLisi in New York and went there for fittings, was sartorially impeccable.

'You asked your question and you received an answer, Mr Birdsong,' the commissioner said. 'We can manage without the theatrics. Proceed, please.'

'Certainly, Mr Chairman.' Birdsong swung back to Eric Humphrey. 'You did say two hundred and fórty-five thousand dollars?'

'Yes, I did.'

'Are there other compensations which go with being the big cheese . . .' (Laughter from the spectators.) 'Excuse me – the chairman of a public utility? A personal limousine perhaps?'

'Yes.'

'Chauffeur-driven?'

'Yes.'

'Plus a fat expense account?'

Humphrey said huffily, 'I would not refer to it as fat.'

'How about enormous?'

More laughter.

J. Eric Humphrey's intense displeasure was beginning to show. Essentially a high-level administrator and in no way a rough-and-tumble fighter, he was ill-equipped to handle the flashy showmanship of Birdsong. He responded coldly, 'My duties involve certain expenses which I am permitted to charge to our company.'

'I'll bet!'

O'Brien was halfway to his feet. The presiding commissioner waved him down and instructed, 'Confine yourself to questions, Mr Birdsong.'

The huge bearded man grinned broadly. 'Yes*sir!*'

Seated in the public section, Nim fumed. Why didn't Humphrey answer bluntly, aggressively, as he could and should? *My salary, Mr Birdsong, is a matter of public record since it is reported to regulatory agencies and the information is easily available. I am certain that you knew it before asking the question; therefore your show of surprise was phony and deceitful. Furthermore, the salary is not out of line for the chairman and chief executive of one of the nation's largest corporations; in fact, it is smaller than in most other companies of comparable size. One*

177

reason for the level of my salary is that industrial organizations like GSP & L are aware they must be competitive in recruiting and retaining executive talent. To be specific: my own experience and qualifications would certainly earn me an equal or larger salary elsewhere. You may not wholly like that system, Mr Birdsong, but while we remain a free enterprise society, that is the way it is. As to a chauffeur-driven car, this was offered to me at the time of my employment on the same competitive basis as salary, and also on the assumption that a chief executive's time and energies are more valuable than the cost of such a car and driver. One more point about that car: like other busy executives I am accustomed to work in it on my way from one place to another and seldom relax there. Finally, if the company's directors and shareholders are dissatisfied with my performance in return for money paid, they have power to remove me . . .

But no! Nim thought glumly: the soft approach, excessive worrying about an elusive public image, pussyfooting, never standing up to the Birdsongs of the world by employing their own tough tactics in reverse – all these were the order of the day. This day and other days to come

It was the second day of hearings on the licence application for Tunipah, first stage. The preceding day had been filled by formalities, including submission by counsel for GSP & L of a mammoth 500-page 'Notice of Intention' (350 copies printed), the first of many similar documents to come. As O'Brien put it sardonically : 'By the time we're through we'll have caused to be chopped down a forest of trees to make the paper we shall use which, put together, could fill a library or sink a ship.'

Earlier today, J. Eric Humphrey was summoned as the applicant's first witness.

O'Brien had led the utility's chairman quickly through a recital of the need for Tunipah and the site's advantages – the promised 'brief appearance'. Then there had been a more lengthy questioning by counsel for the commission, who was followed by Roderick Pritchett, manager-secretary of the Sequoia Club. Both cross-examinations, while occupying more than an hour each, were constructive and low-key. Davey Birdsong, however, who was next and appeared for p & lfp, had already enlivened the proceedings, clearly to the delight of supporters in the audience.

'Now then, Mr Humphrey,' he continued, 'I guess you wake up in the morning figuring you have to do *something* to justify that enormous salary of yours. Is that right?'

O'Brien called out promptly, 'I object!'

'Sustained,' the commissioner pronounced.

Birdsong was unperturbed. 'I'll ask it another way. Do you feel as the main part of your job, Eric baby, that you have to keep dreaming up schemes – like this Tunipah deal – which will make huge profits for your company?'

'Objection!'

Birdsong swung towards the GSP & L counsel. 'Why don't you have a tape made? Then you could press a button without opening your mouth.'

There was laughter and some scattered applause. At the same time the young commissioner leaned over to confer with a second man seated beside him – an elderly administrative law judge, a civil servant with long experience in the type of hearing being conducted. As he spoke softly, the older man could be seen to shake his head.

'Objection denied,' the commissioner announced, then added, 'We allow considerable latitude at these hearings, Mr Birdsong, but you will please address all witnesses with respect, using their correct names, not as' – he tried to suppress a smile but was unsuccessful – 'sport or Eric baby. Another point: we would like some assurance that your line of questioning is relevant.'

'Oh, it's relevant all right! It's *really* relevant.' Birdsong's answer was expansive. Then, as if changing gears, he slipped into the role of supplicant. 'But please realize, Mr Chairman, I'm just a simple person, representing humble people, not an important, fancy lawyer like old Oscar baby here.' He pointed to O'Brien. 'So if I'm awkward, over-friendly, make mistakes . . .'

The commissioner sighed. 'Just get *on*. Please!'

'Yessir! Certainly, sir!' Birdsong swung towards Humphrey. 'You heard the man! You're wasting the commissioner's time. Now quit futzing around and answer the question.'

O'Brien interjected, 'What question? I'll be darned if I remember it. I'm sure the witness can't.'

The commissioner instructed, 'The reporter will read the question back.'

The proceedings halted and those on hard chairs and benches

shifted, making themselves more comfortable while a male steno-typist, who was keeping the official commission record, flipped back through the folded tape of his notes. At the rear of the room several newcomers slipped in as others left. As those participating knew, in months and years to come, long before any decision was reached, this scene and sequence would be repeated count-less times.

The oak-panelled hearing chamber was in a twelve-storey building near the city's centre, occupied by the California Energy Commission, which was conducting the present series of hear-ings. Directly across the street was the building of the California Public Utilities Commission, which would later conduct its own hearings on Tunipah, in large part repetitious. Competition and jealousy between the two separate commissions were intense and, at times, took on an Alice-in-Wonderland quality.

Two additional state agencies would also get into the act soon and conduct hearings of their own; these were the California Water Quality Resources Board and the Air Resources Board. Each of the four government bodies would receive all reports and other papers generated by the remaining three, most of which they would ignore.

Then, at lower level, it was necessary to satisfy an Air Pollu-tion Control District which might impose restrictions even more severe than those of the state agencies.

As O'Brien put it privately, 'No one who isn't directly involved would ever believe the incredible duplication and futility. We who participate, and those who set up this crazy system, should be certified as lunatics. It would be far cheaper for the public purse, and more efficient, if we were locked up in asylums.'

The stenotypist was concluding, '. . . schemes – like this Tuni-pah deal – which will make huge profits for your company?'

'The objective of Tunipah,' Humphrey responded, 'is to pro-vide service to our customers and the community generally, as we always have, by anticipating increased demands for elec-tricity. Profit is secondary.'

'But there *will* be profits,' Birdsong persisted.

'Naturally. We are a public company with obligations to inves-tors . . .'

'Big profits? Profits in the millions?'

'Because of the enormous size of the undertaking and the huge investment, there will be issues of stocks and bonds, which could not be sold to investors unless . . .'

Birdsong cut in sharply, 'Answer "yes" or "no". Will there be profits in the millions?'

The GSP & L chairman flushed. 'Probably – yes.'

Once more his tormentor rocked back and forth on his heels. 'So we only have your word, Mr Humphrey, about whether profits or service comes first – the word of a person who, if this monstrous Tunipah fraud is foisted on the public, stands to profit in every possible way.'

'Objection,' O'Brien said wearily. 'That is *not* a question. It is a prejudicial, inflammatory, unsubstantiated statement.'

'So many big words! – okay, I withdraw it,' Birdsong volunteered before the commissioner could rule. He grinned. 'I guess my honest feelings got the better of me.'

O'Brien looked as if he would object again, then decided not.

As Birdsong and others were well aware, the last exchange would be in the record, despite withdrawal. Also, reporters at the press table had their heads down and were writing busily – something they were not doing earlier.

Still observing from his spectator's seat, Nim thought: no doubt Davey Birdsong's comments would be featured in reports next day because the p & lfp leader was, as usual, making colourful copy.

Among the press group Nim could see the black reporter, Nancy Molineaux. She had been watching Birdsong intently, not writing but sitting upright and unmoving; the pose emphasized her high cheekbones, the handsome if forbidding face, her slim, willowy body. Her expression was thoughtful. Nim guessed that she too was appreciating Birdsong's performance.

Earlier today Ms Molineaux and Nim had passed each other briefly outside the hearing room. When he nodded curtly she raised an eyebrow and gave him a mocking smile.

Birdsong resumed his questioning. 'Tell me, Eric old pal . . . oops, pardon me! – *Mister* Humphrey – have you ever heard of conservation?'

'Of course.'

'Are you aware there is a widespread belief that projects like Tunipah would not be needed if you people got behind conservation seriously? I mean, not just played at conservation in a token way, but *sold* it – with the same hard sell you're using right now in trying for permission to build more plants to make fatter and fatter profits?'

O'Brien was halfway to his feet when Humphrey said, 'I'll answer that.' The lawyer subsided.

'In the first place, at Golden State Power & Light, we do *not* try to sell more electricity; we used to, but we haven't done that kind of selling in a long time. Instead we urge conservation – *very* seriously. But conservation, while helping, will never eliminate steady growth in electrical demand, which is why we require Tunipah.'

Birdsong prompted, 'And that's your opinion?'

'Naturally it's my opinion.'

'The same kind of prejudiced opinion which asked us to believe you don't care whether Tunipah makes a profit or not?'

O'Brien objected. 'That's a misrepresentation. The witness did not say he didn't *care* about profit.'

'I'll concede that.' Abruptly Birdsong swung to face O'Brien, his body seeming to expand as his voice rose. 'We know *all* of you at Golden State care about profits – big, fat, gross, *extortionate* profits at the expense of small consumers, the decent working people of this state who pay their bills and will be stuck with the cost of Tunipah if . . .'

The remainder of the words were drowned in cheers, applause and foot-stomping from the spectators. Amid it all, the commissioner banged his gavel, calling, 'Order! Order!'

A man who had joined in the cheering and was seated next to Nim observed Nim's silence. He enquired belligerently, 'Don't you care, buster?'

'Yes,' Nim said. 'I care.'

Nim realized that if this were a regular court proceeding the chances were that Birdsong would long since have been cited for contempt. But he wouldn't be, now or later, because the courtroom setting was a façade. Hearings of this kind were allowed, deliberately, to operate loosely with occasional disorders tolerated. Oscar O'Brien had explained the reasons at one of his advance briefings.

'Public commissions nowadays are scared shitless that if they don't allow all and sundry to have an unrestricted chance to say their piece, later there could be challenges in the courts on grounds that significant evidence was quashed. If that happened it might mean an overturned decision, undoing years of work because some nut was ordered to shut up or a minor argument disallowed. No one wants that – including us. So, by general consent, the demagogues and kooks *et al* are given their head along with all the time they want. It makes for dragged out hearings but in the end is probably shorter.'

That, Nim knew, was why the experienced administrative law judge had shaken his head a few moments ago, advising the young commissioner not to disallow Birdsong's disputed question.

Something else O'Brien had explained was that lawyers like himself, who were involved on behalf of applicants, raised fewer objections at this type of hearing than they would in court. 'We save them for something that's outrageously wrong and ought to be corrected in the record.' Nim suspected that O'Brien's objections during J. Eric Humphrey's cross-examination by Birdsong were mostly to mollify Humphrey, O'Brien's boss, who had been reluctant to make this appearance anyway.

Nim was sure that when his own turn came to testify and be cross-examined, O'Brien would leave him pretty much to fend for himself.

'Let's get back,' Davey Birdsong was continuing, 'to those huge profits we were talking about. Now take the effect on consumers' monthly bills . . .'

For another half hour the p & lfp leader continued his interrogation. He employed leading, loaded questions unsubstantiated by facts, interrupted by clowning, but hammering home his contention that profits from Tunipah would be excessive and were the major motivation. Nim conceded mentally : while the charge was false, the Goebbels-type repetition was effective. Undoubtedly it would receive prominence in the media, and probably credence, which clearly was among Birdsong's objectives.

'Thank you, Mr Humphrey,' the commissioner said when the GSP & L chairman stepped down from the witness stand. Eric Humphrey nodded an acknowledgment, then departed with evident relief.

Two other GSP & L witnesses followed. Both were specialist engineers. Their testimony and cross-examination were uneventful but occupied two full days, after which the hearing was adjourned until Monday of the following week. Nim, who would have the burden of presenting the main thrust of GSP & L's case, would be next on the witness stand when proceedings resumed.

9

Three weeks ago, when Ruth Goldman startled Nim by announcing her intention to leave home for a while, he considered it likely she would change her mind. However, Ruth hadn't. Now, on Friday evening, during the weekend recess of the Tunipah hearings, Nim found himself alone in their house, Leah and Benjy having been taken by Ruth to their grandparents across town before her departure. The arrangement was that both children would remain with the Neubergers until Ruth's return, whenever that might be.

Ruth had been vague about that, just as she had declined to say where she was going, or with whom. 'Probably it will be two weeks, though it may be less or more,' she had told Nim several days ago.

But there was nothing vague about her attitude towards him; it had been cool and definite. It was, he thought, as if she had reached decisions within herself and all that remained was to implement them. What the decisions were, and how he would be affected, Nim had no idea. At first he told himself he should care, but was saddened to find he didn't. At least, not much. That was why he had raised no protest when Ruth told him her plans were complete and she would be leaving at the end of the week.

It was uncharacteristic, Nim realized, for him merely to 'go along' and let things drift. By nature he was accustomed to make decisions promptly and to plan ahead: that ability, applied to his work, had earned him recognition and advancement. But where his marriage was concerned he still had a curious reluctance to move, perhaps to face reality. He was leaving it all to

Ruth. If she chose to leave permanently and afterwards seek a divorce, which seemed the natural sequence, he would be disinclined to fight or even try to dissuade her. However, he would not take the step himself. Not yet.

He had asked Ruth only yesterday if she was ready to discuss their situation, remembering her words: '... *you and I have only been going through the motions of being married. We haven't talked about it. But I think we should ... Perhaps when I come back.*'

Why wait? Nim reasoned.

But she had answered in a businesslike tone, 'No, *I'll* tell you when I'm ready.' And that had been the end of it.

Leah and Benjy entered frequently into Nim's thoughts along with the possibility of divorce. Both children, he knew, would be devastated by the idea, and he was saddened at the thought of them being hurt. But the fact was, children survived divorces and Nim had observed many who accepted a divorce in the family as a simple facet of life. Nor would there be difficulty about Nim and Leah and Benjy spending time together. He might even end up seeing more of both children than he did now. It had happened to other estranged fathers.

But all that must await Ruth's return, he reflected, as he roamed the empty house on Friday evening.

A half hour ago he had telephoned Leah and Benjy, ploughing through the objections of Aaron Neuberger, who didn't like his telephone to be used, except for emergencies, on the Sabbath. Nim had let the phone ring and ring until his father-in-law gave in and answered. 'I want to talk to my kids,' Nim insisted bluntly, 'and I don't care if it's Mickey Mouse Tuesday.'

When Leah came on the line a few minutes later she reproached him gently. 'Daddy, you've upset Grandfather.'

Nim had felt like saying *Good!* but wisely didn't; and they talked about school, a forthcoming swim meet and ballet class. No mention of Ruth. He sensed that Leah knew something was wrong but was uneasy about asking or knowing.

His conversation with Benjy, which followed, revived the irritation Nim frequently felt about his in-laws.

'Dad,' Benjy had said, 'am I going to have a bar mitzvah? Grandfather said I have to. And Grandmother says if I don't I'll never be a real Jewish man.'

Confound those interfering Neubergers! Couldn't they just be loving grandparents, taking care of Leah and Benjy for a couple of weeks, without grabbing the chance to inject propaganda into the children? It was almost *indecent* to start working on them with such haste, as well as intruding on the rights of Nim and Ruth as parents. Nim had wanted to bring up that subject himself with Benjy, talking it over quietly, intelligently, man-to-man, not having it sprung on him suddenly like this. *Well,* an inner voice inquired, *why didn't you do it? There's been plenty of time. If you had, you wouldn't be wondering right now how to respond to Benjy's question.*

Nim said sharply, 'No one *has* to have a bar mitzvah. I didn't. And what your grandmother said is nonsense.'

'Grandfather says there's a lot I'll have to learn.' Benjy still sounded doubtful. 'He said I ought to have started a long time ago.'

Was there an accusation in Benjy's small precise voice? It was entirely possible – in fact, probable – Nim thought, that Benjy at ten understood a great deal more than his elders assumed. Therefore did Benjy's questions now reflect the same instinctive search for identification with his ancestry which Nim had been aware of in himself, and had subdued, though not entirely? He wasn't sure. Nothing, however, lessened Nim's anger at the way all this had surfaced, though he curbed another sharp answer, knowing it would do harm, not good.

'Look, son, what you said just now simply isn't true. If we decide you should be bar mitzvahed there's plenty of time. You have to realize your grandparents have some views which your mother and I don't agree with.' Nim wasn't sure how true that was of Ruth, but she wasn't around to contradict. He went on, 'As soon as your mother is back, and you come home, we'll talk all this over. Okay?'

Benjy had said 'okay' a touch reluctantly and Nim realized he must keep his promise or lose credibility with his son. He considered the idea of flying his father in from New York and having him stay for a while, which would expose Benjy to a counterbalancing influence. Old Isaac Goldman, while frail and in his eighties, was still acid, cynical and biting about Judaism and enjoyed slamming haymakers into Orthodox Jewish arguments. But no, Nim decided. That would be just as unfair as the Neubergers were being now.

After the phone call, and while mixing himself a scotch and water, Nim caught sight of a portrait of Ruth; it was in oils, painted several years ago. The artist had caught, with remarkable fidelity, Ruth's graceful beauty and serenity. He crossed to the painting and studied it. The face, especially the soft grey eyes, was exceptionally good; so was the hair – shiny black, neatly and impeccably arranged, as always. For the sittings Ruth had worn a strapless evening gown; the flesh tones of her graceful shoulders were uncannily real. There was even, on one shoulder, the small dark mole which she had had removed surgically soon after the portrait was done.

Nim's thoughts returned to Ruth's serenity; it was what the painting showed best. *I could use some of that serenity right now,* he thought, and wished he could talk to Ruth about Benjy and a bar mitzvah. *Dammit! Where in hell has she gone for two weeks and who is the man?* Nim was sure the Neubergers would have some idea. At the very least they would know where Ruth could be contacted; Nim knew his wife too well to believe she would cut herself off completely from the children. Equally certain: her parents would be close-mouthed about the arrangement. The thought refuelled the anger at his in-laws.

Following a second scotch and more perambulating, he returned to the telephone and dialled Harry London's home number. They hadn't talked in a week, which was unusual.

When London answered, Nim asked him, 'Want to drive out to my house and booze a little?'

'Sorry, Nim; I'd like to, but I can't. Got a dinner date. Leaving here soon. Did you hear about the latest bombing?'

'No. When?'

'Happened an hour ago.'

'Anyone hurt?'

'Not this time – but that's the only good part.'

Two powerful bombs had been planted at a GSP & L suburban substation, Harry London reported. As a result more than six thousand homes in the area were now without electric power. Mobile transformers, mounted on flatbed trucks, were being rushed in, but it was unlikely that full service would be restored until tomorrow.

'Those crazies are getting smart,' London said. 'They're learning where we're vulnerable, and where to put their firecrackers to do the most damage.'

'Do we know yet if it's the same group?'

'Yep. Friends of Freedom. They phoned Channel 5 News just before it happened, saying *where* it would happen. Too late to do anything, though. That makes eleven bombings we've had in two months. I just added up.'

Knowing that London, while not directly involved in the investigation, still had pipelines of information, Nim asked, 'Have the police or FBI made any progress?'

'Nil. I said the people doing it are getting smart; so they are. It's a safe bet they study the targets before they hit, then decide where they can get in and out fast, unnoticed, and do the most damage. This Friends of Freedom mob know, just as we do, that we'd need an army to guard everything.'

'And there haven't been clues?'

'Nil again. Remember what I said before? If the cops solve this one it'll be through a lucky break or because somebody got careless. Nim, it ain't the way it is on TV or in novels where crimes always get solved. In the real police world they often don't.'

'I know that,' Nim said, mildly irritated that London was slipping into his lecturer's role again.

'There is one thing, though,' the Property Protection chief said thoughtfully.

'What's that?'

'For a while the bombings slowed down, almost stopped. Now suddenly they've perked up, making it look as if the people doing them have got a new source of explosives, or money, or both.'

Nim pondered, then changed the subject. 'What's new with theft of service?'

'Not a hell of a lot. Oh, sure, we're working hard and catching some small fry. There's a couple dozen new cases of meter tampering we'll take to court. But it's like plugging a hundred leaks when you know there's ten thousand more out there if you just had the people and time to find 'em.'

'How about that big office building? The one where you're keeping watch?'

'Zaco Properties. We still have surveillance on it. Nothing's happened yet. I guess we're going through a flat spell.' Uncharacteristically, Harry London sounded depressed. Maybe it was infectious; perhaps he had transmitted his own low spirits,

Nim thought as he said good night and hung up.

He was still restless, alone in the silent house. So who else could he call?

He considered Ardythe, then dismissed the idea. Nim was not ready yet – if he ever would be – to cope with Ardythe Talbot's onset of religion. But thinking of Ardythe reminded him of Wally Jr, whom Nim had visited in the hospital twice recently. Wally was now out of danger and removed from intensive care, though ahead lay months, perhaps years, of tedious, painful plastic surgery. Not surprisingly, Wally's spirits had been low. They had not discussed his sexual incapacity.

Half guiltily, as he remembered Wally, Nim reminded himself that his own sexual ability was unimpaired. Should he call one of his women friends? There were several whom he had not seen for months but who, quite probably, would be available for drinks, a late dinner somewhere, and whatever followed. If he made the effort, he need not spend the night alone.

Somehow he couldn't be bothered.

Karen Sloan? No. As much as he enjoyed her company, he wasn't in the mood.

Work, then? There was work aplenty piled on his office desk at GSP & L headquarters. If he went there now it would not be the first time he had toiled at night, taking advantage of the quietness to accomplish more than was possible in daytime. It might also be a good idea. The Tunipah hearings were already consuming much of Nim's available time, and the demand would continue, though his normal work load had to be fitted in somehow.

But no, not that either, not desk work in his present mood. How about some other kind of work to occupy his mind?

What could he do, he wondered, to prepare himself for his debut Monday on the witness stand? He was already well briefed. But there was always something more to be prepared for – the unexpected.

An idea jumped into his mind, from out of nowhere, like bread emerging from a pop-up toaster.

Coal!

Tunipah *was* coal. Without coal – to be freighted from Utah to California – no Tunipah electric generating plant was feasible. And yet, while Nim's technical expertise on coal was considerable, his practical experience was limited. There was a simple reason. As yet, no coal-burning electric generating plant existed inside California. Tunipah would be the first in history.

Surely . . . somehow, he thought . . . between now and Monday morning he must go – as if on a pilgrimage – to a coal-fuelled plant. And from it he would return to the Tunipah hearings with the sight, sound, taste and smell of coal fresh in his senses. Nim's instincts, which were often right, advised him he would be a better, stronger witness if he did.

It would also solve the problem of his weekend restlessness.

But a coal-burning plant where?

When the easy answer occurred to him he mixed another scotch and water. Then, with the drink at his side, he sat at the telephone once more and dialled directory assistance in Denver, Colorado.

10

Flight 460 of United Airlines made an on-time departure from the West Coast at 7:15am. As the Boeing 727-200 became airborne and climbed steeply, the morning sun, which minutes before had cleared the eastern horizon, tinted the landscape below a soft red-gold. The world seemed clean and pure, Nim thought, as it always does at dawn, a daily illusion lasting less than half an hour.

While the jet steadied on an easterly course, Nim settled back in his comfortable first-class seat. He had no hesitation in making the trip this way, at company expense, since reflection this morning while driving to the airport in darkness confirmed the good sense of last night's impulse. It would be a two-hour-twenty-minute non-stop flight to Denver. An old friend, Thurston Jones, would meet him there.

A chirpy, personality-packed young hostess – the kind United seemed to have a knack for recruiting – served an omelette breakfast and persuaded Nim to accompany it with California wine, early as it was. 'Oh, come on!' she urged when she saw him hesitate. 'You've "shed the surly bonds of earth," so unzip that psyche! Enjoy!' He *did* enjoy – a Mirassou Riesling, not great but good – and arrived at Denver more relaxed than he had been the previous night.

At Denver's Stapleton International Airport, Thurston Jones shook Nim's hand warmly, then led the way directly to his car since Nim's only baggage was a small overnighter he was carrying.

Thurston and Nim had been students together, as well as room-mates and close friends, at Stanford University. In those days they had shared most things, including women whom they knew, and there was little about either which was unknown to the other. Since then the friendship had endured, even though they met only occasionally and exchanged infrequent letters.

In outward mannerisms the two had differed, and still did. Thurston was quiet, studious, brilliant and good-looking in a boyish way. His manner was self-effacing, though he could exercise authority when needed. He had a cheerful sense of humour. Coincidentally, Thurston had followed the same career route as Nim and now was Nim's opposite number – vice president of planning – for Public Service Company of Colorado, one of the nation's most respected producers and distributors of electricity and natural gas. Thurston also had what Nim lacked – wide practical experience in power generation by coal.

'How's everything at home?' Nim asked on their way to the airport parking lot. His old friend had been married happily for eight years or so to a bubbly English girl named Ursula, whom Nim knew and liked.

'Fine. The same with you, I hope.'

'Not really.'

Nim hoped he had conveyed, without rudeness, a reluctance to discuss his own and Ruth's problems. Apparently so, because Thurston made no comment and went on, 'Ursula's looking forward to seeing you. You'll stay with us, of course.'

Nim murmured thanks while they climbed into Thurston's car, a Ford Pinto. His friend, Nim knew, shared his own distaste for cars with wasteful fuel habits.

Outside it was a bright, dry, sunny day. As they drove towards

Denver, the snowcapped front range of the Rocky Mountains was clear and beautiful to the west.

A trifle shyly, Thurston remarked, 'After all this time it's really good to have you here, Nim.' He added with a smile, 'Even if you did just come for a taste of coal.'

'Does it sound crazy, Thurs?'

Nim had explained last night on the telephone his sudden desire to visit a coal-fired generating plant and the reasoning behind it.

'Who's to say what's crazy and what isn't? Those endless hearings nowadays are crazy – not the idea of having them, but the way they're run. In Colorado we're in the same kind of bind you are in California. Nobody wants to let us build new generation, but five or six years from now when power cuts start, we'll be accused of not looking ahead, not planning for a crisis.'

'The plants your people want to build – they'd be coal-burning?'

'Damn right! When God set up natural resources he was kind to Colorado. He loaded this state with coal, the way he handed oil to the Arabs. And not just any old coal, but good stuff – low in sulphur, clean burning, most of it near the surface and easily mined. But you know all that.'

Nim nodded because he did know, then said thoughtfully, 'There's enough coal west of the Mississippi to supply this country's energy needs for three and a half centuries. *If* we're allowed to use it.'

Thurston continued threading the little car through Saturday morning traffic, which was light. 'We'll go directly to our Cherokee plant, north of the city,' he announced. 'It's our biggest. Gobbles up coal like a starving brontosaurus.'

'We burn seven and a half thousand tons a day here, give or take a little.' The Cherokee plant superintendent shouted the information at Nim, doing his best to be heard above the roar of pulverizer mills, fans and pumps. He was an alert, sandy-haired young man whose surname – Folger – was stencilled on the red hard hat he wore. Nim had on a white hard hat labelled *Visitor*. Thurston Jones had brought his own.

They were standing on a steel plate floor near one side of a gargantuan boiler into which coal – which had just been pulverized to a fine dust – was being air-blown in enormous quantities. Inside the boiler the coal ignited instantly and became white hot; part of it was visible through a glass-enclosed inspection port like a peephole glimpse of hell. This heat transferred itself to a latticework of boiler tubes containing water which promptly became high-pressure steam and ripsnorted to a separate superheater section, emerging at a thousand degrees Fahrenheit. The steam, in turn, rotated a turbine generator which – along with other boilers and turbines at Cherokee – supplied almost three quarters of a million kilowatts to power-hungry Denver and environs.

Only a portion of the boiler's exterior was visible from the enclosed area where the men were standing; the entire height of the boiler was equal to fifteen floors of a normal building.

But all around them were the sight and sound and smell and taste of coal. A fine gravel of black dust was underfoot. Already Nim was conscious of a grittiness between his teeth and in his nostrils.

'We clean up as often as we can,' Superintendent Folger volunteered. 'But coal is dirty.'

Thurston added loudly, with a smile, 'Messier than oil or hydro. You sure you want this filthy stuff in California?'

Nim nodded affirmatively, not choosing to pit his voice against the surrounding roar of blowers and conveyors. Then, changing his mind, he shouted back, 'We'll join the black gang. Don't have any choice.'

He was already glad he had come. It *was* important to acquire a feeling about coal, coal as it would relate to Tunipah, for his testimony next week.

King Coal! Nim had read somewhere recently that 'Old King Coal is striding back towards his throne.' It had to be that way, he thought; there was no alternative. In the last few decades America had turned its back on coal, which once brought cheap energy, along with growth and prosperity, when the United States was young. Other forms of power – notably oil and gas – had supplanted coal because they were cleaner, easier to handle, readily obtainable and, for a while, cheaper. But not any more!

Despite coal's disadvantages – and nothing would wish *those* away – the vast black deposits underground could still be America's salvation, its last and most important natural wealth, its ultimate ace in the hole.

He became aware of Thurston motioning, suggesting they move on.

For another hour they explored Cherokee's noisy, coal-dusty intricacy. A lengthy stop was at the enormous electrostatic dust collectors – required under environmental laws – whose purpose was to remove burned fly ash which otherwise would belch from smokestacks as a pollutant.

And cathedral-like generator halls with their familiar, deafening roar-whine were reminders that whatever the base fuel, electricity in Brobdingnagian quantities was what this place was all about.

The trio – Nim, Thurston, Folger – emerged at length from the plant interior into the open – on a high walkway near the building's peak, two hundred feet above the ground. The walkway, linked to a maze of others beneath it by steep steel stairways, was actually a metal grating with everything below immediately visible. Plant workers moving on lower walkways appeared like flies. At first Nim looked down at his feet and through the grating nervously; after a few minutes he adjusted. The purpose of open gratings, young Folger explained, was for winter weather – to allow ice and snow to fall through.

Even here the all-pervading noise was still around them. Clouds of water vapour, emerging from the plant's cooling towers and changing direction in the wind, blew around and across the walkway. One moment Nim would find himself in a cloud, seemingly isolated, with visibility limited to a foot or two ahead. Then the water vapour would swirl away, leaving a view of the suburbs of Denver spread below, with downtown highrise buildings in the distance. Though the day was sunny, the wind up here was cold and biting and Nim shivered. There was a sense of loneliness, he thought, of isolation and of danger.

'There's the promised land,' Thurston said. 'If you have your way, it's what you'll see at Tunipah.' He was pointing to an area, directly ahead, of about fifteen acres. Covering it completely was a gigantic coal pile.

'You're looking at four months' supply for the plant, not far from a million tons,' Folger informed them.

'And underneath it all is what used to be a lovely meadow,' Thurston added. 'Now it's an ugly eyesore; no one can dispute that. But we need it. There's the rub.'

While they watched, a diesel locomotive on a rail spur jockeyed a long train of freight cars delivering still more coal. Each car, without uncoupling, moved into a rotary dumper which then inverted, letting the coal fall out on to heavy grates. Beneath were conveyors which carried the coal towards the power plant.

'Never stops,' Thurston said. 'Never.'

There would be strong objections, Nim already knew, to transferring this scene to the unspoiled wilderness of Tunipah. In a simplistic way he shared the objectors' point of view. But he told himself: electric power to be generated at Tunipah was essential; therefore the intrusion must be tolerated.

They moved from the high viewing point, descended one of the outside metal stairways to a slightly lower level, and paused again. Now they were more sheltered and the force of the wind had lessened. But the surrounding noise was greater.

'Something else you'll find when you work with coal,' the plant superintendent was saying, 'is that you'll have more personnel accidents than you will with oil or gas or, for that matter, nuclear energy. We've got a good accident prevention programme here. Just the same . . .'

Nim wasn't listening.

Incredibly, with only the kind of coincidence which real life – not fiction – can produce, an accident was happening while he watched.

Some fifty feet ahead of Nim, and behind the backs of the other two who were facing him, a coal conveyor belt was in operation. The belt, a combination of pliant rubber and steel running over cylindrical rolls, carried coal to crushers which reduced it to small pieces. Later still it would be pulverized to a fine powder, ready for instant burning. Now, a portion of the conveyor belt, because of some large coal lumps, was blocked and overflowing. The belt continued moving. New coal was pouring over the side as it arrived. Above the moving belt, a solitary workman, perched precariously on an overhead grating, was probing with a steel rod, attempting to clear the blockage.

Later, Nim would learn the procedure was prohibited. Safety regulations required that the conveyor belt be shut down before a blockage was cleared. But plant workers, conscious of the need to maintain coal flow, sometimes ignored the regulation.

Within one or two seconds, while Nim watched, the workman

slipped, checked himself by grabbing the edge of the grating, slipped again, and fell onto the belt below. Nim saw the man's mouth open as he cried out, but the sound was lost. He had fallen heavily; clearly, he was hurt. The belt was already carrying him higher, nearer the point where the coal crushing machinery, housed in a box-like structure, would cut him to pieces.

No one else was in sight. No one, other than Nim, had seen the accident.

All he had time for was to leap forward, run, and shout as he went, 'Stop the belt!'

As Nim dived between them, Thurston and Folger, not knowing what was happening, spun round. They took in the scene quickly, reacted fast, and raced after Nim. But by the time they moved he was well ahead.

The conveyor belt, at its nearest point to the walkway, was several feet higher and sloping upward. Getting on to it was awkward. Nim took a chance and leaped. As he landed clumsily on the moving belt, on hands and feet, a sharp edge of coal cut his left hand. He ignored the hurt and scrambled forward, upwards, over loose, shifting coal, nearer to the workman who was lying dazed and was stirring feebly on a higher portion of the belt. By now the man was less than three feet from the deadly machinery ahead and moving closer.

What followed was a sequence of events so swift that its elements were inseparable.

Nim reached the workman and grabbed him, trying to pull him back. He succeeded briefly, then heard cloth rip and felt resistance. Somewhere, somehow, the man's clothing was caught in the moving belt. Nim tugged again, to no effect. The clanking machinery was barely a foot away. Nim struggled desperately, knowing it was the last chance. Nothing happened. The workman's right arm, which was ahead of his body, entered the machinery and bone crushed horribly. Blood spurted as the conveyor belt moved on. Then, with unbelieving horror, Nim realized his own clothing was caught. It was too late even to save himself.

At that moment the belt stopped.

After the briefest of pauses the conveyor reversed, brought Nim slowly back to the point where he had launched himself on to it, then stopped again.

Below the conveyor Folger had gone directly to a control box, hit a red 'stop' button hard, then backed the conveyor down.

Now hands reached out, helping Nim return to the walkway. There were shouts and the sound of running feet as more help arrived. Newcomers lifted down the semi-conscious workman, who was moaning and bleeding badly. Somewhere below an alarm bell began ringing. Superintendent Folger, kneeling beside the injured workman, whipped off his leather belt and applied it as a tourniquet. Thurston Jones had opened a metal box and was telephoning, giving orders. Nim heard him say, 'Get an ambulance and a doctor – fast!'

11

'I may not be a blinkin' hero like you,' Thurston declared cheerfully, 'but in this town I do have a little pull.' He had been in another room of his home, telephoning, and had just returned to Nim, who was in the living room, wearing a borrowed bathrobe, his left hand bandaged, the right nursing a stiff scotch and water.

Thurston continued, 'Your suit is being specially cleaned – no mean feat, let me tell you, on Saturday afternoon. It will be delivered here later.'

'Thanks.'

Thurston's wife Ursula had followed her husband in, accompanied by her younger sister Daphne, who, with her infant son, was visiting Denver from Britain. The two women were remarkably similar, Nim had already observed. Neither was conventionally pretty; both were big-boned and tall, with high foreheads and wide generous mouths, a shade too wide for beauty. But their breezy, outgoing personalities were strong and attractive. Nim had met Daphne a half hour ago, for the first time, and liked her immediately.

'There is some other news,' Thurston informed Nim. 'The guy whose life you saved won't lose his arm. The surgeons say they can piece it together, and while it may not be strong enough to use in a coal plant any more, at least he can put it around his wife and three small kids. Oh yes! - and the wife sends a message. She says she and those kids will be in church later today, thanking whatever saint they do business with for one N. Goldman, Esquire, and lighting candles for you. I pass that on in case you believe in any of that stuff.'

'Oh, do stop a minute, Thurs,' Ursula said. 'You're making me cry.'

'If you want the truth,' her husband acknowledged, 'I'm a bit choked up myself.'

Nim protested, as he had earlier, 'I didn't do much, if anything. It was your man Folger who stopped the conveyor and . . .'

'Listen,' Thurston said. 'You saw what happened before anyone else, you acted fast, and that couple of feet you pulled the guy back made all the difference. Besides, the world needs heroes. Why fight it?'

Events, since the dramatic, action-packed few minutes on the high walkway this morning, had moved swiftly. The injured workman, whose name Nim still didn't know, had received efficient first aid; then had been loaded carefully on a stretcher delivered to the walkway on the run by two plant employees. In what seemed only moments after Thurston's telephoned demand for an ambulance, a faint siren could be heard from the direction of downtown Denver and a flashing red light, moving fast, became visible from the high vantage point, even while the vehicle was several miles away.

By the time the ambulance reached Cherokee plant, the stretcher had been taken down in a freight elevator and the injured man was whisked away to a hospital. Because of heavy bleeding and severe shock there had been early fears that he would die, fears that made the latest news welcome.

Only after the serious injury case had been dealt with, and the ambulance gone, had Nim's cut hand been examined There proved to be a deep gash in his palm at the base of the thumb. Thurston had driven Nim to a nearby suburban hospital emergency room where several stitches were put in.

Nim's face, hands and clothing had been black with coal dust and, after the stop at the hospital, he had been driven to Thurston's home, where Nim shed his suit - the only one he had brought - and soaked in a hot bath. Afterwards, and wearing

Thurston's robe, he had been introduced to Daphne, who competently put a fresh dressing and bandage on his hand. Daphne, Nim learned, was a qualified nurse and also a recent divorcee. The second condition was the reason for her current get-away-from-it-all visit to her sister.

Ursula wiped her eyes with a wisp of handkerchief, then said practically, 'Well, now we know there's a happy ending, we can all feel better.' She crossed the room to Nim and impulsively hugged and kissed him. 'There! – that's instead of lighting candles.'

'Hey!' Daphne said. 'Can anybody do that?'

Nim grinned. 'You bet!'

She promptly kissed him. Her lips were full and warm; he liked the feel of them, and a momentary fragrance which came and then was gone.

Daphne announced, 'That's what you get for being a bloody hero, like it or not.'

'That part,' Nim said, 'I like.'

'What we all need now,' Ursula said, 'is a big dose of the jollies.' She addressed her husband. 'Thurs, what are our plans tonight?'

He beamed. 'I'm glad you asked. We're dining and dancing. With my usual brilliant forethought I reserved a table for four at the San Marco Room of the Brown Palace.'

'Sounds marvellous,' Daphne said. 'Can we get a babysitter for Keith?'

'Not to worry,' Ursula assured her. 'I'll arrange it.'

'And *I'm* going dancing,' Nim declared, 'whether my suit comes back or not.'

The music – from a lively, talented combo – plus wine and an excellent dinner, mellowed them all. Earlier, Nim's suit *had* been returned, seemingly none the worse for its sojourn on the coal conveyor. Simultaneously with the cleaners' delivery, a reporter and photographer from the *Denver Post* arrived, wanting an interview, and photographs of Nim. A little reluctantly, he obliged.

Soon after, with Nim and Daphne wedged tightly into the back of Thurston's Pinto, Daphne squeezed his arm. 'I think you're rather super,' she whispered. 'The way you *do* things, and handle yourself, and it's nice you're modest, too.'

Not knowing what to say, he took her hand and continued holding it, already wondering what the later portion of the evening might bring.

Now, dinner was over. Nim and Daphne had danced with each other several times, with an increasing closeness to which Daphne made clear she had no objection.

Once, when the two of them were at the table together, and Thurston and Ursula were dancing, he inquired what had gone wrong with Daphne's marriage.

With the frankness which seemed characteristic of both sisters she answered, 'My husband was older than I am. He didn't like sex much, and most of the time couldn't get it up. There were other things wrong, but that was the main one.'

'I assume that was *not* your problem.'

She threw back her head and laughed. 'How did you guess?'

'But you did have a child?'

'Yes. That was one of the times we managed. Almost the only one. Anyway, I'm glad I have Keith. He's almost two and I love him dearly. By the way, Keith and I are sharing a room, but he's a sound sleeper.'

'All the same,' Nim said, 'I won't come into *his* room.'

'Fair enough. Just leave your door ajar. It's down the hall from mine.'

When, for a change, Nim danced with Ursula she confided, 'I love having Daphne here; we've always been close. The one thing I envy her, though, is having little Keith.'

Nim asked, 'You and Thurs haven't wanted children?'

'We both did. Still do. But we can't have them.' Ursula's voice was clipped, as if she wished she hadn't brought up the subject, and he left it at that.

But later, when the sisters excused themselves and left the table temporarily, Thurston said, 'I understand Ursula told you we can't have kids.'

'Yes.'

'Did she tell you why?'

Nim shook his head.

'The trouble's with me, not Ursula. We both had medical tests, lots of 'em. It seems my pistol will cock and fire, but I feed it only blanks. And I'll never have live bullets, so the doctors tell me.'

200

'I'm sorry.'

Thurston shrugged. 'You can't have everything, I guess, and we've got a lot of other things going, Ursula and I.' He added, 'We considered adopting, but neither of us is sure about that.'

When the women returned they all drank more wine, then danced again. While they were dancing, Daphne murmured in Nim's ear, 'Did I tell you I rather fancy you?'

His arms tightened around her in response. He hoped it would not be too long before they went back to the house.

They had returned an hour and a half ago. Thurston had driven the babysitter home, then all of them sat in the kitchen and talked while Ursula made tea, with Daphne helping. After that they said good night and went to bed. Now, Nim was almost asleep.

A sound aroused him – a creak, unmistakably the bedroom door opening fully, though he had left it ajar as Daphne told him. It was followed by another creak, then the click of a latch as the door closed. Nim lifted his head and strained to see in the darkness but couldn't.

He heard a soft pad of feet and the rustle of a garment; he guessed it was being removed. Then the bedclothes were eased back and a warm, soft, naked body slid in beside him. Arms reached out. In the darkness lips – exciting, welcoming – found his own. The kiss was long; it quickly grew passionate. As limbs pressed closely, Nim's blood surged, he became erect and urgent. His hands began moving gently and he sighed – a mixture of sensual pleasure and contentment.

He whispered, 'Daphne darling, all day I've been wanting this to happen.'

He heard a gurgle of soft laughter. A finger reached out, groping for his lips to bridge them, cautioning silence. A low voice warned, 'Shut up, you idiot! It isn't Daphne. I'm Ursula.'

Shocked, Nim released himself and sat upright. His inclination was to leap from the bed. A hand restrained him.

'Listen to me,' Ursula said urgently and softly. 'I want a baby. And next to Thurs, who can't give me one – and I know he told you about that – I'd rather have it by you, Nim, than anyone else I know.'

He protested, 'I can't do it, Ursula. Not to Thurs.'

'Yes you can, because Thurs knows I'm here, and why.'

'And Thurs doesn't mind?' Nim's voice was unbelieving.

'I swear to you, no. We both want a child. We both decided this is the best way.' Again the soft laugh. 'Daphne minds, though. She's mad as hell at me. She wanted you herself.'

Conflicting emotions swirled within Nim. Then the humour of the situation got to him and he laughed.

'That's more like it,' Ursula said. She pulled him towards her and he stopped resisting as their arms clasped each other again.

She whispered, 'It's the right time of the month. I *know* it can happen. Oh, Nim dear, help me make a baby! I want one so.'

What had he ever done, he wondered, to deserve all the exotic things that happened to him?

He whispered back, 'Okay, I'll do my best.' As they kissed and he became erect again, he asked impishly, 'Do you think it's all right if I enjoy it?'

Instead of answering she held him tighter, their breathing quickened, and she cried out softly with pleasure as he caressed then entered her.

They made love repeatedly and gloriously, Nim finding that his bandaged left hand impeded him not at all. As last, he fell asleep. When he awoke, daylight was beginning and Ursula had gone.

He decided to go back to sleep. Then, once more his bedroom door opened and a figure in a pale pink negligee slipped in. 'I'll be damned,' Daphne said as she took the negligee off, 'if I'm going to be left out altogether. Move over, Nim, and I hope you have some energy left.'

Together, happily, they discovered he had.

Nim's return flight to the West Coast, again with United, was in late afternoon. Thurston drove him to the airport; Ursula and Daphne came along, Daphne bringing her small son, Keith. Though conversation during the drive was friendly and relaxed, nothing was said about the happenings of the night. Nim kissed both sisters goodbye at the car. While the women waited, Thurston accompanied Nim into the terminal.

At the passenger security checkpoint they stopped to shake hands.

Nim said, 'I appreciate everything, Thurs.'

'Me too. And good luck tomorrow and the other days at the hearings.'

'Thanks. We'll need it all.'

Still clasping Nim's hand, Thurston seemed to hesitate, then said, 'In case you're wondering about anything, I'd like to tell you there are things a man does because he has to, and because it's the best out of limited choices. Something else : there are friends and exceptional friends. You are one of the second kind, Nim. You always will be, so let's never lose touch.'

Turning away towards the aircraft boarding ramp, Nim discovered that his eyes were moist.

A few minutes later, as he settled into his first-class seat for the homeward journey, a friendly air hostess enquired, 'Sir, what will you have to drink after take-off?'

'Champagne,' he told her, smiling. Quite clearly, he decided, nothing else would match his successful weekend.

12

The young, presiding commissioner tapped lightly with his gavel.

'Before the examination of this witness begins, I believe it would be in order to commend him for his conduct two days ago when his prompt action and courage saved the life of a public utility employee in another state.'

In the hearing room there was scattered applause.

Nim acknowledged, with some embarrassment, 'Thank you, sir.'

Until this morning he had assumed that news reports of the drama on the conveyor belt would be confined to Denver. Therefore he had been surprised to find himself the subject of an Associated Press wire story, featured prominently in today's *Chronicle-West*. The report was unfortunate because it drew attention to his visit to the coal-generating plant and Nim wondered what use, if any, the opposition forces would make of this knowledge.

As on previous hearing days, the oak-panelled chamber was occupied by commission staff, counsel for various parties, waiting witnesses, officials of interested groups, press reporters, as well as a sizeable contingent of the public – the last composed mainly of opposition supporters.

Again, on the bench, the same presiding commissioner was flanked by the elderly administrative law judge.

Among those in the hearing room whom Nim recognized were Laura Bo Carmichael and Roderick Pritchett, representing the Sequoia Club; Davey Birdsong of p & lfp, his outsize figure garbed as usual in shabby jeans and open-necked shirt; and, at the press table, Nancy Molineaux, smartly dressed and aloof.

Nim had already been sworn, agreeing to 'tell the truth, the whole truth and nothing but the truth'. Now, the utility's portly general counsel, Oscar O'Brien, on his feet and facing the bench, would lead him through his testimony.

'Mr Goldman,' O'Brien began, as they had rehearsed, 'please describe the circumstances and studies which lead you to believe that the proposal, now being submitted to this commission, is necessary and in the public interest.'

Nim settled himself in the witness chair, aware that his presentation would be long and arduous.

'The studies of Golden State Power & Light,' he began, 'supplemented by those of government agencies, estimate that California's growth by the middle of the next decade, both of population and industry, will substantially exceed the national average. I will deal with specifics later. Parallel with that growth will be an escalating demand for electric power, greater by far than present generating capacities. It is to meet this demand that ...'

Nim strove to keep his tone conversational and easy, to hold the interest of those listening. All the facts and opinions he would present were briefs filed weeks ago with the commission, but spoken evidence was considered important. It was an admission, perhaps, that few would ever read the mountain of paper which grew in size daily.

O'Brien spoke his prompting lines with the confidence of an actor in a long-running play.

'As to environmental effects, will you please explain . . . Can you be specific about those coal deliveries which . . . You stated earlier there would be limits on disturbance of flora and fauna, Mr Goldman. I think the commission would like assurance that

. . . Please enlarge on . . . Would you say that . . . Now let's consider the . . .'

It took slightly more than a day and a half, a total of seven hours during which Nim remained in the witness chair, the focus of attention. At the end he knew he had presented the GSP & L case fairly and thoroughly. Just the same, he was conscious that his real ordeal – a succession of cross-examinations – was still to come.

In mid-afternoon of the second day of the resumed hearings, Oscar O'Brien faced the bench. 'Thank you, Mr Chairman. That concludes my examination of this witness.'

The chairman nodded. 'I think Mr Goldman deserves a break, and the rest of us would welcome one.' He tapped with his gavel. 'This hearing is adjourned until 10am tomorrow.'

Next day the cross-examinations began slowly and easily, like a car moving through low gears on a stretch of level road. The commission counsel, a dry-as-dust middle-aged lawyer named Holyoak, was first.

'Mr Goldman, there are a number of points on which the commissioners require clarification . . .' As it proceeded, Holyoak's questioning was neither friendly nor hostile. Nim responded in the same way, and competently.

Holyoak took an hour. Roderick Pritchett, manager-secretary of the Sequoia Club, was next and the interrogation moved into higher gear.

Pritchett, spare, neat and with mannerisms to match, wore a dark, conservatively tailored three-piece suit. His iron grey hair was precisely parted and in place; occasionally he put up a hand to satisfy himself it remained undisturbed. As he rose and approached the witness stand, Pritchett's eyes appeared to gleam behind his rimless glasses. Shortly before the interrogation he had been conferring intently with Laura Bo Carmichael, seated beside him at one of the three counsel-witness tables.

'Mr Goldman,' Pritchett began, 'I have here a photograph.' He reached back to the counsel table and picked up an eight-by-ten glossy print. 'I'd like you to examine it, then tell me if what you see is familiar to you.'

Nim accepted the photograph. While he studied it, a Sequoia Club clerk was handing additional copies to the commissioner and administrative law judge, counsel, including Oscar O'Brien, Davey Birdsong and the press. Several more copies went to spectators who began passing them around.

Nim was puzzled. Most of the photo was black, but there was a certain familiarity . . .

The Sequoia Club manager-secretary was smiling. 'Please take your time, Mr Goldman.'

Nim shook his head. 'I'm not sure.'

'Perhaps I can help.' Pritchett's voice suggested a game of cat-and-mouse. 'According to what I have read in newspapers, the scene you are looking at is one you personally observed last weekend.'

Instantly Nim knew. The photo was of the Cherokee plant coal pile at Denver. The blackness was explained. Mentally he cursed the publicity which had disclosed his weekend journey.

'Well,' he said, 'I suppose it's a picture of coal.'

'Please give us a little more detail, Mr Goldman. What coal and where?'

Reluctantly Nim said, 'It's stored coal for use by a Public Service Company of Colorado plant near Denver.'

'Precisely.' Pritchett removed his glasses, wiped them briefly, then replaced them. 'For your information, the photograph was taken yesterday and flown here this morning. It isn't a pretty picture, is it?'

'No.'

'Ugly, wouldn't you say?'

'I suppose you could call it that, but the point is . . .'

'The point is,' Pritchett interrupted, 'you have already answered my question – "I suppose you could call it that," you said – which means you agree that the picture is ugly. That's all I asked. Thank you.'

Nim protested, 'But it should also be said . . .'

Pritchett waved an admonitory finger. 'That's *enough*, Mr Goldman! Please remember I am asking the questions. Now let's move on. I have a second photograph for you – and the commissioners – to look at.'

While Nim fumed inwardly, Pritchett returned to the counsel table and this time selected a colour photo. He handed it to Nim. As before the clerk passed out other copies.

Although Nim failed to recognize the specific scene, he had

no doubt where the second photo was taken. It had to be Tunipah, at or near the site of the proposed generating plant. Equally obvious was that the photographer was a skilled professional.

The breathtaking beauty of the rugged California wilderness had been captured under a clear, azure sky. A stark, rocky promontory towered over a stand of majestic pines. Near the base of the trees was dense foliage, in the foreground, a racing, foam-flecked stream. On the nearer bank of the stream a profusion of wild flowers delighted the eye. Further away, in shadows, a young deer had raised its head, perhaps startled by the photographer.

Pritchett prompted, 'A truly beautiful scene, is it not, Mr Goldman?'

'Yes, it is.'

'Do you have any idea where that photograph was taken?'

'I presume it was Tunipah.' There was no point in playing games, Nim decided, or in delaying the point which sooner or later Pritchett was going to make.

'Your presumption is correct, sir. Now I have a further question.' Pritchett's tone sharpened; his voice rose. 'Does it disturb your conscience that what you and your company propose to do at Tunipah is superimpose this, *this hideous ugliness*' – he waved the coal pile picture in the air – 'upon this *serene and glorious beauty*' – now he held up the second, colour photo – 'one of the few remaining unspoilt sanctuaries of nature in our state and country?'

The question – posed with dramatic rhetoric – produced a hum of approval from spectators. One or two applauded.

Nim answered quietly, 'Yes, of course it disturbs me. But I see it as necessary, a compromise, a trade-off. Besides, in proportion to the total area around Tunipah . . .'

'That's *sufficient*, Mr Goldman. A speech is not required. The record will show that your answer was "yes".'

Pritchett paused briefly, then returned to the attack.

'Is it possible that your journey to the State of Colorado last weekend was undertaken *because* your conscience bothered you, because you had to see for yourself the *ugliness* of huge quantities of coal – the kind of quantities there would be at Tunipah – imposed on what was once a beautiful landscape?'

Oscar O'Brien was on his feet. 'Objection!'

Pritchett swung towards him. 'On what grounds?'

Ignoring Pritchett, O'Brien addressed the bench. 'The question has twisted the witness's words. Further, it presumes a state of mind which the witness has not admitted having.'

The presiding commissioner announced blandly, 'The objection is overruled.' O'Brien subsided, glowering.

'No,' Nim said, addressing Pritchett, 'the way you put it was not the reason for my journey. I went because there were technical aspects of a coal-fired generating plant I wished to review in advance of these hearings.' Even to Nim, the reply seemed unconvincing.

Pritchett observed, 'I am sure there are some here who will believe you.' His tone declared: *I don't*.

Pritchett continued with other questions but they were anti-climactic. The Sequoia Club, through its shrewd use of the contrasting photographs, had scored heavily and Nim blamed himself.

At length the club's manager-secretary resumed his seat.

The presiding commissioner consulted a sheet in front of him. 'Does the organization "power & light for people" wish to question this witness?'

Davey Birdsong responded, 'It sure does.'

The commissioner nodded. Birdsong lumbered to his feet.

The big man wasted no time on preliminaries. He asked, 'How did you get here?'

Nim looked puzzled. 'If you mean whom do I represent . . .'

Birdsong snapped, 'We all know who you represent – a rich and greedy conglomerate which exploits the people.' The p & lfp leader slammed a meaty hand on a ledge by the witness chair and raised his voice. 'I mean *exactly* what I said: How did you get here?'

'Well . . . I came in a taxi.'

'You came in a *taxi*! A big, important wheel like you? You mean you didn't use your personal helicopter?'

Nim smiled thinly; it was already obvious what kind of interrogation this would be. He answered, 'I don't have a personal helicopter. And I certainly didn't use one today.'

'But you do use one sometimes – right?'

'On certain special occasions . . .'

Birdsong cut in. 'Never mind all that! You do use one sometimes – yes or no?'

'Yes.'

'A helicopter, paid for with the hard-earned money of gas and electricity consumers in their monthly bills?'

'No, it is not paid for in utility bills. At least, not directly.'

'But consumers pay indirectly – right?'

'You could say that about every piece of working equipment . . .'

Birdsong slammed his hand again. 'We're not talking about other equipment. I'm enquiring about a helicopter.'

'Our company has several helicopters which . . .'

'*Several!* You mean you get a choice – like between a Lincoln and a Cadillac?'

Nim said impatiently, 'They are mainly for operational use.'

'Which doesn't stop you using one when you need it personally, or think you need it – right?' Without pausing for an answer, Birdsong reached into a pocket and produced a newspaper sheet which he unfolded. 'You remember this?'

It was Nancy Molineaux's article in the *California Examiner*, published shortly after the press visit to Devil's Gate Camp.

Nim said resignedly, 'I remember it.'

Birdsong read out details of the newspaper and date, which the stenotypist recorded, then swung back to Nim. 'It says here: '*Mr Goldman . . . is too important to ride on a bus, even though one – privately chartered by Golden State Power – was going his way . . . and had plenty of spare seats. Instead he chose a helicopter . . .*' Birdsong looked up, glaring. 'Is all that true?'

'There were special circumstances.'

'Never mind them. I asked : *is that true?*'

Nim was aware of Nancy Molineaux watching from the press table; a soft smile played about her face. He said, 'It was a prejudiced report, but – more or less – it's true.'

Birdsong appealed to the bench. 'Will the chairman please instruct this witness to respond with a simple "yes" or "no".'

The commissioner said, 'It might save everyone time if you did, Mr Goldman.'

His face set grimly, Nim answered, 'Yes.'

'It took a lot of effort,' Birdsong said, 'like pulling teeth.' He was facing the bench again and, chameleon-like, had slipped from hardness into affability. 'But we finally have an admission from the witness that the contents of this courageous newspaper report are true. Mr Chairman, I would like the article entered into evidence to demonstrate the rich living which officials like Goldman here, and Whatsisname the chairman, accustom themselves to at the expense of poor consumers. Also it shows why expensive boondoggles like Tunipah, aimed at supporting this kind of habit as well as making extortionate profits, are foisted on an unsuspecting public.'

O'Brien, on his feet, protested wearily, 'I object – to inclusion of the report which is irrelevant to this hearing; also to the last remarks which are unsupported by evidence or testimony.'

The commissioner consulted briefly with the administrative law judge, then announced, 'Your objection will be recorded, Mr O'Brien. The document – the newspaper report – will be admitted as an exhibit.'

'Thank *you* sir,' Birdsong said. He returned his attention to Nim.

'Do you, personally, own stock in Golden State Power & Light?'

'Yes,' Nim said. He wondered what came next. He owned a hundred and twenty shares which he had acquired, a few at a time, through a payroll savings plan. Their present market value was slightly more than two thousand dollars – far less than the original cost since the value of GSP & L stock had slumped a month ago after omission of the dividend. But he decided not to volunteer more information than was asked. It proved to be a mistake.

'If this Tunipah deal goes through,' Birdsong continued, 'is it likely the value of all Golden State Power shares will go up?'

'Not necessarily. They could equally well go down.' As he spoke, Nim wondered: should he elaborate, add that with a huge construction programme, to be financed by the sale of securities including new common stock at below book value, the existing GSP & L shares would be diluted and might slump? Such an answer would require complex explanations; it would also – in this context – look like waffling. Nor was Nim sure that the company's treasurer would want the statement made in public. He decided to leave well enough alone.

'Not necessarily,' Birdsong repeated. 'But the market price of those shares *could* go up. Surely you'll admit that.'

Nim said tersely, 'In the stock market, anything can happen.'

Birdsong faced the courtroom and sighed theatrically. 'I suppose that's the best answer I can expect from this *un*cooperative witness, so *I* will make the statement : The shares probably *would* go up.' He swung back to Nim. 'If that happened, isn't it true that *you* would have a vested interest in Tunipah, that you, too, would be a profiteer?'

The notion was so absurd, Nim wanted to laugh. The best he could hope for, for a long time to come, was that the value of his small shareholding would return to its level at the time of purchase.

Birdsong said suddenly, 'Since you seem reluctant to answer, I'll put the question another way : If the value of Golden State shares go up because of Tunipah, will *your* shares be worth more as well?'

'Look,' Nim said, 'I only . . .'

From the bench the commissioner cut in testily, 'It's a simple question, Mr Goldman. Just answer "yes" or "no".'

About to explode at the unfairness, Nim was aware of Oscar O'Brien signalling with a gentle shake of his head. It was a reminder, Nim knew, of the instructions to be patient and resist provocation. He answered with a terse, 'Yes.'

Birdsong declared, 'Now that we have that admission also, Mr Chairman, I wish the record to show that this witness has a vested financial interest in the outcome of this hearing, and therefore his testimony should be judged accordingly.'

'Well, you just put it in the record yourself,' the commissioner said, his irritation still showing. 'So why not move along?'

'Yes*sir!*' The p & lfp leader thrust a hand through his beard as if in thought, then returned to Nim. 'Now then, I have some questions about the effect of Tunipah on the utility bills of ordinary working people, the ones who . . .'

It went on and on. Birdsong concentrated – as he had while cross-examining J. Eric Humphrey – on the suggestion that profit, and nothing else, was the motive behind Tunipah; also that consumers would foot the bill and receive nothing or little in return. What angered Nim, beneath the unruffled surface he struggled to maintain, was that not once were the major, important issues – future power requirements based on growth, industry economics, maintenance of living standards – touched on. Populist froth was being paraded; nothing more. But it would gain attention. Activity at the press table made that clear.

Nim also admitted to himself that the two-pronged attack – the Sequoia Club emphasizing environmental issues and the p & lfp dwelling on rates and finance, however superficially – was effective. He wondered if there had been liaison between the two groups, though he doubted it. Laura Bo Carmichael and Davey Birdsong were on different intellectual planes. Nim still respected Laura Bo, despite their differences, but he despised Birdsong as a charlatan.

During a short recess, after Birdsong had concluded his questioning, Oscar O'Brien warned Nim, 'You're not through yet. After the other witnesses I'll want you back on the stand for redirect, and when I've finished the other people can have at you again if they want.' Nim grimaced, wishing his part was over, thankful that it would be soon.

Laura Bo Carmichael was next on the stand.

Despite her small, slight figure, the Sequoia Club chairman occupied the witness chair with *grande dame* demeanour. She was wearing a severe tailored suit of beige gabardine and, as usual, her greying hair was cut severely short. She wore no ornamentation or jewellery. Her manner was serious. Her voice, as she responded to questions put to her by Roderick Pritchett, was crisp and authoritative.

'We have heard stated in previous testimony, Mrs Carmichael,' Pritchett began, 'that a public need for more electrical power justifies building a coal-powered generating plant in the Tunipah area. Is that your opinion?'

'No, it is not.'

'Will you explain to the commissioners your reasons – and those of the Sequoia Club – for opposing that construction?'

'Tunipah is one of the few, the *very* few, remaining natural wilderness areas in California. It abounds with treasures of nature – trees, plants, flowers, streams, unique geologic formations, animal, bird and insect life, some of those features representing strains which have become extinct elsewhere. The region is, above all, magnificently beautiful. To despoil it with a huge, ugly, high-polluting industrial plant, serviced by a new railroad – itself polluting and intrusive – would be sacrilegious, an ecological stride backwards to the last century, a blasphemy against God and nature.'

Laura Bo had spoken calmly, without raising her voice, which made her statement more impressive. Pritchett paused before his next question, allowing the impact of her words to sink in.

'The spokesman for Golden State Power & Light, Mr Goldman,' Pritchett said, 'has assured the commission that disturbance of the natural state of Tunipah would be minimal. Would you care to comment on that?'

'I have known Mr Goldman for a number of years,' Laura Bo responded. 'He means well. He may even believe what he says. But the truth is: no one can build any kind of a plant at Tunipah without doing tremendous, irreversible environmental damage.'

The Sequoia Club manager-secretary smiled. 'Am I correct in my impression, Mrs Carmichael, that you do not really trust GSP & L where that "minimal damage" promise is concerned?'

'Yes, you are – even if that promise could be fulfilled, which it cannot.' Laura Bo turned her head, directly addressing the two occupants of the bench who had been listening intently. 'In the past, Golden State Power and most other industrial companies have proved themselves *un*trustworthy where environmental choices were concerned. When they were left alone they poisoned our air and water, plundered our forests, squandered mineral resources, scarred our landscapes. Now that we live in another era, where these sins are recognized, they tell us: *Trust us. Our past will not repeat itself.* Well, I, and many others, do *not* trust them – in Tunipah or anywhere else.'

Listening, Nim thought: There was a compelling logic to what Laura Bo was saying. He could, and did, dispute her view of the future; Nim believed that GSP & L and other organizations like it *had* absorbed the lessons of old mistakes, and had learned to be good ecological citizens, if for no other reason than that nowadays it was simply good business. However, no fair-minded person could argue with Laura Bo's assessment of the past. Something else she had already done during her short time on the witness stand, Nim decided, was raise the level of debate far above the gallery-playing pettiness of Davey Birdsong.

'A few minutes ago,' Pritchett said to Laura Bo, 'you stated that some strains of natural life at Tunipah have become extinct elsewhere. Will you tell us what they are?'

The Sequoia Club chairman nodded. She said with authority, 'There are two that I know of: a wild flower, the Furbish louse-

213

wort, and the Microdipodops, otherwise known as the kangaroo mouse.'

Here is where we part company, Nim mused. He remembered his argument with Laura Bo over lunch two months ago when he had objected : *'You'd let a mouse, or mice, prohibit a project which will benefit millions of people?'*

Evidently the same possibility had occurred to Roderick Pritchett because his next question was : 'Do you expect criticism on those two issues – the Furbish lousewort and the Microdipodops? Do you expect people to say that human beings and their desires are more important?'

'I expect a great deal of that kind of criticism, even abuse,' Laura Bo said. 'But nothing changes the shortsightedness and folly of reducing, or eliminating, *any* endangered species.'

'Would you explain that a little more?'

'Yes. A principle is involved, a life-and-death principle which is repeatedly and thoughtlessly violated. As modern society has developed – cities, urban sprawl, industry, highways, pipelines, all the rest – we have upset the balance of nature, destroyed plant life, natural watersheds and soil fertility, banished wild creatures from their habitat or slaughtered them *en masse*, disrupted normal growth cycles, all the while forgetting that every intricate part of nature depends on all the other parts for continuance and health.'

From the bench the commissioner interjected, 'But surely, Mrs Carmichael, even in nature there is flexibility.'

'Some flexibility. But almost always it has been pushed beyond the limits.'

The commissioner nodded politely. 'Please proceed.'

Her regal manner unruffled, Laura Bo continued, 'The point I am making is that past environmental decisions have been based on short-term expediency, almost never a larger view. At the same time, modern science – and I speak as a scientist myself – has operated in self-contained compartments, ignoring the truth that "progress" in one area may be harmful to life and nature as a whole. Automobile emissions – a product of science – are a huge example, and it is expediency which permits them to stay as lethal as they are. Another example is the excessive use of pesticides which, in preserving certain life forms, have wiped out many more. The same is true of atmospheric damage from

214

aerosol sprays. It is a long list. We have all been moving, and still are, towards environmental suicide.'

While the Sequoia Club chairman had been speaking, the hearing room had hushed to a respectful silence. Now no one moved, waiting for her next words.

'It is *all expediency*,' she repeated, her voice rising for the first time. 'If this monstrous Tunipah development is allowed to proceed, expediency will doom the Furbish lousewort and the Microdipodos, and much else besides. Then, if the process continues, I foresee the day when a single industrial project – just like Tunipah – will be ruled as more important than the last remaining stand of daffodils.'

The concluding words brought an outburst of applause from the spectator section. While it persisted, Nim thought angrily: Laura Bo was using her stature as a scientist to make a *non*-scientific, emotional appeal.

He went on seething for another hour as the questions and responses – in similar vein – continued.

Oscar O'Brien's subsequent cross-examination of Laura Bo produced nothing in the way of retraction and in some areas strengthened her earlier testimony. When the GSP & L counsel inquired with a broad smile if she really believed 'that a few populated mouseholes and an unattractive wild flower – almost a weed – are more important than the electrical needs of several million humans', she replied tartly, 'To ridicule is easy and cheap, Mr O'Brien, as well as being the oldest lawyer's tactic in the book. I have already stated why the Sequoia Club believes Tunipah should remain a natural wilderness area and the points which seem to amuse you are two among many. As to the "electrical needs" of which you speak, in the opinion of many, the need for conservation, of making better use of what we have, is a greater need by far.'

O'Brien flushed and snapped back, 'Since you know so much better than experts who have investigated Tunipah, and find it an ideal site for what is proposed, where would *you* build?'

Laura Bo said calmly, 'That is your problem, not mine.'

Davey Birdsong declined to cross-examine Laura Bo, stating grandiosely, 'Power & light for people supports the Sequoia Club view, so well expressed by Mrs Carmichael.'

On the following day, as the last of several more opposition witnesses was concluding, O'Brien whispered to Nim beside him, 'Get yourself together. You're on again next.'

13

Nim felt jaded, anyway. The prospect of new testimony and additional cross-examinations soured him still more.

He had slept only intermittently the night before and, when he did sleep, dreamed he was in a cell-like enclosure, without door or windows, in which all four walls comprised banks of circuit breakers. Nim was trying to keep the circuit breakers switched on and current – which he knew was needed – flowing. But Davey Birdsong, Laura Bo Carmichael and Roderick Pritchett had him surrounded and were determinedly snapping the breakers off. Nim wanted to shout at the others, to argue and plead, but his voice wouldn't work. In desperation he sought to move faster. To offset their six hands against his two he tried kicking switches with his feet. But his limbs resisted; they seemed encased in glue and moved with maddening slowness. With despair Nim realized he was losing, could not keep pace with the others, and soon all the switches would be off. It was then he awoke, soaked in perspiration, and couldn't sleep again.

Now, with Nim once more in the witness chair, the presiding commissioner was saying, 'I remind the witness he is already sworn . . .'

When the preliminaries were over, Oscar O'Brien began, 'Mr Goldman, how many shares of Golden State Power & Light do you own?'

'One hundred and twenty.'

'And their market value?'

'As of this morning, two thousand one hundred and sixty dollars.'

'So any suggestion that you, personally, are likely to make a lot of money out of Tunipah is . . .'

'Ridiculous and insulting,' Nim snapped before the question could be completed. He had personally asked O'Brien to get that into the record, and hoped the press would report it – as they had Birdsong's charge about profiteering. But Nim doubted if they would.

'Quite so.' O'Brien seemed taken aback by Nim's intensity. 'Now let us go back to the environmental impact statement about Tunipah. Mrs Carmichael in her testimony argued that . . .'

The idea was to counteract testimony by opposition witnesses which had been erroneous, excessively prejudiced or incomplete. Nim wondered, while responding to O'Brien's questions, what effect it would all have. He decided: probably none.

O'Brien concluded in less than half an hour. He was followed by Holyoak, the commission counsel, and Roderick Pritchett, neither of whom gave Nim a hard time and both were mercifully brief.

Which left Davey Birdsong.

The p & lfp leader indulged in his characteristic gesture of passing a hand through his bushy, grey-flecked beard as he stood regarding Nim.

'Those shares of yours, Goldman. You said they were worth' – Birdsong consulted a slip of paper – 'two thousand one hundred and sixty dollars. Right?'

Nim acknowledged warily, 'Yes.'

'The way you said it – and I was right here, listening; so were others – made it sound as if that kind of money was just peanuts to you. A "mere" two thousand, you seemed to say. Well, I guess to someone like you who's used to thinking in millions, and riding around in helicopters . . .'

The commissioner interrupted. 'Is this a question, Mr Birdsong? If so, please come to the point.'

'Yes*sir!*' The big man beamed towards the bench. 'I guess it's just that Goldman here gets under my skin because he's such a big cheese, or acts that way, and can't understand how much that kind of money means to poor people . . .'

The commissioner rapped sharply with his gavel. 'Get *on* with it!'

Birdsong grinned again, secure in the knowledge that however much he might be scolded, the chances of being cut off entirely were remote. He turned back to Nim.

'Okay, here's my question: did it occur to you that money like that – "mere thousands," as you put it – means a fortune to a lot of people who will have to foot the bill for Tunipah?'

'In the first place I didn't say "mere thousands," *or* imply it,' Nim retorted. 'You did. In the second, yes it did occur to me, because that kind of money means a lot to me too.'

'If it means that much,' Birdsong said quickly, 'maybe you'd like to double it.'

'Maybe I would. What the hell's wrong with that?'

'*I'm* asking the questions.' Birdsong smiled maliciously. 'So you admit you'd like to double your money, and maybe you will if this Tunipah deal goes through, won't you?' He waved a hand airily. 'No, don't bother answering. We'll draw our own conclusions.'

Nim sat, fuming. He saw O'Brien watching him intently, trying to convey a message: *Watch yourself! Be wary and moderate.*

'You said some things about conservation,' Birdsong resumed. 'I have some questions on that too.'

During the re-examination by O'Brien, conservation had been mentioned briefly. It gave p & lfp a right to raise the subject now.

'Do you know, Goldman, that if big, rich outfits like Golden State Power spent more on conservation instead of on multi-million dollar rip-offs like Tunipah, we could cut the use of electricity in this country by forty per cent?'

'No, I do not know that,' Nim shot back, 'because a forty per cent saving from conservation is unrealistic and a figure you probably pulled out of the air, the way you do most of your other accusations. The best that conservation will do – and *is* doing already – is help to offset a part of new growth and buy us a little time.'

'Time for what?'

'Time to let the bulk of people realize they are facing an electrical crisis which can change their lives – for the worse – in ways they never dreamed of.'

'Is that really true?' Birdsong taunted. 'Or isn't the real truth that Golden Power doesn't *want* conservation because conservation interferes with profits?'

'No, it isn't the truth, not any kind of truth, and it would take a twisted mind – like yours – to suggest or believe it.' Nim knew he was being baited, and was rising to the bait, probably just as Birdsong intended. Oscar O'Brien was frowning; Nim looked the other way.

'I'll ignore that nasty remark,' Birdsong said, 'and ask another question. Isn't the real reason you people aren't working hard at developing solar energy and wind power – which are available now – is because those are cheap power sources, and you wouldn't make the huge profits you expect from Tunipah?'

'The answer is "no", even though your question's a distorted half-truth. Solar electricity is not available in sizeable amounts, and won't be until the turn of the century at the earliest. Costs of collecting solar power are extremely high – far more than electricity from coal at Tunipah; also, solar may be the biggest polluter yet. As to wind power – forget it, except for peripheral, small applications.'

Above Nim, the commissioner leaned forward. 'Did I understand you, Mr Goldman, to say that solar power can pollute?'

'Yes, Mr Chairman.' The statement often surprised those who hadn't considered solar in all its aspects. 'With today's technology, a solar power plant with the same output that we are proposing for Tunipah would need one hundred and twenty square miles of land just to house its collectors. That's roughly seventy-five thousand acres – two thirds the size of Lake Tahoe – compared with three thousand acres required by a conventional power plant such as we are proposing now. And remember – land used for those solar collectors would be shut off to any other use. If that isn't pollution . . .'

He left the sentence unfinished as the commissioner nodded. 'An interesting point, Mr Goldman. One, I suppose, that many of us hadn't thought of.'

Birdsong, who had been standing impatiently during the exchange, resumed his attack. 'You tell us, Goldman, that solar power won't be ready until the next century. Why should we believe you?'

'You don't have to.' Nim slipped back into his earlier manner, making his contempt for Birdsong clear. 'You can believe or disbelieve anything you want. But a concensus of the best technical judgements, made by experts, says that large-scale use of solar electricity is twenty-plus years away; even then it may not fulfil expectations. That's why, in the meantime, there *must* be

219

coal-burning plants like Tunipah – *and in a lot more places than just Tunipah* – to meet the coming crisis.'

Birdsong sneered, 'So we're back to that fake, makebelieve, phony crisis.'

'When it happens,' Nim told him heatedly, 'you can read those words back and eat them.'

The commissioner reached for his gavel to command order, then hesitated; perhaps curious to see what would happen next, he let his hand fall back. Birdsong's face reddened, his mouth tightened angrily.

'*I* won't be eating any words. *You* will!' he spat at Nim. 'You'll *choke* on words – you and that capitalist gang at Golden State Power. *Words, words, words!* From these hearings, which those of us who stand against you will keep going as long as we can, and from other hearings like them. After that, still more words because we'll drag this Tunipah boondoggle through the courts, and tie you up with appeals, injunctions, and every other legal blockage in the book. Then if that isn't enough we'll raise new objections, so the whole cycle will start again and, if we have to, we'll go on for twenty years. The *people* will stop your profiteering schemes, *and the people will win!*'

The p & lfp leader paused, breathing heavily, then added, 'So maybe solar energy will get here first after all, *Mister* Goldman. Because let me tell you, you won't get those coal-burning plants. Not Tunipah or any others. Not now or ever.'

As the commisioner hesitated again, seeming fascinated by the verbal duel, a burst of applause erupted in part of the spectator section. At the same moment, Nim exploded. He slammed a fist down hard on an arm of the witness chair, then leaped to his feet. Eyes blazing, he faced Davey Birdsong.

'So maybe you *will* stop those plants being built – Tunipah and others – just the way you say. And *if* you do it, it will be because this crazy, self-defeating system gives limitless power to egomaniacs and kooks and charlatans like you.'

Suddenly the hearing room had fallen silent. Nim's voice rose as he continued. 'But spare us any sanctimonious drivel, Birdsong, about *you* representing the people. You don't. *We* represent the people – ordinary, decent, normal-living people who rely on power companies like ours to light and heat their homes, and keep factories working, and do the million other things *you'll* cut people off from if you and your kind have their selfish, short-sighted way.'

Nim swung towards the bench, directly addressing the commissioner and administrative law judge. 'What's needed now, in this state and most others, is intelligent compromise. Compromise between the "no-growth-at-any-pricers" like the Sequoia Club and Birdsong, and those who call for maximum growth and damn the environment! Well, I – and the company I work for – admit the need for compromise, and urge it on ourselves and others. We recognize there are no easy, simple choices, which is why we seek the middle ground, namely : let there be *some* growth, but for God's sake grant us the means – electrically – to accommodate it.'

He turned back to Birdsong. 'What *you'll* do for people in the end is make them suffer. Suffer from desperate shortages, from massive unemployment, from all the big and small things which won't work without electric power – all of it when the crisis hits, a crisis which isn't phony but is real, a crisis which will sweep across North America, and probably a lot of other places in the world.'

Nim asked the silent, surprised figure in front of him, 'And where will you be then, Birdsong? In hiding, probably. Hiding from the *people* who'll have found out what you really are – a cheat and faker who misled them.'

Even while speaking, Nim knew he had gone too far, had broken recklessly the normal constraints of public hearings, as well as restrictions placed on him by GSP & L. Perhaps he had even given Birdsong grounds for claiming libel. Yet another part of Nim's mind argued that what he had said *needed* to be said, that there were limits to patience and reasonableness, and that *someone* had to speak out plainly, fearlessly, accepting whatever consequences came.

He stormed on. 'You sound off about forty per cent conservation, Birdsong. That isn't conservation; that's *deprivation*. It would mean a whole new way of life, and a damn sight poorer one.

'Okay, there *are* some who say we ought to have lower standards of living, all of us, that we live too well and *should* be deprived. Well, maybe that's true, maybe not. But, either way, that kind of decision for change isn't for power companies like

GSP & L to make. Our responsibility is to maintain the living standards which people – through their elected governments – tell us that they want. It's why we'll go on protecting those standards, Birdsong, until ordered otherwise – but ordered officially, not by overinflated, self-appointed pecksniffs like you.'

As Nim paused for breath, the commissioner enquired coolly, 'Have you quite finished, Mr Goldman?'

Nim swung to face the bench. 'No, Mr Chairman, I haven't. While I'm on my feet there are a couple of other things I'd like to say.'

'Mr Chairman, if I might suggest a recess . . .' It was Oscar O'Brien, competing for attention.

Nim said firmly, 'I intend to finish, Oscar.' He observed that everyone at the press table was scribbling and the official steno-typist had his head down, fingers racing.

'There will be no recess for the moment,' the commissioner said, and O'Brien subsided unhappily, with a shrug. Birdsong was still standing, silently, but a half-smile now replaced his surprised expression. Perhaps he was reasoning that Nim's out-burst had harmed GSP & L's cause and was helping p & lfp. Well, Nim thought, whether that was true or not, having gone this far he was damned if he would get fainthearted. He addressed the commissioner and the administrative law judge, both watching him curiously.

'This entire exercise, Mr Chairman – and I mean this hearing and others like it – is a futile, time-wasting, costly charade. It's futile because it takes years to accomplish what ought to be done in weeks, and sometimes even longer to do nothing. It's time-wasting because those of us who are *real* producers, not paper-eating bureaucrats, could spend the endless hours we're required to be here a helluva lot more usefully to the companies we work for and society as a whole. It's outrageously costly because tax-payers and power users – who Birdsong claims to represent, but doesn't – get stuck with paying millions for this crazy, counter-productive, comic-opera pseudo-system. And it's a charade be-cause we pretend that what we are doing here makes sense and reason when all of us on our side of the fence know damn well it doesn't.'

The commissioner's face flushed crimson. Decisively, this time, he reached for his gavel and slammed it down. Glaring at

Nim, he pronounced, 'That is *all* I will allow on that subject, but I give you due warning, Mr Goldman: I intend to read the transcript carefully and consider other action later.' Then to Birdsong with equal coldness: 'Have you concluded your questioning of this witness?'

'Yes*sir!*' Birdsong grinned broadly. 'If you ask me, he just pissed in his own nest.'

The gavel slammed. 'I am *not* asking you.'

Oscar O'Brien was on his feet again. Impatiently the commissioner waved him down and announced, 'This hearing is adjourned.'

There was a buzz of excited conversation as the hearing room emptied. Nim did not share in it. He had glanced towards O'Brien, who was stuffing papers into a briefcase, but the lawyer shook his head – a gesture combining disbelief and sadness – and a moment later stalked out alone.

Davey Birdsong joined a group of supporters who were noisily congratulating him, and they all went out, laughing.

Laura Bo Carmichael, Roderick Pritchett, and several others from the Sequoia Club regarded Nim curiously but made no comment as they, too, left.

The press table emptied quickly, except for Nancy Molineaux, who appeared to be reviewing her notes and making more. Her head came up as Nim passed by. She said softly, 'Baby, oh *baby*! Did you ever crucify yourself!'

'If I did,' he told her, 'I'm sure you'll make the most of it.'

She shook her head and smiled lazily. 'Don't need to make anything, man. You stuck your own ass in the blender. Man, oh man! *Wait* till you see tomorrow's papers.'

He didn't answer and left Ms Molineaux still working on her notes, no doubt seeking the sharpest quotes with which to impale him. Nim was sure the bitch would slant her story, to make him look as bad as possible and she would enjoy it, he thought, even more than her report about the helicopter at Devil's Gate.

A sense of loneliness engulfed him as he left the hearing room alone.

Outside he was surprised to find several TV reporters with mini-cameras awaiting him. He had forgotten how fast the visual media, once tipped off, could cover a breaking story.

'Mr Goldman,' one of the TV men called out, 'we heard about some things you said in there. Would you repeat them so we can have a story on the news tonight?'

For a second Nim hesitated. He didn't have to do it. Then he decided: he was in so much trouble already that nothing more which might be said or done could make things worse. So why the hell not?

'Okay,' he responded, 'here's the way it is.' He began speaking forcefully, heatedly, once more as cameras rolled.

14

'From this moment on,' J. Eric Humphrey said, his voice with a cutting edge like steel, 'you will cease to be a spokesman for this company about *anything*. You will not appear on TV or radio. You will not give interviews to the press or respond to a reporter's question, even if asked the time of day. Is that clear?'

'Yes,' Nim said, 'it's clear.'

The two faced each other, the chairman's desk between them. The setting was unusually formal since Humphrey had chosen not to use the more casual conference area where he and Nim normally had discussions.

It was the afternoon of the day following Nim's outburst at the California Energy Commission hearing.

'As to public hearings,' Humphrey went on, 'you will, of course, no longer appear at any. Other arrangements will be made.'

'If you want my resignation, Eric, you can have it.'

Nim had been thinking about that possibility all day. His departure, he reasoned, might relieve GSP & L of some embarrassment, and he was aware of owing a loyalty to the utility which in the past had treated him well. Also, from his own point of view he was not sure he wanted to continue working with some kind of stigma, expressed through a restriction of his activities. His pride was involved there, and why not?

One thing Nim knew for sure: he would have no trouble getting a senior appointment elsewhere. Plenty of public utilities would jump at the chance of recruiting someone with his background and experience, as he had learned from job offers before now. On the other hand, he was reluctant to leave California, which Nim, and a multitude of others, believed to be the most agreeable and exciting place in the world to live and work. Someone had said: if something happens – good or bad – it happens in California first. Nim agreed wholeheartedly.

There was also the problem of Ruth and Leah and Benjy. Would Ruth want to move – to Illinois, for example – the way things were between them? Probably not.

'No one said anything about resigning,' Eric Humphrey acknowledged huffily.

Nim resisted an impulse to smile. This was not the moment. But he knew, without indulging in egotism, that he was valuable to the chairman in a host of ways, entirely apart from public appearances. His planning role was one. In fact, being a GSP & L policy spokesman had not been part of Nim's original duties, but had been added later and increased as time went by. In a way, Nim thought, he would be glad to be rid of the public aspect, so maybe he could put the pieces together and carry on. Anyway, he decided, for the moment he would do nothing rash.

'That is all for now,' Humphrey said coldly, returning to papers he had been studying when Nim was summoned. It was clear that the chairman would need time to get over his personal displeasure.

Teresa Van Buren was waiting in Nim's office.

'I want you to know,' the PR director said, 'that I spent an hour with Eric this morning arguing against his decision not to let you loose in public any more. At one point he got as angry with me as he is with you.'

'Thanks, Tess.' Nim dropped into a chair. He felt exhausted physically, as well as mentally.

'What truly sent our esteemed chairman up the wall, and made him unpersuadable, was your doing your thing on television *after* the hearing. That really guaranteed maximum exposure.' Van Buren chuckled. 'If you want the truth, I don't object to that, though you could have been more tactful, then and at the hearing. But the main thing is, I think you'll be vindicated eventually.'

'In the meantime,' Nim said, 'I'm gagged.'

'Yes, and I'm afraid that's going to be known outside of here. Do you mind?' Without waiting for an answer, Van Buren produced a *California Examiner*. 'Have you seen the afternoon paper?'

'I saw an early edition.'

At lunchtime Nim had read a front-page Nancy Molineaux story which was headed:

**Tirade by GSP & L's Goldman
Disrupts Energy Hearing**

The report began:

An intemperate attack by Nimrod Goldman, a Golden State Power & Light vice president, on opposition witnesses and the California Energy Commission itself, created turmoil yesterday at a public hearing called to consider a proposed new generating plant at Tunipah.

A shocked Commissioner Hugh G. Forbes, who presided, later dubbed Goldman's remarks as 'insulting and unacceptable' and said he will consider possible legal action . . .

The later *Examiner* edition which the PR chief had brought contained a new lead and heading:

**GSP & L Disciplines Goldman
And Disavows His Outburst**

Nimrod Goldman, former 'fair-haired boy' at Golden State Power & Light, today stands in disgrace, his future with the giant utility uncertain because of a public temper trantrum yesterday. Meanwhile his GSP & L bosses have disassociated themselves from Goldman's vitriolic attack on . . .

And so on.

Van Buren said apologetically, 'There was no way to stop the news getting out about your being cut off as a spokesman. If it hadn't come from my office – and, as it was, I only answered questions – someone else would have leaked it.'

Nim nodded glumly. 'I understand.'

'By the way, don't take seriously any of that stuff about the commission taking action. I talked to our legal department and it's just hot air. There's nothing they can do.'

'Yes,' he told her, 'I already figured that.'

'But Eric did insist on a repudiation statement. He's also writing a private letter of apology to the commission.'

Nim sighed. He still did not regret having spoken out; he had thought about that, too, since yesterday. But it was depressing to be treated like an outcast by colleagues. It also seemed unfair that most press reports – including that of the morning *Chronicle-West* and other California papers – had focused on the sensational aspects of yesterday, glossing over or ignoring the serious points which Nim had made. Nor had Davey Birdsong's antics – the insults and provocation – been given more than the briefest mention, and even then not critically. The press, it seemed to Nim, operated on its own double standard. However, that was nothing new.

Van Buren glanced at the *Examiner* again. 'Nancy made the most of it all, and has given you the hardest time; she goes for the jugular as a habit. You two don't seem to like each other.'

Nim said feelingly, 'I'd gladly cut that bitch's heart out. If she had one.'

The PR director frowned. 'That's pretty strong, Nim.'

'Maybe. But it's how I feel.'

Nim thought: It was Nancy Molineaux's description, '*Nimrod Goldman . . . today stands in disgrace,*' which had really got to him a moment ago, had really hurt. Not least, he admitted to himself, because it was true.

Part Three

1

'Daddy,' Leah said, addressing Nim across the dinner table, 'will you get to spend more nights at home now?'

There was a moment's silence in which Nim was aware that Benjy had put down his knife and fork and was watching him intently, silently endorsing his sister's question.

Ruth, too, who had been reaching for the pepper mill, changed her mind and waited with the children for Nim's answer.

'I might,' he said; the suddenness of the question, and having three pairs of eyes focused on him, were disconcerting. 'That is, if I'm not given a lot of other work which could keep me at the office late.'

Benjy, brightening, said, 'And at weekends too – will you get more time with us, Dad?'

'Maybe.'

Ruth intervened. 'I think you are being given a message.'

She smiled as she said it, something she had done infrequently since her return home several days ago. She was more serious than before, Nim was aware, at times preoccupied. The two of them still had not had their definitive, heart-to-heart talk; Ruth seemed to be avoiding it and Nim, still depressed from his recent experiences, had not felt like making the effort on his own.

Nim had wondered in advance : how did a husband and wife treat each other on the wife's return after she had been away for two weeks, almost certainly with another man? In their own case the answer seemed : exactly as before she left.

Ruth had arrived back without fuss, had collected the children from her parents, then picked up the threads of life at home as if she had never dropped them. She and Nim continued to share a bedroom, as they always had – though not a bed; it seemed a long time since Nim had left his own twin bed to join Ruth in hers. But in other respects their regular life resumed. Of course, Nim reminded himself, in the past there had been similar situations – in reverse – when *he* returned from extra-marital excursions which, at the time, he believed Ruth had not known about, but now suspected that she had. And one final reason for the quietus was, again, Nim's bruised ego – bruised elsewhere. He simply wasn't ready for more emotion yet.

Now they were all at home, having a family evening meal, the third in three days, which, in itself, was unusual.

'As you all know,' Nim said, 'there have been some changes at the office but I don't know yet how everything is going to work out.' He noticed something about Benjy and leaned forward, inspecting him more closely. 'What happened to your face?'

Benjy hesitated, his small hand going up to cover a bruise on his left cheek and a cut beneath the lower lip. 'Oh, it was just something at school, Dad.'

'What kind of something? Were you in a fight?'

Benjy appeared uncomfortable.

'Yes, he was,' Leah said. 'Todd Thornton said you're a fink, Daddy, because you don't care about the environment and want to spoil it. So Benjy hit him, but Todd's bigger.'

Nim said severely to Benjy, 'No matter what anyone says about *anything*, it's wrong and stupid to go around hitting people.'

His son looked crestfallen. 'Yes, Dad.'

'We had a talk,' Ruth said. 'Benjy knows that now.'

Beneath his outward reaction Nim was startled and shocked. It had not occurred to him until now that criticism directed at himself would find a target in his family also. He said softly, 'I'm truly sorry if anything that happened to me has hurt any of you.'

'Oh, that's all right,' Leah assured him. 'Mommy explained to us how what you did was honourable.'

Benjy added eagerly, 'And Mom said you had more guts, Dad, than all the others put together.' Benjy made clear, by the way he snapped his teeth together, that he enjoyed the word 'guts'.

Nim had his eyes fixed on Ruth. 'Your mother told you that?'

'It's true, isn't it?' Benjy asked.

'Of course it's true,' Ruth said; she had flushed slightly. 'But your father can't say it about himself, can he? Which is why *I* told you.'

'So that's what we tell the other kids when they say anything,' Leah added.

For an instant Nim felt a surge of emotion. The thought of Benjy fighting with his small fists to defend his father's reputation, then Ruth, rising above the differences between the two of them, to protect his honour with the children, left Nim with a choked-up feeling close to tears. He was saved from more embarrassment by Ruth's exhortation, 'All right, now let's everyone get on with dinner.'

Later, while Nim and Ruth were still at the dining table sipping coffee, and the children had left to watch TV, he said, 'I'd like you to know that I appreciate what you told Leah and Benjy.'

Ruth made a dismissing gesture. 'If I hadn't believed it, I wouldn't have told them. Just because you and I aren't Romeo and Juliet any more, doesn't mean I've stopped reading and thinking objectively about outside things.'

'I've offered to resign,' he told her. 'Eric says it isn't necessary, but I may still.' He went on to speak of the various possibilities he was considering, including a move to another power company, perhaps in the Midwest. If that happened, Nim asked, how would Ruth feel about moving there with the children?

Her answer was quick and definite. 'I wouldn't do it.'

'Do you mind telling me why?'

'I should think it's obvious. Why should three members of our family – Leah, Benjy, me – be uprooted, go to live in a strange place, and mostly for your convenience, when you and I haven't yet discussed our own future together – *if* we have one, which seems unlikely.'

So there it was, out in the open, and he supposed the signal for their serious talk had come. How strange, he thought, that it should happen at a moment when briefly they had seemed closer than in a long time!

He said, with the sadness that he felt, 'What the hell happened to us?'

Ruth answered sharply, 'You should be the one best able to answer that. I'm curious about one thing, though – just how many other women have there been in our fifteen years of marriage?' He was aware of the recent hardness he had observed in Ruth as she continued. 'Or maybe you've lost count, the way I did. For a while I could always tell when you had something new going – or should I say "someone" new? Then later on I wasn't so sure, and I guessed that you were overlapping, playing the field, with two or even more at once. Was I right?'

Having trouble in meeting Ruth's eyes directly, he answered, 'Sometimes.'

'Well, that's one point settled anyway. So my guess was right.

But you haven't answered the first question. How many women altogether?'

He said unhappily, 'I'll be damned if I know.'

'If that's true,' Ruth pointed out, 'it isn't exactly complimentary to those other females you must have felt something for, however briefly. Whoever they were, I'd say they deserved better from you than not even to be remembered.'

He protested, 'It was never serious. None of it. Not with any of them.'

'That I *do* believe.' Ruth's cheeks were flushed with anger. 'For that matter, you were never serious about me.'

'That isn't true!'

'How can you possibly say that? After what you've just admitted. Oh, I could understand one other woman; maybe two. Any wife with sense knows that happens sometimes in the best of marriages. But not *scores* of women, the way it's been with you.'

He argued, 'Now you're talking nonsense. It was never scores.'

'One score then. At *least*.'

Nim was silent.

Ruth said thoughtfully, 'Maybe that was Freudian – my saying "scores" just now. Because that's what you like to do, isn't it? – score with as many women as you can.'

He admitted, 'There's probably some truth in that.'

'I *know* there's truth.' She added quietly, 'But it doesn't make a woman – a wife – feel any better, or less belittled, dirty, cheated, to hear it from the man she loved, or thought she did.'

'If you've felt that way so long,' he asked her, 'why did you wait until now to bring it up? Why have we never had this kind of talk before?'

'That's a fair question.' Ruth stopped, weighing her answer, then went on, 'I suppose it was because I kept on hoping you would change; that you'd grow out of wanting to fornicate with every attractive woman you set eyes on, grow out of it the way a child learns to stop being greedy about candy. But I was wrong; you haven't changed. And, oh yes, since we're being honest with each other, there was another reason. I was a coward. I was afraid of what being on my own might mean, of what it could do to Leah and Benjy, and afraid – or maybe too proud – to admit that *my* marriage, like so many others, wasn't working.' Ruth stopped, her voice breaking for the first time. 'Well, I'm not afraid, or proud, or anything any more : I just want out.'

'Do you mean that?'

Twin tears coursed down Ruth's cheeks. 'What else is there?'

A spark of resistance flared in Nim. Did he need to be so totally defensive? Weren't there two sides to everything, including this?

'How about your own love affair?' he asked. 'If you and I go separate ways, does your man friend move in as soon as I step out?'

'What man?'

'The one you've been seeing. The one you went away with.'

Ruth had dried her eyes. She regarded him now with an expression which seemed part amused, part sorrowing. 'You really believe that. That I went away with a man.'

'Well, didn't you?'

She shook her head slowly. 'No.'

'But I thought . . .'

'I know you did. And I let you go on thinking it, which probably wasn't a good idea. I decided – spitefully, I suppose – that it would do no harm, and might even achieve some good, if you had a taste of what I'd been feeling.'

'Then how about those other times? Where were you?'

Ruth said, with a trace of her earlier anger, 'There *is* no other man. Can't you get that through your thick head? There never has been. I came to you a virgin – you know that, unless you've forgotten or have me confused with one of your other girl friends. And there hasn't been anyone else but you since.'

Nim winced because he did remember, but persisted, 'Then what were you doing . . . ?'

'That's my private business. But I'm telling you again : it wasn't a man.'

He believed her. Absolutely.

'Oh Christ!' he said, and thought : everything was coming apart at once; most of what he had done and said recently had turned out to be wrong. As to their marriage, he wasn't sure if he wanted it to go on or not. Maybe Ruth was right, and getting out would be the best thing for them both. The idea of personal freedom was attractive. On the other hand, there was a good deal he would miss – the children, home, a sense of stability, even Ruth, despite their having grown apart. Not wanting to be forced

234

to a decision, wishing that what was happening could have been postponed, he asked almost plaintively, 'So where do we go from here?'

'According to what I've heard from friends who travelled this route' – Ruth's voice had gone cold again – 'we each get a lawyer and begin staking out positions.'

He pleaded, 'But do we have to do it now?'

'Give me one single, valid reason for waiting any longer.'

'It's a selfish one, I'll admit. But I've just been through one difficult time . . .' He let the sentence trail off, realizing it sounded like self-pity.

'I know that. And I'm sorry the two things have come together. But nothing is going to change between us, not after all this time. We both know that, don't we?'

He said bleakly, 'I suppose so.' There was no point in promising to revise his own attitudes when he wasn't sure he could, or even wanted to.

'Well, then . . .'

'Look . . . would you wait a month? Maybe two? If for no other reason than that we'll have to break the news to Leah and Benjy, and it will give them time to get used to the idea.' He was not sure that the argument made sense; it probably didn't. Nor did it seem plausible that a delay would achieve anything. But instinct told him that Ruth, too, was reluctant to take the final, irrevocable step to end their marriage.

'Well . . .' She hesitated, then conceded, 'All right. Because of what's happened to you just now, I'll wait a little while. But I won't say two months, *or* one. If I decide to make it less, I will.'

'Thank you.' He had a sense of relief that there would be an interval, however brief.

'Hey!' It was Benjy, appearing at the dining room door. 'I just got a new cassette from the Merediths. It's a play. Wanna watch?'

The Merediths were next door neighbours. Nim glanced at Ruth. 'Why not?'

In the basement recreation room Ruth and Nim sat side by side on a sofa, with Leah sprawled on a rug, while Benjy deftly inserted a video cassette into their Betamax tape deck, connected to a colour TV. A group of residents in the area had an agreement which was becoming widespread : one family recorded a television programme – usually the children of the house, or a babysitter, took care of it – hitting the 'stop' button whenever commercials appeared. The result was a high-quality recording, *sans* commercials, which the adults and other families watched later at their leisure, the cassettes being rotated among a dozen or so households.

Knowing that the practice was growing as increasing numbers of people shared the discovery, Nim wondered how long it would be before it affected TV network revenues. Perhaps it had already. In a way, Nim thought, the TV networks and stations were going through the same shoal waters power companies like GSP & L had already navigated. The TV people had abused their public privileges by flooding the airwaves with a vulgar excess of advertising and low-grade programming. Now Betamax and comparable systems were giving the public a chance to strike back by being selective, and eliminating advertising from their viewing. In time, perhaps, the development would cause those in charge of TV to grasp the need for public responsibility.

The two-hour play on the borrowed cassette was *Mary White*, a tragic, moving story about the family of a loved teenager who had died. Perhaps because he had seldom been more aware of his own family, yet realized how little time was left in which it was likely to remain a unit, Nim was glad the lights were low, his sadness and his tears unobserved by the other three.

2

On a dark, lonely hill above the suburban community of Millfield, Georgos Winslow Archambault crawled on his belly towards a chain link fence protecting a GSP & L sub-station. The precaution – against being observed – was probably unneeded, he reasoned; the sub-station was unattended, also there was no moon tonight and the nearest main road, which carried traffic over the sparsely inhabited hill, was half a mile away. But recently, Golden State Piss & Lickspittle had hired more security pigs and set up mobile night patrols which varied their operating hours and routes – clearly so they would not create a pattern. So it made sense to be cagey, even though crawling while carrying tools and explosives was awkward and uncomfortable.

Georgos shivered. The October night was cold and a strong wind knifed around crags and boulders of the rocky hill, making him wish he had worn two sweaters beneath his dark blue denim jumpsuit instead of one. Glancing back the way he had come, he saw that his woman, Yvette, was just a few yards behind, and keeping up. It was important that she did. For one thing she had the wire and detonators; for another, Georgos was running behind schedule due to a traffic delay in getting out here from the city, a journey of twenty miles. Now he wanted to make up time because tonight's operation involved the destruction of three sub-stations by the entire Friends of Freedom force. At one of the other sites Ute and Felix were working together; at the third Wayde was operating alone. Their plan called for all three explosions to occur simultaneously.

When he reached the fence, Georgos detached a pair of heavy wire-shears from his belt and began cutting. All he needed was a small hole, close to the ground. Then if a patrol came around, after the two of them had gone and before the explosion, the cut fence might escape attention.

While Georgos worked he could see the widespread, shimmering lights of Millfield below him. Well, all of them would be out soon; so would a lot of others further south. He knew about Millfield and the other townships nearby. They were bourgeois communities, peopled mainly by commuters – more capitalists and lackeys! – and he was glad to be causing them trouble.

The hole in the fence was almost complete. In a minute or so Georgos and Yvette could wriggle through. He glanced at the luminous dial of his wristwatch. Time was tight! Once inside, they would have to work fast.

The targets of tonight's triple strike had been chosen carefully. There used to be a time when Friends of Freedom bombed transmission towers, toppling two or three at once in an attempt to knock out service over a wide area. But not any more. Georgos and others had discovered that when towers were toppled, power companies rerouted their power, so that service was restored quickly, often within minutes. Also, fallen towers were immediately replaced by temporary poles, so even *that* power highway was soon in use again.

Large sub-stations, though, were something else. They were vulnerable, critical installations and could take weeks to repair or replace completely.

The damage which would be done tonight, if all went well, would cause a widespread blackout, extending far beyond Millfield, and it could be days, perhaps a lot longer, before everything was switched back on. Meanwhile the disruption would be tremendous, the cost enormous. Georgos gloated at the thought. Maybe, after this, more people would take the Friends of Freedom seriously.

Georgos thought: his small but glorious army had learned a lot since their early attacks on the despicable enemy. Nowadays, well ahead of any operation, they studied GSP & L's layout and working methods, seeking areas of vulnerability, situations where the greatest havoc could be caused. This aspect had been helped recently by an ex-GSP & L engineer, dismissed for stealing, who now nursed a hatred of the company. While not an active member of Friends of Freedom, the former employee had been bought with some of the fresh money supplied by Birdsong. Other money from the same source had been used to buy more and better explosives.

Birdsong had let slip one day where the cash was coming from – the Sequoia Club, which believed it was financing p & lfp. It greatly amused Georgos that a fat-cat, establishment outfit was unknowingly footing the bill for revolution. In a way it was a pity that the dimwitted Sequoia crowd would never find out.

Click! The last strand of wire was severed and the cut portion of the fence fell away. Georgos pushed it inside the sub-station enclosure so it would be less noticeable, then followed it with three packets of plastic explosive, after which he wriggled through himself.

Yvette was still close behind. Her hand had healed – after a fashion – since her loss of two fingers when a blasting cap exploded prematurely a couple of months ago. The stumps of the fingers were ugly, and not sewn up neatly as would have happened if a surgeon had attended her. But Georgos had done his best to keep the wounds clean and, largely through luck, infection was avoided. Also avoided were the dangerous questions certain to have been asked at a hospital or doctor's office.

Damn! His jumpsuit had caught on an end of wire. Georgos heard the denim rip and felt a sharp pain as the wire penetrated his undershorts and sliced into his thigh. In being cautious, he had made the aperture too small. He reached back, felt for the wire and managed to dislodge it, then continued through the fence with no further trouble. Yvette, who was smaller, followed without difficulty.

No talk was necessary. They had practised beforehand and knew exactly what to do. Cautiously, Georgos taped plastic explosive to the three large transformers the sub-station housed. Yvette handed him detonators and played out wire to be connected to timing devices.

Ten minutes later all three charges were in place. Yvette passed him, one by one, the clockwork fuse mechanisms with attached batteries which he had carefully assembled yesterday for himself and the other two teams. Handling each one gingerly, making sure there would be no premature explosion, Georgos connected the wires from the detonators. Again he checked his watch. By working fast they had made up some, but not all, of the lost time.

The three explosions would occur, more or less together, eleven minutes from now. It barely gave Georgos and his woman time to make it back down the hill to where their car was hidden, off the road, in a stand of trees. But if they hurried – ran most of the way – they would be safely *en route* to the city before a response to the massive power failure could be mounted. He commanded Yvette, 'Get going! Move it!' This time she preceded him through the fence.

It was while Georgos himself was crawling out that he heard the sound of a car, not far away and ascending the hill. He paused to listen. Unmistakably it was using the private gravel road, owned by GSP & L, which provided access to the sub-station.

A security patrol! It had to be. This late at night no one else would come here. As Georgos finished scrambling through and stood upright, he could see the reflection of headlights on some trees below. The road was winding, which explained why the car was not yet in sight.

Yvette had heard and seen too. As she started to say something, he motioned her to silence and snarled, 'Over here!' He began running – towards the gravel road, then across it to a clump of bushes on the far side. In the bushes he dropped and flattened himself, Yvette beside him doing the same. He sensed her trembling. He was reminded of what he forgot sometimes – that she was little more than a child in many ways; also, she had never been quite the same, despite her devotion to him, since the incident of the hand.

Now the headlights were in sight as the car rounded the last bend before the sub-station. It was approaching slowly. Probably the driver was being careful because the service road had no reflective markers and the edges were hard to see. As the headlights came nearer, the entire area was illuminated brightly. Georgos pressed down, raising his head only slightly. Their chances of remaining concealed, he calculated, were good. What worried him was the nearness of the explosion. He checked his watch. Eight minutes to go.

The car stopped, only a few feet from Georgos and Yvette, and a figure got out on the passenger side. As the figure moved forward into the range of headlights, Georgos could see a man in security guard uniform. The guard had a flashlight with a powerful beam which he directed at the fence surrounding the sub-station. Moving the beam from side to side, he began walking, making a circuit of the fence. Now Georgos could distinguish the shape of a second man – the driver – who seemed to be staying in the car.

The first man had gone part way around when he stopped, directing the flashlight downward. He had found the opening where the fence was cut. Moving closer, he used the flashlight to inspect inside the fence. The light moved over power lines, insulators and transformers, paused at one charge of plastic explosive, then followed the wires to the timing device.

The guard swung around and shouted, 'Hey, Jake! Call in an alarm! Something's funny here.'

Georgos acted. He knew that seconds counted, and there was no alternative to what had to be done.

He leaped to his feet, at the same time reaching to his belt for a hunting knife he carried in a sheath. It was a long, sharp, vicious knife, intended for an emergency such as this, and it came out smoothly. The leap had carried Georgos almost to the car. One more pace and he wrenched open the driver's door. The startled occupant, an elderly man with grey hair, also in security guard uniform, turned. He had a radio mike in his hand, close to his lips.

Georgos lunged forward. With his left hand he pulled the guard from the car, spun him around, then with a powerful upward thrust buried the knife in the man's chest. The victim's mouth opened wide. He began a scream which almost at once subsided to a gurgle. Then he fell forward to the ground. Pulling hard, Georgos retrieved the knife and returned it to the sheath. He had seen a gun in a holster as the guard fell. Now, snapping open the holster, he grabbed it. Georgos had learned about guns in Cuba. This was a .38 Smith & Wesson revolver and, in the reflection from the headlights, he broke the gun and checked the chambers. All were loaded. He snapped the gun closed, cocked it, and released the safety.

The first guard had heard something and was returning to the car. He called out, 'Jake! What was that? Are you okay?' His gun was drawn but he had no chance to use it.

Already Georgos had slipped like a silent shadow around the rear of the car, making use of darkness behind the lights. Now he was down on his knees, taking careful aim, the muzzle of the .38 cradled on his left elbow for stability, his right forefinger beginning to squeeze the trigger. The sights were lined on the left side of the approaching guard's chest.

Georgos waited until he was sure he would hit his target, then fired three times. The second and third shots were probably unnecessary. The guard pitched backwards without a sound and lay still where he had fallen.

There was no time, Georgos knew, even to check his watch. He grabbed Yvette, who had risen to her feet at the sound of the shots, shoving her forward as they began running. They raced together down the hill, taking a chance on missing the roadway in the darkness. Twice Georgos stumbled and recovered; once he trod on a loose rock and felt his ankle twist, but he ignored the pain and kept moving. Despite his haste he made certain that Yvette stayed close. He could hear her breath, coming in sobs.

They were a third of the way down when the sound of an explosion reached them. The ground vibrated first, then the sound wave followed – a loud, reverberating *cruump!* Seconds later there was another explosion, and then a third, and the sky lit up with a bright, yellow-blue flash. The flash repeated itself, then the reflection of flames, from fiercely burning oil from the transformers, lighted the sky. Rounding a bend in the gravel road, Georgos had a sudden sense of something being different. Then he realized what it was; his objective had been fulfilled. All the lights of Millfield were out.

Aware of the urgent need to get clear, not knowing if the security guard in the car had radioed a message or not, Georgos continued running, leading the way.

With relief, and both of them near exhaustion, he found their car where they had left it – in the stand of trees near the foot of the hill. Minutes later they were on their way, headed for the city, with blacked-out Millfield behind them.

'You killed those men! You murdered them!'

Yvette's voice, from the front seat of the car beside him, was hysterical as well as still breathless from her exertion.

'I had to.'

Georgos answered tersely, without turning his head, keeping his eyes directed at the freeway which they had just reached. He was driving carefully, making sure to stay slightly below the legal speed limit. The last thing he wanted was to be stopped by the Highway Patrol for some driving infraction. There was blood, Georgos knew, on his clothing from the man he had knifed, and there would be blood on the knife also, identifiable by type. He had discovered, too, that he was bleeding copiously himself – from his left thigh where the wire had penetrated more deeply than he had realized earlier. And he could feel his ankle swelling from when it twisted on the rock.

Yvette whined, 'You didn't have to *kill* them!'

He shouted at her fiercely, 'Shut up! Or I'll kill *you*.'

He was thinking back, mentally running over every detail that had happened, trying to remember if there were any clues left behind which would identify either him or Yvette. They had both worn gloves at the fence and in laying the charges. He had slipped his off to connect the timer, and later when he fired the gun. But the gloves had been on when he attacked with the knife, so there would be no fingerprints on the car door handle. Prints on the gun? Yes, but he had had the presence of mind to bring the gun with him and would dispose of it later.

Yvette was snivelling again. 'That one in the car. *He was an old man!* I saw him.'

'He was a dirty fascist pig!'

Georgos said it forcefully, in part to convince himself, because the memory of the grey-haired man had been eating at him too. He had tried to push out of his mind the recollection of the shocked, open mouth and stifled scream as the knife went in deeply, but he had not succeeded. Despite his anarchist training and the bombings since, Georgos had not killed anyone at close quarters before and the experience sickened him. He would never admit it though.

'You could go to prison for murder!'

He snarled back, 'So could you.'

There was no point in explaining that he was indictable for murder already – for the seven deaths resulting from the La Mission plant explosion and the letter bombs mailed to GSP & L, but he could set his woman straight about tonight, and would.

'Get this, you stupid whore! You're in this as much as I am. You were there, a part of it all, and you killed those pigs just as if you pulled the knife or fired the gun. So whatever happens to me happens to you. Don't ever forget it!'

He had got through to her, he could tell, because she was sobbing now, choking on words, burbling something incoherent about wishing she hadn't got into this. For an instant he felt compassion and a surge of pity. Then self-discipline reasserted itself; he dismissed the thought as being weak and counter-revolutionary.

He estimated they were almost halfway to the city, then realized something he had been too preoccupied to take in earlier. The area they were passing through, normally brightly lighted and well beyond Millfield, was also in darkness; even street lights were out. With sudden satisfaction he thought: it meant that the other freedom fighters had succeeded in their objectives. *The entire battle, fought under his generalship, had been won!*

Georgos began humming a little tune, composing in his mind a communiqué to acquaint the world with one more glorious victory by Friends of Freedom.

3

'When the power failure happened,' Karen Sloan said from her wheelchair, 'Josie and I were on our way home in Humperdinck.'

'Humperdinck?' Nim was puzzled.

Karen gave him one of her warm, glowing smiles. 'Humperdinck is my beautiful, beautiful van. I love it so much I just couldn't call it "van", so I gave it a name.'

They were in the living room of Karen's apartment and it was early evening in the first week of November. Nim had accepted – after several postponements because of pressures of work – an invitation from Karen to join her for dinner. Josie, Karen's aide-housekeeper, was in the kitchen preparing the meal.

The small apartment was softly lighted, warm and comfortable. Outside, in contrast, most of northern California was enduring a Pacific gale, now in its third day, which had brought strong winds and torrential rain. As they talked, rain pounded against the windows.

Other sounds merged softly; the steady hum of the respirator mechanism which kept Karen breathing, and an accompanying hiss of air, inward and out; small clatters of dishes, the noise of a cupboard door opening, then closing, from the kitchen.

'About the power failure,' Karen resumed. 'I'd been to a movie, at a theatre where they have facilities for wheelchairs – I can do so many things now with Humperdinck that I couldn't before – and, while Josie was driving, all the street lights, and lights in buildings, went out.'

'Almost one hundred square miles,' Nim said with a sigh. 'Everything went. Everything.'

'Well, we didn't know that then. But we could see it was widespread, so Josie drove directly to Redwood Grove Hospital, which is where I go if I ever have problems. They have an emergency generator. The staff took care of me, and I stayed at the hospital for three days until the power was back on here.'

'Actually,' Nim told her, 'I already knew most of that. As soon as I could after those explosions and the blackout, I phoned your number. I was at the office; I'd been called in from home. When there was no answer I had someone contact the hospital, which is listed on your info sheet. They told us you were there, so I stopped worrying because there was lots to do that night.'

'It was an awful thing, Nimrod. Not just the blackout, but those two men murdered.'

'Yes, they were old-timers,' Nim said, 'pensioners who were brought back in because we were short of experienced security help. Unfortunately their experience belonged to another era and we found out later that the worst they'd ever dealt with was an occasional trespasser or small-time thief. They were no match for a killer.'

'Whoever did it hasn't been caught yet?'

Nim shook his head. 'It's someone we, and the police, have been looking for for a long time. The worst thing is, we still haven't the slightest idea who he is or where he operates from.'

'But isn't it a group – Friends of Freedom?'

'Yes. But the police believe the group is small, probably no more than a half-dozen people, and that one man is the brains and leader. They say there are similarities in all the incidents so far which point to that – like a personal handwriting. Whoever he is, the man's a homicidal maniac.'

Nim spoke feelingly. The effect of the latest bombing on the GSP & L system had been far worse than any other preceding it. Over an unusually wide area, homes, businesses and factories had been deprived of electric power for three to four days in many cases, a week in others, reminding Nim of Harry London's observation several weeks earlier that, *Those crazies are getting smart.*'

Only by a massive, costly effort which required bringing in all of GSP & L's spare transformers, borrowing some from other utilities, and diverting all available personnel to effect repairs, had power been restored as quickly as it was. Even so, GSP & L was being criticized for failing to protect its installations adequately. *The public is entitled to ask,* the *California Examiner* pontificated in an editorial, *if Golden State Power & Light is doing all it can to prevent a recurrence. Judging by available evidence, the answer is 'no'.* However, the newspaper offered no suggestion as to how the enormous, widespread GSP & L network could be protected everywhere twenty-four hours a day.

Equally depressing was the absence of any immediately usable clues. True, the law enforcement agencies had obtained another voice print, matching earlier ones, from the bombastic tape recording received by a radio station the day after the bombings. As well, there were some threads of denim material snagged on a cut wire near the site of the double murder, almost certainly from a garment worn by the attacker. The same wire also revealed dried blood which had been typed and found to differ from the blood of both dead guards. But, as a senior police detective told Nim in a moment of frankness, 'Those things can be useful when we have someone or something to match them with. Right now we're no nearer to having that than we were before.'

'Nimrod,' Karen said, interrupting his thoughts. 'It's been almost two months since we were together. I've truly missed you.'

He told her contritely, 'I'm sorry. I really am.'

Now that he was here, Nim wondered how he could have stayed away so long. Karen was as beautiful as he remembered her and, when they kissed a few minutes ago – a lingering kiss – her lips were loving, just as they had seemed before. It was as if, in a single instant, the gap in time had closed.

Something else Nim was aware of: in Karen's company he experienced a sense of peace, as happened with few other people he knew. The feeling was hard to define, except perhaps that Karen, who had come to terms with the limitations of her own life, transmitted a tranquillity and wisdom suggesting that other problems, too, could be resolved.

'It's been a difficult time for you,' she acknowledged. 'I know because I read what the newspapers said about you, and saw reports on television.'

Nim grimaced. 'The Tunipah hearings. I've been told I disgraced myself.'

Karen said sharply, 'You don't believe that, any more than I do. What you said was sensible, but most reports played that part down.'

'Any time you like, you can handle my public relations.'

She hesitated, then said, 'After it happened I wrote some poetry for you. I was going to send it, then thought maybe you were tired of hearing from everybody, no matter what they said.'

'Not everybody. Just most people.' He asked, 'Did you save it – the poem?'

'Yes.' Karen motioned with her head. 'It's over there. In the second drawer down.'

Nim rose from his seat and crossed to a bureau beneath book-shelves. Opening the drawer he had been told to, he saw a sheet of Karen's blue stationery on top, which he took out, then read what was typewritten.

The moving finger sometimes does go back,
Not to rewrite but to reread;
And what was once dismissed, derided, mocked,
May, in the fullness of a moon or two,
Or even years,
Be hailed as wisdom,
Spoken forthrightly at that earlier time,
And having needed courage
To face the obloquy of others less perceptive,
Though burdened with invective.

Dear Nimrod!
Remind yourself: A prophet's seldom praised
Before sunset
Of the day on which he first proclaimed
Unpalatable truths.
But if and when *your* truths
In time become self-evident,
Their author vindicated,
Be, at that harvest moment, forgiving, gracious,
Broad of mind, large-purposed,
Amused by life's contrariness.

For not to all, only the few,
Are presbyopic gifts: long vision, clarity, sagacity,
By chance, through lottery at birth,
Bestowed by busy nature.

Silently, Nim read the words a second time. At length he said, 'Karen, you never cease to surprise me. And whenever you do this I'm not sure of what to say, except I'm moved and grateful.'

At that moment, Josie – short and sturdy, her dark features beaming – marched in with a loaded tray. She announced, 'Lady and gentleman, dinner is served.'

It was a simple but tasty meal. A Waldorf salad, followed by a chicken casserole, then lemon sherbet. Nim had brought wine – a hard-to-get Heitz Cellar Cabernet Sauvignon – superb! As on the last occasion, Nim fed Karen, experiencing the same sense of sharing and intimacy that he had before.

Only once or twice did he remember with a trace of guilt the excuse he had used for not being at home tonight – an evening business engagement for GSP & L. But he rationalized that spending the time with Karen was different from other occasions when he had cheated, and lied to Ruth, or tried to. Perhaps, even now, he thought, Ruth didn't believe him, but if so she had given no indication when he left this morning. Also in his favour, Nim reminded himself: during the past four weeks there had been only one other occasion when he was not at home in time for family dinner, and then he genuinely *had* been working late.

Easily, leisurely, during their intensely personal dinner, Nim and Karen talked.

Josie had removed dishes and brought them coffee when, for a second time, the subject of Karen's van came up. Humperdinck. The special van, adapted under Ray Paulsen's direction to convey a quadriplegic's elaborate, powered wheelchair, and purchased from GSP & L by Karen's parents.

'Something I haven't explained,' Karen told him, 'is that I don't really own Humperdinck. I can't afford to. It has to be registered to my father, even though I use it.'

Insurance was the reason. 'Insurance rates for a disabled person are astronomical,' Karen said, 'even though someone like me will never drive. With the van in my father's name, the rates are lower, so that's why I don't own Humperdinck officially.'

She went on, 'Apart from the insurance, I was worried – still am a little – about Daddy borrowing the money to pay for Humperdinck. His bank said no, so he went to a loan company and they agreed, but at higher interest. I know it will be hard for him to make the loan payments because his business is not doing well, and he and Mother already help me with money when my allowances won't stretch. But they insisted I shouldn't concern myself, and to let them do the worrying.'

Nim said thoughtfully, 'Maybe there's something I could do. I could contribute a little money myself, then see if our company would donate . . .'

Karen cut in sharply, 'No! Absolutely not! Nimrod, our friendship is wonderful and I cherish it. But I won't take money from you – ever – and that includes your asking someone else. If my own family does something for me, that's different and we work it out together, but that's all. Besides, you already helped us enough with Humperdinck.' Her voice softened. 'I'm a proud and independent person. I hope you understand.'

'Yes,' he said, 'I understand, and I respect you.'

'Good! Respect is important. Now, Nimrod dearest, you'll only believe what a difference Humperdinck has made to my life if you let me show you. May I ask you something bold?'

'Ask me anything.'

'Could we have a date outside – perhaps go to the symphony?'

He hesitated only momentarily. 'Why not?'

Karen's face lighted with a smile and she said enthusiastically, 'You must tell me when you can be free and I'll make arrangements. Oh, I'm so happy!' Then, impulsively: 'Kiss me again, Nimrod.'

As he went to her, she tilted up her face, her mouth seeking his eagerly. He put a hand behind her head, running his fingers gently through her long blonde hair. She responded by pressing her lips closer. Nim found himself emotionally and sexually stirred and the thought came to him: how much promise the next few minutes might hold if Karen were whole in body instead of what she was. Then he dismissed the thought and broke off the kiss. For a moment he caressed her hair again, then returned to his chair.

'If I knew how,' Karen said, 'I'd purr.'

Nim heard a discreet cough and turned his head to see Josie standing at the doorway. The aide-housekeeper had changed from the white uniform she wore while serving dinner to a brown wool dress. He wondered how long she had been there.

'Oh, Josie,' Karen said, 'are you ready to go?' For Nim's benefit she added, 'Josie's visiting her family tonight.'

'Yes, I'm ready,' the other woman acknowledged. 'But shouldn't I put you to bed before I go?'

'Well, I suppose so.' Karen stopped, a faint flush suffusing her cheeks. 'Or perhaps, later on, Mr Goldman wouldn't mind . . .'

He said, 'If you'll tell me what to do, I'll be glad to.'

'Well, then, that's settled,' Josie said. 'So I'll be going, and good night.'

A few minutes later they heard the sound of the outer door closing.

When Karen spoke there seemed a nervousness in her voice. 'Josie won't be back until tomorrow morning. Normally I have a relief aide-housekeeper, but she's not well, so my big sister is coming for the night.' She glanced at a wall clock. 'Cynthia will be here in an hour and a half. Can you stay until then?'

'Of course.'

'If it's inconvenient for you, Jiminy – he's the janitor you met the first time – will come in for a while.'

Nim said firmly, 'The hell with Jiminy! I'm here and I'm staying.'

'I'm glad.' Karen smiled. 'There's some wine left. Shall we kill the bottle?'

'Good idea.' Nim went into the kitchen, found glasses and the recorked Cabernet. Returning, he divided the remaining wine and held one of the glasses while Karen sipped.

'I feel a wonderful glow,' she said. 'The wine helped, but that isn't all of it.'

On impulse he leaned over, raised Karen's face in his hand, and kissed her once more. She responded as ardently as the other times, except that the kiss was longer. At length, reluctantly, he moved back, though their faces remained close.

'Nimrod.' It was a whisper.

'Yes, Karen.'

'I think I'm ready to go to bed.'

He found his pulse beating faster. 'Tell me what to do.'

'Unplug my wheelchair first.'

Nim went to the rear of the chair and did so. The power cord retracted into a housing as the battery on the chair took over.

A sudden smile of mischief flashed across Karen's face. 'Follow me!'

Using the electric wheelchair's blow-sip tube control, and with a speed and dexterity which amazed him, Karen manoeuvred herself from the living room, down a small hallway, and into a bedroom. There was a single bed, neatly turned down. Beside it a low-wattage light burned dimly. Karen swung her chair so it was at the foot of the bed, facing away.

'There!' She looked at Nim expectantly.

'All right. What next?'

'You lift me out of the chair, then just pivot – the way you would if you were playing golf – and put me on the bed. When Josie does it we use a body sling that winds up like a crane. But you're strong, Nimrod. You can lift me in your arms.'

He did so, gently but surely, aware of the warm softness of her body, and afterwards followed instructions which Karen gave him about her breathing apparatus. He switched on a small Bantam respirator already at the bedside; at once he could hear it cycling – a dial showed fifteen pounds of pressure; the rate was eighteen breaths a minute. He put a tube from the respirator into Karen's mouth; as she began breathing the pressure went to thirty. Now she could dispense with the pneumo-belt she had been wearing beneath her clothes.

'Later,' Karen said, 'I'll ask you to put a chest respirator on me. Not yet, though.'

She was horizontal on the bed, her long hair spread over the pillow. The sight, Nim thought, would have excited Botticelli.

He asked, 'What do I do now?'

'Next . . .' she said, and in the soft, dim light he saw a blush bloom again on her cheeks. 'Next, Nimrod, you undress me.'

Karen's eyes were partly closed. Nim's hands were shaking and he wondered if what he thought was happening could be true. Not long ago, he remembered, he had told himself that falling in love with Karen would involve love without sex – in contrast to sex without love which he had experienced so often before. Was he wrong? With Karen could there conceivably be love *and* sex? But if it happened, surely he would be despicable, taking brutish advantage of her helplessness. Could he? Should he? The ethical issues seemed a nightmare tangle of unanswered questions, a moral labyrinth.

He had unbuttoned Karen's blouse. Now he raised her shoulders while he eased it from her arms. She wore no brassiere. Her small breasts were superbly shaped, the tiny nipples slightly raised.

'Touch me, Nimrod.' It was a soft command. Responding, he moved his hands lightly over her breasts, his fingertips caressing, then knelt and kissed them. At once he felt her nipples harden. Karen murmured, 'Oh, that's wonderful!'

A moment later she told him, 'The skirt unfastens on the left side.' Still gentle, he unbuttoned and removed it.

When Karen was naked, doubts and anxiety still plagued him. But he moved his hands, slowly and with skilful sensuality, as he knew by now she wanted. Soft murmurings made her pleasure clear. After a while she whispered, 'I want to tell you something.'

251

He whispered back, 'I'm listening.'

'I'm not a virgin. There was a boy . . . it happened when I was fifteen, just before I . . .' She stopped, and he saw that tears were rolling down her cheeks.'

'Karen, don't!'

She shook her head. 'I *want* to tell you. Because I want you to know there hasn't been anyone else in all those years; no one, between then – and you.'

He waited, letting the purport of what she had said sink in before he asked, 'Are you telling me . . . ?'

'I *want* you, Nimrod. *All the way*. Now!'

'Oh Christ!' Nim breathed the words, aware that his own desires – never difficult to unleash – were making themselves known in urgent terms. Then he threw the complex equations overboard and started taking off his clothes.

Nim had wondered, like others he supposed, how it would be for an unimpaired man to make sexual love to a quadriplegic woman. Would someone like Karen be totally passive? Would the man make all the effort, obtaining no response? And in the end would there be pleasure for one, or both, or neither?

He was discovering the answers, and all were unexpected.

Karen was demanding, responsive, exciting, satisfying.

Yes, in one sense she was passive. Her body, other than her head was unable to move. Yet Nim could feel the effect of their lovemaking transmitting itself through her skin, vagina, breasts, and most of all her passionate cries and kisses. It was not, he thought in a flash of whimsy, at all like having sex with a mannequin, as some might suppose. Nor was the pleasure brief. It was prolonged, as if neither wanted it to end. He had a sense, over and over, of glorious eroticism, of floating and soaring, of joy and loving, until at last, as always, the ending came. Attainment of a summit; climax of a symphony; the zenith of a dream. *And for them both*. Could a quadriplegic woman have an orgasm? Emphatically, *yes*!

And afterwards . . . once more . . . a return to tenderness and kindly loving.

Nim lay still, carefully considerate of Karen, blissful, spent. He wondered what she was thinking and if, in the aftermath, she had regrets.

As if telepathy had delivered both questions, Karen stirred.

She said drowsily but happily, 'Nimrod, a mighty hunter of the Lord.' Then : 'This day has been the best in all my life.'

4

Cynthia said, 'I had a hard day and I could use a drink. There's usually scotch around here. How about you?'

Nim told her, 'Count me in.' It was an hour since he had made love to Karen, who was now sleeping. He felt the need for a drink too.

Karen's older sister had come to the apartment twenty minutes ago, using her own key. Nim had finished dressing sometime earlier.

She had introduced herself as Cynthia Woolworth. 'Before you ask the question, no, my husband – unfortunately – is not connected with that wealthy family. I used to spend half my life answering that; now I get it out of the way at the beginning. Sloan was simpler.'

'Thank you,' he said. 'I'll never mention it again.'

Cynthia, he observed, was different from Karen, but also similar. Where Karen was blonde and slim, Cynthia was brunette, her figure full, though not excessively. Clearly, too, Cynthia's personality was more forceful and outgoing, though perhaps, Nim thought, the misfortune which life had dealt Karen early, and their differences in life styles since, could account for that. What both had in common was a rare natural beauty – the same delicate symmetry of features, full lips, wide blue eyes, a flawless skin and – more developed in Cynthia – elegant, slim hands. It occurred to Nim that both Sloan girls had inherited their charms from their mother, Henrietta, in whom traces of an earlier loveliness still lingered. Nim remembered that Cynthia was three years older than Karen, which made her forty-two, although she appeared younger.

Cynthia located the scotch, then ice and soda, and mixed two drinks efficiently. The quick economy of her movements showed she was used to managing for herself. She had demonstrated that from the time she arrived at the apartment, shook out her dripping raincoat and hung it in the bathroom, then following mutual introductions, instructed Nim, 'All right, you sit down and relax – here, I brought the evening paper – and I'll do what's needed for my sister.'

She had walked into Karen's bedroom, closing the door so that Nim could hear a murmur of voices, but no more.

When Cynthia came out fifteen minutes later, moving quietly, she announced that Karen was asleep.

Now, seated facing Nim, Cynthia swirled the liquor and ice in her glass and informed him, 'I know what happened here tonight. Karen told me.'

Startled by the directness, all he could think of in response was, 'I see.'

Cynthia threw back her head and laughed. She pointed an accusing finger. 'You're scared! You're wondering if I'll be the avenging elder sister. Or if I'll call the cops maybe, and holler "rape!" ' '

He said stiffly, 'I'm not sure I want, or need to discuss with you . . .'

'Oh, *come on*!' Cynthia had continued to laugh; now suddenly she stopped. Her face became serious. 'Look, Nimrod – if I can call you that – I'm sorry if I embarrassed you, and I can see I did. So now let me tell you something. Karen thinks you're a kind, sweet, gentle, loving man, and the best thing that's ever happened to her. And if you're interested in an outside opinion, I feel the same way.'

Nim stared at her. As he did, he realized that for the second time tonight he was seeing a woman cry.

'Damn! I didn't mean to do that.' With a tiny handkerchief Cynthia wiped her tears away. 'But I guess I'm as happy and satisfied as Karen is herself.' She regarded Nim in frank approval. 'Well, almost.'

Nim's tension of a moment earlier dissolved. Grinning, he acknowledged, 'I can only say one thing. I'll be damned!'

'I can say more than that, and will,' Cynthia said. 'How about another drink first?'

Without waiting for an answer she scooped up Nim's glass

and replenished it, along with her own. Returning to her seat, she sipped the scotch before continuing, carefully choosing her words.

'For your sake, Nimrod, as much as Karen's, I want you to realize something. What happened between you and my sister tonight was wonderful and beautiful. You may not know this, or understand it, but some people treat quadriplegics the way they would a leper. I've seen it happen sometimes; Karen sees it more. That's why, in my book, you come out as Mr Nice Guy. You've never thought of her, or treated her, as anything but a woman . . . Oh, for God's sake! . . . Here I am crying again.'

Cynthia's handkerchief was clearly inadequate. Nim handed her his own and she glanced at him gratefully. 'It's the little things you do . . . Karen told me that . . .'

He said humbly, 'It all started, you know – my coming to see Karen – accidentally.'

'Most things do.'

'And what went on between us tonight . . . well, I didn't plan it. I didn't even think . . .' Nim stopped. 'It simply happened.'

'I know that,' Cynthia said. 'And while we're about it, let me ask you something else. Did you – do you – have any guilt feelings?'

He nodded. 'Yes.'

'Don't! I read something once, when I was finding out how I could best help Karen, by a man named Milton Diamond. He's a medical professor in Hawaii who made a study of sex and disabled people. I may not have the words exactly right, but the sense of what he wrote was : *The disabled have enough problems without having conventional guilt-laden values forced on them . . . private sexual satisfaction takes precedence over public approval; therefore any guilt is wrong . . . and sexually, for disabled people, anything goes.*' Cynthia added almost fiercely, 'So don't *you* have any guilts either. Wipe them out!'

'I'm not sure,' Nim said, 'if I can take any more surprises tonight. Just the same, I'm glad we talked.'

'I am too. It's a part of learning, and I had to learn about Karen, just as you have.' Cynthia continued sipping her scotch, then said meditatively, 'Would you believe me if I told you that when Karen was eighteen and I was twenty-one I hated her?'

'I'd find it hard to believe.'

'Well, it's true. I hated her because she got all the attention from our parents and their friends. Some days, at home, it was as if I didn't exist. It was always, *Karen this, and Karen that! What can we do for dear, poor Karen?* Never, *What can we do for healthy, normal Cynthia?* It was my twenty-first birthday. I wanted a big party, but my mother said it was "inappropriate" because of Karen. So we had a little family tea – just my parents and me; Karen was in the hospital then – a lousy *tea*, and a shoddy, cheap little cake. As for my birthday presents, they were just tokens because guess where all the available money was going, every cent. I'm ashamed to say it, but that night I prayed for Karen to die.'

In the silence which followed, even through drawn curtains, Nim could hear wind-driven rain against the window. He had understood what Cynthia had told him, and was moved. Yet, in a corner of his mind he thought: glorious rain! To a utilities man, rain, sleet or snow meant stored-up hydroelectric power for the dry season ahead. He pulled back his thoughts and spoke to Cynthia.

'So when did your feelings change?'

'Not for years, and even then slowly. Before that I went through my own guilt period. I felt guilty because I was whole and Karen wasn't. Guilty because I could do the things she couldn't – play tennis, go to parties, neck with boys.' Cynthia sighed. 'I wasn't a good sister.'

'But you are now.'

'As much as I can be – after taking care of a husband, house and kids. It was after my first child was born that I began to understand and appreciate my little sister and we became close. Now the two of us are dear, loving friends, sharing ideas and confidences. There isn't anything I wouldn't do for Karen. And there isn't anything she doesn't tell me.'

Nim said drily, 'I'd gathered that.'

They talked on. Cynthia told him more about herself. She had married at twenty-two; one reason was to get away from home. Since then her husband had held a succession of jobs; his present one was as a shoe salesman. Nim surmised that the marriage was barely adequate, if that, and Cynthia and her husband stayed together for lack of an alternative and the sake of their three children. Before her marriage, Cynthia had taken singing lessons;

now, four nights a week she sang in a second-rate night club to supplement her husband's meagre pay. Tonight was a non-singing night and Cynthia would stay with Karen, her husband taking care of their one child still at home. Cynthia had two more scotches while they talked; Nim declined. After a while her voice became slightly slurred.

At length Nim stood up. 'It's late. I have to go.'

'I'll get your raincoat,' Cynthia said. 'You'll need it, even going to your car.' She added, 'Or you can stay if you want. There's a couch makes up into a bed.'

'Thanks. I'd better not.'

She helped him on with the coat and, at the apartment front door, kissed him fully on the lips. 'That's partly for Karen,' Cynthia said, 'partly for me.'

Driving home, he tried to push the thought away as being predatory and disloyal, but it persisted: so many attractive, desirable women in the world, and so many available and willing to share sexual pleasures. Experience, instinct, her own unmistakable signals told him: Cynthia was available too.

5

Among other things, Nim Goldman was a wine buff. He had a keen nose and palate and especially liked varietal wines from the Napa Valley, which were California's finest and in good years rated with the premium wines of France. So he was glad to go to the Napa Valley with Eric Humphrey – even in late November – though he wondered why the chairman had invited him along.

The occasion was to celebrate a homecoming. An honoured, victorious, sentimental homecoming of one of California's most distinguished sons.

The Honorable Paul Sherman Yale.

Until two weeks earlier he had been a revered Associate Justice of the United States Supreme Court.

If ever a single individual merited the accolade 'Mr California', unquestionably it was Paul Sherman Yale. All that a Californian might wish or strive to be had been exemplified in his distinguished career, now drawing to a close.

Since his early twenties when – two years ahead of most contemporaries – he was graduated with honours from Stanford Law School, until his eightieth birthday, which he recently celebrated, Paul Yale had filled a succession of increasingly important public roles. As a young lawyer he established a statewide reputation as a champion of the poor and powerless. He sought, and won, a seat in the California Assembly and, after two terms there, moved up to become the youngest member ever elected to the state Senate. His legislative record in both houses was remarkable. He was the author of early legislation to protect minorities and outlaw sweat-shops. He also sponsored laws which aided California farmers and fishermen.

Moving on from the Senate, Paul Sherman Yale was elected the state's Attorney General, in which office he declared war on organized crime and sent some of its big-name practitioners to jail. A logical next step was to Governor, a post he could have had for the asking. Instead he accepted President Truman's invitation to fill a vacancy on the US Supreme Court. His Senate confirmation hearings were brief, their outcome a foregone conclusion since – both then and later – no breath of scandal or corruption ever touched his name, and another sobriquet sometimes applied to him was 'Mr Integrity'.

While serving on the highest court, he wrote many opinions which reflected his broad humanity, yet were praised by legal scholars as being 'pure law'. Even his dissents were widely quoted, and some prompted legislative changes. Amidst it all, Mr Justice Yale never forgot that he and his wife Beth were Californians and, at every opportunity, declared his continuing affection for his native state.

When in due season, he concluded that his work was done, he resigned quietly and the Yales left Washington, typically without fuss, returning – as Paul Yale expressed it to *Newsweek* – 'westward and home'. He turned down the suggestion of a massive testimonial banquet in Sacramento, yet consented to a more modest welcome luncheon in his beloved birthplace, the Napa Valley, where the Yales planned to live.

Among the guests – at Yale's suggestion – was the chairman of Golden State Power & Light. Humphrey requested, and obtained, an extra invitation for his assistant, Nim.

En route to Napa Valley in the chairman's chauffeur-driven limousine, Humphrey was affable while he and Nim worked on plans and problems, as was usual on such journeys. It was obvious that the chairman had put his displeasure with Nim behind him. The purpose of their present journey was not mentioned.

Even with winter close at hand, and several weeks after harvest time, the valley was extraordinarily beautiful. It was a clear, crisp, sunny day, following several days of rain. Already early shoots of bright yellow mustard weed were growing between the rows of grapevines – now stark and leafless, and soon to be pruned in readiness for next season. Within the next few weeks the mustard would grow in profusion, then be ploughed under to fertilize and, some said, add a special pungency to the flavour of grapes and wine.

'Notice the spacing of the vines,' Humphrey said; he had put aside his work as they entered the central portion of the valley where vineyards stretched far into the distance to the lush green hills on either side. 'The spacing's much wider than it used to be. That's for mechanical harvesting – the grape growers' way of beating the unions. The union leaders cheated their own members out of jobs by empire building and intransigence, so labour will soon be minimal here, with most jobs done by machine, and more efficiently.'

They passed through the township of Yountville. A few miles further, between Oakville and Rutherford, they turned through an entranceway, framed by adobe-coloured curving walls, into the mission-style Robert Mondavi Winery, where the luncheon would be held.

The guest of honour and his wife had arrived early, and were in the winery's elegant Vineyard Room, ready to greet others as they came. Humphrey, who had met the Yales several times before, introduced Nim.

Paul Sherman Yale was small, spry and upright, with thinning white hair, intense grey eyes which seemed to bore into whatever they were looking at, and a general liveliness which belied his eighty years. To Nim's surprise he said, 'I've been looking forward to meeting you, young man. Before you go back to the city we'll find a corner somewhere and have a talk.'

Beth Yale, a warm, gracious woman who had married her husband more than fifty years ago when he was a young Assemblyman, and she his secretary, told Nim, 'I think you'll enjoy working with Paul. Most people do.'

As soon as he could, Nim eased Humphrey aside. Low-voiced, he asked, 'Eric, what's happening? What's all this about?'

'I made a promise,' Humphrey said. 'If I told you, I'd be breaking it. Just wait.'

As the arriving guests multiplied and the line of those waiting to shake hands with the Yales lengthened, the sense of occasion grew. It seemed as if the entire Napa Valley had turned out to pay its homage. Nim recognized faces attached to some of the great names of California wine making: Louis Martini, Joe Heitz, Jack Davies of Schramsberg, today's host Robert Mondavi, Peter Mondavi of Krug, André Tchelistcheff, Brother Timothy of Christian Brothers, Donn Chappellet, others. The Governor, who was out of the state, had sent the Lieutenant Governor as his representative. The media had arrived in force, including TV camera crews.

The occasion, which had been billed as private and informal, would be viewed or read about by most Californians tonight and tomorrow.

Lunch – with Napa Valley wines, of course – was followed by introductory speeches, mercifully brief. A toast to Paul and Beth Yale was drunk; a spontaneous standing ovation followed. The guest of honour rose, smiling, to respond. He spoke for a half hour – warmly, simply, eloquently – a casual, easy talk with friends. There was nothing earth-shattering, no strident revelations, simply the words of the local boy at last come home. 'I am not entirely ready to die,' he said. 'Who is? But when I leave for eternity, I want to board the bus from here.'

The kicker came at the end.

'Until that bus arrives, I intend to be active and, I hope, useful. There is a job I have been told that I can do and which may be of service to California. After due thought, and consultation with my wife, who was uneasy about having me at home all day anyway ... [*Laughter*] ... I have agreed to join the staff of Golden State Power & Light. Not as a meter reader; unfortunately my eyesight is failing ... [*More laughter*] ... but as a member of the board and a public spokesman for the company. In deference to my hoary old age I am being allowed to set my own office hours, so I shall probably arrive – on the days I choose to show up at all – in time for an expense account lunch . . . [*Loud laughter*] . . . My new boss, Mr Eric Humphrey, is here today, probably to collect my Social Security number and employment record . . . [*Laughter and cheers*].'

There was more of the same.

Afterwards, Humphrey would inform Nim: 'The old boy insisted on secrecy while he and I were negotiating, and then he wanted to make the announcement himself in his own way. It's why I couldn't tell you in advance, even though you are the one who will work with him in helping him get oriented.'

Meanwhile, as Mr Justice Yale (he would retain the title for the remainder of his life) concluded his speech and sat down to sustained applause, reporters crowded around Eric Humphrey. 'We have yet to work out full details,' Humphrey told them, 'but essentially Mr Yale's role will be as he described it – a spokesman for our company, both to the public and before commissioners and legislators.'

Humphrey looked pleased as he answered reporters' questions – as well he might, Nim thought. Lassoing Paul Sherman Yale, bringing him into the GSP & L orbit, was a tremendous coup. Not only did Yale have built-in public credence, but every official door in California, from the Governor's downwards, was open to him. Clearly, what he would be was a lobbyist of highest calibre, though Nim was certain the word 'lobbyist' would never be spoken in his presence.

Already, the TV crews were manoeuvring GSP & L's new spokesman into position for a statement. It would be one of many, Nim supposed – some of them the kind of statements Nim himself might have continued making if he hadn't blown it. Watching it happen, he felt a pang of envy and regret.

6

'Apart from anything else,' Beth Yale told Nim with a frankness he would later find characteristic, 'we can use the money. No one gets rich being on the Supreme Court, and living in Washington is so expensive we rarely managed to save anything. Paul's grandfather did set up a family trust fund, but it's been horribly mismanaged . . . Would you mind putting on another log?'

They were seated before a fieldstone fireplace in a small, comfortable house located in a vineyard, a mile or so from where they had had lunch. The house had been loaned to the Yales by its owner, who used it during summers, until they were able to locate a place of their own.

Nim added a log to the fire and stirred two others, partially burned, to a cheerful blaze.

A half hour ago Mr Justice Yale had excused himself to have, as he put it, 'a battery charge catnap'. He explained, 'It's a trick I learned many years ago when I found my attention wandering. Some of my colleagues even do it on the bench.'

Before that they had talked for more than two hours about the affairs of Golden State Power & Light.

The 'talk in a corner' with Nim, which Paul Yale had spoken of before the luncheon, and had not happened for the reason that there was no way he could escape his admirers while he remained at the Mondavi winery. He had therefore suggested that Nim come back to the house. 'If I'm going to do something, young man, I like to get moving. Eric tells me you can supply the best overall view of your company, so let us start viewing.'

They had done precisely that. While Nim described the status, policies and problems of GSP & L, Paul Yale injected sharp, pertinent questions. Nim found it a stimulating mental exercise, in a way like playing chess with a skilled opponent. And Yale's remarkable memory astounded him. The old man seemed to have forgotten nothing of his earlier days in California and his knowledge of GSP & L history at times exceeded Nim's.

While her husband was having his 'battery charge', Beth Yale served tea before the fire. Soon after, Paul Yale reappeared.

He announced, 'I heard you talking about the family trust.'

His wife put fresh water into the teapot and set a cup before him. 'I've always said you have ears which reach around corners.'

'That's from years in court – straining to hear lawyers when they mumble. You'd be surprised how many do.' Paul Yale addressed Nim. 'That trust fund Beth spoke of was set up because my grandfather hoped public service would become a tradition in our family. He believed anyone who travelled that route should not have to worry about having an adequate income. It's not a fashionable viewpoint nowadays, but I happen to agree. I've seen too many people in Washington's high places have to scratch around for extra money. It leaves them open to temptations.'

The Justice drank the tea his wife had poured, and observed, 'A civilized custom, afternoon tea. It's something we owe the British; that, and the great body of our law.' He put his cup down. 'Anyway, as Beth said, the trust fund has been mismanaged. While I was on the Court there was nothing I could do, but now I've begun to repair some of the damage.' He chuckled. 'That is, as well as working for GSP & L.'

'It isn't for ourselves,' Beth Yale added. 'But we have grandchildren who show signs of going into public life. It may help them later.'

Nim sensed that the family trust fund was a sore point with the Yales. Confirming this, Paul Yale grumbled, 'The trust owns a winery, a cattle feedlot, two apartment buildings in the city and – can you believe it? – all of them have been losing money, creating debts, eating into capital. Last week I leaned hard on the administrator – read him the riot act about cutting down expenses.' He stopped abruptly. 'Beth, we're boring this young man with our family problems. Let's get back to God's Power & Love.'

Nim laughed at the name, used by old-timers in the state for GSP & L.

'I'm concerned, as I'm sure you are, about all the sabotage and killings that have been going on,' Paul Yale said. 'The people who claim responsibility – what is it they call themselves?'

'Friends of Freedom.'

'Ah, yes. An interesting exercise in logic : "Be free *my* way or I'll blow you to pieces." Are the police any closer to tracking them down, do you know?'

'Apparently not.'

'Why do those people do it?' Beth Yale asked. 'That's what's so hard to understand.'

'A few of us at the company have done some thinking and talking about that,' Nim told her.

Paul Yale asked, 'What kind of thinking?'

Nim hesitated. He had mentioned the subject on impulse and now, under Mr Justice Yale's penetrating gaze, he wished he hadn't. However, the question had to be answered.

Nim explained the police theory that the Friends of Freedom group was small, with one man the brains and leader. 'Assuming that to be true, we thought that if we could get, even partially, inside the mind of the leader – we call him "X" – we'd improve our chances of catching him. We might even get lucky, guess what he would plan next, and be ready.'

What Nim did not say was that the idea had occurred to him after the latest bombings when the security guards were murdered. Since then he, Harry London, Teresa Van Buren and Oscar O'Brien had met three times for lengthy brainstorming sessions and, while nothing positive had developed, all four felt they were moving closer to an understanding of the unknown saboteurs and 'X'. O'Brien, who still harboured hostility to Nim because of the Tunipah hearings, had opposed the suggestion at first, calling it 'time wasting'. But later the general counsel relented and joined in. He was something of a scholar and, with his sharp lawyer's mind, contributed substantially to the discussions.

'You've assumed your "X" is a man,' Paul Yale said. 'Have you considered the possibility of a woman?'

'Yes, but the odds favour a man, mainly because those tape recordings, received after every bombing, are of a man's voice and it's a reasonable assumption he is "X". Also we concluded that in history almost all leaders of armed revolutions have been men; psychologists say women's minds are too logical and the details of revolution seldom make sense. Joan of Arc was an exception.'

Paul Yale smiled. 'What other theories do you have?'

'Well, even though the leader isn't a woman, we're convinced there is a woman in the so-called Friends of Freedom, and almost certainly she's close to "X".'

'Why do you believe that?'

'For several reasons. Number one, "X" is extremely vain. The tape recordings show that clearly; our "think group" played all of them many times. Number two, he's strongly masculine. One thing we listened for was any hint of homosexuality, either in intonation or words. There wasn't any. On the contrary the tone, the choice of words . . . well, the description we all came up with after playing the tapes over and over was "a young, robust male".'

Beth Yale had been listening intently. Now she said, 'So your "X" is macho. Where does that lead you?'

'To a woman, we believe,' Nim answered. 'Our reasoning was that a man like "X" would need to have a woman around; he couldn't exist without one. Also, she has to be a confidante – for the practical reason that she would be close, also because his vanity demands it. Look at it this way : "X" sees himself as a heroic figure, which is something else the tapes show. Therefore he would want his woman to view him the same way. So that's another reason she has to know about, and probably share in, what he's doing.'

'Well,' Paul Yale said, 'you certainly have an abundance of theories.' He sounded amused and sceptical. 'I'd say, though, you've pushed supposition – pure conjecture, unsubstantiated – to the limits and beyond.'

Nim conceded, 'Yes, I suppose we have.' He felt embarrassed, foolish. In light of a Supreme Court Justice's reaction, all that he had just related seemed unconvincing, even absurd – especially now that he was away from the other three. He decided not to pass on the remainder of the think group's conclusions, though they were clear in his own mind.

The police were convinced, because of the modus operandi and a hint in the latest tape recording, that the Friends of Freedom leader, 'X', was the actual murderer of the two guards. The quartet of Nim, London, Van Buren and O'Brien, after discussion, shared that view. Furthermore, they had argued at length among themselves and now believed that 'X''s woman was at the murder site. Their eventual reasoning: The project had been 'X''s most ambitious to date and, consciously or subconsciously, he would have wanted her to see him in action. Which made her not only a witness but an accessory to murder.

So how did that knowledge – or, rather, supposition – put them closer to learning the identity of 'X'?

The answer: It didn't. But it revealed a potential weakness, a

vulnerability, of 'X', to be exploited. How to exploit it, if at all,
was something unresolved.

Now, Nim thought, it all seemed way, way out.

He decided: Paul Yale's assessment was probably the kind of cold douche they all needed. Tomorrow he would consider dropping the whole 'think tank' idea, leaving detective work where it belonged – with the police, FBI, and various sheriff's departments, all of whom were working on the Friends of Freedom case.

His thoughts were interrupted by arrival of the Yales' housekeeper, who reported, 'A car for Mr Goldman has arrived.'

'Thank you,' Nim said. He rose to leave. A second company limousine had been ordered for him from the city since Eric Humphrey, who had a later engagement, had left the valley immediately after lunch.

Nim told the Yales, 'It was a privilege to meet you both. And when you need me again, sir, I'm available.'

'I'm sure I will soon,' Paul Yale said, 'and I enoyed our talk.' His eyes twinkled. 'At least, the substantial part of it.'

Nim resolved mentally that in future, when dealing with someone of Paul Sherman Yale's stature, he would confine himself to solid facts.

7

The big break, for Harry London, came swiftly and unexpectedly.

The Property Protection chief was in his small, glass cubicle office – the department had still not been given permanent quarters and continued to operate in makeshift space – when he heard his secretary's telephone ring outside. A moment later his own extension buzzed.

He picked up the phone lazily because that was how he felt. The past two months had been a desultory period in which nothing major had occurred concerning theft of service. Routine pre-

vailed. In late summer a computer study had revealed a stagger-
ing thirty thousand possible cases of power theft and, since then,
London, his deputy Art Romeo, and their staff – now increased
to five investigators – had been checking out the suspect cases
one by one. As Harry London knew from his experience as a
Los Angeles detective, it was like most police work – plodding,
repetitious, wearying. And results were mixed.

About ten per cent of the investigations so far had produced
sufficient evidence for GSP & L to charge customers with cheating and to claim payment for estimated arrears. Another ten per
cent showed changes in consumption levels to be for valid
reasons, such as genuine conservation, the consumers innocent.
The remainder of cases were inconclusive.

Of the provable cases, only a handful had been sufficiently
serious to merit prosecution.

To all concerned the task seemed slow and endless. Which was
why Harry London, his chair tilted back, feet up on the desk,
had reached a state of ennui on this particular mid-December
afternoon.

'Yeah?' he said into the phone.

A whispering, barely audible voice inquired, 'This Mr London?'

'Yes, it is.'

'This here's Ernie, janitor at the Zaco Building. Mr Romeo
said to call him or you if them guys come back. They're here
now.'

Harry London's feet hit the floor like slingshots. He snapped
upright in his chair. 'The same ones who bypassed the meters?'

'It's them all right. They come in a truck, same's before.
They're workin' now. Listen, cain't stay on this phone more'n a
minute.'

'You don't have to,' London said, 'so listen carefully. Get the
licence number of that truck.'

'Already got it.'

'Great! Now, some of us will be down there as fast as we can
make it. While we're on the way, don't do anything to make those
men suspicious, but if they start to leave, try to keep them talking.' While speaking, London pressed a button summoning his
secretary.

The caller, still whispering, sounded doubtful. 'Do it if I can.
Listen, Mr Romeo said I'd get paid if . . .'

'You'll get yours, my friend. That's a promise. Now just do what I said. I'm leaving now.' London slammed down the phone.

His secretary, a young, bright Chinese-American named Suzy, was standing in the doorway. He told her, 'I need help from the city police. Phone Lieutenant Wineski; you know where to get him. If Wineski isn't available, ask someone else in the Detective Division to meet me at the Zaco Building. Say the case I told Wineski about is breaking. Then try to get Art Romeo. Tell him the same thing, and to bust his ass and get to Zaco. Got it?'

'I have it, Mr London,' Suzy said.

'Good kid!' London hurried out and ran for the elevator which would take him to the basement parking garage.

Going down, he calculated that with fast driving and reasonable traffic he could be at the Zaco Building in ten minutes or less.

Harry London's estimate overlooked two factors – early commuter traffic out of the city and Christmas shoppers, clogging downtown streets and slowing movement to a crawl. It took him a frustrating twenty minutes to reach the Zaco Building, which was on the opposite side of the city's business district.

As he pulled up, he recognized an unmarked police car which had preceded him by seconds only. Two men in plain clothes were getting out. One was Lieutenant Wineski. London blessed his good luck. Wineski was a friend, a police officer whom London had cultivated and whose presence would save time-wasting explanations.

Lieutenant Wineski had seen London and was waiting, the other officer beside him. The second man was a detective named Brown whom London knew slightly.

'What gives, Harry?' Wineski was young, smart, ambitious; he kept his body trim and, unlike most of his detective colleagues, dressed well. He also liked unusual cases because, more often than not, they brought publicity. Around police headquarters the guessing was that Boris Wineski would go high in the force, possibly to the top.

London answered, 'A hot tip, Boris. Let's go.' Together the trio hurried across the forecourt of the building.

Two decades earlier the twenty-three storey, reinforced-concrete Zaco Building had been modern and fashionable, the kind of place where a topflight brokerage house or advertising agency might have rented several floors. Now, like other office structures of its genre, it was showing signs of seediness, and some of the first-class tenants had moved to newer buildings where glass and aluminium predominated. Most of the Zaco Building's space was still rented, but to less prestigious tenants. It was a safe assumption that the building was less profitable than in its heyday.

All of this Harry London knew from earlier investigation.

The building's lobby, of imitation marble, with a bank of elevators facing the main entrance, was beginning to fill with departing office workers. Dodging the outgoing flow, London led the way to an inconspicuous metal door which he knew, from a surreptitious previous visit, opened onto a stairway providing access to three lower floors.

On the way in he had given the two detectives a quick summary of the phone call twenty-five minutes earlier. Now, hurrying down cement stairs shielded by fire doors, he found himself praying that the men they were seeking had not already left.

Something else the Property Protection chief knew was that the extensive electric and gas metering and controls were on the lowest floor. From there the building's general power supplies were monitored – for heating, elevator operation, air conditioning and lighting.

Near the foot of the last stairway a thin, gaunt man in coveralls, with unkempt sandy hair and a stubble of beard, appeared to be inspecting garbage cans. He looked up, then abandoned what he was doing and came forward as Harry London and the detectives clattered down.

'Mr London?' Unmistakably it was the same weak voice as on the telephone.

'Right. You Ernie, the janitor?'

The man in coveralls nodded. 'Sure took your time.'

'Never mind that. Those men still here?'

'Inside.' The janitor motioned to a metal door, similar to others on the floors above.

'How many?'

'Three. Listen, how 'bout my money?'

'For Chrissake!' London said impatiently. 'You'll get it.'

Lieutenant Wineski cut in. 'Is anybody else in there?'

The janitor, looking surly, shook his head. 'Ain't nobody else down here but me.'

'All right.' Wineski moved forward, taking command. He told the other detective and London, 'We'll do this fast, Harry, you come in last. When we're inside, stay back by the door until I tell you.' To the janitor: 'You wait out here.' Wineski put a hand on the metal door then ordered, 'Now!'

As the door flew open, the trio rushed in.

Inside, against an interior wall some twenty-five feet away, three men were working. Afterwards Harry London would report with relish: 'If we'd mailed 'em a list, with specifications of how we'd like the evidence laid out, they couldn't have done better.'

An electric current transformer cabinet – installed, then locked by GSP & L – was open. Several transformer switches, it was discovered later, had been opened, bound with insulating tape, then closed. The effect was to reduce electric meter recordings by a third. A few feet away a gas meter had an illegal bypass partially exposed. Supplies and tools for the work being done were spread around – insulated pliers, socket wrenches, lead disc seals and a mechanic's seal press (both stolen from GSP & L), and the transformer cabinet casing with a key – also stolen – in its lock.

Wineski announced in a loud, clear voice, 'We are police officers.' He ordered, 'Don't move! Leave everything where it is.'

At the sound of the opening door, two of the men working had spun around. The third, who was lying full length and working on the gas meter bypass, rolled sideways to see what was happening, then shifted quickly to a crouch. All three were wearing neat, uniform-type coveralls with shoulder patches bearing the intertwined initials QEGC which later inquiry would enlarge to Quayle Electrical & Gas Contracting.

Of the two men nearest the entry door, one was huge, bearded, and with the physique of a wrestler. His forearms, where the sleeves were rolled back, showed bulging muscles. The other was young – he seemed little more than a boy – with a narrow, sharp-featured face. It registered instant fright.

The big, bearded man was less intimidated. Ignoring the command not to move, he grabbed a heavy pipe wrench, raised it, and leaped forwards.

Harry London, who had stayed back as instructed, saw Wineski reach swiftly under his coat; an instant later a gun was in his hand. The detective rapped out, 'I'm a crack shot. If you move another foot I'll put a bullet in your leg.' As the bearded giant hesitated: 'Drop the wrench – *now*!'

The other detective, Brown, had produced a gun also, and reluctantly the would-be attacker obeyed.

'You by the wall!' Wineski snapped; the third man, older than the other two, was now standing upright and looked as if he would try to run. 'Don't start anything! Just turn around and face that wall! You other two – join him, do the same.'

Scowling, with hatred in his eyes, the bearded man moved back. The youthful workman, his face white, his body visibly trembling, had already hurried to comply.

There was a pause in which three sets of handcuffs clicked.

'All right, Harry,' Wineski called over. 'Now tell us what all this stuff means.'

'It's the kind of solid evidence we've been looking for,' the Property Protection chief assured him. 'Proof of big-time electric and gas stealing.'

'You'll swear to that in court?'

'Sure will. So will others. We'll give you as many expert witnesses as you want.'

'Good enough.'

Wineski addressed the three handcuffed men. 'Keep facing the wall but listen carefully. You are all under arrest and I am required to advise you of your rights. You are not obliged to make a statement. However, if you do . . .'

When the words of the familiar Miranda ritual were finished, Wineski motioned Brown and London to join him by the outer door. Keeping his voice low, he told them, 'I want to split these birds. From the look of him, the kid's ready to break; he may talk. Brownie, get to a phone. Call in for another car.'

'Right.' The second detective put away his gun and went out. The door to the stairway was now open and, moments later, hurrying feet could be heard coming down. As London and Wineski swung towards the doorway, Art Romeo appeared and the two relaxed.

Harry London told his deputy, 'Pay dirt. Take a look.'

The little man who, as usual, looked like a shifty underworld character himself, surveyed the scene and whistled softly.

Lieutenant Wineski, who had known Romeo before he worked for GSP & L, told him, 'If that's camera equipment you've got, better start shooting.'

'Will do, Lieutenant.' Romeo unslung a black leather case

from his shoulder and began assembling a photoflash unit.

While he was taking several dozen photographs, from various angles, of the spread-out equipment and uncompleted illegal work, police reinforcements arrived – two uniformed officers, accompanied by the returning Detective Brown.

A few minutes later the arrested men were led out – the youngest, still frightened, first and separately. While one uniformed officer remained to guard the evidence. Wineski followed. He told Harry London with a wink, 'Want to question that kid myself. Let you know what happens.'

8

'Wineski was dead right,' Harry London informed Nim Goldman. 'The kid – he was eighteen, by the way, and not long out of trade school – broke down and spilled his guts. Then Wineski and Brown used what he told them to pry more information out of the other two.'

It was four days after the confrontation and arrests at the Zaco Building. Immediately following those events London had reported briefly to Nim. Now, as Nim's guest at lunch in the officers' dining room at GSP & L headquarters, he was supplying further details.

'Go ahead,' Nim said, 'tell me more.' They had paused to enjoy large mouthfuls of lamb stew – a popular 'special of the day' for which the chef was noted.

'Well, according to Boris Wineski, when they questioned the big guy – his name is Kasner – he didn't talk much. He's streetwise, has an arrest record, no convictions. The older one, who was working on the gas bypass, let out a few things we didn't know, then he clammed up too. By that time, though, it didn't matter. The police had all the important information – and their truck.'

'Oh, yes, the truck. Did the police impound it?'

'Damn right!' Not surprisingly, London sounded happy; he

had been in an upbeat mood for the past few days. 'That truck was loaded up with even more evidence of illegality than was left around in the Zaco Building. There were electric meters, seals, locking rings and keys, meter-size jumper cables, you name it. And almost all the stuff was stolen – naturally. You can't buy those items on the open market. One thing we now believe is that the Quayle people have a helper right here in the company who has been their source of supply. We're working on the accomplice angle.'

'That Quayle outfit,' Nim queried. 'What's been found out about them?'

'Plenty. First, there was enough damaging stuff on the truck and in the Zaco Building for Wineski to ask for a warrant to search the Quayle offices. He did ask, and he got it fast. Result: the police were in there before the Quayle people even knew their men had been arrested.'

'Don't let your stew get cold,' Nim said. 'It's good.'

'Sure is. Fix it so that I eat here more often, would you?'

'Go on getting the kind of results you did last week, and you could be up here regularly before you know it.'

The dining room, reserved for company vice presidents and above, and their guests, was modest in size and decor, so as not to create an impression of opulence when outsiders were brought in. But the food was exceptional. Its quality far exceeded that of the general staff cafeteria located on a lower floor.

'Getting back to Quayle Electrical & Gas,' London said, 'first they've got a legit business – good size, with a fleet of twenty-five trucks. They also have a string of subcontractors, smaller firms, to whom they farm out work. The way it looks now – and again I'm quoting Lieutenant Wineski – is that Quayle has used the legitimate side of its business as a cover for power stealing, which they've been into in a big way. There was a lot more material on their premises – the same kind of stuff that was on the truck they sent to Zaco.'

'Tell me one thing,' Nim said. 'If a company like Quayle was legit to begin with, why in God's name would they get into power theft?'

London shrugged. 'The oldest reason: money. Some of this is guesswork, but the way the pieces are coming together it looks as if Quayle – like a lot of businesses nowadays – has had trouble

273

making a profit because of high costs. But the illegal stuff shows a *big* profit. Why? Because they can charge maybe five, six, seven times what they would for ordinary work. And the outfits they do it for – like the Zaco Building – are glad to pay because they expect even bigger savings in *their* costs. Something else you have to remember, Nim, is that until recently it's all been easy, a pushover; they've gotten away with it.'

'The way it all sounds,' Nim said, 'there's still a good deal to unravel?'

'A big ball of yarn,' London acknowledged. 'And it could be months before the whole picture becomes clear. Right now, though, two things are helping. One, the DA's office is really interested; they've put a prosecutor on the case and Wineski's working with him. Two, the Quayle outfit kept detailed records of all its jobs, and those of subcontractors too.'

Nim asked, 'And the police have those records?'

'Right – except the DA may have them by now. They turned up in the search. Only trouble is, there's nothing to show what work was legitimate, and what was illegal. That's where my department, my people, are helping out.'

'In what way?'

'We're checking every job that the Quayle outfit did in the past year. Something their records – work orders – show is precisely what materials were used in each case. If we can show they were stolen or used for illegal purposes – and in a lot of instances it looks as if we can – the DA will have a big, fat, prosecutable case.'

Nim ruminated, digesting the information he had been given. He asked, 'How about the company that owns the Zaco Building, and other people Quayle did illegal work for? Presumably we'll be going after them too?'

'Damn right we are! There should be records of payments to Quayle Electrical in the books of Zaco and the others, which opens up another whole side to the case.' London's voice reflected mounting enthusiasm. 'I'm telling you, Nim, we've uncovered a fat rat's nest. I predict some big names in this town will have mud on them before all this is over.'

'The chairman will want a detailed report,' Nim said. 'And progress reports later.'

'He'll get them. So will you.'

'How about staff? Can you handle all this with the people you have now?'

'Not sure yet, Nim. I may need some help. If so, I'll let you know next week.'

'What's happened to the three men who were arrested?'

'They're out on bail. The police are protecting the kid, hiding him, because they intend to use him as a prosecution witness. By the way, one thing he let out was that only *some* of the Quayle crews – the trusted ones – have been doing power theft installations. If we can narrow that down to *which* crews, it should make investigation easier.'

'Just one thing puzzles me,' Nim said. 'Since the illegal work at the Zaco Building was already done, why did the Quayle crew go back?'

'That's one great big laugh,' London answered. 'A laugh on them. That way the kid heard it, and told Wineski, somebody in charge at Zaco heard a rumble about our snooping – Art Romeo's and mine. It had them worried. So they decided *not to steal as much,* and what those three guys were doing was modifying the work they'd done earlier. If they'd left well enough alone, we could have stewed for ever, waiting.'

'Speaking of stew,' Nim said, 'have some more.'

Later that afternoon, while Nim was with J. Eric Humphrey in the chairman's office suite, he described the substance of the Property Protection chief's report. 'You could think of it as a small Christmas present,' Nim said.

Humphrey expressed brief approval, smiled at the reference to Christmas, which was five days away, then let the subject drop. As Nim was aware, other matters were weighing more heavily on the chairman's mind.

One was Tunipah. Another was water. A third was oil.

Hearings on GSP & L's Tunipah licence application before the California Energy Commission were proceeding even more slowly than anticipated, their pace described by Oscar O'Brien the day before : 'A snail by comparison is supersonic.' Clearly it would be months before the present, first stage of hearings was concluded, with the prospect of subsequent stages stretching on for years. Coupled with that, the other related hearings – before the Public Utilities Commission, Water Quality Resources

Board, and Air Resources Board – had not even begun.

As a result, O'Brien had now revised his earlier estimate that licensing procedures would take six to seven years. 'The way things are going,' he reported yesterday, 'it could be eight years, even ten, before we get permission to start construction. Assuming we ever do.'

As to other proposed generating plants, including Devil's Gate pumped storage and Fincastle geothermal, progress was equally, dispiritingly slow.

And all the while, as Eric Humphrey, Nim, and others in the GSP & L hierarchy realized, a day of reckoning was drawing closer; a day when public demands for electric power would surpass by far what could be produced with existing facilities. On that day and beyond, the unbuilt plants of Tunipah, Fincastle, Devil's Gate, *et al*, would be desperately, but vainly, longed for.

Water was the second reason for the chairman's concern.

Despite two winter storms with accompanying rainfall, seasonal precipitation in California so far had been alarmingly small. Reservoirs, depleted by an earlier drought, were far below normal levels for the third week of December. And snow, which usually fell heavily in the Sierra Nevada and elsewhere, had been exceptionally light or non-existent.

In a good precipitation year, winter snow was money in the bank for a huge public utility like Golden State Power & Light. When the snow melted in the spring, great rivers and streams cascaded downward, filling reservoirs which would fuel a vast network of hydro-electric power stations during the summer ahead.

Now, according to estimates which Eric Humphrey had been given, hydro-electric power next year might be reduced by twenty-five per cent because of the lack of run-off water.

Then oil.

For Golden State Power & Light, as well as other public utilities along both coasts, oil loomed as the largest question mark, the biggest potential worry of them all.

Only that morning, in the *Chronicle-West*, a syndicated business columnist had summed up the situation:

The danger about oil has been creeping up, like a tiger in the grass, while we haven't noticed or maybe didn't want to.

It began with the decline of the US dollar several years ago – our once respected 'greenback', but no longer strong, no longer 'good as gold' because the dollar's gold backing was cancelled out during the Nixon presidency.

Then, while the dollar plunged because of ineptitude and politics in Washington, the oil exporting nations of the Middle East, North and West Africa, Indonesia and Venezuela raised their dollar prices in an attempt to stay even.

That didn't work. The dollar continues to sink like the setting sun, worth less and less in terms of real value because the US has paid (and goes on paying) far more for imported oil than it earns from exports. And, as more dollars departed for Saudi Arabia, Iran and elsewhere, more were printed by the US Treasury – depleting the dollar's value even further.

After that we witnessed some interim experiments – payment for oil through a 'basket of currencies' was one. (That's a highfalutin' name for a mixture including deutschmarks, guilders, French and Swiss francs, pounds sterling, yen and dollars.) But that, too, proved ineffective because the ailing dollar and pound tipped the basket downward.

Finally, the oil nations demanded payment in the only money which, in this world's long history, has never failed to keep its value – gold.

The United States refused. It still does. (Of course you can see the Treasury's viewpoint. The US doesn't *have* that much gold left, having squandered enormous amounts in futile attempts to 'demonetize' gold. In fact, there's only sufficient in Fort Knox and the Fed Reserve banks to pay one year's oil bill with a bit left over.)

Instead the US Treasury, which for more than a decade has relied on printing-press money – backed by nothing – to pay its way, has offered to run the presses faster and produce more paper dollars.

But this time the oil nations have been adamant. They have said, in effect, 'If we want paper money we can print our own – without giving away our oil to get it.' And, like the mythical Chinese laundryman who insisted, 'No tickee, no washee,' they now threaten: 'No gold, no oil.'

So, it seems, an impasse is imminent.

True, the oil has not stopped flowing – yet! Equally true: it could be a year or more before it does.

Meanwhile, discussions between governments are continuing, so a compromise is possible.

We'll wait and see.

The general uncertainty about oil was an ominous, overhanging cloud for GSP & L because nearly half of the company's generating capacity was dependent on oil fuel, the bulk of it imported.

Natural gas, which used to be available to generate electricity, was already in short supply.

Thus, the prospect of an oil, gas and water shortage simultaneously was something which Eric Humphrey, Nim and other executives preferred not to think about – and shuddered when they did.

'Is there any chance, do you think,' Eric Humphrey asked Paul Sherman Yale, 'of the Governor's changing his mind and coming out with an endorsement of our Tunipah plans? After all, with an ongoing oil and gas crisis, and with nuclear still in limbo, what stronger argument is there for a coal-burning plant?'

Mr Justice Yale had joined Humphrey and Nim shortly after Nim's report on theft of service. The previous day, GSP & L's new and distinguished spokesman had been in Sacramento at the state capital.

'The Governor acknowledges that argument,' Yale said, 'and he's vacillating. I saw him yesterday and urged him to make a pro-Tunipah statement. I'd say the chances are sixty–forty that he will.'

'I'm pleased to hear it.' Humphrey noticeably brightened and Nim thought: once more the chairman's wisdom in hiring Paul Yale was being demonstrated. Yale seemed able to walk into the Governor's office without advance notice whenever he chose and the same was true of his access to senior legislators.

'I can tell you, gentlemen,' Yale said, 'that there's plenty of worrying in Sacramento about oil. Those I talked with yesterday, including the Governor, see gasoline rationing as inevitable soon, whether the present crisis is settled or not.'

'Personally,' Humphrey said, 'I'd consider that a good thing. The way North Americans have used cars, especially big cars, squandering gasoline as if there were no tomorrow, has been gross and disgusting. The Europeans – rightly so – believe we're irresponsible.'

Nim resisted an impulse to remind the chairman about his own big car. Instead, he told Yale, 'I hope Sacramento realizes that producing electricity is a much more economical use of oil than in an automobile.'

Paul Sherman Yale smiled. 'I assure you I lose no opportunity – public and private – to make that clear.'

Nim remembered that Yale *had* made that point publicly a week ago. It was on a TV programme, *Meet the State Press*, where, considering the short time since his appointment, the former Associate Justice showed himself adroitly knowledgeable about GSP & L affairs. Watching the show at home, Nim had again felt regret at not being the utility's policy spokesman any more. But honesty made him admit that Yale did the job superbly.

Eric Humphrey's mind had swung back to their discussion about oil. 'I sometimes think if I were an Arab I'd refuse paper dollars for my oil and demand gold, or at least a gold-backed currency. I wonder if the United States will give in and use some of our gold, even though it would not last long.'

'Do we even have as much gold as we're supposed to?' Nim asked. 'There seems some doubt about it.'

Humphrey looked surprised. Mr Justice Yale didn't; a soft smile played around his lips.

'I subscribe to a financial newsletter – *The International Harry Schultz Letter*,' Nim said. 'There are often things in there which prove to be true but newspapers don't seem to want to publish. Schultz has been writing about two men – a Washington lawyer, Dr Peter Beter, who used to be counsel for the United States Export-Import Bank, and Edward Durell, an American industrialist. Both are shouting "fraud" about Fort Knox gold, claiming there may be a lot less there than the world believes.'

Paul Sherman Yale nodded. 'Quite a few in Washington have heard of both men, but not many will admit it. Incidentally, I subscribe to Schultz's letter too.'

'What Beter and Durell argue,' Nim explained to Humphrey, 'is that Fort Knox gold hasn't been audited properly since 1953. They also claim that most of the remaining gold is impure – from melted-down coins containing silver, copper and antimony, which President Roosevelt called in when gold ownership for Americans was made illegal. That alone would mark the gold holdings down by twenty per cent, possibly more.'

'I've not heard that before,' Humphrey said. 'It's interesting.'

Nim went on, 'There's more. It's believed that in the 1960 dollar crisis a whole lot of US gold was used to support the dollar, with the intention it would be replaced. It never was.'

'In that case,' Humphrey asked, 'why keep it a secret?'

Paul Yale interjected, 'That's easy to answer. If the rest of the world believed the United States doesn't have the gold it claims to, there would be a fresh run on the dollar – panic selling.' He added thoughtfully, 'I've heard rumours in Washington about that missing gold. They say every new Treasury Secretary is sworn to secrecy, then told the facts. One thing *is* clear: the government won't permit an independent audit of Fort Knox gold.' He shrugged. 'I have no means of knowing if any of what Beter and Durell claim is true. But stranger things have happened, especially in Washington.'

Eric Humphrey sighed. 'There are days,' he told Yale, 'when I find myself wishing my assistant were less well informed, that he read less widely, and once in a while reined in that searching mind of his. As if I didn't have enough to worry about – Tunipah, coal, water, gas, oil – now he's added gold.'

9

In the chairman's mahogany-panelled office in the Sequoia Club's Cable Hill headquarters, Laura Bo Carmichael hesitated, her pen poised over a cheque in front of her. It was for twenty-five thousand dollars.

The cheque was drawn on the club's special projects account. It was payable to power & light for people.

The money would be the second instalment of the total – fifty thousand dollars – pledged to Davey Birdsong's organization last August, five months ago. The first payment had been made immediately following the confidential agreement between the Sequoia Club and p & lfp. Now the second half was due.

The signature of Roderick Pritchett, the Sequoia Club's manager-secretary, was already on the cheque, one line below where the chairman's was required. With a squiggle of Laura Bo's pen

– her signature was usually unreadable – she could make the cheque official. Yet still she hesitated.

The decision to ally the Sequoia Club with p & lfp had plagued her with doubts, immediately after it was made and ever since.

These doubts were reinforced at the Tunipah hearings where Davey Birdsong, she thought, had behaved abominably. All of Laura Bo's intellect rebelled against what she saw as his cheap, shoddy tactics, his clownish playing to the gallery, his cynical appeal to the lowest levels of intelligence.

Now she asked herself again: had she been wrong in casting the deciding vote which approved the alliance and made the money available? Had the respected Sequoia Club debased and dis-honoured itself by an association, for which – if the truth became public, as it might – Laura Bo, as chairman, would be held res-ponsible?

Shouldn't she have sided, after all, with Priscilla Quinn, who had laid her opinion about Birdsong on the line? Laura Bo could remember – clearly and uncomfortably – Priscilla's words : '*All my instincts are against trusting him . . . I have principles, some-thing that disgusting man appears to lack.*' And afterwards : '*I think you will all regret that vote. I wish my dissent to be re-corded.*'

Laura Bo Carmichael regretted her vote already.

She put her pen down, the cheque still unsigned, and reached for an intercom handset. When the manager-secretary answered, she asked, 'Roderick, could you come in, please?'

'It occurs to me,' she told him a few minutes later, 'that we might reconsider making this second payment. If the first was a mistake, then at least we need not compound it.'

Pritchett, dapper and well groomed as usual, seemed surprised. He took off his rimless glasses and polished them with a hand-kerchief, a time-honoured, time-consuming tactic.

'Has it occurred to you, Madam Chairman,' he said, replacing the glasses, 'that if we withheld those funds we would be violat-ing an agreement, honourably entered into, and fulfilled – so far – by the other side?'

'But *has* it been fulfilled? What did we get for the first twenty-five thousand – Birdsong's histrionics at the Tunipah hearings?'

'I'd say,' Pritchett said, picking his way carefully among the words, 'that Birdsong has achieved a good deal more than histrionics. His tactics, while rough – certainly rougher than we could resort to ourselves – have been shrewd. So far he has caused most of the media's attention to be focused on *opposition* to Tunipah while the arguments of Golden State Power have received only trifling attention. He also succeeded in demolishing their key witness, Goldman – first by provoking him, then standing back while Goldman antagonized everyone in sight, including his own company.'

'I felt sorry for him,' Laura Bo said. 'I've known Nim Goldman for a long time and, while he may be misguided, he's honest and sincere. He did not deserve what happened.'

Pritchett said primly, 'In these kind of contests some of those involved – and their reputations – are apt to get bruised. The important thing, from the point of view of the Sequoia Club, is to win. Where Tunipah is concerned I believe we will.'

'And *I've* never believed,' Laura Bo responded, 'in winning *at all costs*. I listened to that argument many years ago. To my dying day I will regret not contesting it.'

The manager-secretary felt like sighing but restrained himself. He had encountered Mrs Carmichael's recurring guilt about Hiroshima–Nagasaki many times before and had learned to cope with it. Nimbly backtracking, he assured her, 'My choice of words was unfortunate. What I should have said is that the agreement with Birdsong will help attain our objectives, which are admirable, as we both know.'

'But *where* is all that money going?'

'Some of it to Birdsong himself, of course. After all, he's putting in many hours personally – still attending those hearings every day, cross-examining new witnesses, at the same time keeping himself and opposition to Tunipah in the news. Then there are his supporters. He's managed to pack the hearing room with them continuously; that alone gives an impression of strong, spontaneous opposition to Tunipah from the public.'

'Are you suggesting it is *not* spontaneous? That Birdsong pays those people to be there?'

'Not all.' Again Pritchett chose his words warily; he knew how it was being done because he had talked to Birdsong, but was reluctant to be specific. 'Let's say some of those people have expenses, they have to absent themselves from work, and so on. Also those same supporters, or others Birdsong recruited, staged demonstrations at the Golden State Power & Light annual meeting. He told us about his plans there, if you remember, when we met.'

Laura Bo Carmichael appeared shocked. '*Paid* demonstrators! A *paid* disruption of an annual meeting! All of it with *our* money. I *do not like it.*'

'May I remind you of something, Madam Chairman,' Pritchett remonstrated. 'We entered into this arrangement with p & lfp with our eyes open. When our committee met – Mr Irwin Saunders, Mrs Quinn, you, me – we were aware that Birdsong's methods might be, well . . . unorthodox compared with our own. A few days ago I went over my notes of that August meeting and we agreed there could be certain things "we'd be better off not knowing". Those, incidentally, were Mr Saunders' exact words.'

'But did Irwin, at that time, understand Birdsong's methods?'

'I think,' Pritchett said drily, 'as an experienced lawyer he had a pretty good idea.'

The point was valid. As his friends and enemies knew, Irwin Saunders was a rough-and-tumble fighter in the courts and was not noted for ethical niceties. Perhaps more accurately than anyone, he had judged in advance how Birdsong would work.

The manager-secretary, though not mentioning it to Laura Bo, was also concerned about another matter involving lawyer Saunders.

Roderick Pritchett was due to retire soon. Saunders was the influential chairman of the Sequoia Club's finance committee, which would decide how large a pension – or how small – Pritchett would receive.

The club's pensions for retired staff were neither automatic nor fixed, but based on years of service and the committee's opinion of an individual's performance. Roderick Pritchett, who knew he had had his critics across the years, particularly wanted to look good to Saunders in these final months, and the Tunipah hearings and Davey Birdsong could be critical factors.

He told Laura Bo, 'Mr Saunders is delighted with Birdsong's efforts in opposing Tunipah. He telephoned to say so and reminded me that Birdsong promised 'continual harassment of Golden State Power & Light on a broad front'. The p & lfp has delivered on that. Another thing agreed to was no violence – you may recall I raised that point specifically. Birdsong has also kept his promise there.'

283

Laura Bo asked, 'And have you heard from Priscilla Quinn?'

'No.' Roderick Pritchett smiled. 'But, of course, Mrs Quinn would be elated, even triumphant, if you backed down now and refused to make that second payment. I imagine she would go around telling everyone she was right and you were wrong.'

It was a shrewd thrust. Both of them knew it.

If the original decision were reversed at this late stage, it would be remembered that Laura Bo Carmichael had cast the pivotal vote; therefore her embarrassment would be acute, not least because of the accompanying admission that twenty-five thousand dollars of the club's money had been spent unwisely. And Priscilla Quinn's sharp tongue would make the most of *that*.

Woman versus woman. For all her disdain of femininity, her determination not to let her sex influence her decisions, in the end it was Laura Bo's womanly pride which proved persuasive.

Picking up her pen, she scribbled a signature on the p & lfp cheque and handed it to a smiling Roderick Pritchett.

The cheque was mailed to Birdsong later that same day.

10

'We need more violence! More, more, *more*!' Davey Birdsong thumped a clenched fist angrily, his voice raised to a shout. 'A pisspotful more, to shake people up! *And* some bloody, messy deaths; a lot of them. It's the only way, the *absolute only way*, to stir the goddamn dumb public off their complacent asses and get action. You don't seem to realize it.'

Across the rough wooden table which divided them, Georgos Winslow Archambault's thin, ascetic face flushed at the final accusation. He leaned forward and insisted, 'I do realize that. But what you are talking about requires organization and time. I'm doing my best, but we can't take on a target *every* night.'

'Why in hell not?' The big, bearded man glared at Georgos. 'For Chrissakes! All you do now is let off some dinky firecrackers, then laze around her for a goddamn month's vacation.'

Their discussion, which had quickly developed into an argument, was taking place in the basement workshop of the rented East Side house – the Friends of Freedom hideaway. As usual the workshop was cluttered with tools and hardware of destruction – wires, metal parts, chemicals, timing mechanisms, and explosives. Birdsong had arrived ten minutes ago after taking his usual precautions against being followed.

'I told you before, there's enough bread for whatever you need,' the p & lfp leader continued. The trace of a smile lighted his face. 'And I just got more.'

'The money is important,' Georgos conceded. 'But we take the risks here. You don't.'

'Goddammit! – you're *supposed* to take risks. You're a soldier of the revolution, aren't you? And I take risks too – of a different kind.'

Georgos shifted uncomfortably. He resented this entire dialogue, just as he did the increasing dominance of Birdsong, which had happened since Georgos' own source of funds dried up and Birdsong's replaced it. More than ever Georgos hated his movie-actress mother, who, without knowing it, had financed Friends of Freedom in the beginning, then had ceased to do so with the ending of Georgos' allowance through the Athens law firm. He had read in a newspaper recently that she was seriously ill. He hoped it was something painful and terminal.

'The last attack on the enemy,' Georgos declared stiffly, 'was our most successful. We caused a power failure over one hundred square miles.'

'Sure. And what effect did it have?' Contemptuously, Birdsong answered his own question. 'Nil! Were any of our demands met? No! You killed two lousy pig security guards. Who cares? Nobody!'

'I'll admit it was surprising and disappointing that none of our demands . . .'

Birdsong cut him off. 'They *won't* be met! Not until there are bodies in the streets. Blood-drenched, putrefying piles of bodies. Not until the dead cause panic among the living. That's the lesson of *every revolution*! It's the only message the docile, moronic bourgeois understand.'

'I know all that.' Then, sarcastically, 'Perhaps you have some better ideas for . . .'

'You're damn right I do! Now listen to me.'

Birdsong lowered his voice; his anger and contempt appeared to dissipate. It was as if, like a schoolmaster, he had impressed the need to learn upon a pupil. Now the lesson itself, in lower key, would follow.

'First,' he said, 'we state some articles of faith. We ask ourselves: why are we doing what we are? And the answer is: because the existing system in this country is stinking, rotten, corrupt, oppressive, spiritually bankrupt. What's more, the system can't be changed – that's been tried; it doesn't work. So everything existing, the whole geared-to-the-rich, grind-the-poor capitalist system, has to be destroyed to allow *us* – the true believers, we who love our fellow men – to build anew and decently. The revolutionary is the *only one* who sees that clearly. And the destruction, piece by piece, is what Friends of Freedom – along with others like us – are beginning to do.'

While he talked, Davey Birdsong showed – as he had elsewhere – his chameleon quality. In part he had become the university lecturer – persuasive, eloquent; in part he was a mystic, speaking to his own inner soul as much as to Georgos.

He continued, 'So where does the destruction begin? Ideally, everywhere. But because, so far, we are few in numbers, we choose a common denominator – electricity. It affects all the populace. It lubricates the wheels of capitalism. It makes the bloated rich more bloated still. It allows minor comforts – palliatives – to the proletariat, deluding the masses into believing they are free. It is capitalism's tool, an opiate. Cut off the electricity, disrupt the core of its system, and you thrust a dagger in capitalism's heart!'

Brightening, Georgos injected, 'Lenin said, "Communism is Soviet government plus the electrification of . . ." '

'Don't interrupt! I know *exactly* what Lenin said, and it was in another context.'

Georgos subsided. This was a new and different Birdsong from the several variants he had seen before. Also there seemed little doubt, at this moment, about who was in command.

'But,' the big man resumed – he had risen and was striding back and forth – 'we have seen that more is required than disruption of electricity alone. We must draw greater attention to Friends of Freedom, and our objectives, by disrupting – destroying – electricity's *people*.'

'We already did some of that,' Georgos pointed out. 'When we blew up their La Mission plant; then the letter bombs. We killed their chief engineer, their president . . .'

'Piddling numbers! Penny ante! I mean something big, where the killing will not be in ones and twos but hundreds. Where bystanders will be wiped out too, proving there's no safety on the sidelines of a revolution. *Then* our aims get attention! That's when fear will set in, followed by panic. When all in authority and below, *everyone*, will be scurrying to do *exactly what we want*!'

Davey Birdsong's eyes were focused on the distance, clearly far beyond the dismal, disordered basement. It was as if he were seeing a dream, a vision, Georgos thought – and found the experience heady and infectious.

The prospect of more killing excited Georgos. The night of the bombing at Millfield, after he had slain the two security guards, he had been briefly sickened; it was, after all, the first time he had killed another human being face to face. But the feeling quickly passed, to be replaced by a sense of elation and – curiously, he thought – sexual arousement. He had taken Yvette that night and used her savagely, reliving, while he did, the powerful upward knife thrust with which he had killed the first guard. And now, remembering, listening to Birdsong's talk about mass killings, Georgos felt his sexual organs stir again.

Birdsong said quietly, 'The opportunity we need is coming soon.'

He produced a folded newspaper page. It was from the *California Examiner* of two days earlier and a single-paragraph item had been ringed in red crayon.

POWER GROUP TO MEET

Possible nationwide shortages of electric power will be discussed next month when the National Electric Institute holds a four-day convention in the city's Christopher Columbus Hotel. A thousand delegates from public utilities and electrical manufacturers are expected to attend.

'I scratched around for more details,' Birdsong said. 'Here are the exact dates of the convention and a preliminary programme.' He tossed two typewritten sheets on the workshop table. 'It will be easy to get the final programme later. That way we'll know where everybody is, and when.'

Georgos' eyes were agleam with interest, his resentment of a few minutes earlier forgotten. He gloated, 'All those big wheels from power outfits – social criminals! We can mail letter bombs to selected delegates. If I begin work now . . .'

'No! At best you'd kill half a dozen – probably not that many because after the first explosion they'd get wise and take precautions.'

Georgos conceded, 'Yes, that's true. Then what do you . . . ?'

'I have a better idea. Much, much better; also bigger.' Birdsong permitted himself a thin, grim smile. 'During the second day of that convention, when everybody has arrived, you and your people will plant two series of bombs in the Christopher Columbus Hotel. The first set of bombs will be exactly timed to go off during the night – say at 3am. That stage of bombing will concentrate on the main floor and mezzanine. The objective will be to block or destroy all exits from the building as well as every stairway, every elevator. So no one can escape from the floors above when the second stage begins.'

Georgos nodded his understanding, listening intently as Birdsong continued.

'A few minutes after the first bombs have exploded, other bombs – also exactly timed – will go off on the floors above. Those will be fire bombs – as many as you can plant and all containing gasoline, so as to set the hotel on fire and keep it burning.'

A wide, anticipatory smile spread over Georgos' face. He said breathlessly, 'It's brilliant! *Magnificent!* And we can do it.'

'*If* you do it right,' Birdsong said, 'not one person on those upper floors will leave that building alive. And at three in the morning, even those who stayed out late will be in bed. We will execute everybody: Those convention delegates – our main target for punishment – and their women, children, and all others in the hotel who have chosen to get in the way of a just revolution.'

'I'll need more explosives; a whole lot.' Georgos' mind was working fast. 'I know how and where to get them, but it will cost.'

'I already told you we have plenty of money. For this time out, and more.'

'Getting the gasoline is no problem. But clockwork mechanisms – I agree with you the timing will have to be exact – those ought to come from out of town. Bought in small numbers from

288

several places. That way we won't attract attention.'

'I'll do that,' Birdsong said. 'I'll go to Chicago, it's far away. Get me a list of what you need.'

Still concentrating, Georgos nodded. 'I must have a floor p of the hotel – at least the main floor and mezzanine where we'll set the first explosives.'

'Does it have to be exact?'

'No. Just a general layout.'

'Then we'll draw our own. Anyone can walk in there, anytime.'

'Something else which will have to be bought,' Georgos said, 'is several dozen fire extinguishers – portable ones, the red-painted kind that stand on their own base.'

'Fire *extinguishers*! For Chrissakes, we want to start a fire, not put one out.'

Georgos smiled slyly, knowing it was his turn to be superior. 'The fire extinguishers will be emptied, their casings weakened, and our time bombs put inside them. It's something I've been working on. You can set down a fire extinguisher anywhere – especially in a hotel – without it being suspect or, most times, even noticed. If it *is* noticed, it simply looks as if the management is taking extra safety precautions.'

Grinning broadly, Birdsong leaned forwards and thumped Georgos on the shoulders. 'That's diabolical! *Beautifully* diabolical!'

'We can work out later how to get the extinguishers into the hotel.' Georgos was still thinking aloud. 'It shouldn't be difficult. We could rent a truck or buy one, and paint a fake company name on it, so it looks official. We'd print up some kind of authorization – maybe get a hotel purchase order and copy it – which our people would carry, in case they were stopped by anyone, asking questions. Then we'll want uniforms – for me, the others . . .'

'No problem about a truck or uniforms,' Birdsong said, 'and we'll work on the purchase order thing.' He mused. 'It's all coming together. I have that feeling. And when it's over, people will see our strength and fall over themselves to obey our orders.'

'About the explosives,' Georgos said. 'I'll need ten thousand dollars cash – small bills – in the next few days, and after that . . .'

With mounting enthusiasm, they continued planning.

'If there's an obscure Jewish holiday which no one else ever heard of,' Nim told Ruth, speaking from the driver's seat of his Fiat, 'you can be sure your parents will dust it off and use it.'

His wife, in the seat beside him, laughed. He had noticed, earlier this evening, when he came home from work and while they were getting ready to go out, that Ruth was in an easy, cheerful humour. It contrasted with the moodiness, and sometimes outright depression, she had exhibited in recent weeks.

It was now mid-January, and even though three months had passed since their talk about a possible divorce, and Ruth's concession that she would wait 'a little while', neither had raised the subject again directly. But, clearly, it would have to be discussed soon.

Basically, their relationship – an uncertain truce – remained unchanged. Nim, however, had consciously been more considerate, continuing to spend increased time at home and with the children, and perhaps Leah's and Benjy's obvious enjoyment of their father had caused Ruth to hold back from a final confrontation. Nim, for his part, was still unsure how he wanted their dilemma to be resolved. Meanwhile, the problems of GSP & L kept him intensely occupied, with little room for personal concerns.

'I can never remember all those Jewish holidays,' Ruth said. 'What did father say this one was?'

'Rosh Hashanah L'Elanoth – or Jewish Arbor Day. I did some research in the office library, and literally it means New Year of the Trees.'

'New year for Jewish trees? Or just any trees?'

He chuckled. 'Better ask your old man.'

They were travelling across town, heading west, and Nim threaded the car through traffic which never seemed to lessen, whatever time of day it was.

A week ago Aaron Neuberger had telephoned Nim at work to suggest he bring Ruth for a Tu B'Shvat party – the more common name of the same holiday. Nim had accepted immediately, partly because his father-in-law was unusually friendly on the phone, partly because Nim had mild guilt feelings about his own behaviour to the Neubergers in the past and it seemed an opportunity to expiate them. His scepticism, though, about his parents-in-laws' almost fanatic Jewishness had not changed.

When they arrived at the Neubergers' home – a spacious, comfortable duplex apartment in a well-to-do area of the city's west side – several cars were already parked outside and, nearer the house, they could hear the sound of voices from the upper level. Nim was relieved to know there were other guests. The presence of strangers might prevent the usual barrage of personal questions, including the inevitable one about a bar mitzvah for Benjy.

Going in, Ruth touched the mezuzah at the doorway, then kissed her hand, as she usually did out of deference to her parents. Nim, who in the past had scoffed at the custom as being – among other things – superstitious, on impulse did the same.

Inside, there was no doubt about their welcome – especially Nim's.

Aaron Neuberger, who was apple-cheeked, stocky and totally bald, had sometimes regarded Nim with thinly veiled suspicion. But tonight his eyes were friendly behind thick-lensed glasses as he pumped his son-in-law's hand. Rachel, Ruth's mother, a voluminous woman who disapproved of diets for herself and others, clasped Nim in her arms, then held him back appraisingly. 'Is my daughter not feeding you at all? All I feel is bones. But we will put some meat on them tonight.'

Nim was amused and, at the same time, touched. Almost certainly, he thought, word had reached the Neubergers that his and Ruth's marriage was in jeopardy; therefore the older couple had set aside other feelings in an attempt to hold the family together. Nim glanced sideways at Ruth, who was smiling at the demonstrative reception.

She was wearing a softly draped dress of blue-grey silk, with pearl earrings of the same shade. As always, her black hair was elegant, her skin soft and unblemished, though paler than normal, Nim thought.

As Nim and Ruth moved forward to meet those who had arrived earlier, he whispered, 'You look beautiful tonight.'

She looked at him sharply and said, low-voiced, 'Have you any idea how long it is since you told me that?'

There was no time for any more. They were surrounded by faces, going through introductions, and shaking hands. Among the two dozen or so guests there were only a few whom Nim knew. Most were already eating, plates piled high with delicacies from an elaborate buffet.

'Come with me, Nimrod!' Ruth's mother seized his arm in an iron grip and propelled him from the living room to the dining room where the buffet was set up. 'The rest of our friends, you can meet later,' she instructed. 'For now, have something to fill that emptiness inside before you faint from hunger.' She took a plate and began piling food on it generously, as if it were the day before the fast of Yom Kippur. Nim recognized several varieties of knishes, kishke cooked in cholent, lokshen kugel, stuffed cabbage and pitcha. Set out ready as sweets were honey cake, strudel and apple pirushkes.

Nim helped himself to a glass of white Israeli Carmel wine.

As he returned to the living room, the purpose of the occasion became clear. Rosh Hashanah L'Elanoth, their host explained, is celebrated in Israel by the planting of trees and in North America by eating fruit of a kind not partaken of, thus far, in the Jewish year. To make the point, Aaron Neuberger and others were nibbling on figs from several dishes spread around.

Something else the Neubergers made plain was that they expected donations from their guests, and the money collected would be sent to Israel to pay for tree plantings. Already, several fifty- and twenty-dollar bills had been deposited on a silver tray, put out for the purpose. Nim added twenty dollars of his own, then helped himself to figs.

'If you'll pardon an atrocious pun,' a voice behind him said, 'I suppose it all shows we give a fig.'

Nim turned. The speaker was an elderly, gnomish man with a cherubic, cheerful face beneath a cloud of white hair. Nim remembered him as a doctor – an internist – who sometimes attended the Neubergers. He groped in memory for a name and found it.

'Good evening, Dr Levin.' Raising his glass of wine, Nim offered the toast, '*L'Chaim.*'

'*L'Chaim* . . . how are you, Nim? Don't see you often at these Jewish wingdings. I'm surprised at your interest in the Holy Land.'

'I'm not religious, Doctor.'

'Nor am I, Nim. Never have been. Know my way around a sanatorium a whole lot better than a synagogue.' The doctor finished the fig he had been eating and selected another. 'But I like the forms and ceremonies, all the ancient history of our people. It isn't religion, you know, that holds Jewish people together. It's a sense of community going back five thousand years. A long, long time. Ever think about that, Nim?'

'Yes, since you ask. I've been thinking quite a lot about it.'

The older man regarded him shrewdly. 'Troubles you sometimes, does it? Wondering how much of a Jew you can be? Or if you can be one at all without observing all that labyrinthine ritual stuff old Aaron does?'

Nim smiled at the reference to his father-in-law, who, across the room, had manoeuvred a newly arrived guest into a corner and was earnestly describing Tu B'Shvat: '... has its roots in the Talmud ...'

'Something like that,' Nim said.

'Then I'll give you some advice, son: don't let it worry you worth a damn. Do what I do: enjoy being a Jew, be proud of all the achievements of our people, but as to the rest – pick and choose. Observe the High Holy Days if you like – personally I take them off and go fishing – but if you don't observe them, that's allowable in my book too.'

Nim found himself warming towards the cheerful little doctor and told him, 'My grandfather was a rabbi, a sweet old man I remember well. It was my father who broke away from religion.'

'And you wonder sometimes if you should go back?'

'In a vague way. Not too seriously.'

'In any way – forget it! It's a mental impossibility for someone at your stage – or mine – to become a practising Jew. Start going to synagogue, you'll find that out in five minutes. What you feel, Nim, is nostalgia, an affection for things in the past. Nothing wrong with it, but that's what it is.'

Nim said thoughtfully, 'I suppose so.'

'Let me tell you something else. People like you and me have the same concern for Judaism that we might have for old friends – an occasional sense of guilt for not having seen them more often, plus emotional attachment. I felt that way when I went with a group to Israel.'

'A religious group?'

'Nope. Mostly businessmen, a few other doctors, couple of lawyers.' Dr Levin chuckled. 'Hardly any of us took a yarmulke. I didn't. Had to borrow one when I went to the Wall in Jerusalem. Just the same, it was a deeply emotional experience, something I'll never forget. Had a sense of belonging and pride. I felt Jewish then. Always will.'

Nim asked, 'Do you have children, Doctor?'

The other shook his head. 'Never did. My dear wife – she's dead now, bless her memory! . . . she and I both regretted it. One of the few things I do regret.'

'We have two children,' Nim said. 'A girl and a boy.'

'Yes, I know. And because of them you started thinking about religion?'

Nim smiled. 'You seem to know all the questions as well as answers.'

'Heard 'em before, I guess. That, and I've been around a long time. Don't worry about your kids, Nim. Teach them decent human instincts – I'm sure you have. Beyond that, they'll find their own way.'

There was an obvious next question. Nim hesitated, then asked it, 'Would a bar mitzvah help my son find his way?'

'Won't harm him any, will it? You wouldn't be exposing him to some social disease if you sent him to Hebrew school. Besides, a bar mitzvah's always followed by a damn good party. You meet old friends, eat and drink more than you should, but everybody loves it.'

Nim grinned. 'That's more sense on the subject than I've heard anywhere else.'

Dr Levin nodded sagely. 'Here's some more. Your boy is entitled to make a choice – that's his right, his heritage. Studying for a bar mitzvah gives him that. It's like opening a door; let *him* decide if he wishes to go through it. Later on, he'll either go Aaron's way, or yours and mine, or maybe somewhere between. Whichever he chooses, it's not for us to worry.'

'I'm grateful to you,' Nim said. 'You've helped my thinking.'

'Glad to. There's no charge.'

While they had been talking, the number of guests had increased while the hubbub of other conversations swelled in volume. Nim's cherubic companion glanced around, nodding and smiling; obviously he was acquainted with almost everyone who had come. His eyes stopped at Ruth Goldman, now chatting with another woman; Nim recognized her as a concert pianist who often performed for Israeli causes.

'Your wife looks beautiful tonight,' Dr Levin observed.

'Yes,' Nim said, 'I told her that as we came in.'

The doctor nodded. 'She conceals her problem, and her anxiety, well.' He stopped, then added, 'My anxiety, too.'

Nim regarded him, puzzled. 'You're speaking of Ruth?'

'Of course.' Levin sighed. 'Sometimes I wish I didn't have to treat patients I care about as much as I do your wife. I've known her since she was a little girl, Nim. I hope you realize that everything possible is being done. Everything.'

'Doctor,' Nim said; he had a sudden sense of alarm, a cold contraction in his stomach. 'Doctor, I don't have the slightest idea what you are talking about.'

'You don't?' Now it was the older man's turn to be startled; an expression of guilty confusion crossed his face. 'Ruth hasn't told you?'

'Told me *what*?'

'My friend,' Dr Levin put a hand on Nim's shoulder, 'I just made a mistake. A patient, any patient, is entitled to have confidence respected, to be protected against a gabby doctor. But you're Ruth's husband. I assumed . . .'

Nim protested, 'For God's sake, what are we discussing? What's the mystery?'

'I'm sorry. I can't tell you.' Dr Levin shook his head. 'You'll have to ask Ruth. When you do, tell her I regret my indiscretion. But tell her also – I think you ought to know.'

Still with some embarrassment, and before he could be subjected to more questioning, the doctor moved away.

For Nim, the next two hours were agony. He observed the social rituals, met guests whom he had not already talked with, joined in conversations, and answered questions from a few people who knew his role at GSP & L. But all of the time his thoughts were on Ruth. What in hell did Levin mean by: '*She conceals her problem, and her anxiety, well*'? And: '*Everything possible is being done. Everything*'?

Twice he eased his way through talkative groups to be beside Ruth, only to find that private conversation was impossible. 'I want to talk to you,' he managed to say once, but that was all. Nim realized he would have to wait until they were on their way home.

At last the party began to wane, the number of guests to thin. The silver tray was piled high with money for more trees in Israel. Aaron and Rachel Neuberger were at the outer doorway, bidding good night as people left.

'Let's go,' Nim said to Ruth. She retrieved her wrap from a bedroom and they joined the exodus.

They were almost the last to leave. As a result, the four had a moment of intimacy which had not been possible earlier.

As Ruth kissed her parents, her mother pleaded, 'Couldn't you stay a little longer?'

Ruth shook her head. 'It's late, Mother; we're both tired.' She added, 'Nim has been working very hard.'

'If he works so hard,' Rachel shot back, 'then feed him better!'

Nim grinned. 'What I ate tonight will hold me for a week.' He held out his hand to his father-in-law. 'Before we go, there's something I think you'd like to know. I've decided to enroll Benjy in Hebrew school so he can have a bar mitzvah.'

For brief seconds there was a silence. Then Aaron Neuberger raised his hands to the level of his head, palms outwards, as if in prayer. 'Praise be to the Master of the Universe! We should all live and be well until that glorious day!' Behind the thick-lensed glasses his eyes were wet with tears.

'We'll talk about specifics . . .' Nim began, but failed to finish because both of Ruth's parents, together, hugged him tightly in their arms.

Ruth said nothing. But a few minutes later when they were in the car, and as Nim pulled away, she turned towards him. 'That was a beautiful thing you just did, even though it goes against your beliefs. So why?'

He shrugged. 'Some days I'm not sure what I believe. Besides, your friend Dr Levin helped straighten my thinking.'

'Yes,' Ruth said quietly, 'I saw you talking with him. For a long time.'

Nim's hands tightened on the steering wheel. 'Is there anything you want to tell me?'

'Such as?'

His pent-up frustration poured out. 'Such as why you've been going to Dr Levin, what it is you are anxious about, and why you've kept it from me. And, oh yes, your doctor asked me to say he was sorry for being indiscreet, but that I ought to know – whatever the hell that means.'

'Yes,' Ruth said, 'I suppose it's time you did.' Her voice was flat, the earlier cheerfulness gone. 'But will you wait until we are home? I'll tell you then.'

They drove the rest of the way in silence.

'I think I'd like a Bourbon and soda,' Ruth said. 'Do you mind getting it for me?'

They were in the small, cosy living room of their house, the lights turned low. It was almost 1am, Leah and Benjy, who had gone to bed several hours ago, were asleep upstairs.

'Sure,' Nim said. It was unusual for Ruth, who rarely drank anything stronger than wine, to ask for hard liquor. He crossed to a sideboard which did duty as a bar, mixed a Bourbon and soda, and poured a cognac for himself. Returning, he sat facing his wife while she gulped a third of her drink, then, with a grimace, put the glass down.

'All right,' he said. 'Now give!'

Ruth took a deep breath, then began. 'You remember that mole I had removed – six years ago?'

'Yes, I do.' Strangely, Nim had recalled it only recently – the night he had been alone in the house, with Ruth away, when he made the decision to visit Denver. He had noticed the mole in the oil painting of Ruth which hung in their living room, the portrait where she was wearing a strapless evening gown. Nim glanced at it now. There was the mole, just as he remembered it before it was removed: small and dark, on the left shoulder. He asked, 'What about it?'

'It was a melanoma.'

'A what?'

'A melanoma is a mole which may have cancer cells. That's why Dr Mittelman – you remember, he was the one who took care of me then – advised me to have it removed. I agreed. Another doctor – a surgeon – did the cutting. It wasn't a big deal, and afterwards both of them said the mole came away cleanly; there was no sign of anything having spread.'

'Yes, I do remember Mittelman saying that.' Nim had been

mildly concerned at the time, but the physician was reassuring, insisting the procedure was a long-shot precaution, nothing more. As Ruth had just pointed out, it all happened six years ago; Nim had forgotten the details until now.

'Both doctors were wrong,' Ruth said; the level of her voice dropped until it was barely a whisper. 'There *were* cancer – melanoma – cells. They *had* spread. Now . . . they've spread still more . . . through my body.'

She barely managed to get the last words out. Then, as if a dam pent up too long had burst, her control dissolved totally. The breath went out of her in a wail, her body shook with violent sobbing.

For moments Nim sat helpless, numb, unable to comprehend, much less believe, what he had just heard. Then reality penetrated. With a whirlwind jumble of emotions – horror, guilt, anguish, pity, love – he went to Ruth and took her in his arms.

He tried to comfort her, holding her tightly, her face pressed hard against his own. 'My darling, my dearest love, why have you never told me? In God's name – *why*?'

Her voice came weakly, muffled by tears. 'We weren't close . . . not loving any more, the way it used to be . . . I didn't want just pity . . . you had other interests . . . other women.'

A wave of shame and self-disgust swept over him. Instinctively, releasing Ruth, he fell to his knees before her and, taking her hands, he pleaded, 'It's late to ask forgiveness, but I do. I've been a goddamn fool, blind, selfish . . .'

Ruth shook her head; characteristically, some of her control returned. 'You don't have to say all that!'

'I want to say it because it's true. I didn't see it before. I see it now.'

'I already told you I don't want . . . only pity.'

He urged, 'Look at me!' When she lifted her head he said softly, 'I love you.'

'Are you sure you're not just saying it because . . . ?'

'I said I love you, *and I mean it*! I always have, I guess, except I got mixed up and stupid. It needed something like this to make me realize . . .' He stopped, then pleaded again, '*Is* it too late?'

'No.' Ruth gave the ghost of a smile. 'I never did stop loving you, even though you've been a bastard.'

'I admit it.'

'Well,' she said, 'maybe we owe Dr Levin something.'

'Listen, dearest.' He groped for words, wanting to offer reassurance. 'We'll fight this thing together. We'll do everything that's medically possible. And there'll be no more talk of separation or divorce.'

She said loudly, strongly, 'I never wanted either. Oh, Nim darling, hold me! Kiss me!'

He did. Then, as if it had never been, the gulf between them disappeared.

He asked, 'Are you too tired to tell me everything? Tonight? Now?'

Ruth shook her head. 'I want to tell you.'

For another hour she talked while Nim listened, occasionally interjecting questions.

About eight months ago, he learned, Ruth became aware of a small lump on the left side of her neck. Dr Mittelman had retired from practice the year before. She went to Dr Levin.

The doctor was suspicious of the lump and ordered a series of tests, including chest x-ray, liver scan, and bone scan. The extensive tests explained Ruth's daytime disappearances which Nim had noticed. Results showed that melanoma cells, after lying dormant for six years, had suddenly spread throughout Ruth's body.

'The day I heard,' she said, 'I didn't know what to do or think.'

'Whatever else was wrong between us,' Nim protested, 'you should have told me.'

'You seemed to have so much else on your mind. It was about the time that Walter was killed in that explosion at La Mission. Anyway, I decided to keep it to myself. Afterwards, I took care of the insurance forms, all the rest.'

'Your parents don't know?'

'No.'

After the test results, Ruth explained, she had begun attending a local hospital once a week, as an outpatient, for chemotherapy and immunotherapy treatments. That, too, explained more daytime absences.

She suffered occasional nausea and some weight loss because of the treatments, but managed to conceal both. Nim's repeated absences from home had made it easier.

Nim put his head in his hands, his shame deepening. He had

assumed Ruth was meeting another man, while all of the time . . .

Later, Ruth went on, Dr Levin informed her of a new treatment being used at the Sloan-Kettering Institute in New York. He believed she should go there to learn about it. Ruth went – for a two-week stay and another battery of tests.

That was the time of her prolonged absence from home which Nim had thought of with indifference, or as an inconvenience to himself.

He was bereft of words.

'What's done is done,' Ruth told him. 'You couldn't possibly have known.'

Nim asked the question he had been dreading. 'What do they say about the future – the prognosis?'

'First of all, there is no cure; second, it's too late for surgery.' Ruth's voice was steady; most of her normal poise was back. 'But I could have a lot of years left, though we'll never know until they run out. Also I don't know about the Sloan-Kettering Institute yet – whether I'll be better off taking their treatment or not. The doctors there are working on a method which uses microwaves to raise the temperature of a tumour, followed by radiation which may – or may not – destroy the tumour tissue.' She smiled wanly. 'As you might imagine, I've found out as much about it as I can.'

'I'd like to talk to Dr Levin myself – tomorrow,' Nim said, then corrected himself. 'That is, later today. Do you mind?'

'Mind?' Ruth sighed. 'No, I don't mind. It's so wonderful to have someone to lean on. Oh, Nim, I've needed you so much!'

He held her again. Soon afterwards, he turned out the lights and led the way upstairs.

For the first time in many months Nim and Ruth shared a bed and, in the early morning as dawn was breaking, they made love.

12

A knife blade flashed. Blood spurted. Watching the procedure of castration, Nim felt slightly sick.

Beside him, Mr Justice Yale chuckled, 'Be thankful you were destined to be a man, not a steer.'

The two were on a narrow catwalk above an animal pen, part of a cattle feedlot in California's agricultural heartland – the San Joaquin Valley. The feedlot was one of the properties of the Yale Family Trust.

'The thought of any male being cut off from sex depresses me,' Nim said.

He had flown here early this morning, his purpose to brief Paul Yale on electric power as it related to agriculture. California farmers were enormous users of electricity; agriculture and associated industry consumed a tenth of everything GSP & L generated. Without electricity, farming – indispensable to the state's well-being – would wither.

Later today the ex-Supreme Court Justice would appear as GSP & L's spokesman at a regional hearing on the utility's plans for Tunipah. It was one of an Energy Commission series – some called it a travelling road show – at which local leaders and citizens were invited to testify about power needs in their areas. The San Joaquin Valley farmers, who saw their livelihood threatened by power shortages, were already among Tunipah's staunch advocates.

Inevitably, there would be opposition too.

Still watching the activity below them, Yale told Nim, 'I know what you mean about eliminating manhood – even in animals. In a way it's a pity; it's also necessary. When you're a farmer you don't even think about those things.'

'Are you enjoying being one?'

'A part-time farmer? I'm not sure.' The old man frowned. 'Mostly I've been looking at balance sheets, trying to find out why this operation and others in that family trust of ours won't show a profit.'

'What's happening right now,' Nim said, 'seems to be efficient.'

301

'Efficient but damned costly.'

They were observing the 'check in' process in which calves, born on a grazing range and raised for six months there, were brought to the feedlot to be fattened for market.

Five cowboys – middle-aged men garbed in denims – kept the operation moving.

It began with herding a half-dozen calves into a circular pen. Inside, the animals were prodded, by electric cattle prods, into a narrow cement corridor, the walls extending above their heads but open at the top. A grubicide solution, to kill grubs and insects, was poured generously over each animal.

The corridor led – with an awful inevitability, Nim thought – to a hydraulic squeeze. This was a metal cage. As each calf entered, the cage contracted so the creature was held tightly with its head protruding and body lifted from the ground. The frightened animal bellowed lustily – with good reason, as the next few minutes proved.

First procedure was the discharge into each ear of a syringe containing motor oil. It would remove ticks. Next a huge hypodermic was shoved into the bellowing mouth and a worming solution injected. After that, the sharp extremities of both horns were clipped off with a heavy shear, leaving the soft and bloody insides exposed. Simultaneously came a strong, sickening smell of burning hair and flesh as a red-hot electric branding iron was pressed into the creature's side.

Then, at the touch of a lever, and with a hiss of air, the cattle squeeze rotated ninety degrees on to its side. In what had been the bottom, a small 'gate' was exposed, which a cowboy opened. Inserting an aerosol can containing disinfectant, the man sprayed the calf's genitals, then put the can down and picked up a knife. Reaching inside, he slit the scrotum, probed with fingers, then pulled out and cut the testicles, which he tossed into a container beside him. Another application of the aerosol spray on the now bleeding, gaping wound, and the operation was complete.

The steer, having been deprived of all desires other than to eat, would fatten nicely.

The hydraulic squeeze was opened. Still bellowing, the animal ran out into a further holding pen.

From beginning to end it had taken less than four minutes.

'It's faster and simpler than it used to be,' Yale told Nim. 'In my grandfather's day, and even recently, the calves would have to be lassoed and roped up before the things you're watching could be done. Nowadays our cowboys rarely ride horses; some of them don't even know how.'

Nim asked, 'Is the modern way cheaper?'

'It ought to be, but isn't. It's the inflated cost of everything that does us in – labour, materials, feed, electricity – *especially* electricity. This operation runs on it. We use electric power for the mill which mixes feed for forty thousand cattle. And did you know that in the pens there are bright lights on all night?'

'As I understand it,' Nim said, 'it's so the cattle can see to eat.'

'Right. They sleep less, feed more, and fatten faster. But our power bills are astronomical.'

Nim hummed 'It seems to me I've heard that song before,' and Yale laughed.

'Sound like a bellyaching consumer, don't I? Well, today I am. I've told the trust manager, Ian Norris, to cut down, economize, search out waste, conserve. We have to.'

Nim had met Norris briefly, earlier this morning. He was a dour, humourless man in his late fifties who had an office in the city and managed other estates as well as the Yale Family Trust. Nim guessed that Norris had preferred it when Paul Sherman Yale was in Washington and uninvolved in trust business.

'What I'd like to do,' Yale said, 'is sell off this property and some of the others my grandfather left. But right now is a bad time.'

While they talked, Nim had continued watching the procession below. Something puzzled him.

'That last calf,' he said. 'And the one before it. They weren't castrated. Why?'

A cowboy nearby, overhearing Nim's question, turned. He had a swarthy Mexican face and was grinning broadly. So was Mr Justice Yale.

'Nim, my boy,' the old man said. He leaned nearer, speaking confidentially. 'There's something I should tell you. Those last two were girls.'

They had lunch in Fresno, in the Windsor Room of the Hilton Hotel. During the meal Nim continued the briefing he had come for. It proved an easy task. As soon as any fact or statistic was presented, Mr Justice Yale appeared to have it memorized. He rarely asked for repetition and his sharp, probing questions showed a quickness of mind, plus a grasp of the big picture. Nim hoped that when he was eighty his mental powers would be as good.

Much of their talk was about water. Ninety per cent of electric power used by farmers in the lush San Joaquin Valley, Nim reported, was to pump water from wells for irrigation. Therefore, interruptions in power supply could be disastrous.

'I remember this valley when it was mostly desert,' Paul Yale reminisced. 'That was in the 1920s. There was a time when nobody believed anything would grow here. The Indians called it "Empty Valley".'

'They hadn't heard of rural electrification.'

'Yes, it wrought miracles. What's that line from Isaiah? – "*The desert shall rejoice and blossom as the rose*." Yale chuckled. 'Maybe I can slip that into my testimony. A line or two from the Bible adds a touch of class, don't you think?'

Before Nim could answer, the maître d' came to their table. He announced, 'Mr Yale, there's a telephone call for you. You may take it at the hostess's desk if you wish.'

The older man was gone several minutes. Nim could see him across the room, writing in a notebook as he listened intently to whatever was being said on the telephone. When he returned to the table, he was beaming and had the notebook open.

'Some good news from Sacramento, Nim. Excellent news, I think. An aide to the Governor will be at the hearing here this afternoon; he'll read a statement that the Governor now strongly supports the plans for Tunipah. A confirming press release is going out now from the Governor's office.' Yale glanced at his notes. 'It speaks of "a personal conviction, after study, that the Tunipah development is essential to the growth and prosperity of California".'

'Well,' Nim said, 'you really pulled it off. Congratulations!'

'I'll admit I'm pleased.' Pocketing the notebook, Yale glanced at his watch. 'What do you say we get some exercise and walk over to that hearing?'

'I'll walk with you, but I won't come in.' Nim grinned. 'You may remember – at the Energy Commission I'm still *persona non grata*.'

Their destination was the State Building, some ten minutes away.

It was a bright, pleasant day and Paul Yale, spry in walking as in much else, stepped out briskly. After the flow of talk before and during lunch, both fell silent.

Nim's thoughts returned, as they had so often lately, to Ruth. A week and a half had passed since the soul-searing night when he learned that Ruth's life was endangered by cancerous cells at large in her body. Apart from a talk with Dr Levin, Nim had kept the knowledge to himself. There seemed no point in turning Ruth – as he had seen happen with other families – into an object of gossip and speculation.

Dr Levin's attitude had been neither defeatist nor reassuring. 'Your wife may have many years of normal life,' he had said. 'But you must also know that her condition could deteriorate suddenly and rapidly. Treatment, though – whether it's chemotherapy or immunotherapy – will tilt the odds in her favour.'

As to possible additional therapy, Ruth was to make another trip to New York soon; it would be decided then if the newer, in-part-experimental method at the Sloan-Kettering Institute was likely to help her. For Nim, as well as Ruth, the waiting was like living on the loose ledge of a precipice, wondering if it would collapse or hold.

'The only advice I can give,' Dr Levin had added, 'is what I've told your wife already: live one day at a time, and use it to the full. Don't let her put things off that she wants to do, and can. Come to think of it, that's good counsel for us all. Remember that you or I could drop dead from a heart attack or be killed in a traffic accident tomorrow, with your wife surviving us by many years.'

The doctor had sighed. 'I'm sorry, Nim; maybe that sounds like a load of bull. I know you want something definite. Everybody does. But the advice I've given you is the best I have.'

Nim had taken Dr Levin's advice by spending as much time with Ruth as possible. Today, for example, he could have stayed on overnight in Fresno; there were local developments about which he might usefully inform himself. Instead, he had arranged to take an afternoon flight back, and would be home for dinner.

His thoughts were jerked into the present by Mr Justice Yale, who observed, 'There seems to be an extraordinary number of people around for this time of day.'

Nim had been preoccupied; now he looked about him. 'You're right. There are.'

The streets within immediate view contained large numbers of pedestrians, all apparently heading in the same direction – towards the State Building. Some were hurrying, as if anxious to get ahead of others. Cars, too, were streaming in and a traffic jam was developing. Among occupants of the cars and those on foot, women and teenagers seemed to predominate.

'Perhaps,' Nim said, 'word got around that you were coming here.'

The old man chuckled. 'Even if it did, I don't have the charisma to pull a crowd this size.'

They reached the grassy mall which fronted on the State Building. It was packed with people.

'If you want to find something out, a good way is to ask,' Yale said. He touched the arm of a middle-aged man in workman's clothes. 'Excuse me. We are curious to know why so many people are here.'

The other looked at him incredulously. 'You ain't heard?'

Yale smiled. 'It's why I asked.'

'It's Cameron Clarke. He's coming here.'

'The movie actor?'

'Who else? Gonna speak his piece at some gumment hearing. Bin on radio all morning. On TV too, so my old lady says.'

Nim asked, 'What government hearing?'

'How should I know? Who cares? Just wanna get a look at him, is all.'

Paul Yale and Nim exchanged glances as the same thought occurred to them.

'We'll know soon enough,' Yale said.

They began easing their way closer to the State Building, a functional, uninteresting edifice with steps in front. At the same time a black limousine with a police motorcycle escort approached from the opposite direction. A cry went up, and was repeated, 'There he is!' The crowd surged forward.

More policemen appeared. They cleared a way for the limousine to reach the sidewalk near the steps. As the car stopped, a uniformed chauffeur jumped out and opened the rear door. A short, slight, young man emerged. He had a shock of blond hair and was wearing a lightweight tan suit. The crowd cheered.

'Cameron! Hi there, Cameron!' Someone began the cry and others took it up.

Like royalty, Cameron Clarke waved in response.

He was Hollywood's current gold-plated box office guarantee. His handsome, boyish, amiable face was known to fifty million worshipping fans from Cleveland to Calcutta, from Seattle to Sierra Leone, from Brooklyn to Baghdad. Even august justices of the US Supreme Court had heard of Cameron Clarke, as Paul Sherman Yale had demonstrated moments earlier. The mere presence of Clarke anywhere was sufficient to set off a near-riot of adulation. The Fresno police, undoubtedly aware of this, were doing their best to control the crowd now.

Press photographers, who had begun shooting as the limousine stopped, were continuing as if film were inexhaustible. A TV crew, which had been waiting, moved in closer to the movie star.

An interview ensued.

Interviewer (*with great respect*): Mr Clarke, why are you here?
Cameron Clarke: I am here, as an ordinary humble citizen, to protest an ill-conceived, sordid and totally unneeded scheme which would desecrate the magnificent, unspoiled area of California known as Tunipah.
I: Sir, those are strong words. Would you explain why you feel that way?
CC: Certainly. The Tunipah plan is ill-conceived because it is anti-environment. It is sordid because the objective is to make profits for Golden State Power & Light, which doesn't need them. It is unnecessary because another source of power is available; furthermore, conservation could reduce power needs by more than Tunipah would generate.

Nim and Paul Yale were within hearing. 'He's reciting lines,' Nim muttered angrily. 'I wonder what uninformed idiot wrote them for him.'

I: What is that other source of power, Mr Clarke?
CC: Solar energy.
I: You believe that solar could be available now?
CC: Absolutely. However, there is no hurry, even for solar. The

307

talk we hear of electrical shortages is just a scare tactic –
propaganda put out by the power companies.

A spectator shouted, 'Attaboy, Cameron! That's telling the
bastards! Stick it to 'em!'

The actor looked up, waved an acknowledgment, and smiled.

Nim told his companion, 'I think I've heard enough. If you
don't mind, Mr Yale, I'll start back north and leave you to the
hearing. It looks as if it will be quite a production.'

'I know who'll be the star, and it isn't me,' Yale said ruefully.
'All right, Nim; you go. Thanks for all your help.'

As Nim elbowed his way outwards through the crowd, Yale
beckoned a policeman and identified himself. A moment later,
unnoticed, he was escorted into the State Building.

The TV interview with Cameron Clarke was continuing.

'Actually,' Oscar O'Brien said next day, 'when you get Cameron
Clarke by himself, you find out he's a pretty decent guy. I talked
to him; I also know a couple of his friends. He has a solid marriage and three kids he's crazy about. The trouble is though,
whenever he opens his mouth in public, what he says gets treated
as if it came from Mount Olympus.'

The general counsel, who had appeared at the Fresno hearing,
was reporting – at an inquest session – to J. Eric Humphrey,
Teresa Van Buren, and Nim.

'As it turned out,' O'Brien said, 'the main reason Clarke is
opposed to Tunipah is that he owns property near there – a hideaway place he and his family use in summers. They keep horses,
ride the trails, fish, sometimes camp out overnight. He's afraid
our Tunipah development would spoil all that, and he's probably right.'

Eric Humphrey asked, 'Was the point not made that the welfare of millions of Californians outweighs the holiday privileges
of one individual?'

'It was made all right,' O'Brien said. 'Christ knows, I tried on
cross-examination. But do you think anyone cared? No! Cameron Clarke objected to Tunipah and the god of the silver screen
had spoken. That was all that mattered.'

The lawyer stopped, remembering, then said, 'When Clarke
spoke his piece at the hearing about despoiling nature – and, by
God, I have to admit he was good, it was like Mark Antony

orating over Caesar's corpse – there were people, among those crowded in, who were crying. I mean it – crying!'

'I still think someone wrote his lines,' Nim said. 'From all I hear, he doesn't know that much about anything.'

O'Brien shrugged. 'It's academic.'

He added, 'I'll tell you something else. When Clarke had finished testifying and was ready to leave, the presiding Commissioner sent word he would appreciate an autograph. Wanted it for his niece, he said. Damn liar! It was for himself.'

'Whichever way you slice it,' Teresa Van Buren pronounced, 'Cameron Clarke has done our cause a lot of harm.'

No one mentioned what scarcely needed saying: that TV, radio and print reviews of the movie actor's brief appearance had eclipsed all other news about Tunipah. In the *Chronicle-West* and *California Examiner*, the statement by the Governor of California in support of the project rated a brief paragraph near the end of the Clarke-dominated report. On TV it was not mentioned at all. As to Paul Sherman Yale's appearance, that was totally ignored.

13

Instinct told Nancy Molineaux she was on to something. Possibly a major story, though so far it was shapeless and insubstantial. There were other problems. One was that she didn't really know what she was looking for. Another was the practical need to do other, regular reporting jobs for the *California Examiner*, which limited the time available for her nebulous quest. Making it even more difficult was the fact that she had not confided in anyone yet, particularly the *Examiner*'s city editor, who was always in a mad rush for results and could never understand that finesse and patience could sometimes be important tools of a good reporter. Nancy had both.

She had been using them since the Golden State Power & Light annual shareholders' meeting when Nim Goldman suggested to her in anger, 'Why not investigate *him*?'

'Him' was Davey Birdsong.

Goldman, of course, had blown his cool and did not expect her to take the suggestion seriously. But, after thinking about it, Nancy had.

She had been curious about Birdsong before. Nancy mistrusted people who were always on the side of righteousness and the downtrodden, or would like you to think they were, as Davey Birdsong did. Nancy's experience was that those kinds of liberal-populist do-gooders were usually looking out for number one first, with all others trailing a long way behind and getting the leftover crumbs. She had seen a lot of that at first hand – in black communities as well as white.

Mr Milo Molineaux, Nancy's father, was *not* a liberal do-gooder. He was a building contractor who, throughout his life, had pursued one forthright, stated objective: to transform himself from a poor boy, born of black parents in rural Louisiana, into a rich man. He had succeeded, had done it honestly, and nowadays Mr Molineaux was very rich indeed.

Yet her father, Nancy had observed, had done more for people of his own race – by providing steady employment, fair wages and human dignity – than a thousand political activists and their kind who (as the saying went) 'had never had to meet a payroll.'

She despised some of the liberals, including white ones who acted as if they were trying to atone personally for three hundred years of black slavery. The way those idiots behaved was as if a black person could do nothing wrong – ever. Nancy amused herself by being rude and bitchy to them, watching them take it and smile, and letting her get away with the inexcusable just because she was black. While they did, her contempt for them grew.

She did not despise Nim Goldman. In fact – though the knowledge would have amazed Nim – she had come to like and admire him.

Goldman hated her guts, and Nancy knew it. He hated her straightforwardly, making no effort to conceal it. He hated her as a reporter and as a woman. Nancy was perfectly sure her colour had nothing to do with Goldman's hatred, which would have been just as intense had she been white, yellow or a shade of purple. Where his hatred of Nancy Molineaux was concerned, Goldman was colour-blind.

Which was as it should be. Ergo, Nancy respected him.

In a perverse way – which she recognized as perverse – she rather enjoyed arousing Goldman's anger. It was so goddamn refreshing! Just the same, enough was enough. Twice she had impaled him well and truly, but it wasn't fair to go on doing it. Besides, the son-of-a-bitch had guts and was honest, which was more than you could say for most of those sleazy pontificators at the hearing where Goldman had spoken his mind and afterwards got gagged.

About that hearing, Nancy had written the story she had to because she prided herself in being – first and foremost – a good journalist. Which meant being ruthless, putting emotions, personal feelings, second. But none of it had stopped her feeling sorry for Goldman and mentally wishing him well.

If she ever got to know him better – which was unlikely – someday she might tell him all of that.

Meanwhile there was a certain logic and justice, Nancy Molineaux thought, in that having abandoned Goldman as a target, she had switched attention to Davey Birdsong.

Birdsong she most certainly did *not* admire, being certain – even at this early stage of her inquiries – that he was a phony and probably a crook.

She had begun, soon after the GSP & L shareholders' meeting, by quietly investigating Birdsong's p & lfp. That had taken several months because she worked in her spare time and there were some extended periods when she didn't have any. But results, while slow, were interesting.

Birdsong, Nancy learned, had founded p & lfp four years earlier, at a time when inflation, plus increased oil prices, had forced electricity and gas rates substantially higher. Without question, the rate increases caused hardship to lower- and middle-income families. Birdsong had proclaimed himself the people's champion.

His flamboyance earned him instant media attention and he capitalized on it by recruiting thousands of members into p & lfp. To accomplish this, Birdsong employed a small army of university students as canvassers and Nancy had managed to locate several – now *ex*-students – who had worked for him. All, without exception, were soured by the experience.

'We thought we were doing something noble, helping the underprivileged,' one of the former students, an architect, told Nancy. 'But we discovered what we were mostly doing was helping Davey Birdsong.'

Her informant continued, 'When we went out canvassing we were given petitions to take with us which Birdsong had had printed up. The petitions were addressed to the Governor, State Senate and House, the Public Utilities Commission . . . you name it. They urged "reduced utility rates for hard-pressed residential users", and we went door-to-door, asking people to sign. Hell! – who *wouldn't* sign that? Just about everybody did.'

Another ex-canvasser – a young woman who had consented to talk to Nancy at the same time – took up the story.

'As soon as we had a signature – not before – we were told to explain that organizing petitions cost money. So would everyone please help by donating three dollars to the campaign, which included a year's membership in p & lfp? By that time, the people we'd been talking to figured they owed us something for our trouble – it was smart psychology, Birdsong's good at that – and there were very few, even poor families, who didn't come through with the three bucks.'

'There was nothing really dishonest, I guess,' the young architect said, 'unless you call collecting a whole lot more money than was needed to run p & lfp dishonest. But what really *was* cheating was what Birdsong did to the students who worked for him.'

'Birdsong promised us, as wages,' the young woman said, 'one dollar out of every three collected. But he insisted *all* the money must go to him first – as he explained it – to be entered in the books, then we would be paid later. Well, it *was* later, much later. Even then we only got a fourth of what he'd promised – twenty-five cents instead of a dollar out of every three. We argued with him, of course, but all he would say was that we had misunderstood.'

Nancy asked, 'You didn't have anything in writing?'

'Nothing. We trusted him. After all, he was on the side of the poor against big business – or so we thought.'

'Also,' the architect added, 'Birdsong was careful – as we realized later – to talk to each of us separately. That way . . . no witnesses. But if there *was* a misunderstanding, all of us made the same one.'

'There was no misunderstanding,' the young woman informant said. 'Birdsong is a con man.'

Nancy Molineaux asked those two canvassers and others for estimates of how much money was collected. In his own public statements, Birdsong had reported p & lfp as having twenty-five thousand members. But most whom Nancy talked to believed the real figure was substantially higher – probably thirty-five thousand. If so, and allowing for the amount paid out to canvassers, the first year's receipts of p & lfp were probably close to a hundred thousand dollars, mostly in cash.

'You're not kidding,' the architect had said when informed of Nancy's estimate. 'Birdsong has a profitable racket.' He added ruefully, 'Maybe I'm in the wrong one.'

Something else Nancy discovered was that collection of money by p & lfp was continuing.

Davey Birdsong was still hiring university students – there was always a new generation which needed part-time work and money – and the objective was to get more p & lfp annual memberships, as well as have existing ones renewed. Apparently Birdsong was no longer cheating the students; probably he realized he couldn't get away with it indefinitely. But, for sure, a potful of cash was flowing into p & lfp.

What did Birdsong do with it? There seemed no simple answer. True, he *did* provide an active, vocal opposition to Golden State Power & Light on several fronts – at times successfully – and many who belonged to p & lfp believed they were getting their money's worth. But Nancy questioned that.

With help from an accountant she had done the arithmetic and, even allowing for the most generous expenses and a personal salary for Birdsong, there was *no way* he could have spent more than half of what was coming in. So how about the remainder? The best guess was that Birdsong, who controlled p & lfp totally, was siphoning it off.

Nancy couldn't prove it, though. Not yet.

Her accountant adviser said that eventually the Internal Revenue Service might demand an accounting from p & lfp and Birdsong. But the IRS, he pointed out, was notoriously understaffed. Therefore lots of so-called non-profit organizations were never audited and got away with financial skulduggery.

The accountant asked: did Nancy want him to tip off the IRS confidentially?

Her emphatic answer: no. She wasn't ready to tip off anybody.

313

The accountant's services were available to Nancy because her father was an important client of his firm. The same applied to a lawyer often retained by Milo Molineaux, Inc, and Nancy took the ex-university students to him and had them swear out affidavits. They cooperated willingly.

university lecturing and writing. There was nothing wrong with She was building her dossier carefully.

Nancy Molineaux knew about Birdsong's other income from that, or even unusual, but it reinforced her curiosity about what Davey Birdsong did with all that money.

Then there was a vague rumour – she overheard it at a cock-tail party – that Birdsong and p & lfp had appealed to the Sequoia Club for financial support. Nancy considered that unlikely and, even if true, was certain the wealthy and prestigious Sequoia Club would have no truck with the likes of Davey Birdsong. Just the same, because she made a habit of covering all bases, Nancy had put out feelers. So far, no results.

The most intriguing question of all came up one day in January when Nancy was driving her Mercedes 450SL and happened to see Davey Birdsong walking on a downtown street. Without stopping to reason why, she decided to follow him. She whisked her car into a handy self-serve parking lot and went after him on foot, keeping a discreet distance behind. What came next was like something out of an espionage novel.

Although Nancy was positive Birdsong had not seen her, he behaved as if he expected to be followed and was determined to shake off pursuit. First, he walked into the busy main lobby of a hotel. After glancing around, he ducked into a men's room and a few minutes later came out wearing dark glasses and a soft felt hat, whereas before he had been bareheaded. The change did not fool Nancy. However, his appearance *was* different and she realized that, if Birdsong had been dressed that way to begin with, she probably would not have noticed him. He left the hotel by a side door. Giving him a comfortable start, Nancy followed.

She almost lost him then because, further along the street from the hotel, he was boarding a bus which promply closed its doors and moved away.

There was no time to return to her car, but luckily a taxi was approaching. Nancy hailed it. She flashed a twenty-dollar bill and told the driver, a young black, 'Keep that bus in sight, but don't make it obvious we're following it. Every time it stops, though, I want to see who gets off.'

The driver was instantly with it. 'Will do, lady! Just sit back. Leave the action to me.'

He was smart and resourceful. He passed the bus twice, then each time eased into the right lane traffic so the bus, in an outside lane, would pass him. While both vehicles were close, Nancy kept her head averted. But whenever the bus stopped to take on or disembark passengers, the taxi was positioned so she could see clearly. For what seemed a long time, Birdsong did not appear and Nancy wondered if she had missed him after all. Then, about four miles from his point of boarding, he got off.

She could see him looking around.

'That's the one – with the beard,' she told her driver.

'I see him!' The cabby accelerated past, without glancing in Birdsong's direction, then eased into the kerb. 'Don't turn around, lady. I got him in the mirror. Now he's crossing the street.' After a minute or two: 'Be damned if he ain't getting on another bus.'

They followed the second bus too. It was going in an opposite direction from the first and retraced some of the original route. This time Birdsong got off after a few blocks, again looking around him. Close by were several parked taxis. Birdsong took the first and, as it pulled away, Nancy could see his face peering through the rear window.

She made another decision and instructed, 'Let him go. Take me back downtown.'

Nancy reasoned: there was no sense in pushing her luck. She hoped Birdsong had not detected her taxi trailing him, but if she persisted he undoubtedly would. Solving the mystery of where he went, and why, would have to be done some other way.

'Geez, lady, kinda hard to figure you out,' the cabby complained when they had changed direction. 'First you wanna tail the guy, so we do okay. Then you quit.' He went on grumbling, 'Didn't even get close enough to see the other hack's number.'

Because he had done his best, she decided to explain why she didn't want to be that close, and possibly be seen. He listened, then nodded. 'Gotcha!'

A few minutes later the young driver turned his head. 'You still wanna find out where the beard goes?'

'Yes,' Nancy said. The more she thought about Birdsong's elaborate precautions, the more convinced she became that something important was happening. Something she *had* to know.

The driver asked, 'Know where the guy hangs out mostly?'

'His home address? No, but it wouldn't be hard to find.'

'Maybe we could work a deal,' the driver said. 'Me and two buddies. They ain't working, and they got cars with CB radios. I got a CB too. Three of us could take turns following the beard, pulling a switcheroo so he don't keep seeing the same heap. We'd use the radios. That way, when one guy eased off, he'd call another in.'

'But to do that', Nancy pointed out, 'you'd have to keep watch on him all the time.'

'Can do. Like I said, my friends ain't working.'

The idea had possibilities. She asked, 'How much would it cost?'

'Have to figure that out, lady. But not as much as you'd think.'

'When you've done your figuring,' Nancy said, 'call me.' She scribbled her apartment phone number on the back of a business card.

He called late that night. By then she had looked up Birdsong's home address which was in the phone book.

'Two hunnert and fifty a week,' the cabby said. 'That's for me and the other two.'

She hesitated. Was it important enough to go to all that trouble and expense? Again her instincts told her yes.

So should she ask the *Examiner* for the money? Nancy was doubtful. If she did, she would have to disclose everything she had uncovered so far, and she was certain the paper would want to publish immediately the material on Davey Birdsong and his p & lfp. In Nancy's opinion that would be premature; she believed strongly there was more to come and it was worth waiting for. Another thing: the newspaper's penny-pinching management hated to spend money unless it had to.

She decided to go ahead on her own. She would pay the money herself and hope to get it back later. If she didn't, it would be no great disaster, though it would violate one of the rules she lived by.

By most standards, Nancy Molineaux was wealthy. Several years ago her father established a trust fund which provided her with a regular, comfortable income. But, as a matter of pride, she kept her private finances and professional earnings separate.

For once, pride would have to be humbled.

The cabby said he would like something in advance, which was reasonable, and Nancy told him to drop by and pick it up.

After he did, she heard nothing for six days. At the end of that time, the young cabdriver, whose name was Vickery, brought her a report. To Nancy's surprise it was detailed and neatly written. All of Birdsong's movements were described; they were routine and innocuous. At no point had he shown awareness of being followed. Most significant: he made no attempt to throw any follower off.

'Goesta show one week ain't enough,' Vickery said. 'Wanna try another?'

Nancy thought : *What the hell, why not?*

In another seven days Vickery was back. He had the same kind of detailed report, with similarly negative results. Disappointed, she told him, 'Okay, that's all. Forget it.'

The young man regarded her with unconcealed contempt. 'You gonna give up now? Look whatcha got invested!' When he sensed her wavering, he urged, 'Go for broke! Try one more week.'

'You should be a frigging salesman,' Nancy said, 'not driving a hack.'

She thought about it. She had proof that Birdsong was a fraud; did she still believe he was a crook? And would finding where he went so mysteriously help the story she intended to write? Finally, should she cut her losses or – as the smartass kid put it – go for broke?

Her instincts again. They told her all three answers should be yes.

'Okay, hotshot,' she told Vickery. 'One extra week. But no more.'

They hit pay dirt on the fourth day.

Vickery phoned, then came to her apartment, that night. 'Figured you'd wanna know right away. This aft the beard tried to shake anybody off, the way he did that day with you and me.' He added smugly, 'We beat the sonovabitch.'

'For what it's cost me,' Nancy said, 'I should goddamn hope so.'

The young man grinned as he presented the usual written report. It showed that Davey Birdsong had driven his own car from his apartment garage and parked it on the opposite side of the city. Before leaving the car, he had put on dark glasses and a hat. Then he had taken a taxi back across town, followed by two bus rides in differing directions, and finally a walk – a round-about route to a small house on the city's east side.

He went into the house. The address was given.

'The beard stayed inside two hours,' Vickery said.

After that, the report continued, Birdsong took a taxi to a point a few blocks from where his car was parked. From there he walked to the car and drove home.

Vickery asked hopefully, 'Wannus to watch the beard some more?' He added. 'Them buddies of mine still ain't working.'

'With you for a friend,' Nancy said, 'they shouldn't worry.' She shook her head. 'No more.'

Now, two days later, Nancy was seated in her car, observing the house which Davey Birdsong had visited so secretively. She had been there nearly two hours. It was approaching noon.

Yesterday, the day after Vickery's final report, she spent completing an *Examiner* feature assignment, though she had not yet turned in her copy to the city desk. She would do so tomorrow. Meanwhile her time was her own.

The house she was watching was number 117 Crocker Street. It was one of a dozen identical row houses built in the 1920s and, a decade ago, refurbished by a speculative builder who believed the district was destined for revival and upgrading. The builder was wrong. Crocker Street remained what it had been – an unimpressive, drab thoroughfare where people lived because they could not afford something better. And the refurbished houses were slipping back into their former state, attested to by chipped masonry, cracked windows and peeling paint.

To Nancy's eyes, number 117 seemed no different from the rest.

Cagily, she had parked her Mercedes a block and a half away, where she had a clear view of the house but believed she would not be observed herself. The presence of several other parked cars helped. She had brought binoculars but had not used them for fear of arousing the curiosity of some passer-by.

So far there had been little activity on the street, none whatever at number 117.

Nancy had no idea what to expect, if anything, nor had she

any plan. As the morning passed she wished she might see something of the occupants of the house, but the wish went unfulfilled. She wondered if she had stayed long enough. Perhaps she should leave now and return another day.

A vehicle passed her parked car, as had several others during the preceding two hours. She noticed casually that it was a beat-up Volkswagen van, painted brown and with a broken side window. The window was roughly patched with cardboard and masking tape.

Abruptly Nancy became alert. The VW had swung across the street and was stopping in front of 117.

A man got out. Nancy risked using her binoculars. She saw that he was lean, with close-cropped hair and a bushy moustache: she judged him to be in his late twenties. In contrast to the van, he was neatly dressed in a dark blue suit and wore a tie. He went to the rear of the vehicle and opened its door. The binoculars were powerful – she used them in her apartment to watch shipping in the harbour – and she caught a glimpse of the man's hands. They appeared to be badly stained in some way.

Now he was reaching inside the van and he lifted out a substantial red-coloured cylinder. It seemed to be heavy. Setting the object down on the sidewalk, he reached inside again and produced another, then carried the two towards the house. As he did, Nancy realized they were fire extinguishers.

The man made two more journeys between the VW and the house, each time carrying in two more red fire extinguishers. Six altogether. After the final pair he stayed in the house for about five minutes, then re-emerged and drove away.

Nancy wavered about following, then decided not to. Afterwards she sat wondering: why would so small a house need so much fire protection? Suddenly she exclaimed, 'Shit!' She had not thought to note the VW's licence number, which she could have done easily. Now it was too late. She chided herself for being a lousy detective and thought maybe she should have followed the van after all.

Time to go anyway? She supposed so. Her hand went to the ignition switch, then stopped. Something else was happening at 117. Once more she reached for the binoculars.

A woman had come out of the house; she was young, slight in build, and carelessly dressed in faded jeans and a pea coat. She glanced around her momentarily, then began walking briskly – in the opposite direction from the parked Mercedes.

This time Nancy did not hesitate. She started the car and eased out from her parking space. Keeping the woman in sight, she followed slowly, warily, pulling into the kerb occasionally so as not to overtake her quarry.

The woman did not look back. When she turned a corner, Nancy waited as long as she dared before doing the same. She was in time to see the woman enter a small supermarket. It had a parking lot and Nancy drove on to it. She locked the car and followed inside.

The supermarket was averagely busy, with perhaps twenty people shopping. Nancy caught sight of the woman she had followed – at the far end of an aisle, putting cans into a shopping cart. Nancy got a cart herself, dropped in a few items at random from nearby shelves, then moved casually towards the other woman.

She appeared even younger now than she had at a distance – little more than a girl. She was pale, her fair hair untidy, and she wore no makeup. On her right hand she had what looked like an improvised glove. Clearly it covered some kind of deformity or injury for she was using only her left hand. Reaching out, she selected a jar of Mazola Oil and read the label.

Nancy Molineaux manoeuvred her cart past, then abruptly turned, as if she had forgotten something. Her eyes met the other woman's. Nancy smiled and said brightly, 'Hi! Don't we know each other?' She added, 'I think we have a mutual acquaintance, Davey Birdsong.'

The response was immediate and startling. The young woman's face went ashen white, she visibly trembled, and the Mazola Oil fell from her hand, shattering on the floor.

There was a silence lasting several seconds in which nothing happened except that a pool of oil spread rapidly across the shopping aisle. Then the store manager hurried forward, clucking like a worried hen. 'My goodness! What a mess! Whatever happened here?'

'It was my fault,' Nancy said quickly. 'I'm sorry and I'll pay for what was broken.'

The manager objected, 'It won't pay for the cleaning up, will it?'

'No,' Nancy told him, 'but think of the exercise you'll get.' She took the arm of the other woman, who was still standing transfixed, as if in shock.

'Let's get out of here,' Nancy said. Unresisting, abandoning her shopping cart, the girl in the pea coat and jeans went with her.

On the parking lot, Nancy steered the girl towards the Mercedes. But as the passenger door was unlocked and opened she seemed to come alert.

'I can't! Oh, I can't! I have to get back to the house.' Her voice was nervously high-pitched, the trembling, which had stopped as they emerged from the supermarket, began again. She looked at Nancy wildly. 'Who *are* you?'

'I'm a friend. Look, there's a bar around the block; I saw it on the way. Why don't we go there, have a drink? You look as if you need one.'

'I tell you I can't!'

'Yes you can, and you will,' Nancy said. 'Because if you don't, I'm going to phone your friend Davey Birdsong this afternoon and tell him . . .'

She had no idea how she would have finished the sentence but its effect was electric. The girl got into the car without further protest. Nancy shut the door alongside her, then went around to the driver's side.

It took only a few minutes to drive to the bar and there was parking space outside. They left the car and went in. The interior was dark and smelled of mildew.

'Christ!' Nancy said. 'We need a guide dog.' She groped her way to a corner table, away from the few other people already drinking. The girl followed.

As they sat down, Nancy said, 'I have to call you something. What?'

'Yvette.'

A waiter appeared and Yvette ordered a beer, Nancy a daiquiri. They were silent until the drinks came.

This time the girl spoke first. 'You haven't told me who you are.'

There seemed no reason to conceal the truth. 'My name is Nancy Molineaux. I'm a newspaper reporter.'

Twice before, Yvette had exhibited shock, but this time the

effect was even greater. Her mouth fell open, the drink slipped in her hand and, if Nancy had not grabbed it, would have gone the way of the Mazola.

'Take it easy,' Nancy urged. 'Reporters only eat people when they're hungry. I'm not.'

The girl whispered, having trouble with the words, 'What do you want from me?'

'Some information.'

Yvette moistened her lips. 'Like what?'

'Like, who else lives in the house you came out of? What goes on there? Why does Davey Birdsong visit? That's for starters.'

'It's none of your business.'

Nancy's eyes were becoming accustomed to the gloom and she could see, despite the flash of spirit, that the other woman was still frightened. She tried a random shot. 'Okay, I guess I should have gone to the police in the first place and . . .'

'No!' Yvette half rose, then fell back. Suddenly she put her face in her hands and began to sob.

Nancy reached across the table. 'I know you're in some kind of trouble. If you'll let me, I'll help.'

Through the sobbing: 'Nobody can help.' A moment later, with an obvious effort of will, Yvette stood up. 'I'm going now.' Even in her acute distress, she possessed a certain dignity.

'Listen,' Nancy said. 'I'll make a deal. If you'll agree to meet me again, I won't say or do anything in the meantime.'

The girl hesitated. 'When?'

'Three days from now. Right here.'

'Not three days.' Again the mix of doubt and fear. 'Maybe a week.'

It would have to do. 'All right. A week from today, next Wednesday – same time, same place.'

With a nod of agreement, Yvette left.

Driving away, Nancy was unsure whether she had handled the situation well or badly. And what the hell was it all about? Where did Davey Birdsong and Yvette fit in? Nancy's reference to the police during her conversation with Yvette had been an offhand, impulsive remark. Yet the girl's near-hysterical reaction suggested that something illegal was going on. If so, what kind of illegality? It was all frustrating, with too many questions, too few answers – like trying to assemble a jigsaw puzzle without the slightest notion of what the end result might be.

14

For Nancy Molineaux, another piece of the jigsaw fell into place next day. It concerned the vague, overheard rumour – which Nancy hadn't believed – that Birdsong's p & lfp was seeking financial help from the Sequoia Club.

Despite her scepticism, she had put out feelers. One produced results.

A mailroom employee of the Sequoia Club, an elderly black woman named Grace, had once asked Nancy Molineaux's help in obtaining city-subsidised housing. At the time, all it had taken was a single telephone call and use of the *California Examiner*'s influence to get her near the top of an official waiting list. But Grace had been grateful and insisted that if she could ever return the favour, she would.

Several weeks ago Nancy called at her home and mentioned the p & lfp–Sequoia Club rumour. Would she try to discover, Nancy asked, whether there was any substance to it and, if so, whether anything had come of p & lfp's request?

A few days later she received a report: as far as Grace could learn, the rumour was untrue. She added, though, 'Something like that could be secret, with not more than two or three at the top, like Prissy Pritchy [which was what the Sequoia Club staff called Roderick Pritchett] knowing about it.'

Today, Grace had used her lunch hour to go to the *Examiner* Building and make her way to the newsroom. Nancy happened to be in. They went into a soundproof glass cubicle where they could talk. Grace, who was heavily built, overflowed a tight, brightly coloured print dress and wore a floppy hat. She was carrying a string bag and reached into it.

'Found out something, Miss Molineaux. Don't know if it has to do with what you wanted, but here it is.'

'It' was a copy of a Sequoia Club memo.

Grace explained: three outward-bound envelopes, all marked *Private and Confidential*, had come through the mailroom. That was not unusual. What *was* unusual was that one of the envelopes had arrived unsealed, probably through a secretary's carelessness. Grace slipped it aside and later, when she was unobserved, read the contents. Nancy smiled, wondering how much other mail got perused the same way.

Grace had used one of the Sequoia Club's Xerox machines to make the copy. Nancy read the confidential memo carefully.

From: Manager-Secretary
To: Members of Special Executive Committee
For your information, the second donation to B's organization from the contingency fund, and agreed to at our August 22 meeting, has now been paid.

It was initialled 'R.P.'

Nancy asked, 'Who was the envelope addressed to?'

'Mr Saunders. He's a board member and . . .'

'Yes, I know.' Irwin Saunders, the well known lawyer-about-town, was a Sequoia Club wheel. 'How about the other two envelopes?'

'One was to Mrs Carmichael, our chairman. The other was addressed to Mrs Quinn.'

That would be Priscilla Quinn. Nancy knew her slightly. A snob and socialite.

Grace asked anxiously, 'Is it what you wanted?'

'I'm not sure.' Nancy read the memo again. Of course, 'B' *could* mean Birdsong, but it might also mean other things. For example, the mayor, whose last name began with 'B', headed an organization called 'Save Old Buildings', which the Sequoia Club supported actively. But in that case would a memo be 'private and confidential'? Perhaps. The Sequoia Club had always been close-mouthed about its money.

'Whatever you do,' Grace said, 'you won't let on where that came from?'

'I don't even know you,' Nancy assured. 'And you've never been here.'

The older woman smiled and nodded. 'I need that job. Even though it don't pay much.' She stood up. 'Well, I'll be getting back.'

'Thanks,' Nancy said. 'I appreciate what you did. Let me know when *you* need anything.'

Favours for favours, she had discovered early, were part of journalism's commerce.

Returning to her desk, still wondering if the memo referred to Birdsong and p & lfp, or not, she met the city editor.

'Who was the old lady, Nancy?'

'A friend.'

'You hatching a story?'

'Maybe.'

'Tell me about it.'

She shook her head. 'Not yet.'

The city editor regarded her quizzically. He was a greying veteran of newspaperdom, good at his job but, like many of his kind, he had reached the outer limits of promotion. 'You're supposed to be part of a team, Nancy, and I'm the coach. I know you prefer being a loner, and you've got away with it because you get results. But you can push that game too far.'

She shrugged. 'So fire me.'

He wouldn't, of course, and they both knew it. Leaving him frustrated, as she did so many men, she returned to her desk and began telephoning.

She tried Irwin Saunders first.

A secretary declared he was not available, but when Nancy mentioned the *Examiner*, he came cheerfully on the line.

'What can I do for you, Miss Molineaux?'

'I'd like to discuss the Sequoia Club's donation to Mr Birdsong's power & light for people.'

There was a second's silence. 'What donation?'

'It's our understanding . . .'

Saunders laughed aloud. 'Bullshit! Nancy . . . may I call you that?'

'Sure.'

'Nancy, that kind of I-already-know-but-would-like-some-confirmation statement is the oldest reporter's ploy in the book. You're talking to a wily old fish who doesn't take those baits.'

She laughed with him. 'I'd always heard you were sharp, Mr Saunders.'

'Damn right, kiddo.'

She persisted, 'But how about a link-up between the Sequoia Club and p & lfp?'

'That's a subject, Nancy, about which I'm unlikely to know anything.'

Score *one* for me, she thought. He had not said *I don't know.*

Only *I'm unlikely to know*. Later, if he had to, he could claim he hadn't lied. He probably had a recorder going at this moment.

'My information,' she said, 'is that a Sequoia Club committee decided . . .'

'Tell me about that alleged committee, Nancy. Who was on it? Name names.'

She thought quickly. If she mentioned the other names she knew – Carmichael, Quinn – he would be on the phone immediately to caution them. Nancy wanted to get there first. She lied, 'I don't have any names.'

'In other words, you don't have a damn thing.' His voice was suddenly less friendly. 'I'm a busy lawyer, Miss Molineaux, with a heavy case load. Clients pay me for my time and you're wasting it.'

'Then I won't waste any more.'

Without replying, he hung up.

Even while talking, Nancy had been leafing through a phone directory in search of 'Quinn'. Now she found it : *Quinn, Dempster W. R.* Trust Priscilla Quinn's old man to have one more name than most other people. Nancy dialled and after the second ring was informed by a male voice, 'This is the Dempster Quinn residence.' It sounded like the soundtrack of *Upstairs, Downstairs*.

'Mrs Quinn please.'

'I'm sorry. Madam is at lunch and may not be disturbed.'

'Disturb her,' Nancy said, 'by telling her the *California Examiner* intends to mention her name; and does she want to help us get the facts straight?'

'One moment, please.'

Not only moments passed, but several minutes. Eventually a cool female voice inquired, 'Yes?'

Nancy identified herself.

'What is it you want?'

'Mrs Quinn, when the Sequoia Club executive committee, of which you are a member, met last August and decided to team up with Davey Birdsong's power & light for people, what was . . .?'

Priscilla Quinn said sharply, 'That committee meeting, and the entire arrangement, are supposed to be confidential.'

Bingo! Unlike lawyer Saunders, Quinn was *not* a wily fish.

326

Nancy now had the confirmation she had sought, a confirmation she would never have obtained by asking direct questions.

'Well,' Nancy said, 'word seems to be around. Maybe Birdsong talked.'

She heard what sounded like a sniff. 'Very likely. I would never trust that man in the slightest degree.'

'Then may I ask why you agreed to support his . . .'

'I did not agree. I was the one who voted against the whole idea. I was defeated by the others.' A note of alarm entered Priscilla Quinn's voice. 'Are you planning to print any of this?'

'Naturally.'

'Oh, dear. I don't want to be quoted.'

'Mrs Quinn,' Nancy pointed out, 'when you came on the line I identified myself, but you said nothing about any of our conversation being off the record.'

'Well, I do now.'

'It's too late.'

The other woman said indignantly, 'I shall telephone your publisher.'

'Who won't do a thing,' Nancy shot back, 'except tell me to go ahead and write the story.' She paused, considering. 'What I *will* do is make a deal.'

'What kind of deal?'

'I have to use your name as a member of the Sequoia Club executive committee. There's no way I can avoid that. But I won't mention that I spoke to you *if* you'll tell me how much money was paid by the Sequoia Club to p & lfp.'

'But that's blackmail!'

'Call it a trade – fair exchange.'

There was a brief silence followed by, 'How do I know I can trust you?'

'You can. Go on – take a chance.'

A pause again. Then, very quietly : 'Fifty thousand dollars.'

Nancy's lips pursed in a silent whistle.

As she hung up, instinct told her she had spoiled Mrs Dempster W. R. Quinn's lunch.

An hour or two later, having handled some other, routine news chores, Nancy sat at her desk thinking, calculating. So how much did she know?

Fact one: Davey Birdsong had cheated students and collected considerably more money than was needed to run p & lfp.

Fact two: the Sequoia Club was backing Birdsong with money – a lot of it. That alone was a news scoop which would raise many eyebrows and almost certainly damage the club's reputation as a high-level, prestigious body.

Fact three: Birdsong was involved in something he didn't want found out, hence his elaborate precautions when he visited that East Side house. *Question one:* what did he do there; did it relate to the large amounts of money he had accumulated; and what went on in the house? Nancy still hadn't the faintest idea.

Fact four: the girl from the house, Yvette, was scared shitless about something. *Question two:* what? Same answer as to question one.

Fact five: number 117 Crocker Street was owned by the Redwood Realty Corporation. Nancy had found that out earlier today from the tax assessor's office. Later, posing as a credit bureau investigator, she had telephoned Redwood and learned the property had been rented for the past year to a Mr G. Archambault, about whom nothing was known except that he paid the rent promptly. *Question three:* who and what was Archambault? Go back to question one.

Conclusion: the jigsaw was incomplete, the story not ready to break.

Nancy mused: She would have to wait and be patient until her meeting with Yvette six days from now. At this moment she was sorry she had agreed to delay that long, but having made the promise she would keep it.

Briefly Nancy wondered: Would she be in any danger, having tipped off Yvette about her interest, and then going back? She didn't think so. Anyway, fear of consequences seldom bothered her.

And yet . . . Nancy had an uncomfortable feeling she ought to share her knowledge with someone else, talk over what she had, and ask a second opinion about what to do next. Logically, she should go to the city editor. She might have done it, too, if the son-of-a-bitch hadn't handed her that coach-and-team crap earlier today. Now it would look as if she was sucking around him because of it. Screw you, Mr Charlie!

For the time being, Nancy decided, she would continue to keep the whole ball of wax to herself.

It was a decision which later, looking back, she would bitterly regret.

15

In his office, Nim was going through the morning mail. His secretary, Victoria Davis, had already opened and sorted most of the letters and memos, putting them into two folders, one green, the other red – the latter reserved for urgent or important subjects. Today the red file was full to overflowing. There were also, placed separately, a few unopened letters marked *Personal*. Among these Nim recognized a familiar, pale blue envelope with a typewritten address. Karen Sloan's stationery.

Lately, Nim's conscience had troubled him about Karen – in two ways. On the one hand he cared about her very much indeed, and felt guilty because he had not visited her since the night they made love, even though they had talked by telephone. And on the other hand, there was Ruth. How did his love affair with Karen fit in with his reconciliation and new rapport with Ruth? The truth was: it didn't. Yet he could not suddenly toss Karen aside like a used Kleenex. If it had been some other woman he could, and would, have done it instantly. But Karen was different.

He had considered telling Ruth about Karen, then decided nothing would be gained by it. Besides, Ruth had enough problems without adding to them; also, he would be the one who would have to decide about Karen.

He was ashamed to admit it, even to himself, but for the time being he had put Karen on a mental shelf and, for that reason, delayed opening her letter now.

The thought of Ruth, though, reminded him of something else.

'Vicki,' he called through the open office door, 'did you get those hotel reservations?'

'Yesterday.' She came in, pointing to the green folder. 'I wrote you a note; it's in there. The Columbus had a cancellation, so you have a two-bedroom suite. They promised me it will be high and with a view.'

'Good! How's that last revision of my speech coming?'

'If you'll stop asking questions to which I've already given you answers,' Vicki told him, 'I'll have it ready this afternoon.'

He grinned. 'Get out of here!'

In a week's time Nim was due to address the annual convention of the National Electric Institute. His paper, which had already gone through several drafts, would be about future power demands and was entitled 'Overload'.

The big national NEI convention, important to the public utility industry and its suppliers, was being held locally this year – in the Christopher Columbus Hotel. It would last four days. Because there were numerous social events, it occurred to Nim it would be an interesting change for his family if they moved with him into the hotel for the duration of the convention. He had put the suggestion to Ruth, Leah, and Benjy, who reacted enthusiastically.

The idea of getting a high room with a view was Nim's. He thought the children would enjoy it.

His promise to speak at the NEI convention had been made nearly a year ago, long before his removal from the role of company spokesman. When Nim mentioned the commitment recently to Eric Humphrey, the chairman told him, 'Go ahead, but stay away from controversy.' In fact, Nim's paper would be heavily technical, intended mainly for other power company planners like himself. Whether or not he would season it – despite the chairman's warning – with a soupçon of controversy, he had not yet decided.

As Vicki closed the office door behind her, Nim went back to his red file, then decided he would open Karen's letter after all.

He was sure the envelope contained verses – the verses Karen so painstakingly typed with a stick held in her mouth. And, as always, he was moved by the thought of her labouring long and patiently on his behalf.

He was right.

TOP SECRET (as the military say);
For your eyes only, darling Nimrod,
(Such dear, kind eyes).

No others should alight
On this communiqué –
Un-military,
Very private, intimate, adoring.

My sensual delectation lingers:
A swirling, heady, Cyprian mixture,
At once
So sweetly light, robustly carnal.

My mind, my flesh
My nerve ends, toes, lips, fingers,

Tingling with joyous residues,
Remember – Oh my precious lover! –
The rich fulfillment of your loving.
Such ecstasy!
From this day forth
I'll vote for hedonism!

You are indeed a noble knight
In burnished armour,
Whose shining sword
(Especially that sword)
Brings golden happiness.
I thrill to it,
And you,
Forever.

Karen, he thought, when he had finished, *you turn me on! Oh, how you turn me on!*

His best intentions seemed to melt. He would see Karen again, no matter what. And soon.

First, though, he reminded himself, he had a heavy work schedule, including his convention speech. He settled down again to the official mail.

Moments later the telephone buzzed. When Nim answered impatiently, Vicki informed him, 'Mr London is on the line and would like to talk to you.'

Conscious of the bulging red folder, Nim told her, 'Ask if it's important.'

'I already did. He says it is.'

'Put him on, then.' A click and the Property Protection chief's voice said, 'Nim?'

'Harry, this is a full week for me. Is it anything that will keep?'

'I don't think so. Something tricky has come up, something I think you ought to know about.'

'Okay, go ahead.'

'Not on the phone. I need to see you.'

Nim sighed. At times Harry London acted as if everything in his department rated top priority compared with the rest of GSP & L. 'All right. Come up now.'

Nim resumed work until London arrived some five minutes later.

Pushing his chair back from the desk, Nim said, 'I'm listening, Harry. But make it brief.'

'I'll try.' The short, craggy Property Protection chief settled down in a facing chair. In dress and demeanour he still looked the smart, sharp ex-Marine, but there were more lines on his face than a few months ago, Nim thought.

'You'll remember,' London began, 'that soon after we caught those Quayle guys stealing power at the Zaco Building, I told you we'd uncovered a rat's nest. I predicted there was a lot more to come, and that some big names might be involved.'

Nim nodded.

'Try this big name on: Mr Justice Paul Sherman Yale.'

Nim shot upright. 'You have to be kidding!'

'I wish I were,' London said dolefully. 'Unfortunately, I'm not.'

All of Nim's impatience had vanished. He instructed, 'Tell me everything you know. Everything.'

'That day you and I had lunch,' Harry London said, 'something else I told you was that my department would check the records of Quayle Electrical & Gas Contracting – working with the DA's office – to review all the work Quayle did in the past year. After that we'd do more investigating to discover how much of it, if any, was illegal.'

'I remember.'

'We did all that. My people have worked like the devil and we found a bundle. You'll get the details in a report I'm writing. The gist of it is that the DA has many more cases to prosecute, with big dollar numbers attached.'

'Get to Mr Yale,' Nim said. 'How does he fit in?'

'I'm coming to that.'

Among the Quayle company work orders, the Property Protection chief reported, were an unusual number initiated for the same person – an Ian Norris.

Though the name seemed familiar, Nim couldn't place it.

'Norris,' London said, 'is a lawyer who works as some kind of financial adviser. He has an office in town – it's in the Zaco Building, wouldn't you know it? – and he looks after trusts and estates. One of them is called the Yale Family Trust.'

'I know about the Yale Trust.' Now Nim remembered Norris. They had met briefly at the cattle feedlot near Fresno.

'We have solid proof,' London continued, 'that Norris is in power theft up to his hairline. He controls a lot of property – office and industrial buildings, apartments, stores, that kind of stuff. Apparently Norris discovered some time ago that he could do a better job for his clients – save them money and make some for himself – if he lowered electricity and gas bills by cheating. He figured he could get away with it – at least, that's the way it looks – so he went into stealing power on a grand scale, using Quayle Electrical & Gas Contracting.'

'But it doesn't follow,' Nim pointed out, 'that the people Norris represents had the slightest idea of what was going on.' He had a sense of relief. Even though the Yale Family Trust might be involved, he was confident that Paul Sherman Yale would never be a party, personally, to anything dishonest.

'What you say is true enough,' London said, 'and even if any of Norris's clients did know, I doubt if we could ever prove it. But the DA is building a case against Norris and the Yale name is bound to be in it. That's why I thought you should know. It ain't going to look good, Nim, for him or for us.'

Harry was right, Nim thought. The name of Yale and Golden State Power & Light were now closely linked and there would be those who – despite all evidence to the contrary – would believe some kind of conspiracy existed. Never mind that it didn't make sense. It would not stop rumour-mongers, and there could be resulting embarrassment all around.

'I haven't finished,' Harry London said, 'and maybe this is the most important bit of all.'

Nim listened, wondering what was coming next.

'A lot of the illegal work the Quayle people did for Norris – or rather, for the people Norris represents – began nearly a year ago. But everything for the Yale Family Trust, which includes illegal wiring in two apartment buildings in the city, a winery in the

Napa Valley, and at a cattle feedlot near Fresno, has been done within the past three months. And, in case you hadn't noticed, that's *since* Mr Justice Yale left the Supreme Court, and *since* he came to work for Golden State Power.'

'Give me a minute, Harry,' Nim said. He had a sense of shock and bewilderment. 'Let me think about that.'

'Take your time,' London told him. 'Been doing plenty of thinking myself.'

Nim couldn't believe it. Simply could not believe that Paul Sherman Yale would be a participant in power theft, even peripherally, even as a silent spectator. And yet . . . Nim was reminded uneasily of their conversation at the cattle feedlot. What was it Paul Yale had said? *'It's the inflated cost of everything that does us in . . . especially electricity. This operation runs on it. We use electric power for the mill . . . for forty thousand cattle . . . in the pens there are bright lights on all night . . . our power bills are astronomical.'* And later: *'I've told the trust manager, Ian Norris, to cut down, economize . . . We have to.'*

Even before then; on that day in the Napa Valley when Nim first met the Yales, Beth Yale betrayed her husband's bitterness, and her own, that their family trust was mismanaged and losing money.

Nim addressed Harry London. 'One more question. Do you know if anyone – from your department, the police, or the DA's office – has contacted Mr Yale about any of this?'

'I do know. No one has.'

Nim paused, once more assessing all that he had heard. Then he announced, 'Harry, this is too big for me. I'm going to hand it to the chairman.'

The Property Protection chief nodded his agreement. 'I figured you'd have to.'

At 11am next day they assembled in the chairman's office suite: J. Eric Humphrey, Nim, Harry London, Paul Sherman Yale.

Mr Justice Yale, who had just been chauffeured from the Napa Valley, was especially jovial. His lined face beaming, he told the others, 'Coming back to California has made me feel younger and happier. I should have done it years ago.' Suddenly aware that no one else was smiling, he turned to Humphrey. 'Eric, is anything wrong?'

Humphrey, while outwardly dapper and composed as usual, was inwardly uncomfortable, Nim could tell. He knew the chairman had approached this meeting with misgivings.

'Frankly, I'm not sure,' Humphrey replied. 'But some information has been reported to me which I believe you should be told about. Nim, please fill in the background for Mr Yale.'

In a few sentences Nim explained about the high incidence of power theft and the role in the company of Harry London, whom Mr Justice Yale had not met previously.

While Nim talked, the old man's brow furrowed. He appeared puzzled and during a pause inquired, 'How does my own work fit in with this?'

'Unfortunately,' Humphrey said, 'what we're discussing does not concern your work. There appear to be . . . well, some personal aspects.'

Yale shook his head in a gesture of perplexity. 'Now I'm even more at a loss. Will someone please explain?'

'Harry,' Nim instructed, 'you take over.'

'Sir,' London said, addressing Yale, 'I believe you know an Ian Norris.'

Was it imagination, Nim wondered, or had an expression of alarm for the briefest instant crossed Mr Justice Yale's face? Probably not. Nim cautioned himself: don't look for shadows that don't exist.

'Certainly I know Norris,' Yale acknowledged. 'He and I have business dealings. But I'm curious about *your* connection with him.'

'My connection, sir, is that Norris is a thief. We have definite proof.' Harry London went on, describing what he had revealed to Nim yesterday about Norris's power stealing and the Yale Family Trust.

This time Paul Sherman Yale's reaction was unmistakable: in succession – incredulity, shock, anger.

At the end of London's recital, Eric Humphrey added, 'I hope you understand, Paul, why I decided that this matter – painful as it is – had to be brought to your attention.'

Yale nodded, his face flushed, still revealing the conflict of emotions. 'Yes, that part I understand. But as to the rest . . .' He spoke sternly to Harry London. 'This is a serious accusation. Are you certain of your facts?'

'Yes, sir. Absolutely sure.' London met the old man's gaze unflinchingly. 'The DA is definite, too. He believes he has ample evidence to convict.'

Eric Humphrey interjected, 'I should explain to you, Paul, that Mr London's record with us has been outstanding. He has put teeth into our Property Protection programme and shown himself to be a responsible executive. He is not given to making accusations lightly.'

Nim added, 'Especially one this serious.'

'It is certainly serious.' Mr Justice Yale had regained his composure and was speaking in measured tones as if, Nim thought, he were once more occupying the highest judicial bench. 'For the moment I accept what you gentlemen say, though later I will insist on examining the evidence.'

'Naturally,' Eric Humphrey said.

'Meanwhile,' Yale continued, 'I assume it is clearly understood and accepted that, until this moment, I had no knowledge myself of anything you have described.'

Humphrey assured him, 'That goes without saying. None of us had the slightest doubt of it. Our main concern was about embarrassment to you.'

'And to Golden State Power,' Nim added.

Yale shot him a quick, shrewd glance. 'Yes, there is that to be considered.' He permitted himself a slight smile. 'Well, I thank you for your confidence in me.'

'It never wavered,' Humphrey said.

Briefly Nim wondered: wasn't the chairman overdoing it a bit? Then he thrust the thought away.

Paul Yale seemed to want to go on talking. 'Apart from this unfortunate incident, I find the entire concept of power theft interesting. Frankly, I had no idea such a thing existed. I have never heard of it before. Nor did I know there were such people in the public utility business as Mr London.' He told the Property Protection chief, 'On some other occasion I would be interested to hear more about your work.'

'Be glad to fill you in anytime, sir.'

They went on talking, the initial strain gone. It was arranged that later in the day Harry London would disclose to Mr Justice Yale the detailed evidence relating to Ian Norris and the Yale Family Trust properties. Yale announced his intention to retain private legal counsel to protect his interests *vis-à-vis* Norris. He explained, 'The question of succession of trustees for that family trust has always been something of a problem. My grandfather made provisions which were inelastic and have not worn well with time. It will require a court order to have Norris removed. In the circumstances, I shall seek it.'

Nim contributed little to the discussion. Something, somewhere in his mind, was bothering him. He wasn't sure what.

Two days later, Harry London returned to Nim.

'Got some news you'll like about that Norris case.'

Nim looked up from the latest draft of his NEI convention speech. 'Such as?'

'Ian Norris has made a statement. He swears your friend Paul Sherman Yale knew nothing whatever about what was going on. So the old boy's story is confirmed.'

Nim asked curiously, 'Why would Norris make a statement?'

'Deals within wheels. I'm not sure the scales of justice are dead level, but here's the way it is: Norris's lawyer has been talking with the DA. First, it's been agreed GSP & L will be paid what's owing – or rather, what we estimate is owing, which is a helluva lot of money. After that, Norris will plead "no contest" to a charge of criminal stealing under Section 591.'

'What's that?'

'Part of the California Penal Code. Covers stealing from public utilities like us and the phone companies, and allows for a fine and a prison term of up to five years. Anyway, the DA will ask for the maximum fine but will agree not to press for imprisonment. Put it all together and there'll be no evidence presented in court, so the name of the Yale Family Trust won't be in the record.'

Harry London stopped.

'Getting information from you,' Nim complained, 'is like drawing corks. Tell me the rest of that under-the-counter deal.'

'Some of it I don't know; probably never will. One thing that comes through is that our Mr Yale has powerful friends. The DA has been under pressure to get the case settled and keep the Yale name under wraps.' London shrugged. 'I suppose that's best for dear old GSP & L.'

'Yes,' Nim agreed, 'it's best.'

Afterwards, with London gone, Nim sat, silent, thinking. It was true: there would have been harmful publicity for the company if one of its directors and its official spokesman had been involved in a case of power theft, however innocently. Nim supposed he should feel relieved. Yet something continued to nag at him, as it had for two whole days, a burr in his subconscious, a conviction that he knew something important if he could only remember what.

There was something else. This time not subconscious.

Why should Mr Justice Yale have made such a heavy-handed point – as he did at the meeting with Eric Humphrey, Harry London and Nim – about never having heard of power theft? Of course, it was entirely possible he hadn't. True, there had been reports in the press and an occasional mention on TV, but no one person could be expected to know everything in the news, even a Supreme Court judge. Just the same, the insistence had seemed – to Nim – overdone.

He returned to his first thought: the nagging doubt. *What in hell was it that he knew?* Maybe if he didn't try so hard it would drop quietly into his mind.

He continued working on his speech for the National Electric Institute convention, only four days away.

16

A day of glory nears!

The valiant people's army, Friends of Freedom, fighting the vile capitalists who keep Amerika in chains, will strike a blow to be acclaimed in history.

All preparations are A-okay for countdown . . .

Georgos Winslow Archambault, writing in his journal, hesitated. Then, using his stub of pencil (it was getting uncomfortably short and he would have to discard it soon, Gandhi's precepts or not), he crossed out the last four words. They had capitalist overtones, he realized, as he substituted:

. . . have been brilliantly executed by the Friends of Freedom high command . . .

Better. Much better! He went on writing.

. . . The people's enemies, consorting under the infamous, fascist-front banner of the National Electric Institute, begin assembling in two days' time.
  They are in for a grand surprise – and a deserved punishment.

Georgos smiled as he put the pencil stub down and rested from composing, which, as usual, tired him mentally. Standing, he surveyed the basement workshop, now jammed tightly with new supplies and equipment. He stretched his lean, lithe body. Then he dropped to the floor in a space he had deliberately kept clear and did forty push-ups rapidly. It pleased Georgos that he sailed through the exercise easily and his breathing was normal at the end. Three days from now he might be glad of his physical fitness.

He would get back to the journal in a minute. With significant history in the making, it must not be neglected because someday it should find an honoured place in the archives of revolution.

He reflected: everything for the impending operation was knitting together perfectly – planning, supplies, the logistics of getting explosive and incendiary bombs into the Christopher Columbus Hotel. The first set of bombs (containing high explosive) would detonate at 3am during the second night of the NEI convention, the fire bombs from five to ten minutes later. Both sets of bombs, disguised as fire extinguishers, would be placed in position the preceding day – roughly sixteen hours before detonation.

Thanks to Georgos' resourceful leadership, all was proceeding like . . . he groped for a metaphor . . . like those excellent clockwork mechanisms Davey Birdsong bought in Chicago and delivered here.

Georgos had revised his earlier opinions about Birdsong. Now he felt admiration and love for the big, bearded man.

Not only was Birdsong's original idea sheer genius, but in helping implement it he was taking active risks. In addition to the shopping trip to Chicago, Birdsong had helped to buy up fire extinguishers locally, a few at a time from different sources. In the basement workshop there were now almost three dozen – ample for the Friends of Freedom plan. Georgos had been cautious in bringing them to the house, mostly after dark. He had taken one calculated risk in delivering six extinguishers in daylight – he urgently needed the space in his VW van to pick up more – but had surveyed the street carefully first, then moved quickly, and was satisfied afterwards that he had not been observed.

As well as collecting the thirty-odd extinguishers, Georgos had already done the needed work on half of them. First he had emptied the original contents, then machined the insides of the casings to weaken them. After that, in those which were to be fire bombs, he inserted plastic bottles filled with gasoline, plus explosive charges with detonators, and timing mechanisms. In the case of the high explosive bombs, which would block off exits from the hotel, he substituted four pounds of dynamite for the gasoline.

Soon, when he had finished writing his journal, he would continue with the remaining extinguishers. It would be necessary to work steadily through the next forty-eight hours – *and* with great care because the amount of explosive now in the workshop was sufficient to wipe out the entire block if anything went wrong. But Georgos had confidence in his own ability and that he could finish in time.

His thin, ascetic face lighted in gleeful contemplation as he recalled Birdsong's words when they first discussed their plan to block off escape from the hotel, then start fierce fires on the upper floors : *'If you do it right, not one person on those upper floors will leave that building alive.'*

A further plus for Birdsong : he had come through with all the money Georgos asked for, even though the cost of everything had been greater than expected.

Then there was the diversion Birdsong had planned. It would help Georgos, aided by the other freedom fighters, to get the bombs safely into the hotel.

As he had done several times already, Georgos went over the details in his mind.

With some more of Birdsong's money, Georgos had bought a Dodge pick-up truck – used, but in good condition and by happy coincidence painted red. He had made the purchase with cash and employed fake identity papers, so later the ownership would not be traceable.

The truck was now hidden in a locked, private garage adjoining a second Friends of Freedom hideaway – a recently rented apartment in the city's North Castle district which only Georgos knew about. The apartment would serve as a location to fall back on if the Crocker Street house became unusable for any reason.

The red truck was already lettered neatly on both sides : *Fire Protection Service, Inc.* A masterstroke (another of Georgos' ideas) was the choice of an open pick-up rather than a closed van. The vehicle's contents – seemingly innocent fire extinguishers – would be exposed for all to see.

Georgos' own regular transportation – his old VW van – was in private parking not far from the Crocker Street house and would not be used in the NEI attack.

How Birdsong's diversionary scheme would work was that he, with about a hundred p & lfp supporters, would stage an anti-GSP & L demonstration at the hotel at the same time that the load of fire extinguishers-cum-bombs would be driven to the service entrance and unloaded. The demonstrators would make themselves sufficiently a nuisance so that any police or security forces on the scene would be kept busy, permitting the red Dodge pick-up to pass unnoticed.

As to other details, Birdsong had come through, as promised, with sketch plans of the Christopher Columbus Hotel main floor and mezzanine. After studying them, Georgos had made three trips himself to the hotel to verify details and decide on exact placement of the high explosive bombs to go off first.

Another thing Georgos learned was that behind-scenes service activity was so busy, at times frantic, that in the daytime almost anyone could walk through the hotel's service areas unquestioned, provided they appeared purposeful and on some business mission. To test this, on the third trip to the Christopher Columbus, Georgos wore one of the neat blue-grey coverall uniforms, embroidered with the words *Fire Protection Service, Inc,* which he and the other freedom fighters accompanying him would wear three days from now.

No sweat. No problem. He had even received friendly nods from several hotel staff members who found his presence unremarkable, and, for his part, Georgos practised the role to be played when the time came to put the bombs in place. Then, he and the others would become obsequious flunkies – the way capitalists liked their serfs to grovel. Chameleons all, the freedom fighters would smile sweetly, mouthing inanities – 'Excuse me',

341

'Yes, sir', 'No, madam', 'Please' – a sickening abasement to inferiors, but one to be suffered for the cause of revolution.

Results would make it all worthwhile!

For extra cover, in case any freedom fighter were stopped and questioned, Birdsong had had some Fire Protection Service, Inc work orders printed. These were now filled in. They instructed that supplementary fire extinguishers were to be delivered to the hotel and left in place for subsequent mounting. Birdsong had also typed, on hotel stationery, an authorization for Fire Protection Service personnel to enter the hotel for that purpose. He acquired the stationery during one of his sorties into the Christopher Columbus where it was available, for use by hotel guests, at desks on the mezzanine.

The two documents replaced Georgos' original idea of getting hotel purchase orders, which had proved too difficult. Neither document would stand up to close scrutiny, Georgos and Birdsong realized, but might make the needed difference in a pinch.

As far as Georgos could see, they had thought of everything.

Only one thing, at this moment, vaguely troubled him and that was his woman, Yvette. Since the night, four months ago, when he executed the two security pigs on the hill above Millfield and afterwards Yvette protested, he had never quite trusted her. Briefly, following Millfield, he considered eliminating her. It would not be difficult, as Davey Birdsong once pointed out, but Georgos decided to postpone action. The woman was useful. She cooked well; also she was convenient when he chose to work off his sexual excitements, which had become more frequent lately as the prospect of killing more people's enemies loomed closer.

As a precaution, Georgos had kept secret from Yvette the plan to bomb the Christopher Columbus Hotel, even though she must realize something important was pending. Perhaps her exclusion was the reason she had been silent and moody these past few weeks. Well, no matter! At this moment he had more important concerns, but soon he would almost certainly have to dispose of Yvette, even at some inconvenience to himself.

Remarkable! Even thinking about killing his woman was giving him an erection.

With growing excitement – in so many agreeable ways – Georgos returned to writing in his journal.

Part Four

1

In a twenty-fifth-floor suite of the Christopher Columbus Hotel, Leah looked up from an exercise book in which she was writing.

'Daddy,' she said, 'can I ask you something personal?'

Nim answered, 'Yes, of course.'

'Are things all right between you and Mommy now?'

It took Nim a second or two to grasp the import of his daughter's question. Then he answered quietly, 'Yes, they are.'

'And you're not . . .' Leah's voice faltered. 'You're not going to break up after all?'

'If you've been worrying about that,' he told her, 'you can stop worrying. That won't happen, I hope, ever.'

'Oh, Daddy!' Leah ran towards him, her arms flung out. She embraced him tightly. 'Oh, Daddy, I'm so glad.' He felt her young face soft against his own and the wetness of her tears.

He held her, and gently stroked her hair.

The two of them were together because Ruth and Benjy had gone down to the lobby floor a few minutes ago – to sample the wares of an ice cream parlour for which the hotel was noted. Leah had chosen to stay with Nim, claiming she wanted to finish some schoolwork she had brought. Or was it, he wondered now, because she saw an opportunity to ask that crucial question?

What parent, Nim reflected, ever knew what went on in children's minds, or the hurts they suffered through parental selfishness or lack of thought? He remembered how Leah had carefully avoided the subject of Ruth's absence while she and Benjy were staying with the Neubergers and they had talked on the telephone. What agony was Leah – a sensitive and aware fourteen-year-old – going through then? The memory left him ashamed.

It also raised the question: when should both children be told the truth about Ruth's condition? Probably soon. True, it would create anxiety, just as it had – and continued to – with Nim. But better Leah and Benjy should know than have it sprung upon them suddenly in a crisis, as might happen. Nim decided he would discuss the subject with Ruth within the next few days.

As if Leah sensed part of his thinking, she said, 'It's all right, Daddy. It's *all right*.' Then, with the adaptability of the young, she wriggled free and went back to what she had been doing.

He walked to the window of the suite living room, observing the panoramic, picture-postcard view; the historic city, it's busy ship-filled harbour and the two world-famed bridges, all touched with gold by the late afternoon sun. 'Hey,' he said over his shoulder, 'that's some fantastic scene.'

Leah looked up, smiling, 'Yeah. Sure is.'

One thing was already clear: bringing his family to the National Electric Institute convention, now in its first day, had been a great idea. Both children were excited when they all checked into the hotel this morning. Leah and Benjy, while excused from school for four days, had been given class assignments, including one to write an essay on the convention itself; Benjy, planning his, expressed a wish to hear his father's speech tomorrow. It was unusual to admit a child to an NEI business session, but Nim managed to arrange it. There were other activities for families – a harbour cruise, museum visits, private movies – in which Ruth and the children would join.

After a while Ruth and Benjy returned to the suite, laughing happily, and reporting that it had been necessary to test two cones each before awarding the ice cream parlour a three-star rating.

The convention's second day.

It dawned bright and cloudless, sun streaming into the suite while Nim, Ruth and the children enjoyed the luxury of a room service breakfast.

Following breakfast, and for the last time before he would deliver it, Nim skimmed through his speech. It was on the programme for 10am. A few minutes after nine he left the others and took an elevator to the lobby floor.

He had a reason for going there first. From a window of the suite he had seen some kind of a demonstration taking place outside and was curious to know who was demonstrating, and why.

As Nim emerged from the hotel's main doorway, he realized it was the same old crowd – power & light for people. About a hundred persons of varying ages were parading, chanting slogans. Didn't they ever get tired, he wondered, or see anything but their own narrow viewpoint?

The usual type placards were being waved.

GSP & L
Cheats
Consumers

Let the People
Not Fat Cat
Capitalists,
Own GSP & L

p & lfp Urges
Public Takeover of
The People's Utilities

Public Ownership
Would Ensure
Lower Electric Rates

What influence, Nim mused, did p & lfp expect to have on the National Electric Institute? He could tell them it would be nil. But, of course, it was local attention they expected and, as usual, were receiving. He could see the ubiquitous TV cameras. Oh yes, and there was Davey Birdsong, looking cheerful and directing it all.

There appeared to be an attempt by the demonstrators to stop vehicular traffic from reaching the hotel. The front driveway was being blocked by a line of p & lfp-ers who had linked arms, preventing several waiting cars and taxis from moving in. Also cordoned off by a second contingent was an adjoining service entrance. Two trucks were held up there. One, Nim saw, was a milk delivery van, the other an open pick-up with a load of fire extinguishers. The drivers of both trucks had got out of their vehicles and were protesting the delay.

Several city policemen now appeared. They moved among the demonstrators, cautioning them. A brief argument followed between police and demonstrators, in which Birdsong joined. Then the big, bearded man shrugged and motioned his supporters away from both entrances while the police, hastening the process, escorted the two trucks in, then the cars and taxis.

'Can you beat that for irresponsibility?' The speaker was another convention delegate, standing beside Nim and identifiable by his NEI lapel badge. 'That dumb bunch would like to cut off the hotel's fire protection and milk. In God's name, why?'

Nim nodded. 'Doesn't make a lot of sense.'

Perhaps it didn't to the demonstrators either for they were now dispersing.

Nim returned inside the hotel and took an elevator to the mezzanine floor, the convention's headquarters.

Like any convention – that unique ritual – the NEI gathering brought together several hundred businessmen, engineers and scientists, their purpose to chew over mutual problems, exchange news of developments, and mingle socially. The theory was that each delegate, afterwards, would do his or her job better. It was hard to put a cash value on such occasions, though one existed.

In an anteroom outside the main convention hall, delegates were assembling for the informal get-together which preceded each day's business session. Nim joined the earlier arrivals, meeting officials of other power companies, some of whom he knew, and some he didn't.

A good deal of the talk was about oil. An overnight news report revealed that the OPEC nations were standing firm in their demand that future payments for oil be in gold, not paper currencies whose value – particularly that of the dollar – diminished almost daily. Negotiations between the United States and OPEC were stalled, with the prospect of a new oil embargo becoming alarmingly real.

If it happened, the impact on public utilities producing electricity could be disastrous.

After a few minutes of sharing in the discussion, Nim felt a pressure on his arm. Turning, he saw Thurston Jones, his friend from Denver. They shook hands warmly.

Thurston asked, 'What news of Tunipah?'

Nim grimaced. 'Building the Pyramids went faster.'

'And the Pharaohs didn't need permits. Right?'

'Right! How's Ursula?'

'Great.' Thurston beamed. 'We're having a baby.'

'That's wonderful. Congratulations! When will the big day be?' Nim was using words to fill in time while marshalling his startled thoughts. He remembered vividly the weekend at Denver and Ursula's arrival in his bed. Ursula, who confided that she and her husband wanted children but couldn't have them, a statement Thurston confirmed. '*We both had medical tests . . . my pistol will cock and fire, but I feed it only blanks. And I'll never have live bullets . . .*'

'The doctor says around the end of June.'

Christ! Nim didn't need a calculator to know it *was* his child. His emotions were whirling, as if in a blender, and what the hell was he supposed to say?

His friend supplied the answer by clapping an arm around Nim's shoulders. 'There's just one thing Ursula and I would like. When the time comes, we want you to be godfather.'

Nim started to say yes, he would, then found he could not get the words out. Instead he clasped Thurston's hand again, tightly, and nodded his agreement. The Jones kid, Nim vowed silently, would have the best, most conscientious godfather there ever was.

They arranged to meet again before the convention ended.

Nim moved on, talking with more power people: from New York's Con Edison – in Nim's view one of the best-run utilities in North America, despite its enforced role as a New York City tax collector and the abuse heaped on it by opportunistic politicians – Florida Power & Light, Chicago's Commonwealth Edison, Houston Lighting & Power, Southern California Edison, Arizona Public Service, others.

There was also a contingent of a dozen delegates from Golden State Power & Light, actively mingling with out-of-towners since theirs was the host company. Among the GSP & L group was Ray Paulsen; he and Nim greeted each other with their usual lack of cordiality. J. Eric Humphrey had not yet appeared at the convention but would do so later.

As he concluded a conversation, Nim observed a familiar face, moving nearer through the growing, increasingly noisy throng of delegates. It was the *California Examiner* reporter, Nancy Molineaux. To his surprise, she came directly to him.

'Hi!' Her manner was friendly and she was smiling, but Nim's memories were too close and sour for him to respond in kind. He had to admit, though, the woman was damned attractive; those high cheekbones and the haughty manner were a part of it. She knew how to dress well; evpensively, too, by the look of her clothes.

He answered coolly, 'Good morning.'

348

'Just picked up your speech in the press-room,' Ms Molineaux said; she had a news release and a full-text copy in her hand. 'Pretty dull stuff. You planning to say anything extra that isn't printed here?'

'Even if I am, I'll be damned if I'd help you by telling you in advance.'

The reply seemed to please her and she laughed.

'Dad,' a voice broke in, 'we're going up to that place now.'

It was Benjy, who had dodged through delegates on his way to a small convention hall gallery where a few visitors could be seated. Over by a stairway Nim could see Ruth and Leah. Both waved and he waved back.

'Okay,' he told Benjy, 'you'd better go get your seats.'

Nancy Molineaux had listened with apparent amusement. She asked, 'You brought your family to the convention?'

'Yes,' he answered curtly, then added, 'My wife and our children are staying with me in the hotel. In case you consider making something of it, I'll tell you that I'm paying their expenses personally.'

'My, my,' she teased, 'what a terrible reputation I have.'

'I'm wary of you,' Nim told her, 'the way I would be of a cobra.'

That Goldman, Nancy thought as she moved away; he was strictly a no-horseshit man.

Coming here today was an assignment she had neither expected nor wanted. But the city editor, spotting Goldman's name on the programme, had sent Nancy, hoping she would find some vulnerability, and thus continue what he saw as a newsworthy vendetta. Well, old I'm-the-coach was wrong. She would report Goldman's speech straight, even give it a build-up if the material were worth it. (The printed version wasn't, which was why she had asked her question.) Apart from that, Nancy wanted to get the hell out of here as quickly as she could. Today was the day she had arranged to meet the girl, Yvette, in the bar where they had talked briefly a week ago. Nancy could make it – she had left her car in the hotel's underground parking garage – though time would be tight. She hoped the girl would show, and would answer some of those puzzling questions.

Meanwhile there was Goldman. She went into the convention hall and took a seat at the press table.

Even while addressing the convention, Nim found himself agreeing with the Molineaux woman: a speech, as heavy with technical material as this one had to be, was unexciting from a press reporter's viewpoint. But as he described the load and capacity problems – present and future – of Golden State Power & Light, the rapt attention of his audience showed that many of those listening shared the problems, frustrations and fears which Nim presented under his title, 'Overload'. They, too, were charged with providing reliable power in their communities. They, too, realized that time was running out, with a major electrical famine a mere few years away. Yet almost daily their honesty was questioned, their warnings disbelieved, their grim statistics scoffed at.

Near the end of his prepared text, Nim reached into a pocket for a page of notes he had made only yesterday. He would use them to conclude.

'Most of us here – probably all of us,' he said, 'share two important beliefs. One belief concerns environment.

'The environment we live in *should* be cleaner than it is. Therefore those who work responsibly towards that objective deserve our support.

'The second belief concerns the democratic process. I believe in democracy, always have, though lately with some reservations. Which brings me back to the environment.

'Some of those who call themselves environmentalists have ceased to be reasonable believers in a reasonable cause and have become fanatics. They are a minority. But by noisy, rigid, uncompromising, often uninformed fanaticism, they are managing to impose their will on the majority.

'In doing so, such people have prostituted the democratic process, have used it ruthlessly – as it was never intended to be used – to thwart everything but their own narrow aims. What they cannot defeat by reason and argument they obstruct by delay and legalistic guile. Such people do not even pretend to accept majority rule because they are convinced they know *better* than the majority. Furthermore, they recognize only those aspects of democracy which can be subverted to their own advantage.'

The last words produced a burst of handclapping. Nim put up a hand for silence, and went on.

'This breed of environmentalist opposes *everything*. There is nothing, absolutely nothing, we of the power industry can propose which does not arouse their ire, their condemnation, their fervent and self-righteous opposition.

'But the fanatics among environmentalists are not alone. They have allies.'

Nim paused, having sudden second thoughts about his notes, aware that what came next could get him into the same kind of trouble as five months ago, after the Energy Commission hearing on Tunipah. It would also run counter to J. Eric Humphrey's 'stay away from controversy' instruction. Well, either way, the worst they could do was hang him. He plunged on.

'The allies I spoke of,' he declared, 'are the growing number of appointees on regulatory boards, put there for political reasons only.'

Nim sensed, among his audience, rapt and immediate interest.

'There was a time, in this state and elsewhere, when the boards and commissions regulating our industry were few in number and could be relied on for reasonably fair, impartial judgements. But not any more. Not only have such boards proliferated to a point where their functions overlap so they now compete brazenly with each other in establishing power bases, but a majority of board members receive their appointments as blatant political rewards. Seldom, if ever, do they get where they are through merit or experience. As a result, such commissioners and board members have little or no business knowledge – indeed, some openly display an anti-business prejudice – and all have political ambitions which govern their every action and decision.

'That is precisely why and how our extremist critics and opponents find themselves with allies. For it is the militant, so-called populist points of view, the anti-power-company stances, which nowdays make news and gain attention. The quiet, balanced, thoughtfully-arrived-at decisions do not, and the commissioners and board members whom I speak of know that lesson very well indeed.

'Expressed another way: what ought to be positions of impartial public trust are being abused and turned against the public interest.

'I have no easy remedy to suggest for these two formidable problems nor, I suspect, have any of you. The best we can do is to let the public know, whenever possible, that their reasonable interests are being undermined by a minority – an insidious

351

alliance of fanatics and self-serving politicians.'

Nim decided to leave it there.

While he was wondering what, after all, would be the reaction to his remarks by Eric Humphrey and other GSP & L colleagues, Nim found to his amazement he was receiving an enthusiastic ovation.

'Congratulations!' . . . 'took guts to say it, but all so true' . . . 'hope what you said gets widest circulation' . . . 'would like a transcript to pass around' . . . 'the industry needs straight shooters like you' . . . 'if you get tired of working for Golden State Power, be sure to let us know'.

As delegates crowded around him, unexpected, incredibly, Nim found he was a hero. The president of a giant Midwest utility assured him, 'I hope your company appreciates you. I intend to tell Eric Humphrey how good you were.'

Amid more handshaking and congratulations, and with a sudden weariness, Nim eased himself away.

Only one thing marred the aftermath: the sight of Ray Paulsen's scowling, hostile face. But the executive vice president said nothing and simply left the convention hall alone.

Nim had reached a doorway to the outer mezzanine when a quiet voice behind him said, 'I came especially to hear you. It was worth it.'

Nim turned. To his amazement he saw the speaker was Wally Talbot Jr. Part of Wally's head was bandaged and he was walking with the aid of sticks, but managed a cheerful grin.

'Wally!' Nim said. 'How great to see you! I didn't know you were out of the hospital.'

'Got out a couple of weeks ago, though not for good. I still have a lot of repair work ahead. Can we talk?'

'Sure. Let's find some place quiet.' He had intended to look for Ruth and the children but could meet them later in the suite.

They went down by elevator to the main floor. In a corner near a stairway two chairs were unoccupied and Nim and Wally went towards them, Wally using his sticks a trifle awkwardly, but obviously preferring to manage by himself.

'Watch it, please!' A figure in smart blue-grey coveralls moved past, manoeuvring a two-wheel trolley on which were balanced three red fire extinguishers. 'Won't be a moment, gentlemen. Just have to put one of these in place.' The man, who was young, lifted aside one of the chairs they were headed for, set down a fire extinguisher behind it, then returned the chair to its original position. He smiled at Nim. 'That's all, sir. Sorry to have held you up.'

'You didn't.' Nim remembered having seen the man earlier this morning, driving one of the trucks which police escorted in during the p & lfp demonstration.

It occurred to Nim that putting a fire extinguisher out of sight behind a chair was a strange arrangement. But it was none of his business and presumably the man knew what he was doing. His coveralls were lettered *Fire Protection Service, Inc.*

Nim and Wally sat down.

'Did you see that guy's hands?' Wally asked.

'Yes.' Nim had noticed that the young man's hands were badly stained, probably from careless use of chemicals.

'He could fix that with a skin graft.' Wally grinned again, this time ruefully. 'I'm getting to be an expert on that subject.'

'Never mind anybody else,' Nim said. 'Tell me about you.'

'Well, just as I said, the skin grafts I'm having will take a long time. A little at a time is how it works.'

Nim nodded sympathetically. 'Yes, I know.'

'But I got some good news. I thought you'd like to share it. I'm getting a new dong.'

'You're *what*?'

'You heard me right. You remember my old one was burned off?'

'Of course I remember.' Nim would never forget the doctor's words the day after Wally's electrocution. '. . . *the electricity passed over the upper surface of his body and exited . . . by the route of his penis . . . It was destroyed. By burning. Totally . . .*'

'But I still have sexual feeling there,' Wally said, 'and it can be used as a base. That's why I was sent to Houston last week – to Texas Medical Center. They're doing wonderful things there, especially for people like me. There's a doctor named Brantley Scott who's been the mastermind; he's going to build me a new penis, and he promises it will work.'

'Wally,' Nim said, 'I'm happy for you, but how the hell can anyone do that?'

'It's done partly by special skin grafts, partly by something called a penile prosthesis. That's a little pump, some tubes and a tiny reservoir, all connected, and implanted in the body surgically. The whole thing is made of silicone rubber, the same stuff that's used for heart pacemakers. Actually, it's a substitute for what nature gave us in the first place.'

Nim asked curiously, 'Does it really work?'

'Damn right it works!' Wally's enthusiasm bubbled on. 'I've seen it. I also found out there are hundreds of people who've been fitted, who've had the surgery, successfully. And, Nim, I'll tell you something else.'

'What?'

'That penile prosthesis isn't only for people like me, people who got injured. It's for others – older men usually, who are normal except they've run out of steam and can't make it with a woman any more. What it does is give them a whole new lease on life. How about you, Nim? Do you need help?'

'Not that kind. Not yet, thank God!'

'But you might someday. Just think of it! No sexual hang-up – ever. You could go to your grave with an erection.'

Nim grinned. 'And what would I do with it there?'

'Hey, there's Mary!' Wally exclaimed. 'She came to pick me up. Can't drive a car myself yet.'

Across the lobby Nim could see Mary Talbot, Wally's wife. She had spotted them and was coming over. Beside her, Nim saw with some concern, was Ardythe Talbot. He had neither seen nor heard from Ardythe since their encounter at the hospital when she hysterically blamed her own and Nim's 'sin' for Wally's troubles. Nim wondered if she had modified her religious fervour.

The signs of strain were on both women. It was, after all, only seven months since Walter Talbot's tragic death during the bombing at La Mission plant, and Wally Jr's accident had happened just a few weeks later. Mary, who had been slim for as long as Nim remembered her, had noticeably put on weight; worry and unhappiness could account for that, of course. And her gamine look had modified, making her seem older. Nim found himself hoping that what Wally had just told him worked. If it did, it should help them both.

Ardythe appeared to be a little better than when he had last seen her, but not much. In contrast to the way she had been immediately before Walter's death – handsome, stylish, athletic – she was now just another elderly woman. But she smiled at

Nim, and greeted him with friendliness, which relieved him.

They chatted. Nim expressed pleasure once more at seeing Wally mobile. Mary said someone had told her, on her way in, about Nim's speech and she congratulated him. Ardythe reported that she had found some more of Walter's old files and wanted GSP & L to have them. Nim offered to collect them if she wished.

'There's no need for that,' Ardythe said hastily. 'I can send them to you. There aren't as many as last time and . . .'

She stopped. 'Nim, what's wrong?'

He was staring at her, startled, his mouth agape.

'Last time . . .' Walter Talbot's files!

'Nim,' Ardythe repeated, 'is anything the matter?' Mary and Wally were looking at him curiously too.

'No,' he managed to say. 'No, it's just that I remembered something.'

Now he knew. Knew what that missing piece of information was which had nagged at his mind, yet eluded him, since that day in Eric Humphrey's office with the chairman, Harry London, and Mr Justice Yale. It was in Walter Talbot's old files, the files Ardythe had given Nim, in several cardboard cartons, shortly after Walter's death. At the time Nim had gone through them briefly; now they were stored at GSP & L.

'I guess we'd better go,' Wally said. 'It was nice seeing you, Nim.'

'The same here,' Nim responded, 'and, Wally - good luck in everything!'

When all three had gone, Nim stood rooted, thinking. He knew what was there now, in those files. He knew, too, what had to be done. But he must verify, authenticate his memory, first.

In another three days. Immediately after the convention.

2

Rush, rush, rush! That was always the way it was, Nancy Molineaux thought as she pushed her Mercedes well past the speed limit, taking chances in the traffic, keeping a wary eye on the rearview mirror for any cruising cops.

The pressures of life never seemed to let up for a single goddamn day.

She had hurriedly phoned in her story on Goldman, which would appear in this afternoon's edition, and now – already ten minutes late – was on the way to meet Yvette. Nancy hoped the girl would have sense enough to wait.

This afternoon Nancy had some loose ends of other work to clear up, for which she would need to return to the *Examiner* office. Oh yes, and somehow she had to sandwich in time to get to the bank because she needed money. She had a dental appointment at four. Then, this evening she had promised to go to two parties, one a 'drop in', early, and another which would groove on for sure until well past midnight.

But she liked a fast tempo, at work and play, though there were days – like this one – when a bit too much happened.

While she drove, Nancy smiled as she thought of her report of Goldman's speech. It would probably surprise him because it was a straightforward, no-slant job, as she had intended.

Several hundred leaders of America's electric power industry today gave a standing ovation to Nimrod Goldman, a Golden State Power & Light vice president, who declared that politically dominated regulatory agencies are abusing public trust and 'compete brazenly with each other in establishing power bases'.

He was addressing the National Electric Institute convention, meeting in this city.

Earlier, Goldman criticized some environmentalists who, he said, oppose everything. 'There is nothing, absolutely nothing, we of the power industry can propose . . .'

Et cetera, et cetera.

She had quoted some of his statements, also, about that electric power famine he claimed was coming, so if Goldman had any beef this time it would have to do with what he had said himself, not the reporting.

Jesus! How did some of those slow-thinking freaks who had cars ever get drivers' licences? She was second in line at a traffic light which had gone to green, but the guy in front hadn't moved yet. Was he *asleep*? She sounded her horn impatiently. *Shit!* The traffic light winked to amber, then red as Nancy reached it. But the cross street seemed clear so she took a chance and ran the red.

After a few more minutes she could see that crummy bar ahead, where she had been last week. How late was she? As she came level with the bar, Nancy glanced at her Piaget watch. Eighteen minutes. And wouldn't you know! – there was no parking space today. She found a spot two blocks away and, after locking the Mercedes, hurried back.

Inside the bar it was dark and mildewy, as before. As Nancy paused, letting her eyes adjust, she had the impression that nothing had changed in seven days, not even the customers.

Yvette had waited, Nancy saw. She was seated alone, a beer in front of her, at the same corner table they had occupied previously. She glanced up as Nancy approached, but gave no sign of interest or recognition.

'Hi!' Nancy greeted her. 'Sorry I'm late.'

Yvette shrugged slightly, but said nothing.

Nancy signalled a waiter. 'Another beer.' She waited until it came, in the meantime covertly inspecting the girl, who had still said nothing. She appeared to be in even worse shape than a week ago – her skin blotchy, hair a mess. The same clothes were dirty and looked as if they had been slept in for a month. On her right hand was the improvised glove, presumably shielding a deformity, which Nancy had noticed at their first encounter.

Nancy took a swig of her beer, which tasted good, then decided to come to the point. 'You said you'd tell me today what goes on in that house on Crocker Street, and what Davey Birdsong does there.'

Yvette looked up. 'No, I didn't. You just hoped I would.'

'Okay, well I'm still hoping. Why don't you start by telling me what it is you're afraid of?'

'I'm not afraid any more.' The girl made the statement in a flat, dull voice, her face expressionless.

Nancy thought: she wasn't getting anywhere and maybe it had been a waste of time coming. Trying again, she asked, 'So what happened between last week and this to make the difference?'

Yvette didn't answer. Instead she seemed to be considering, weighing something in her mind. While she did, as if instinctively and unaware of what she was doing, she used her left hand to rub the right. First with the glove on, then she slipped it off.

With shock and horror Nancy stared at what was exposed.

What had been a hand was an ugly red-white mess of weals and scars. Two fingers were gone, with uneven stubs remaining and loose flesh protruding. The other fingers, while more or less complete, had jagged portions missing. One finger was grotesquely bent, a dried yellow piece of bone exposed.

Nancy said, sickened, 'My God! What happened to your hand?'

Yvette glanced down, then realizing what she had done, covered the hand hastily.

Nancy persisted, 'What *happened*?'

'It was . . . I had an accident.'

'But who left it like that? A doctor?'

'I didn't go to one,' Yvette said. She choked back tears. 'They wouldn't let me.'

'Who wouldn't?' Nancy felt her anger rising. 'Birdsong?'

The girl nodded. 'And Georgos.'

'Who the hell is Georgos? And why wouldn't they take you to a doctor?' Nancy reached out, gripping Yvette's good hand. 'Kid, let me help you! I can. And we can still do something about that hand. There's time.'

The girl shook her head. The emotion had drained from her, leaving her face and eyes as they had been earlier – empty, dull, resigned.

'Just tell me,' Nancy pleaded. 'Tell me what it's all about.'

Yvette let out her breath in what might, or might not, have been a sigh. Then, abruptly, she reached down beside her to the floor and lifted up a battered brown purse. Opening it, she took out two recording tape cassettes which she put on the table and slid across to Nancy.

'It's all there,' Yvette said. Then, in a single movement, she drained what remained of her beer and stood up to go.

'Hey!' Nancy protested. 'Don't leave yet! We only just got started. Listen, why not tell me what's on those tapes so we can talk about it?'

'It's all there,' the girl repeated.

'Yes, but . . .' Nancy found she was talking to herself. A moment later the outer door opened, briefly admitting sunlight, then Yvette was gone.

There seemed nothing to be gained by going after her.

Curiously, Nancy turned the tape cassettes over in her hand, recognizing them as a cheap brand which could be bought in packets for a dollar or so each. Neither cassette was labelled; there was just a pencilled *1, 2, 3, 4* on the various sides. Well, she would play them on her tape deck at home tonight and hope there was something worthwhile there. She felt let down and disappointed, though, not to have got some definite information while Yvette was with her.

Nancy finished her beer and paid for it, then left. A half hour later she was in the *Examiner* city room, immersed in other work.

3

When Yvette told Nancy Molineaux, 'I'm not afraid any more,' the statement was true. Yesterday Yvette had reached a decision which relieved her of concern about immediate affairs, freed her from all doubts, anxiety and pain, and removed the overwhelming fear – which she had lived with for months – of her arrest and life imprisonment.

The decision yesterday was simply that, as soon as she had delivered the tapes to that switched-on black woman who worked for a newspaper, and who would know what to do with them, Yvette would kill herself. When she left the Crocker Street house this morning – for the last time – she carried with her the means to do so.

And now she *had* delivered the tapes, those tapes she put together, carefully and patiently, and which incriminated Georgos and Davey Birdsong, revealed what they had done and what they planned, and disclosed the scenario of destruction and murder intended for tonight – or rather 3am tomorrow – at the Christopher Columbus Hotel. Georgos hadn't thought she knew about that, but all the time she had.

Walking away from that bar, and now that it was done, Yvette felt at peace.

Peace, at last.

It had been a long time since she had known any. For sure there had been none with Georgos, though at first the excitement of being Georgos' woman, of listening to his educated talk and sharing the important things he did, had made everything else seem not to matter. It was only later, much later, and when it was too late to help herself, that she began wondering if Georgos was sick, if all of his cleverness and college learning had become in some way . . . what was that word? . . . perverted.

Now she truly believed it had been, believed that Georgos *was* sick, maybe even mad.

And yet, Yvette reminded herself, she still cared about Georgos; even now, when she had done what she had to. And whatever happened to him, she hoped he wouldn't get hurt too badly, or be made to suffer much, though she knew both things could happen after the black woman played those tapes today and told whoever she decided to – the police most likely – what was on them.

About Davey Birdsong, though, Yvette didn't give a damn. She didn't like him, never had. He was mean and hard, never showing any of the little kindnesses Georgos did, despite Georgos being a revolutionary and not being supposed to. Birdsong could be killed before today was out, or rot in jail for ever, and she wouldn't care; in fact, she hoped one of the two would happen. Yvette blamed Birdsong for a lot of the bad scenes that had happened to her and Georgos. The Christopher Columbus Hotel thing had been Birdsong's idea; that was in the tapes too.

Then she realized she would never know what happened to Birdsong, or Georgos, because she would be dead herself.

Oh God – she was only twenty-two! She had hardly started her life and didn't want to die. But she didn't want to spend the rest of it in prison either. Even dying was better than that.

Yvette kept on walking. She knew where she was going and it

would take roughly half an hour. That was something else she had decided yesterday.

It was less than four months ago – a week after that night on the hill above Millfield when Georgos killed the two guards – that she realized just how much trouble she was in. Murder. She was guilty of it, equally with Georgos.

At first she hadn't believed him when he told her. He was merely trying to frighten her, she thought, when, on the way back to the city from Millfield, he had warned, '*You're in this as much as I am. You were there, a part of it all, and you killed those pigs just as if you pulled the knife or fired the gun. So whatever happens to me happens to you.*'

But a few days later she read in a newspaper about the California trial of three men charged with first-degree murder. The trio had broken into a building together and their leader shot and killed a night watchman. Though the other two were unarmed and did not participate actively in the killing, all three were found guilty and given the same sentence – life imprisonment without possibility of parole. It was then Yvette realized that Georgos had been telling the truth and, from that moment, her desperation grew.

It grew, based on the knowledge that there was no going back, no escaping what she had become. That had been the hardest thing to accept, even while knowing there was no alternative.

Some nights, lying awake beside Georgos in the darkness of that dreary Crocker Street house, she had fantasized that she *could* go back, back to the farm in Kansas where she had been born and lived as a child. Compared with here and now, those days seemed bright and carefree.

Which was bullshit, of course.

The farm was a rocky twenty acres from which Yvette's father, a sour, cantankerous, quarrelsome man, barely scratched enough of a living to feed the family of six, let alone meet mortgage payments. It was never a home of warmth or love. Fierce fights between the parents were a norm which their children learned to emulate. Yvette's mother, a chronic complainer, frequently let Yvette – the youngest – know she hadn't been wanted and an abortion would have been preferable.

Yvette, following the example of her two older brothers and a sister, left home for good as soon as she was able, and never went back. She had no idea where any of the family were now, or if her parents were dead, and told herself she didn't care. She wondered, though, if her parents, or brothers and sister, would hear or read about her death, and if it would matter to them in any way.

Of course, Yvette thought, it would be easy to blame those earlier years for what had happened to her since, but it would be neither true nor fair. After coming west, and despite her legal minimum of schooling, she had got a job as a department store salesclerk – in the infants' wear department, which she liked. She enjoyed helping choose clothes for little kids and, about that time, had the feeling she would like to have children herself someday, though she would *not* treat them the way she had been treated at home.

The thing that happened, which put her on the road she finally walked with Georgos, was being taken, by another girl Yvette worked with, to some left-wing political meetings. One thing led to another, later she met Georgos and . . . Oh God, what was the use of going over it all again!

Yvette was well aware that in some ways she was not bright. She always had difficulty in figuring things out and, at the small country school she attended until aged sixteen, her teachers let her know she was a dunderhead. Which was probably why, when Georgos persuaded her to give up her job and go underground with him to form Friends of Freedom, Yvette hadn't any real idea of what she was getting into. At the time it sounded like fun and adventure, not – as it turned out to be – the worst mistake of her life.

The realization that she – like Georgos, Wayde, Ute and Felix – had become a hunted criminal came to Yvette gradually. When it was implanted fully, she was terrified. What would they do to her if she was caught? Yvette thought of Patty Hearst, and what Hearst had been made to suffer, and she was a *victim* for Chrissakes. How much worse would it be for Yvette, who was not?

(Yvette remembered how Georgos and the other three revolutionaries had laughed and laughed over the Patty Hearst trial, laughed about the way the establishment was falling over itself in a self-righteous effort to crucify one of its own, just to prove it could. Of course, as Georgos said afterwards, if Hearst – in that particular case – had been poor, or black like Angela Davis, she would have got sympathy and a fairer shake. It was Hearst's misfortune that her old man had money. Hilarious, though! Yvette could still see their small group watching TV and breaking up each time the trial reports came on.)

But now the fear from having committed crimes herself hovered over Yvette, a fear which expanded like cancer until, in the end, it filled her every waking hour.

More recently, she realized that Georgos no longer trusted her.

She caught him looking at her in strange ways. He didn't talk as much as before. He became secretive about the new work he was doing. Yvette sensed that, whatever else happened, her days as Georgos' woman were almost over.

It was then, without really knowing why, Yvette started to eavesdrop by making tape recordings. It was not difficult. There was equipment available and Georgos had shown her how to use it. Using a concealed mike, and operating the recorder in another room, she taped conversations between Georgos and Birdsong. That was how, playing the tape back later, she learned about those fire extinguisher bombs at the Christopher Columbus Hotel.

The Georgos-Birdsong conversations were on the cassettes she had given the black woman. So was a long, rambling account of it all, from the beginning, by Yvette herself.

Why had she done it?

Even now she was unsure. It wasn't conscience; no point in kidding herself about that. Nor was it because of any of those people at the hotel; Yvette was too far removed, too far gone, to care. Perhaps it was to save Georgos, to save his soul (if he had one; if any of them did) from the terrible thing he intended to do.

Yvette's mind was getting tired. It always did when she thought too much.

She still didn't want to die!

But she knew she had to.

Yvette looked about her. She had kept on walking, not noticing where she was, and now realized she had come faster and further than she thought. Her destination, which she could already see, was only a short distance ahead.

It was a small, grassy knoll, high above the city, and preserved as a public space. The unofficial name was Lonely Hill, which was appropriate since few people went there, a reason Yvette had chosen it. The final two hundred yards, beyond the last streets and houses, was up a steep, narrow path and she took it slowly. The top, which she dreaded reaching, came all too soon.

Earlier, the day had been bright; now it was overcast with a strong, cool wind knifing across the exposed small peak. Yvette shivered. In the distance, beyond the city, she could see the ocean, grey and bleak.

Yvette sat down on the grass and opened her purse for the second time. The first time had been when she produced the tape cassettes in the bar.

From the purse, where it had weighed heavily, she lifted out a device she had removed several days ago from Georgos' workshop and had hidden until this morning. It was a bangalore torpedo – simple but deadly, a stick of dynamite inside a section of pipe. The pipe was sealed at both ends, but at one end a small hole had been left to allow for entry of a blasting cap. Yvette had inserted the cap carefully herself – something else Georgos taught her – having attached to the cap a short fuse, which now protruded through the end of the pipe. It was a five-second fuse. Long enough.

Reaching into her purse again, Yvette found a small cigarette lighter. As she fumbled with it, her hands were trembling.

The lighter was hard to get going in the wind. She put the pipe bomb down and cupped the lighter with her hand. It sputtered, then flamed.

Now she picked up the pipe bomb again, having difficulty because she was trembling even more, but managed to bring the end of the fuse to the lighter. The fuse ignited at once. In a single, swift movement Yvette dropped the lighter and held the bomb against her chest. Closing her eyes, she hoped it would not be . . .

4

The second day of the National Electric Institute convention was winding down.

All of the day's official business was concluded. The Christopher Columbus Hotel meeting halls were deserted. A majority of delegates and wives, a few with families, were in their rooms and suites. Among them, some hardy spirits were still partying. Many others were already asleep.

Some of the younger delegates and a handful of older roisterers remained spread around the city – in bars, restaurants, discotheques, strip joints. But even they were beginning to drift back to the Christopher Columbus and, when late-night places closed at 2am, the remainder would join them.

'Good night, you characters.' Nim kissed Leah and Benjy, then turned out the lights in the hotel suite's second bedroom, which the children were sharing.

Leah, almost asleep, murmured something inaudible. Benjy, who was more chirpy, even though it was well past midnight, said, 'Dad, living in a hotel is real neat.'

'Gets kind of expensive after a while,' Nim said. 'Especially when someone called Benjamin Goldman keeps signing room service checks.'

Benjy giggled. 'I like doing that.'

Nim had let Benjy sign the breakfast bill this morning, and the same thing happened tonight when Benjy and Leah had steak dinners in the suite while Nim and Ruth attended an NEI reception and buffet. Later, the whole family left the hotel to take in a movie, from which they had just returned.

'Go to sleep now,' Nim said, 'or your signing arm won't be any good tomorrow.'

In the living room, Ruth, who had heard the conversation through the open bedroom door, smiled as Nim returned.

'I may have mentioned it before,' she said, 'but I suppose you know your children adore you?'

'Doesn't everyone?'

'Well . . .' Ruth considered. 'Since you mention it, there could be one or two exceptions. Like Ray Paulsen.'

Nim laughed aloud. 'By golly! You should have seen Ray's face when he came back to the convention with Eric Humphrey, thinking the chairman was going to chew my balls off because of what I said this morning, and instead Eric did the opposite.'

'What did he actually say?'

'Something about having received so many complimentary remarks about my speech, how could he be in a minority and take exception? So he congratulated me instead.'

'If Eric has come around that much, do you think there could be a change in policy now – to more outspokenness, the way you've wanted?'

Nim shook his head. 'I'm not sure. The don't-rock-the-boat faction, led by Ray, is still strong. Besides which, only a few people in our organization understand that a future electric power crisis is almost a certainty.' He stretched, yawning. 'But no more worrying tonight!'

'It's early morning,' Ruth corrected him. 'Nearly one o'clock. Anyway, yesterday was a good day for you, and I'm pleased you got a fair press.' She motioned to a late afternoon edition of the *California Examiner* beside her.

'That was a fat surprise.' Nim had read the *Examiner*'s report of his speech several hours ago. 'Can't figure out that Molineaux dame. I was certain she'd stick in the knife again, and twist it.'

'Don't you know by now that we women are unpredictable?' Ruth said, then added mischievously, 'I should have thought all your research would have shown you that.'

'Maybe I'd forgotten. Perhaps you noticed I've restricted my research lately.' He leaned forward and kissed her lightly on the neck, then sat down in a facing chair. 'How are you feeling?'

'Normal most of the time. I tire easily, though, compared with the energy I used to have.'

'There's something I want to ask you about.' Nim described his conversation with Leah, and his conviction that the children ought to be told about Ruth's health in case a sudden change for the worse should find them unprepared. 'I hope it won't happen, just as much as you do, but it's something we should consider.'

'I've been thinking much the same thing,' she told him. 'You can leave it to me. In the next few days I'll pick a time and tell them.'

He supposed he should have known. Ruth, with her good

judgement, her ability to cope, would always do what was best for the family.

'Thank you,' he said.

They went on talking – quietly, easily, enjoying each other's company – until Nim reached out and took Ruth's hands. 'You're tired and so am I. Let's go to bed.'

They went, hand in hand, into the bedroom where, just before turning out the lights, he noticed the time : 1:30am.

They fell asleep, almost at once, in each other's arms.

A quarter mile from the hotel, Georgos Winslow Archambault was seated alone in the red *Fire Protection Service, Inc* truck. He could hardly wait for 3am and the explosions to begin. Georgos' excitement simmered like a cauldron, arousing him sexually, so that a few minutes ago he had had to masturbate.

It was almost unbelievable how well and smoothly everything had gone. From the moment when the police cleared a way for the Friends of Freedom truck to reach the hotel's service entrance – and, oh, what a priceless joke that was! – only twice had the freedom fighters been stopped as they moved around the hotel. Ute was queried briefly by a plainclothes security man, Georgos by an assistant manager whom he encountered in a service elevator. Both incidents gave Ute and Georgos some nervous moments, but the work orders they promptly showed were glanced at and passed back without further questioning. In neither case was the letter on hotel stationery needed or produced.

The general – and predictable – thinking seemed to be : who would want to stop a fire extinguisher being put in place? The few who might think about it at all would assume that someone else had ordered or approved the extra fire precautions.

Now there was merely the waiting – the hardest part of all. He had deliberately parked some distance from the hotel, partly to avoid the possibility of being noticed, partly to get away quickly when he needed to. He would go closer, on foot, for a better view just before the fun began.

As soon as the hotel was well ablaze, with people trapped inside, Georgos intended to phone a radio station with the communiqué he had already drafted. It contained his new demands – the old ones, plus some more. His orders would be obeyed instantly, of course, when the fascist power structure at last

367

grasped the strength and resourcefulness of Friends of Freedom. In his mind, Georgos could see those in authority grovelling before him . . .

Only one small matter bothered him. That was the sudden disappearance of Yvette; he felt uneasy about it, conscious that where his woman was concerned he had been guilty of weakness. He ought to have eliminated her weeks ago. When she returned, as he was sure she would, he would do it immediately. He was glad, though, that he had kept from Yvette his plans for this latest valiant battle.

Oh, what a day for history to remember!

For what must be the twentieth time since coming here, Georgos checked his watch: 1:40am. Another hour and twenty minutes to go.

Just as a precaution, though he didn't really believe it necessary, Davey Birdsong was giving himself an alibi.

He was outside the city, twenty-odd miles from the Christopher Columbus Hotel, and he intended to keep that distance until the action was over.

Several hours ago he had delivered (for a fee) an hour-long lecture to an adult study group on 'The Socialist Ideal'. Discussion afterwards consumed another ninety minutes. Now he was with a dozen or so tedious, boring people from the group who had adjourned to the house of one of their number to go on gabbing about international politics, of which their knowledge was marginal. As well as talking, there was much drinking of beer and coffee and clearly, Birdsong thought, the whole deal could go on until dawn. Fine, let it! He contributed something himself occasionally, making sure everyone noticed he had stayed.

Davey Birdsong, too, had a typewritten statement he would issue to the press. A copy was in his pocket and it began:

The popular consumers' organization, power & light for people, reaffirms its stand against all violence.

'We deplore violence at all times, and especially the bombing at the Christopher Columbus Hotel last night,' Davey Birdsong, the p & lfp leader, stated.

'p & lfp will continue its peaceful efforts on behalf of . . .'

Birdsong smiled as he thought about it and surreptitiously checked his watch: 1:45am.

Nancy Molineaux was still at her late night party, which had been a good one, but she was ready to leave. For one thing, she was tired; it had been one of those crammed-full days when she scarcely had a minute to herself. For another, her jaw was aching. The goddamn dentist had probed a cavity like he was excavating for a new subway, and when she told him he only laughed.

Despite the ache, Nancy was sure she would sleep well tonight and looked forward to climbing in between her silky Porthault sheets.

After saying goodnight to her host and hostess, who lived in a penthouse not far from the city centre, she took the elevator down to where the doorman already had her car waiting. After she tipped him, Nancy checked the time: 1:50am. Her own apartment block was less than ten minutes' drive. With luck, she could be in bed a few minutes after two.

She remembered, out of nowhere, that she was going to listen tonight to those cassette tapes the girl, Yvette, had given her. Well, she had been working on that story a long time and one more day wouldn't make any difference. Maybe she would get up early, before going to the *Examiner*, and listen to them then.

5

Nancy Molineaux enjoyed life's luxuries and her apartment, in an exclusive, modern high-rise, reflected it.

The beige durrie living room rug by Stark matched vertical linen window blinds. A Pace coffee table of smoked glass, chrome and bleached oak fronted a deep-cushioned sofa in Clarence House suede. The Calder acrylic was an original. So was a Roy Lichtenstein oil on canvas in Nancy's bedroom.

Sliding, full-length windows in the dining room opened on to an outdoor patio with its own small garden and a harbour view.

If Nancy had had to, she could have lived elsewhere and managed adequately on her own earnings; but she came to terms long

369

ago with acceptance of money her father made available. It was there, had been honestly earned, so what was wrong with using it? Nothing.

She was careful, though, not to be ostentatious around her fellow workers, which was why she never brought any of them here.

As she padded around the apartment, getting ready for bed, Nancy located those tape cassettes she had remembered, and put them near her stereo tape deck for playing in the morning.

On coming into the apartment a few minutes ago, she had flipped on an FM radio which she kept tuned to a twenty-four-hour mostly-music station, and was only subconsciously aware, while in the bathroom cleaning her teeth, that the music had been interrupted for a newscast.

'. . . in Washington, deepening gloom about an impending oil crisis . . . Secretary of State has arrived in Saudi Arabia to resume negotiations . . . Senate late yesterday approved raising the national debt ceiling . . . Kremlin again alleged spying by Western newsmen . . . Locally, new charges of city hall corruption . . . bus and rapid transit fares are certain to rise following wage settlements . . . police appealing for help in identifying the body of a young woman, apparently a suicide, discovered this afternoon on Lonely Hill . . . bomb fragments at the scene . . . although the body was badly dismembered, one of the woman's hands had two fingers missing and was further disfigured, apparently from an earlier wound . . .'

Nancy dropped the toothbrush.

Had she heard what she thought she heard?

She considered phoning the radio station to ask for a repeat of the last news item, then realized it wasn't necessary. She had absorbed enough, even while half-listening, to know the young woman's body they were talking about had to be Yvette's. Oh Christ, Nancy thought, she had let the kid walk away and hadn't followed? Could she have helped? And what was it Yvette had said? *'I'm not afraid any more.'* Now it became clear why.

And she still hadn't played the tapes.

Suddenly, Nancy was alert, her earlier tiredness gone.

She slipped on a kimono, turned up the lights in her living room, and inserted the first cassette into her tape deck. There was a pause before the recording began, during which Nancy settled herself in a chair, a notebook on her knees and pencil poised. Then the voice of Yvette, speaking uncertainly, came through Nancy's hi-fi system.

At the first words Nancy sat upright, her attention riveted.

'*This is about the Friends of Freedom, all those bombings and the murders. Where the Friends of Freedom are is 117 Crocker Street. The leader is Georgos Archambault, he has a middle name, Winslow, he likes to use it. I'm Georgos' woman. I've been in it, too. So is Davey Birdsong, he brings the money to buy explosives and the other stuff.*'

Nancy's mouth was agape. She felt shivers passing through her. Her pencil raced.

There was more of Yvette on the tape, then a conversation between two male voices – one presumably the Georgos whom Yvette had spoken of, the other unmistakably Davey Birdsong.

The first side of the first tape ended. Nancy's tape deck had an automatic-reverse feature. The second side began at once.

Still more Yvette. She described the night on the hill above Millfield. The sub-station bombing. The killing of the two guards.

Nancy's excitement mounted. She could scarcely credit what she had – the biggest news scoop of her career and, at this moment, it was all her own. She continued listening, adding to her notes.

Back to Georgos and Birdsong. They were discussing something . . . making arrangements . . . Christopher Columbus Hotel . . . bombs disguised as fire extinguishers . . . a red pick-up truck: Fire Protection Service . . . second night of the National Electric Institute convention . . . 3am . . .

Nancy's skin prickled. She did a swift mental calculation, glanced at her watch, then hurled herself at the telephone.

The news story had ceased to have priority.

Her hand was shaking as she dialled 911 for police emergency.

6

The watch lieutenant presiding at the police department operations centre knew he had to make a fast decision.

A few moments earlier, the male police operator taking Nancy Molineaux's 911 call, and writing down the information, had signalled the lieutenant to cut in on the line. He did so. After listening briefly, he questioned the caller who identified herself by name and as a reporter for the *California Examiner*. She explained about the tapes, how she had acquired them, how they had revealed the information she was now passing on urgently.

'I know of you, Miss Molineaux,' the lieutenant said. 'Are you calling from the newspaper?'

'No. From my apartment.'

'The address, please.'

She gave it.

'Are you listed in the phone book there?'

'Yes. Under *Molineaux, N.*'

'Please hang up your phone,' the lieutenant said. 'You'll be called back immediately.'

The police operator – one of twenty such operators handling emergency calls – had already found the number in a city phone directory. He scribbled it on a piece of paper which he passed to the lieutenant, who tapped the number out, then listened.

Nancy answered on the first ring.

'Miss Molineaux, did you just call police emergency?'

'Yes.'

'Thank you. We had to verify the call. Where will you be if you are required later?'

'At the Christopher Columbus Hotel,' Nancy said. 'Where the hell else?' She hung up.

The police lieutenant debated briefly with himself. He had established that the call was genuine and not from a crank. But was the information strong enough to justify emptying the city's biggest hotel, with resultant chaos, in the middle of the night?

Normally, in the case of a bomb warning – the police received hundreds every year – the procedure was to send an advance squad, consisting of a sergeant and two or three patrolmen, to investigate. If they were suspicious or found merit in the tip, they would phone the operations centre and emergency procedures would begin. (Radio communication was never used at that stage for two reasons. One, if a bomb existed, a radio signal might set it off. Two, since police radios were monitored by all and sundry, the police sought to delay having press and spectators clog the scene.)

But, if the report just received was genuine, the danger real, there was insufficient time for normal methods.

In daytime, with emergency forces from the police and fire departments working together, a big hotel like the Christopher Columbus could be evacuated in half an hour. At night, however, it would take longer – an hour if they were fast and lucky. Night-time evacuation posed special problems; there were always some heavy sleepers, drunks, sceptics, illicit lovers unwilling to be discovered, all requiring room-by-room checks and the use of passkeys.

But there wasn't an hour. The watch lieutenant glanced at the big digital clock above him : 2 : 21am. The newspaperwoman had said a bomb or bombs might go off at 3am. True? False? He wished to hell a more senior officer could be briefed and make the judgement. No time for that either.

The lieutenant made the only decision he could, and ordered, 'Start bomb evacuation procedures – the Christopher Columbus Hotel.'

A half-dozen phones in the operations centre went into use immediately. Alarm calls were placed to central district police and fire units first; fire trucks and all available police cars would roll at once. Next, calls went directly to the police department's night commander and deputy fire chief who, together, would direct the hotel evacuation. Simultaneously, the police tactical unit, which included the bomb squad, was being alerted; they would follow other forces quickly. After that : a call to a nearby Army depot where an explosives ordnance squad would contribute experts in bomb disarming. Police departments in neighbouring municipalities were asked to aid by rushing their bomb squads too. Ambulances – almost certain to be needed – were summoned. Continuing to work down a list, major law enforcement, fire, and city functionaries were notified, most aroused from sleep at home.

The watch lieutenant was speaking by telephone with the night manager of the Christopher Columbus. 'We have a tip, which we believe to be authentic, that bombs have been placed in your hotel. We recommend you evacuate immediately. Police and fire units are on the way.'

The word 'recommend' was used advisedly. Technically, the lieutenant had no authority to order evacuation; any such decision must be the hotel management's. Fortunately, the night manager was neither a hair-splitter nor a fool. 'I'll sound the house alarms,' he said, 'and our staff will do whatever you say.'

Like a war machine set in motion, the command effect spread rapidly, each component gathering momentum, each utilizing specialized techniques to become part of a total effort. The action had already moved away from the operations centre, which would now become a conduit for reports. Meanwhile, answers remained unknown to two vital questions. First: would bomb explosions occur at 3am? Second: assuming they did, could the hotel be effectively cleared in the remaining time – an all-too-inadequate thirty-six minutes?

The suspense would be short-lived. The answers to both questions would be known soon.

She had done her bit for humanity, Nancy Molineaux decided. Now she could go back to being a newspaperwoman.

She was still in her apartment, though getting ready to leave. In between throwing on outdoor clothes hurriedly, Nancy phoned the *Examiner*'s night editor and gave him a fast rundown of what she had. As he asked quick questions, she sensed his excitement at the prospect of a big, breaking story.

'I'm going to the hotel,' Nancy told him. 'Then I'll come in to write.' She knew, without asking, that every available photographer would be dispatched to the scene at once.

'Oh, one other thing,' she told the night man. 'I have two tape cassettes. I had to tell the police about them, and they're sure to be wanted as evidence, which means they'll be impounded. Before that happens, we should make copies.'

They arranged that a messenger would meet Nancy at the hotel and collect the tapes. From there he would rush them to the residence of the paper's entertainment editor, a hi-fi nut who had his own sound lab. The entertainment writer was known to be at home and would be warned that the tapes were on the way.

The copies and a portable playback machine would be in the newsroom, waiting, when Nancy got there.

Nancy had reached the outer door of her apartment, on the run, when she remembered one more thing. Racing back to the phone, she dialled the number of the Christopher Columbus Hotel, which she knew from memory. When the operator answered, she instructed, 'Give me Nimrod Goldman's room.'

In Nim's dream, the GSP & L electric system was in desperate crisis. One by one, the system's generating stations had failed until only one remained – La Mission No 5, Big Lil. Then, exactly as happened last summer on the day Walter Talbot died, the La Mission No 5 panel at Energy Control began emitting warning signals – flashing lights and a high-pitched ringing. The lights diminished but the ringing persisted, filling all of Nim's consciousness until he awoke and found the bedside telephone shrilling. Sleepily, he reached out and picked it up.

'Goldman! Is that you, Goldman?'

Still only partially awake, he answered, 'Yeah.'

'This is Nancy Molineaux. Listen to me!'

'Who?'

'Nancy Molineaux, you idiot!'

Anger fought its way through sleep. 'Molineaux, don't you know it's the middle of the night . . . ?'

'Shut up and listen! Goldman, get hold of yourself and come awake. You and your family are in danger. Trust me . . .'

Raising himself on an elbow, Nim said, 'I wouldn't trust *you* . . .' Then he remembered what she had written yesterday, and stopped.

'Goldman, get your family out of that hotel! *Now!* Don't stop for anything! Bombs are going off.'

Now he was wide awake. 'Is this some sick joke? Because if it is . . .'

'It's no joke.' There was pleading in Nancy's voice. 'Oh, for Chrissakes, believe me! Those Friends of Freedom bastards have planted bombs disguised as fire extinguishers. Get your wife and kids . . .'

The words 'Friends of Freedom' convinced him. Then he remembered the hotel, jammed with conventioneers.

'What about other people?'

'The alarm's gone out. *You* get moving!'

'Right!'

'I'll see you outside the hotel,' Nancy said, but Nim hadn't heard. Instead he had slammed down the phone and was fiercely shaking Ruth.

Only minutes later, with the children crying, sleepily bewildered, and still in nightclothes, Nim rushed them from the suite. Ruth was right behind. Nim headed for the emergency stairs, knowing enough to stay away from elevators in a crisis in case they failed and occupants were trapped. As they began the long journey down twenty-six flights, he could hear the sound of sirens from outside, faint at first, then growing louder.

They were three floors down when fire alarm bells throughout the hotel began ringing stridently.

There were acts of gallantry and heroism that night. Some passed unnoticed, others were conspicuous.

Evacuation of the hotel proceeded swiftly and, for the most part, calmly. Police and firemen moved promptly on to every floor; they thumped on doors, shouted, brushed aside questions with commands, hurried people towards stairwells, cautioning them not to use elevators. Others from the emergency force, assisted by hotel staff, used passkeys to check rooms from which there had been no response. Through it all, the fire alarm bells continued ringing.

A few guests protested and argued, a handful were belligerent but, when threatened with arrest, even they joined the outward exodus. Few, if any, of the hotel guests knew exactly what was happening; they accepted the imminence of danger and moved fast, pulling on a minimum of clothing, abandoning belongings in their rooms. One man, obeying orders sleepily, got as far as the stairway door on his floor before realizing he was naked. A grinning fireman let him go back to put on trousers and a shirt.

The evacuation was already in progress when the police bomb squad arrived in three trucks, tyres and sirens screaming. The bomb men poured into the hotel and, working swiftly but carefully, checked every fire extinguisher in sight. Those which were suspect had ropes looped over them, after which – paying out rope as they went – the bomb men retreated around corners,

376

getting as far away as was practical. When someone had made sure the immediate area was clear of people, the ropes were tugged. This jogged the extinguishers and toppled them – normally enough movement to set off any booby traps. However, there were no explosions and, after each extinguisher was dealt with, a bomb man lifted it and carried it outside. That represented the greatest risk of all, but was accepted because of the special circumstances.

From the street in front of the hotel, the extinguisher bombs were rushed, by a hastily assembled fleet of trucks, to a disused waterfront pier where they were dumped into the bay.

Soon after deployment of the police bomb squad, they were joined by an Army ordnance unit of a half-dozen officers and NCOs – bomb experts who helped speed the removal process.

Twenty minutes after the alarm was given, it became evident to those in charge that evacuation was going well, and faster than expected. The chances of having most guests out of the hotel before 3am looked good.

By now, every street leading to the Christopher Columbus was jam-packed with vehicles – fire equipment, police cars and wagons, ambulances, all with dome lights flashing. A huge van, operated by the city's Office of Emergency Services, had just moved in and was setting up an on-site command post. Two GSP & L heavy-duty service trucks were among recent arrivals, one crew standing by in case of power problems, the other disconnecting gas service at the street main.

Representatives of press, TV and radio were arriving in growing numbers, eagerly asking questions of anyone who might answer. Two local radio stations were broadcasting live from the scene. The news was already international; AP and UPI had flashed bulletins nationwide and overseas.

Among the press corps, Nancy Molineaux was the centre of attention by a group composed of several police detectives, an FBI special agent, and a young Assistant District Attorney. (The Assistant DA had been on the police operations centre list.) Nancy answered as many questions as she could, but was evasive about the two cassette tapes which had already been collected from her as arranged. Under a stern near-threat from the Assistant DA, she promised they would be handed to him within the next two hours. One detective, following discussions between his superiors and the Assistant DA, left the group to telephone two instructions: raid the house at 117 Crocker Street. Arrest Georgos Archambault and Davey Birdsong.

Through it all, police and firemen continued to hasten evacuation of the hotel.

Inevitably, as the hotel emptied, there were casualties. An elderly woman tripped on the concrete emergency stairs and fell heavily, breaking her hip and wrist. An ambulance crew carried her away, moaning, on a stretcher. A New England power company official had a heart attack after descending twenty flights and died on the way to the hospital. Another woman fell and suffered a concussion. Several more had minor cuts and bruises resulting from haste and congestion on the stairs.

There appeared to be no panic. Strangers helped each other. Boorishness or bad manners were almost nil. Some hardy spirits made jokes, helping others overcome their fear.

Once outside the hotel, evacuees were herded to a side street, two blocks away, where police cars had been parked to form a barricade. Fortunately, the night was mild and no one seemed to be suffering because of scanty clothing. After a while, a Red Cross van appeared and volunteer workers passed out coffee, doing what else they could to console people while they waited.

Nim Goldman and his family were among the early groups to reach the cordoned-off area. By then, Leah and Benjy were thoroughly awake, and now excited by what was happening. When he was satisfied that Ruth and the children were safe, and despite Ruth's protests, Nim returned to the hotel. Afterwards he realized he was foolhardy in the extreme, but at the time was prompted by the general heady excitement and the remembrance of two things. One was Nancy Molineaux's hasty reference on the phone to 'bombs disguised as fire extinguishers', the other, the young man who, only yesterday, had placed a fire extinguisher behind a lobby chair while Nim and Wally Talbot watched. Nim wanted to make sure, with many people still in the hotel: had that particular extinguisher been found?

By now it was close to 3am.

Despite a stream of agitated guests emerging from the hotel's main entrance, Nim managed to force his way back in. Once inside the lobby, he tried to get the attention of a passing fireman, but the man brushed him aside with a 'not now, buddy', and raced upstairs towards the mezzanine.

378

There seemed no one else in authority who was unoccupied; and Nim headed to where he had seen the fire extinguisher placed.

'Mr Goldman! Mr Goldman!' The call came from his right and a small man in civilian clothes, with a metal badge pinned to his breast pocket, hurried forward. Nim recognized Art Romeo, the shifty-appearing little deputy to Harry London in the Property Protection Department. The shield, Nim realized, was that of a GSP & L security officer, but it appeared to be giving Romeo authority.

Much later, Nim would discover that Art Romeo had been visiting the hotel, and was sharing a nocturnal poker game with out-of-town cronies from another utility, when the alarm was given. He had promptly pinned on his security badge and helped with the evacuation.

'Mr Goldman, you *must* go outside!'

'Forget that! I need help.' Nim hurriedly explained about the fire extinguisher which he suspected was a bomb.

'Where is it, sir?'

'Over here.' Nim strode to where he had been seated yesterday and pulled a chair aside. The red extinguisher was where the young man in coveralls had left it.

Art Romeo's voice took on authority. 'Move away! Get out! Go!'

'No, it has to be . . .'

What happened next occurred so quickly that Nim had trouble afterwards recalling the sequence of events.

He heard Romeo shout, 'Officers! Over here!' Suddenly two brawny policemen were beside him, and Romeo was telling them, 'This man refuses to leave. Take him outside!'

Without questioning the order, the policemen seized Nim and roughly frog marched him towards the main front door. As Nim was thrust through it he managed to glance back. The little figure of Art Romeo had lifted the fire extinguisher and, with it clasped in his arms, was following.

Ignoring Nim's protests, the policemen continued shoving him towards the evacuation area two blocks distant. When he was within a few yards of it, they released him. One said, 'If you come back, mister, we'll arrest you and you'll be taken downtown and charged. We're doing this for your own good.'

At that same instant there was the mighty roar of an explosion, followed by a cacophony of shattering glass.

In the days which followed, based on eyewitness accounts and official reports, it was possible to piece the various happenings together.

Using the information Nancy Molineaux had given the police operations centre, obtained from the tape recordings and her notes, the bomb squad knew they had to look for high explosive bombs on the hotel's main floor and mezzanine, incendiary bombs on the floors above. They had located – or so they thought – all the high explosive bombs and, with Army aid, removed them.

A bomb squad spokesman said next day, 'In the circumstances, we and the Army boys took chances we wouldn't have normally. We gambled that we'd have time to do what we did, and the gamble paid off. If we'd been wrong about the timing, God help us all!'

The bomb squad had been wrong, however, in believing they had located all the high explosive bombs. The one they missed was the one Nim remembered.

By the time Art Romeo had bravely picked up the bomb, staggered with it from the hotel, and taken it to the area from where the disposal trucks had been shuttling, all the bomb squad members were on upper floors of the hotel, working frantically to clear the fire bombs.

Consequently, after Art Romeo set the high explosive bomb down, no one else was close when, seconds later, it exploded. Romeo was blown to pieces instantly. Almost every window in adjoining blocks was shattered, as was the glass in nearby vehicles. But miraculously, incredibly, no one else was hurt.

As the roar of the explosion died, several women screamed and men cursed.

The explosion also marked a psychological turning point. No one, any more, questioned the need for the emergency exodus. Talking, among the displaced hotel guests, was noticeably more subdued. Some, abandoning any idea of returning to the Christopher Columbus, began to leave the scene quietly, making their own arrangements for the remainder of the night.

But within the hotel, although no guests remained, the action was not yet over.

Out of the nearly twenty fire bombs which Georgos Archambault and his fellow terrorists placed on upper floors, eight were not located and removed in time; they detonated shortly after 3am. Fierce fires resulted. It was more than an hour before all were brought under control; by then the floors where they occurred were a sodden, burned out shambles. It was clear to all concerned that, without the advance warning and evacuation, the death toll would have been enormous.

As it was, two policemen and three firemen died. Two more firemen were badly injured. All were close to the fire bombs which exploded.

As dawn succeeded darkness, mopping up continued.

Most former guests of the Christopher Columbus were provided with makeshift accommodation elsewhere. Later in the day, those who could would return to collect their belongings and begin a dispirited trek home.

By unanimous agreement, which no one even bothered discussing, the NEI convention was abandoned.

Nim took Ruth, Leah and Benjy home in a taxi. He had wished to thank Nancy Molineaux for her phone call, but observing her still a centre of attention for some reason, he decided to do it later.

As Nim and his family left, morgue wagons were joining the other vehicles at the scene.

Soon after the explosion which killed Art Romeo, Georgos Archambault was sobbing as he ran towards where his *Fire Protection Service* truck was parked.

It had all gone wrong! Everything!

Georgos couldn't understand it.

Some thirty-five minutes earlier, just after 2:25am, he had been puzzled to hear many sirens approaching the area where he was waiting in the pick-up. Moments later, fire engines and police cars sped past, obviously headed for the Christopher Columbus. As minutes went by, the activity increased and more vehicles followed. Georgos was now thoroughly alarmed.

At twenty to three he could wait no longer. He got out of the truck, locked it, and walked towards the hotel, getting as close as he could before a barrier of police cars stopped him.

He was near enough to see – to his great dismay – people streaming from the hotel, many in nightclothes, and being urged by police and firemen to move faster.

Those people were supposed to stay inside until the bombs

went off and the hotel was burning! Then it would be too late to leave.

Georgos wanted to wave his arms and shout, 'Go back! Go back!' But, despairingly, he knew it would have no effect and only draw attention to himself.

Then, while he watched, some of his carefully planted fire extinguisher bombs were carried from the hotel by people who had no right to interfere with them, and then were rushed away in trucks, preventing what Georgos had so painstakingly planned. He thought: if he had *only* booby trapped the bombs, as he could have done with extra work, they could never have been moved. But he had been so confident that nothing would go wrong. Now it had, robbing Friends of Freedom of their glorious victory.

That was when Georgos began to cry.

Even when he heard the high explosive bomb go off in the street, it did not console him and he turned away.

How had it happened? Why had he failed? In what devious way had the enemy found out? He watched the firemen and police – blind, ignorant slaves of fascist capitalism – with bitterness and anger.

At that point, Georgos realized that his own identity might now be known, that perhaps he was in personal peril, and he began to run.

The pick-up truck was just as he had left it. No one seemed to notice him as he unlocked the truck and drove away, though lights were going on in nearby buildings and sightseers were hurrying towards the hotel, attracted by the sound and activity.

Instinctively Georgos headed for Crocker Street, then wondered: was it safe?

The question was quickly answered. As he turned into Crocker at the far end from number 117, he saw that the street further on was blocked by police cars. A moment later he heard the sound of gunfire – a fusillade of shots, a pause, then a second fusillade as if fire was being returned. Georgos knew that Wayde, Ute and Felix, who had elected to stay in the house tonight, were trapped; he wished desperately he was with them, if necessary to die nobly. But there was no way now that he could fight his way in – or out.

As quickly as he could, hoping not to attract attention, he

382

turned the truck around and returned the way he had come. There was only one place left to go: the apartment in North Castle, intended for a crisis such as this.

While he drove, Georgos' mind worked quickly. If his identity was known, the police would be searching for him. Even at this moment they might be spreading a dragnet, so he must hurry to get underground. Something else: in all probability, the pigs knew about the *Fire Protection Service* truck and would be on the lookout for it; therefore the truck must be abandoned. But not until he was nearer the North Castle hideaway. Taking a chance, Georgos increased his speed.

One chance must not be taken, he reasoned. The truck could not be left too close to the apartment; otherwise it would betray his whereabouts. He was approaching North Castle. How near to his destination dare he drive? He decided: within one mile.

When Georgos estimated he was that distance away, he pulled to the kerb, switched off the engine and got out, not bothering to lock the truck or take the ignition key. He reasoned further: the police might well assume he had had a parked car waiting and changed vehicles, or he had boarded a late night bus or taxi, any of which assumptions would leave his general whereabouts in doubt.

What Georgos did not know was that a drunk, recovering from a quart of cheap wine consumed earlier, was propped up in a doorway opposite where the *Fire Protection Service* truck had stopped. The drunk was sufficiently lucid to observe the truck's arrival and Georgos' departure on foot.

For his part, Georgos began walking briskly. The streets were silent, almost deserted, and he was aware of being conspicuous. But no one accosted or appeared to notice him and, in a quarter of an hour, he was unlocking the apartment door. With relief he went inside.

At about the same time, a cruising police patrol spotted the red pick-up for which an alert had gone out a short time earlier. The patrolman who transmitted a radio report noted that the radiator was still warm.

Moments later, the same officer noticed the drunk in the doorway opposite and elicited the information that the driver of the truck had left on foot, and in which direction. The police car sped away, but failed to locate Georgos.

The police patrol did return, however, and – with base ingratitude – took their informant into custody, charging him with being drunk in public.

Davey Birdsong was arrested, shortly after 5 : 30am, outside the apartment building where he lived.

He had just returned there by car after the lecture and study group session which kept him outside the city through the night.

Birdsong was shocked. He protested heatedly to the two plain-clothes detectives who made the arrest, one of whom promptly informed him of his legal right to remain silent. Despite the warning, Birdsong declared, 'Listen, you guys, whatever this is all about, I want to tell you I've been away since yesterday. I left my apartment at six o'clock last night and haven't been back since. I have plenty of witnesses to that.'

The detective who had cautioned Birdsong wrote the statement down, and – ironically – the 'alibi' proved Birdsong's undoing.

When Birdsong was searched at police headquarters, the p & lfp press statement deploring 'the bombing at the Christopher Columbus Hotel last night' was found in a jacket pocket. The statement was later proved to have been typed on a machine kept in Birdsong's apartment – *the apartment he claimed he had not entered since six o'clock the previous evening, nearly nine hours before the bombing became public knowledge.* As if this were not enough, two torn-up, earlier drafts of the statement, in Birdsong's handwriting, were also discovered in the apartment.

Other evidence proved equally damning. The cassette tape recordings of conversations between Georgos Archambault and Davey Birdsong matched a voiceprint of Birdsong, made after his arrest. The young black taxi driver, Vickery, whom Nancy Molineaux employed, made a statement confirming Birdsong's devious journey to the house at 117 Crocker Street. Birdsong's purchase of fire extinguishers, which had been converted to bombs, was also attested to.

He was charged with six counts of first-degree murder, conspiracy to commit a felony, and a 'shopping list' of other charges. Bail was set at one million dollars, a sum which Birdsong could not raise and no one else seemed inclined to. Hence, he remained in custody, pending his trial.

*

Of the remaining Friends of Freedom, Wayde, the young Marxist intellectual, and Felix, from Detroit's inner city, were killed in the gun battle with police at 117 Crocker Street. Ute, the embittered Indian, turned a gun on himself and died as police stormed the house.

The evidence of revolutionary activity at number 117 was captured intact, including the journal of Georgos Winslow Archambault.

7

Around the *California Examiner* newsroom and the Press Club bar, they were already saying that Nancy Molineaux was a dead cert for a Pulitzer.

She had it all.

As the managing editor was heard to tell the publisher: 'That classy broad has come through with the whole goddamn, zipped-up, total Erector set of the hottest story this side of the second coming.'

After leaving the Christopher Columbus Hotel, and going to the paper, Nancy wrote continuously right up to the *Examiner*'s 6:30am first deadline. Through the remainder of the morning and early afternoon, she updated and amplified the earlier material for the later three editions. And, as reports of new developments came in, they were funnelled through her.

In case of any query about Friends of Freedom, Georgos Archambault, Davey Birdsong, p & lfp, the Sequoia Club's money, the hotel bombing, the life and death of Yvette, the password was, 'Ask Nancy'.

Just as in a reporter's dream, almost the entire front page under a banner headline, was Nancy Molineaux's.

The newspaper put a copyright slug over her story, which meant that any TV or radio station or other newspaper using her exclusive coverage was obliged to quote the *Examiner* as its source.

Because Nancy was an integral part of the story herself – her discovery of 117 Crocker Street, the meetings with Yvette, and her possession of the only copy of the tapes established that – she achieved personal celebrity status.

The day the story broke she was interviewed, at her newsroom desk, for TV. That night the film appeared on the national network news of NBC, ABC and CBS.

Even so, the *Examiner* management made the TV crews wait, fuming, until Nancy had finished her own reporting and was good and ready.

Newsweek and *Time,* following the TV crowd, got the same treatment.

Over at the *Chronicle-West,* the city's morning, competitive paper, there was unconcealed envy and much scurrying to catch up. The *Chronicle*'s editor, however, was big enough to send Nancy a half-dozen roses next day (a dozen, he thought, would be overdoing it) with a congratulatory note, delivered to her *Examiner* desk.

The effects of the news story spread outwards, not in ripples, but in waves.

To many who read Nancy Molineaux's report, the most shocking revelation was that the Sequoia Club, even if indirectly, had financed the Christopher Columbus bombing.

Indignant Sequoia Club members across the nation telegraphed, phoned or mailed their resignations.

'Never again,' thundered California's senior senator in an interview with the *Washington Post*, 'will I trust that despicable organization or listen to anything it advocates.' The statement found a thousand echoes elsewhere.

It was generally conceded that the Sequoia Club, its name disgraced and influence diminished, could never be the same again.

Laura Bo Carmichael resigned immediately as the club's chairman. After doing so, she went into seclusion, refusing to take telephone calls from the press or anyone else. Instead, a private secretary read to callers a short statement which concluded, 'Mrs Carmichael considers her public life to be at an end.'

The only Sequoia Club figure to emerge with honour was Mrs Priscilla Quinn, who, Nancy accurately reported, had been the sole opponent of paying fifty thousand dollars to Birdsong's p & lfp.

Nancy took satisfaction in recording that the big-league lawyer,

Irwin Saunders, was one of those who voted 'yes'.

If the Sequoia Club attempted to rehabilitate itself, it was predicted that Priscilla Quinn would be the new chairman, with the club's emphasis directed towards social work rather than environmental matters.

Following Nancy's exposé of Georgos Archambault, and later reports of his disappearance, a small army of police detectives and FBI special agents fanned out through the North Castle district in search of the Friends of Freedom leader. They had no success.

A thorough police search of 117 Crocker Street produced large amounts of evidence, further incriminating Georgos and Davey Birdsong. Among the clothes left by Georgos was a denim jumpsuit; lab tests showed that, where the garment was torn, a missing portion matched a small piece of material found at the Millfield sub-station, snagged on a cut wire, the night the two security guards were killed. Also in the house were voluminous written records, including Georgos' journal; all were turned over to the District Attorney. The existence of the journal was revealed to the press, though its contents were not disclosed.

After Davey Birdsong's part in the whole affair was described in print, Birdsong, in jail, was segregated from other prisoners for his own safety.

Before some of that happened, however, Nancy Molineaux went through a personal crisis of her own. It occurred shortly before noon the day during which her major story broke.

She had been working under deadline pressure since before dawn and, having had no sleep the night before and being sustained only by coffee and orange juice, was tiring. It showed.

Several times since 7:30am, when the city editor came on duty in time for the second edition, old 'I'm-the-coach' had stopped by Nancy's desk with quiet words of encouragement. Apart from that, there was little need for editorial discussion. Nancy was assembling the facts capably – her own, and others fed to her. She also had a reputation for writing 'clean' copy which required little, if any, rewrite.

Occasionally, when she stopped typing and glanced up, Nancy caught the city editor looking over at her. Though his expression was inscrutable, she had a notion they were both thinking the same thing – something which, through most of the past few hours, she had pushed determinedly from her mind.

The last thing Nancy had observed before leaving the Christopher Columbus was the shrouded bodies of the dead policemen and firemen being wheeled from the hotel on trolleys to waiting morgue wagons. There were also two men, outside the hotel, putting pieces of something into a plastic bag; it took her a minute to realize they were collecting the remains of the sixth dead man, the one blown to pieces by a bomb.

It was then Nancy faced the stark, grim truth which, until now, she had evaded: that for an entire week she had been in possession of information which, if shared, could have prevented all six deaths and much else.

The same thought bored into her consciousness each time she caught the city editor looking at her. That, and his words of a week ago: *'You're supposed to be part of a team, Nancy, and I'm the coach. I know you prefer being a loner, and you've gotten away with it because you get results. But you can push that game too far.'*

At the time she had dismissed the advice with a mental, *Screw you, Mr Charlie!* Now, she wished vainly, desperately, she hadn't.

At 11:55am, with two hours and twenty minutes still to go before the final edition deadline, the thought of the six dead bodies could no longer be thrust away, and Nancy was ready to crack.

'Take a break and come with me,' a voice said quietly. When she looked up, old I'm-the-coach was again beside her.

She hesitated and he added, 'That's an order.'

With unusual docility, Nancy stood up and followed him as he left the newsroom.

A short way down the corridor was a small room, normally kept locked, and sometimes used for management meetings. The city editor used a key to open it and held the door for Nancy to precede him.

Inside, the furnishings were comfortable but simple, a boardroom-type table and upholstered chairs, a pair of matching walnut cabinets, soft brown curtains.

With another key the city editor opened one of the cabinets. He motioned Nancy to sit down.

'There's a choice of brandy or scotch. Not the best brands; we don't compete with the Ritz here. I suggest the brandy.'

Nancy nodded, suddenly unable to find words.

Her superior poured California brandy into two glasses and

sat down facing her. When they had sipped he said, 'I've been watching you.'

'Yes, I know.'

'And we've both been thinking the same thing. Right?'

Again she nodded without speaking.

'Nancy,' the city editor said, 'as I see it, by the end of today you'll go one of two ways. Either right over the edge, which means a mental breakdown and ending up on some shrink's couch twice a week, *ad infinitum*, or you'll get a grip on yourself and let what's in the past stay there. I'll say this about the first route: it will louse up your life and benefit nobody except the shrink. As to the second, you've got spunk and intelligence, and you can handle it. But you'll have to make a positive decision, not just let things slide.'

Relieved, at last, to say it aloud, she told him, 'I'm responsible for last night. If I'd told someone what I knew, the police could have been warned and they'd have investigated that Crocker Street house.'

'The first statement is false,' he told her, 'the second true. I'm not saying you won't live with last night for the rest of your life. I think you will. But you're not the first to make an error in judgement which harmed others; you won't be the last either. Also in your defence: you didn't know what would happen; if you had, you'd have acted differently. So my advice is this, Nancy: face up to it, accept what you did and didn't do, and remember it – for experience and learning. But otherwise put it behind you.'

When she remained silent, he went on, 'Now I'll tell you something else. I've been a lot of years in this business – some days I think too many. But in my opinion, Nancy, you're the best damn reporter I've ever worked with.'

It was then that Nancy Molineaux did something which had happened only rarely in the past, and even then she had never let others see. She put her head in her arms, broke down, and cried.

Old I'm-the-coach went to the window and decently turned his back. Looking down at the street outside, he said, 'I locked the door when we came in, Nancy. It's still locked and will stay that way until you're ready, so take your time. And, oh yes – something else. I promise that no one but you and me will ever know what went on in here today.'

In a half hour Nancy was back at her desk, with her face washed and makeup repaired, writing once more, and totally in control.

Nim Goldman telephoned Nancy Molineaux the next morning, having tried to reach her, unsuccessfully, the day before.

'I wanted to say thank you,' he said, 'for that call you made to the hotel.'

She told him, 'Maybe I owed you that.'

'Whether you did or didn't, I'm still grateful.' He added, a trifle awkwardly, 'You pulled off a big story. Congratulations.'

Nancy asked curiously, 'What did you think of it all? The things that went into the story, I mean.'

'For Birdsong,' Nim answered, 'I'm not in the least sorry, and I hope he gets everything he deserves. I also hope that phony p & lfp never surfaces again.'

'How about the Sequoia Club? Do you feel the same way?'

'No,' Nim said, 'I don't.'

'Why?'

'The Sequoia Club has been something we all needed – part of our societal system of checks and balances. Oh, I've had disputes with the Sequoia people, so have others, and I believe the club went too far in opposing everything in sight. But the Sequoia Club was a community conscience; it made us think, and care about the environment, and sometimes stopped our side from going to excesses.'

Nim paused, then went on, 'I know the Sequoia Club is down right now, and I'm genuinely distressed for Laura Bo Carmichael who, despite our disagreements, was a friend. But I hope the Sequoia Club isn't out. It would be a loss to everyone if that happened.'

'Well,' Nancy said, 'sometimes a day is full of surprises.' She had been scribbling while Nim talked. 'May I quote all that?'

He hesitated only briefly, then said, 'Why not?'

In the *Examiner*'s next edition, she did.

8

Harry London sat brooding, looking at the papers Nim had shown him.

At length he said glumly, 'Do you know the way I feel about all this?'

Nim told him, 'I can guess.'

As if he had not heard, the Property Protection chief went on, 'Last week was the worst in a long time. Art Romeo was a good guy; I know you didn't know him well, Nim, but he was loyal, honest, and a friend. When I heard what happened, I was sick. I'd figured when I left Korea and the Marines I was through with hearing about guys I know being blown to bits.'

'Harry,' Nim said, 'I'm desperately sorry about Art Romeo too. What he did that night was something I'll never forget.'

London waved the interruption away. 'Just let me finish.'

Nim was silent, waiting.

It was Wednesday morning, in the first week of March, six days after the trauma at the Christopher Columbus Hotel. Both men were in Nim's office, with the door closed for privacy.

'Well,' London said, 'so now you show me this, and to tell the truth, I wish you hadn't. Because the way I see it, what else is there left to believe in any more?'

'Plenty,' Nim answered. 'A lot to care about and plenty to believe in. Not any more, though, the integrity of Mr Justice Yale.'

'Here, take these.' Harry London handed the papers back.

They comprised a batch of correspondence – eight letters, some with copies of enclosures attached, and all were from the files of the late Walter Talbot, until his death last July, chief engineer of GSP & L.

The three cardboard cartons from which the letters had been taken were open in Nim's office, their other contents spread around.

Locating the letters, which Nim suddenly recalled to mind at the NEI convention, had been delayed because of last week's tragedy and aftermath. Earlier today, Nim had had the files brought up from a basement storage vault. Even then it had taken him more than an hour to find the particular papers he sought – those he remembered glancing at seven months ago, the day at Ardythe's house when she gave him the cartons for safe-keeping.

But he had found them. His memory had been right.

And now the letters must inevitably be used as evidence at a confrontation.

Exactly two weeks earlier, at the meeting between J. Eric Humphrey, Nim, Harry London and Justice Paul Sherman Yale on the subject of power stealing, the former Supreme Court justice had stated unequivocally, '. . . *I find the entire concept of power theft interesting. Frankly, I had no idea such a thing existed. I have never heard of it before. Nor did I know there were such people in the public utility business as Mr London.*'

The correspondence Nim had found showed all four statements to be deceitful and untrue.

It was, in the oft-used phrase of Watergate, 'the smoking gun'.

'Of course,' London said abruptly, 'we'll never know for sure whether the old man gave his approval to the power thievery by the Yale Trust, or even if he knew about it and did nothing. All we can prove is that he's a liar.'

'And was worried as hell,' Nim said. 'Otherwise he would never have trapped himself by those statements.'

The facts of the matter were simple.

Walter Talbot had been a pioneer in drawing attention to huge financial losses incurred by electric and gas utilities as a result of theft. He had written articles on the subject, made speeches, been interviewed by news media, and had appeared as an expert witness in a New York State criminal trial which wended its way, via appeals, through higher courts. The case had generated wide interest. Also correspondence.

Some of the correspondence had been with a member of the United States Supreme Court.

Justice Paul Sherman Yale.

It was clear from the exchange that Walter Talbot and Paul Yale had known each other well during earlier years in California.

The first letter was on a distinguished letterhead.

$$\mathfrak{Supreme\ Court\ of\ the\ United\ States}$$
$$\mathfrak{Washington,\ D.C.\ 20543}$$

It began : *My dear Walter.*

The writer expressed his interest, as a legal scholar, in a burgeoning new field of law enforcement, namely, that related to the stealing of electricity and gas. He asked for more details of the types of offences involved and methods being used to combat them. Also requested were any known facts about prosecutions, and their outcomes in various parts of the country. The letter inquired after the health of Ardythe and was signed *Paul.*

Walter Talbot, with a sense of decorum, had replied more formally : *My dear Justice Yale.*

His letter was four pages long. Accompanying it was a photocopy of one of Walter's published articles.

Several weeks later Paul Yale wrote again. He acknowledged the letter and article and posed several pertinent questions which demonstrated he had read the material carefully.

The correspondence continued through five more letters, spaced over eight months. In one of them Walter Talbot described the function of the Property Protection Department in a typical public utility, and the duties of an individual heading it - such as Harry London.

Not surprisingly, the letters pointed up the sharp, inquiring mind, the lively interest in everything, of Paul Sherman Yale.

And the entire correspondence had taken place *only two years before Mr Justice Yale's retirement from the bench.*

Could Paul Yale possibly have forgotten? Nim had already asked himself that question and decided the answer was an emphatic 'no'. The old man had demonstrated, too many times, his remarkable memory – both for large issues and for detail – to make that believable.

It was Harry London who raised the key issue Nim had been debating. 'Why did the old boy do it? Why did he lie to us the way he did?'

'Probably,' Nim said thoughtfully, 'because he knew Walter was dead, and because the chance of any of the three of us – the chairman, you, me – knowing about that correspondence was remote. In fact, it must have been obvious that we didn't. Also, the odds on those letters ever surfacing were a million to one against.'

London nodded his agreement, then said, 'The next question, I reckon, is : how many other times has the Honorable Paul done the same thing and gotten away with it?'

'We'll never know, will we?'

The Property Protection chief motioned to the letters. 'Of course, you'll show these to the chairman.'

'Yes, this afternoon. I happen to know Mr Yale is coming in later today.'

'Which brings up something else.' Harry London's voice was bitter. 'Will we go on trying as hard as we have to keep that precious Yale name out of those court proceedings which are coming up? Or, in view of this new information, will "Mr Integrity" take his chances like anybody else?'

'I don't know.' Nim sighed. 'I simply don't know. And, in any case, it won't be my decision.'

The showdown with Mr Justice Yale occurred shortly after 4pm in the chairman's office suite.

When Nim arrived, having been summoned by J. Eric Humphrey's secretary, it was obvious that tension already existed. The chairman's expression could best be described, Nim thought, as 'wounded old Bostonian'. Humphrey's eyes were cold, his mouth tightly set. Paul Yale, while unaware of precisely what was afoot, clearly shared the knowledge that it was something disagreeable and his normal cheerfulness had been replaced by a frown. The two were seated at a table in the conference area and neither man was speaking when Nim joined them.

Nim took the chair on Eric Humphrey's left, facing Mr Justice Yale. He placed on the table before him the file containing the Talbot-Yale correspondence.

Earlier, Eric Humphrey and Nim, after some debate, had agreed on the sequence of procedure. They also decided that Harry London need not, this time, be included.

'Paul,' Humphrey began, 'on the previous occasion when the three of us were together, we had a discussion about certain problems of power stealing. In part, they involved the Yale Family Trust. I'm sure that you remember.'

Mr Justice Yale nodded. 'Yes, of course.'

'At that time you made a number of statements. All were to the effect that you had no idea, prior to that moment, that such a thing as power theft existed.'

'Now stop this!' Paul Yale's face flushed angrily. 'I do not like your tone or attitude, Eric. Nor am I here to be questioned about what I may, or may not, have said . . .'

Humphrey's voice cut acidly across the protest. 'There is no "may" about it. What you told us was precise and unambiguous. Moreover, it was repeated several times. I remember it that way. So does Nim.'

It was plain to Nim that Paul Yale's mind was working at high speed. The old man said sternly, 'Whatever was said, it does not follow from it . . .'

'Nim,' the chairman ordered, 'show Mr Yale the contents of our file.'

Opening the folder, Nim slid the small pile of letters and attachments across the table. The earliest dated letter – on Supreme Court stationery – was on top.

Paul Yale picked it up, glanced at it, then dropped it hastily. He did not bother with the others. His face, which had been flushed before, suffused an even deeper red.

Afterwards, replaying the scene in his mind, Nim guessed that while Yale expected some kind of unfavourable revelation, the possibility of being confronted with his old correspondence had not occurred to him. If Nim's conjecture was true, it would explain the old man's abject, total shock.

His tongue moistened his lips. He seemed unable to find the words he wanted.

Then he said awkwardly, defensively, 'Sometimes, especially in Washington . . . with so much happening, so many papers, the unending correspondence . . . one forgets . . .' The statement trailed off. Obviously it sounded as false and unconvincing to Mr Justice Yale as it did to the other two.

'Strike that,' he said abruptly, and stood up. Pushing back his chair, he walked away from the table and, without looking at Nim or Humphrey, asked, 'Please give me a moment to collect my thoughts.'

Briefly the old man paced the chairman's broadloom. Then he turned, though continuing to stand.

'It is plain, gentlemen, as only documentary evidence can make it, that I have been guilty of deception and – no doubt deservedly – been caught.' Paul Yale's voice was lower than normal; his face reflected pain as he continued. 'I will not compound my error by explanations or excuses, either by describing my considerable anxiety at the time of our earlier talk, or my urgent and natural desire to protect my good name.'

Just the same, Nim thought, *you've managed to do both while saying that you wouldn't.*

'I will, however,' Yale went on, 'swear to you that I neither participated in power theft by the Yale Family Trust, nor had any knowledge of it prior to our first discussion here.'

Eric Humphrey, who, Nim remembered, had been eager to accept Paul Yale's word before, remained silent. Probably the chairman was thinking, as was Nim, that anyone who would lie once to protect his reputation would lie again for the same reason.

Inevitably, Nim was reminded of Harry London's question: *'How many other times has the Honorable Paul done the same thing and gotten away with it?'*

As the silence hung, the pain in the old man's eyes deepened.

'Nim,' Eric Humphrey said quietly, 'I don't believe it's necessary for you to stay any longer.'

With relief, Nim gathered up the papers on the table and returned them to the file while the other two watched. Taking the file with him, and with no further word spoken, Nim left.

He did not know it then, but it was the last time he would ever meet Mr Justice Yale.

Nim never learned what else transpired in the chairman's office that day. He didn't ask, nor did Eric Humphrey volunteer the information. But the end result was revealed the next morning.

At 11am Humphrey sent for Nim and Teresa Van Buren. Seated at his desk, and holding a letter, he informed them, 'I have received the resignation of Justice Paul Sherman Yale as our public spokesman and a director of this company. The resignation has been accepted with regret. I would like an announcement made immediately to that effect.'

Van Buren told him, 'We should state some reason, Eric.'

'Ill health.' Humphrey referred to the letter in his hand. 'Mr Yale's doctors have advised him that, at his age, the strain of his new duties at GSP & L has proven too arduous. They have advised him to discontinue them.'

'No problem,' the PR director said. 'I'll have it on the wires this afternoon. I have another question, though.'

'Yes?'

'That leaves us without a spokesman for the company. Who takes over?'

For the first time the chairman smiled. 'I'm too busy to search for someone else, Tess, so I suppose there's no alternative. Put the saddle back on Nim.'

'Hallelujah!' Van Buren said. 'You know the way I feel. It should never have been taken off.'

Outside the chairman's office Teresa Van Buren lowered her voice, 'Nim, give me the straight dope behind this Yale thing. What went wrong? You know I'll find out sooner or later.'

Nim shook his head. 'You heard the chairman, Tess. Failing health.'

'You bastard!' she shot at him. 'For that, I may not put you on TV until next week.'

Harry London read the published report of Paul Yale's departure and came to Nim the next day.

'If I had any guts,' he declared, 'I'd resign in disgust at that fiction about ill health and acceptance with regret. It makes all of us liars, just the way he is.'

Nim, who had not slept well, said irritably, 'So go ahead - resign.'

'I can't afford to.'

'Then knock off the holier-than-thou crap, Harry. You said yourself there's no way we could prove Mr Yale was into power theft personally.'

London said dourly, 'He was though. The more I think about it, the more I believe it.'

'Don't forget,' Nim pointed out, 'that Ian Norris, who ran the Yale Family Trust, swore he wasn't.'

'Yes, and the whole thing smells like a deal. Norris will get his payoff in some way later - maybe by staying on as trustee. Besides, Norris wouldn't have gained anything himself by involving the great man.'

'Whatever we think, or don't,' Nim said, 'it's over and finished. So get back to work and catch more power thieves.'

'I already have. There's a bunch of new cases, as well as others developing from the Quayle inquiry. But Nim, I'll tell you one thing for the future.'

Nim sighed. 'Go ahead.'

'We've been part of a cover-up, you and me; a cover-up to protect that high-and-mighty Yale name. It goes to show there are still special rules and laws for those with pull and power.'

'Look, Harry . . .'

'No, hear me out! What I'm doing, Nim, is serving notice that if I have *clear evidence* in any case in the future, no matter *who* it is, no one is going to stop me from bringing it out in the open and doing what has to be done.'

'Okay, okay,' Nim said. 'If there's clear evidence, I'll fight it with you. And now we've settled that, please go, and let me get some work done.'

When he was alone, Nim regretted having vented his bad humour on Harry London. Most of what London had said, about the resignation statement being a lie and part of a cover-up, had already occurred to Nim, and troubled him last night, when he slept only fitfully. Were there degrees of lying? Nim didn't believe so. As he saw it, a lie was a lie. Period. In which case, wasn't GSP & L – in the persons of Eric Humphrey, who authorized a public falsehood, and Nim, who endorsed it by his silence – equally culpable as Paul Sherman Yale?

There could be only one answer: yes.

He was still thinking about it when his secretary, Vicki Davis, buzzed and told him, 'The chairman would like to see you immediately.'

J. Eric Humphrey, Nim could tell at once, was unusually perturbed.

When Nim came in, the chairman was moving restlessly around his office, something he rarely did. He continued standing as he talked and Nim listened.

'There is something I wish to say to you, Nim, and shortly I will explain why,' the chairman said. 'Recently I have been ashamed and disgusted at certain events which have happened in this company. I do not *like* to feel ashamed of the organization which pays me a salary and which I head.'

Humphrey paused, and Nim remained silent, wondering what was coming next.

'One matter for shame,' the chairman continued, 'has been dealt with within the past twenty-four hours. But there is another, larger issue which persists – the outrageous attacks upon the lives and property of this company.'

'The FBI and police . . .' Nim began.

'Have accomplished nothing,' Humphrey snapped. 'Absolutely nothing!'

'They have Birdsong in jail,' Nim pointed out.

'Yes – and why? Because one intelligent, determined woman reporter was more resourceful than a veritable army of professional law enforcers. Remember also that it was information from the same young woman which resulted in those other blackguards at that Crocker Street house being shot and killed – their just deserts.'

Only J. Eric Humphrey, Nim thought, would use words like 'blackguards' and 'just deserts'. All the same, Nim had seldom seen Humphrey so openly emotional. He suspected that what was being said now had been bottled up inside the chairman for a long time.

'Consider this,' Humphrey resumed. 'For more than a year we have suffered the indignity of having our installations, even this headquarters, bombed by a ragtag, small-time band of terrorists. Worse still, it has cost the lives of nine of our own good people, not including Mr Romeo who died at the Christopher Columbus Hotel. And that is something else! I am *deeply ashamed* that while we were the host city, the host company, to the NEI convention, that terrible episode was allowed to happen.'

'I really don't believe, Eric,' Nim said, 'that anyone could, or does, blame GSP & L for what occurred at the Columbus.'

'*I* blame us, and I blame myself, for not having been more insistent, earlier, that the law enforcement agencies *do something*. Even now, that vile man, the leader, Archambault, is still at large.' Humphrey's voice had risen in pitch. 'An entire week has gone by. *Where* is he? *Why* have the law enforcement agencies failed to find him?'

'I understand,' Nim said, 'that they're still searching, and they believe he's somewhere in the North Castle area.'

'Where he is doubtless plotting to kill or maim more of our people, and do our company more injury! Nim, *I want that villain found*. If necessary I want us – GSP & L – to find him.'

Nim was about to point out that a public utility was not equipped to perform police work, then had second thoughts. He asked instead, 'Eric, what do you have in mind?'

'I have in mind that we are an organization employing many high calibre people with an abundance of brainpower. Judging by results, the law enforcement agencies lack both. Therefore, Nim, these are my instructions to you: bring your own brain and those of others to bear on this problem. Call on whoever you require to help you; you have my authority. But I want results. For the sake of our people who were killed, for their families, and for the rest of us who take pride in GSP & L, I want that despicable person, Archambault, caught and brought to justice.'

The chairman stopped, his face flushed, then said tersely, 'That's all.'

It was a coincidence in timing, Nim thought, after his encounter with Eric Humphrey, that he, too, had been thinking about brain-power.

Four months ago, largely because of scepticism by Mr Justice Yale, Nim had abandoned the 'think group' approach to the problem of terrorist attacks by the so-called 'Friends of Freedom'.

Following Paul Yale's criticism that they had 'pushed supposition – pure conjecture, unsubstantiated – to the limits and beyond', Nim had summoned no further 'think meetings' between himself, Oscar O'Brien, Teresa Van Buren and Harry London. And yet, reviewing what was now known, the quartet's ideas and guesswork had been uncannily close to the truth.

In fairness, Nim reasoned, he could only blame himself. If he had persisted, instead of becoming overawed by Yale, they might have anticipated, possibly even prevented, some of the tragic events which had since occurred.

Now, armed with Eric Humphrey's instructions, there might still be something they could do.

Originally, in discussing the then-unknown leader of Friends of Freedom, the 'think group' labelled him 'X'. The identity of 'X' was now known, and the man – Georgos Archambault – dangerous, an overhanging threat to GSP & L and others, was believed to be hiding somewhere in the city.

Could intensive thought and probing discussion somehow penetrate that hiding?

Today was Friday. Nim decided that sometime during the weekend, using the chairman's authority if needed, he would bring the four 'thinkers' together once again.

9

'As it turned out,' Nim said, consulting notes, 'we were remarkably accurate. Let me remind you of just *how* accurate.'

He paused to sip the scotch and soda which Oscar O'Brien had poured for him a few minutes ago, before they started.

It was Sunday afternoon. At the general counsel's invitation, the 'think group' had assembled in his home and was sprawled around an informal comfortable garden room. The other three had been cooperative when approached by Nim, even more so when informed of J. Eric Humphrey's wishes.

The O'Brien house, high above the shoreline and with a beach below, afforded a magnificent waterfront view which, at the moment, included a multitude of sailboats, their weekend sailors endlessly beating, reaching or running, and miraculously avoiding each other, amid a flurry of whitecaps raised by a stiff westerly breeze.

As on previous occasions when the group had met, a tape recorder was running.

'On the basis of the then-available information,' Nim continued, 'information which was sketchy at best, we hypothesized that one man – 'X' – was the leader and brains of Friends of Freedom, that he was strongly masculine and vain, and that he had a woman confidante who worked closely with him. We also believed that "X" personally murdered those two guards at Millfield, and that the woman was present at the time. Furthermore, we concluded the woman might be a source of weakness and prove the undoing of "X".'

'I'd forgotten some of that,' Teresa Van Buren interjected. 'By God, we were right on target!'

The PR director, appearing as if she had come unchanged from a lazy weekend at home, was wearing a rumpled green caftan over her ample figure. Her hair, as usual, was untidy, probably because she ran her fingers through it whenever she was thinking. Her feet were bare; the pair of dilapidated sandals she had slipped off were beside her chair.

'Yes,' Nim acknowledged, 'I know. And I'll admit to you all, it was my fault we failed to continue. I guess I lost faith, and I was wrong.' He decided to say nothing about the influence of Mr Justice Yale, who, after all, had done no more than express an opinion.

Nim proceeded, 'Now that we know the identity of X, and a good deal more about him, perhaps we can use the same mental process in helping track him down.'

He stopped, conscious that three pairs of eyes were focused on him intently, then added, 'Perhaps not. But the chairman believes we should try.'

Oscar O'Brien grunted and removed from between his thick lips the cigar he had been smoking. The air was already thick with smoke, a condition distasteful to Nim, but it was O'Brien's home and objecting seemed unreasonable.

'I'm willing to give it a whirl,' the lawyer said. 'Where do we start?' He was wearing old grey slacks, loosely belted below his bulging belly, a baggy sweater, and loafers without socks.

'I've prepared a memo,' Nim said. Opening a briefcase, he produced copies and passed them around. The memo contained a summary of all information, published since the NEI convention, about Friends of Freedom and Georgos Archambault. The bulk of it was from Nancy Molineaux's reports.

Nim waited until the others had finished reading, then asked, 'Is there anything additional, which any of you know, that isn't in there?'

'I might have an item or two,' Harry London volunteered.

The Property Protection chief had been cool today when meeting Nim, probably remembering their sharp words two days ago. But his tone was normal as he said, 'I have friends in the law enforcement agencies. As Nim knows, they sometimes tell me things.'

In contrast to the others – including Nim, who was also dressed casually – London was impeccable in beige slacks with a knife-edge crease, and a starched bush jacket. He wore socks which matched the ensemble. His leather shoes were gleaming.

'The newspapers mentioned that Archambault kept a journal,' London said, 'and it was found among his other papers. That's in here.' He tapped Nim's memo with a fingernail. 'What isn't here, and wasn't let out because the DA hopes to use it in evidence at Archambault's trial, is what was *in* the journal.'

Van Buren asked, 'Have you seen the journal?'

'No. But I was shown a Xerox copy.'

As usual, Nim thought, Harry London was moving at his own pedantic pace.

O'Brien asked impatiently, 'Okay, what was in the damn thing?'

'I don't remember.'

There was obvious disappointment, then revived interest as London added, 'At least, not all of it.' He paused, then continued, 'There are two things, though, you can tell from reading what the guy put down. First, he's every bit as vain and conceited as we figured, maybe more so. Also – and you get this right away from reading all the garbage that's in there – he has what you'd call a compulsion to write things.'

'So have thousands of others,' Van Buren said. 'Is that all?'

'Yep.'

London seemed deflated and Nim put in quickly, 'Tess, don't knock that kind of information. Every detail helps.'

'Tell us something, Harry,' Oscar O'Brien said. 'Do you remember anything about the handwriting in that journal?'

'What kind of thing?'

'Well, was it distinctive?'

The Property Protection chief considered. 'I'd say, yes.'

'What I'm getting at,' the general counsel said, 'is this : if you took a sample of the journal handwriting, and then another turned up from someplace else, would it be easy to match the two and know they were both from the same person?'

'I see what you mean,' London said. 'No doubt of it. Very easy.'

'Um.' O'Brien was stroking his chin, drifting off into a reverie of his own. He motioned to the others. 'Carry on. I only have a half-baked idea that isn't ready yet.'

'All right,' Nim said, 'let's go on to talk about North Castle, the part of town where that *Fire Protection Service* truck was found abandoned.'

'With the radiator still warm,' Van Buren reminded them. 'And he was seen to go on foot from there, which makes it likely he couldn't have gone far.'

'Maybe not,' Harry London said, 'but that whole North Castle area is a rabbit warren. The police have combed it and got nothing. If anybody wanted to choose a place in this city where they could disappear, that's the district.'

'And from what I've read or heard,' Nim added, 'it's a reasonable guess that Archambault had a second hideaway prepared, to fall back on, and is now in it. We know he wasn't short of money, so he could have arranged everything well ahead of time.'

'Using a phony name, of course,' Van Buren said. 'The same way he did to buy the truck.'

Nim smiled. 'I doubt if the phone company has him listed in *Directory Assistance*.'

'About that truck registration,' London said. 'It's been checked on, and it's a dead end.'

'Harry,' O'Brien queried, 'has anyone estimated the size of the area in which Archambault has apparently been swallowed up? In other words, if you drew a circle on a map, and stated "the man is probably hiding somewhere in there", how big would the circle be?'

'I believe the police have made an estimate,' London said. 'But of course it's only a guess.'

'Tell us,' Nim prompted.

'Well, the thinking goes something like this: when Archambault abandoned that truck, he was in one helluva hurry. So, assuming he was heading for a hideaway, while he wouldn't have left the truck close to it, it would not have been far either. Say a mile and a half at the most. So if you take the truck as the centre, that means a circle with a one-and-a-half-mile radius.'

'If I remember my high school geometry,' O'Brien mused, 'the area of a circle is pi times the radius squared.' He crossed to a small desk and picked up an electronic calculator. After a moment he announced, 'That's a bit over seven square miles.'

Nim said, 'Which means you're talking about roughly twelve thousand homes and small businesses, with probably thirty thousand people living within that circle.'

'I know that's a lot of territory,' O'Brien said, 'and looking for Archambault in there would be like searching for the proverbial needle. Just the same, we might smoke him out, and here's a thought for the rest of you to kick around.'

Nim, London and Van Buren were listening carefully. As all of them knew, it was the lawyer's ideas which had led to most of the conclusions at their earlier sessions.

O'Brien continued, 'Harry says Archambault has a compulsion to write things. Taken with the other information we have about the man, it adds up to him being an exhibitionist with a need to "sound off" constantly, even in small ways. So my thought is this: if we could get some kind of public questionnaire circulating in that seven-square-mile area – I mean the kind of thing with a string of questions to which people write in answers – our man might not be able to resist answering too.'

There was a puzzled silence, then Van Buren asked, 'What would the actual questions be about?'

'Oh, electric power, of course – something to arouse Archambault's interest, if possible, to make him angry. Like: how do you rate the service which GSP & L gives the public? Do you agree that continued good service will require higher rates soon? Do you favour a public utility remaining under private enterprise? That sort of thing. Of course, those are rough. The real questions would have to be thought out carefully.'

Nim said thoughtfully, 'I suppose your idea, Oscar, is that as the questionnaires came back, you'd look for some handwriting matching the sample in that journal.'

'Right.'

'But supposing Archambault used a typewriter?'

'Then we couldn't identify,' the lawyer said. 'Look, this isn't a foolproof scheme. If you're looking for that, you won't find one.'

'If you did get a returned questionnaire where the handwriting matched,' Teresa Van Buren objected, 'I don't see what good it would do you. How would you know where it came from? Even if Archambault was dumb enough to answer, you can be sure he wouldn't give his address.'

O'Brien shrugged. 'I already admitted it was a half-baked notion, Tess.'

'Wait a minute,' London said. 'There *is* one way a thing like that could be traceable. Invisible ink.'

Nim told him, 'Explain that.'

'Invisible ink isn't just a trick for kids; it's used more often than you'd think,' the Property Protection chief said. 'Here's the way it works: on every questionnaire would be a number, but it wouldn't be visible. You print it with a luminescent powder dissolved in glycol; the liquid's absorbed into the paper so there's no trace of it in view. But when you find the questionnaire you want, you hold it under a black light scanner and the number shows up clearly. Take it away from the scanner, the number disappears.'

Van Buren exclaimed, 'I'll be damned!'

Harry London told her, 'It's done often. On lottery tickets is one example; it proves a lottery ticket is genuine and not a fake which some crook printed. Also, half the so-called anonymous questionnaires floating around are done that way. Never trust any piece of paper which says you can't be identified.'

'This begins to get interesting,' O'Brien said.

'The big problem, though,' Nim cautioned, 'is how to distribute those questionnaires widely, yet keep a record of where each one went. I don't see how you'd do it.'

Van Buren sat up straight. 'I do. The answer is under our noses. Our own Billing Department.'

The others stared at her.

'Look at it this way,' the PR director said. 'Every house, every building, in that seven-square-mile area is a customer of GSP & L, and all that information is stored in our billing computers.'

'I get it,' Nim said; he was thinking aloud. 'You'd programme the computer to print out the addresses in that area, and no more.'

'We could do even better,' O'Brien put in; he sounded excited. 'The computer could produce the questionnaires ready for mailing. The portion with a customer's name and address could be detached so only the non-identifiable part would be sent back.'

'*Apparently* non-identifiable,' Harry London reminded him. 'But while the regular printing was being done, that invisible ink number would be added. Don't forget that.'

O'Brien slapped a thigh enthusiastically. 'By Jupiter, we're on to something!'

'It's a good idea,' Nim said, 'and worth trying. But let's be realistic about two things. First, even if the questionnaire reaches Archambault, he might be smart and throw it away, so what we're backing is a long shot.'

O'Brien nodded. 'I agree.'

'The other thing,' Nim continued, 'is that Archambault – under whatever name he's using in his hideaway – may not be on our direct billing system. He could be renting a room. In that case someone else would get the electricity and gas bills – and the questionnaire.'

'That's a possibility,' Van Buren conceded, 'though I don't believe it's likely. Think of it from Archambault's point of view. For any hideaway to be effective, it has to be self-contained and private. A rented room wouldn't be. Therefore chances are, he has a house or apartment, the way he did before. Which means separate metering with separate billing. So he *would* get the questionnaire.'

O'Brien nodded again. 'Makes sense.'

They continued talking for another hour, refining their idea, their interest and eagerness growing.

10

GSP & L's Computer Center, Nim thought, bore a striking resemblance to a movie set of *Star Wars*.

Everything on the three floors of the company's headquarters building which the centre occupied was futuristic, clinical and functional. Aesthetic frills which appeared in other departments – decorative furniture, carpets, paintings, curtains – were forbidden here. There were no windows; all light was artificial. Even the air was special, with humidity controlled and temperature at an even seventy degrees. All who worked in the Computer Center were subject to closed-circuit TV surveillance and no one knew when he or she was being watched by the utility's equivalent of Big Brother.

Movement of individuals in and out of the centre was rigidly controlled. Security guards, operating inside bulletproof glass cubicles, and speaking through microphones, scrutinized every arrival and departure. Their orders allowed them to assume nothing. Not even a known, friendly face which they saw each working day was permitted to pass without an inspection of credentials.

Each person moving through the security area (always singly; more than one at a time was not allowed) was enclosed in an 'air lock' – in effect, a small prison, also of bulletproof glass. After entry, a heavy door at the rear clanged shut and was bolted electronically. Another door in front, equally formidable, was opened when a guard was satisfied that all was well. If suspicions were aroused, as sometimes happened, both doors remained closed and locked until reinforcements, or proof of identity, arrived.

No exceptions were made. Even the company's chairman, J. Eric Humphrey, never got in without a temporary visitor's badge and careful scrutiny.

The reason for ultra-precautions was simple. The centre housed a priceless treasure trove: a computerized record of eight and a half million GSP & L customers, with their meter readings, billings, and payments – all going back years – plus details of shareholders, employees, company equipment, inventories, technical data, and a multitude of other intelligence.

One strategically placed hand grenade in the Computer Center could have wreaked more havoc to the giant utility's system than a wheelbarrow load of high explosive employed against high voltage lines or sub-stations.

The centre's information was stored on hundreds of magnetic disc packs. There were twenty discs to a pack, and each disc – twice the size of a normal LP recording – contained the records of one hundred thousand customers.

Value of the computers was about thirty million dollars. Value of the recorded information was incalculable.

Nim had come to the Computer Center with Oscar O'Brien, their purpose to observe the dispatch of what was officially a 'Consumer Survey' mailing but what, in fact, was the baited trap in which it was hoped to snare the Friends of Freedom leader, Georgos Archambault.

It was Thursday, four days after the Sunday 'think group' session in the general counsel's home.

Many hours had been spent since then, working on the questionnaire scheme. Nim and O'Brien had decided eight questions would be posed. The first few were simple. For example:

Does Golden State Power & Light provide you with satisfactory service? Please answer yes or no.

Further on, there was room for more expansive answers.

In what ways do you believe that Golden State Power & Light service could be improved?

And:

Do you have trouble understanding the details on your Golden State Power & Light bills? If so, please tell us your problem.

Finally:

Golden State Power & Light apologises to its customers for inconveniences as a result of cowardly attacks on company installations by small-time, would-be terrorists who act in ignorance. If there are ways in which you think such attacks could be ended, please give us your views.

As Oscar O'Brien observed, 'If that doesn't make Archambault hopping mad, and tempt him into replying, nothing will.'

Law enforcement authorities – the city police, FBI, and the District Attorney's office – when informed of GSP & L's idea, had reacted favourably. The DA's office offered help in examining the thousands of questionnaires when they began coming back.

Sharlett Underhill, executive vice president of finance, whose responsibilities included the Computer Center, met Nim and O'Brien after they were checked through Security. Mrs Underhill, dressed smartly in a light blue tailored suit, told them, 'We are running your Consumer Survey now. All twelve thousand copies should be out of here and in the mail tonight.'

'Eleven thousand nine hundred and ninety-nine of the damn things,' O'Brien said, 'we don't care about. There's just one we're hoping to get back.'

'It would cost us a lot less money,' the finance chief said tartly, 'if you knew which it was.'

'If we knew that, my dear Sharlett, we wouldn't be here.'

The trio walked deeper into computer country, past rows of softly humming metal and glass cabinets, stopping beside an IBM 3800 laser printer which was spitting out questionnaires, ready for mailing in window envelopes.

The top of the single page read:

Golden State Power & Light
CONSUMER SURVEY
We would appreciate your answers,
in confidence, to some important questions.
Our objective is to serve you better.

The name and address followed, then a perforation across the entire page. Below the perforation was the instruction:

TO PRESERVE YOUR ANONYMITY
TEAR OFF AND DISCARD THE TOP
PORTION OF THIS FORM.
NO SIGNATURE OR ANY OTHER
IDENTIFICATION IS REQUIRED.
THANK YOU!

A return business-reply envelope, requiring no stamp, would accompany each questionnaire.

Nim asked, 'Where is the invisible ink?'

O'Brien chuckled. 'You can't see it, meat-head. It's invisible.'

Sharlett Underhill went closer to the printer and opened the top. Leaning forward, she pointed to a bottle containing a clear, apparently oily liquid; the bottle was inverted and from it a plastic tube ran downwards. 'This is a special assembly put on for this job. The tube feeds a numbering device linked with the computer. The bottom half of each page is being imprinted with the invisible number. At the same time, the computer is recording which number goes to what address.'

Mrs Underhill closed the cover. At the back of the machine she removed one of the completed questionnaires and carried it to a metal desk nearby. There she switched on a portable light on a small stand. 'This is a "black" light.' As she placed the paper under it, the number 3702 leaped out.

'Damned ingenious,' O'Brien said. 'Okay, so now we have a number. Then what?'

'When you give me the number which requires identifying,' Mrs Underhill informed him, 'it will be entered into the computer along with a secret code, known only to two people – one of our trusted senior programmers and me. The computer will immediately tell us the address to which that particular questionnaire was mailed.'

Nim pointed out, 'We're gambling, of course, that we'll have a number to give you.'

Sharlett Underhill fixed the two men with a steely glare. 'Whether you do or not, I want you both to understand two things. I was not in favour of what is being done here because I do not like my department's equipment and records used for what is essentially a deceitful purpose. I protested to the chairman, but he seems to feel strongly about what is being done and I was overruled.'

'Yes, we know that,' O'Brien said. 'But for God's sake, Sharlett, this is a special case!'

Mrs Underhill remained unsmiling. 'Please hear me out. When you have given me the number you hope to get – *and I will accept one number only* – the information you want will be drawn from the computer, using the secret code I mentioned. But, *the moment that has happened,* the computer will be instructed to forget all the other numbers and related addresses. I want that clearly understood.'

'It's understood,' the lawyer acknowledged. 'And fair enough.'

Nim said, 'Changing the subject, Sharlett, did your people have trouble defining and separating that seven-square-mile area we specified?'

'None whatever. Our programming method makes it possible to divide and subdivide our customers into many categories and any geographic area.' The executive vice president relaxed as she warmed to a subject she clearly enjoyed. 'When properly used, a modern computer is a sensitive and flexible tool. It's also totally reliable.' She hesitated. 'Well, almost totally.'

As she spoke the last words, Mrs Underhill glanced towards another IBM printer, flanked by a table at which two men were seated. They appeared to be checking computer printouts, one by one, by hand.

O'Brien was curious. 'What's happening over there?'

For the first time since they had come in, Sharlett Underhill smiled. 'That's our "VIP anti-goof squad". Many public utilities have one.'

Nim shook his head. 'I work here and I've never heard of it.'

They strolled to where the work was being done.

'Those are bills,' Mrs Underhill said, 'based on latest meter readings, and due to go out tomorrow. What the billing computer does is separate the bills of several hundred people who are on a special list – the mayor, supervisors, councilmen in the various cities we serve, senior state officials, Congressmen, newspaper editors and columnists, broadcasters, judges, prominent lawyers – others like that. Then each bill is inspected, as you're seeing now, to make sure there's nothing unusual about it. If there is, it's sent to another department and double-checked before mailing. That way, we avoid fuss and embarrassment if a computer, or a person who programmed it, does slip up.'

They watched the inspection continue, an occasional bill being extracted and put aside, while Sharlett Underhill reminisced.

'We once had a computer print a monthly bill for a city councilman. The computer tripped and added a string of extra zeros. His bill should have been forty-five dollars. Instead, it went to him as four million, five hundred thousand dollars.'

They all laughed. Nim asked, 'What happened?'

'That's the point. If he'd brought the bill in, or phoned, everyone would have had a good laugh, after which we'd have torn it up and probably given him a credit for his trouble. Instead, he called a press conference. He showed the bill around to prove how incompetent we are at GSP & L, and said it proved we ought to be taken over by the city.'

O'Brien shook his head. 'I can hardly believe it.'

'I assure you it happened,' Mrs Underhill said. 'Politicians are the worst people to magnify a simple mistake, even though *they* make more than most of us. But there are others. Anyway, it was about then we started our own "VIP anti-goof squad". I'd heard about it from Con Edison in New York. They have one. Now, whenever we come across anyone important or pompous or both, we add his – or her – name. We even have a few people in this company on the list.'

O'Brien conceded, 'I can be pompous at times. It's one of my weaknesses.' He pointed to the pile of bills. 'Am I in there?'

'Oscar,' Sharlett Underhill told him as she led the way out, 'that is something you will never know.'

11

Ruth Goldman was in New York.

She had gone to begin treatments at the Sloan-Kettering Institute and would be away two weeks. Other trips would be necessary later.

The decision had been taken by Dr Levin after studying the test results from Ruth's previous visit and discussing them by telephone with the New York doctors. He told Nim and Ruth together, 'I can't make promises; no one can, and nothing is definite. But I'll go so far as to say that I, and the Sloan-Kettering people, are cautiously optimistic.' That was as much as they could get from him.

Nim had taken Ruth to the airport early yesterday morning for an American Airlines non-stop flight. They had said an emotional goodbye.

'I love you,' he declared just before Ruth boarded. 'I'll miss you, and I'll be doing whatever's the equivalent of praying.'

She had laughed then, and kissed him once more. 'It's a strange thing,' she had said, 'but even with all this, I've never been happier.'

In New York, Ruth was staying with friends and would attend the Institute several days a week as an outpatient.

Leah and Benjy had again gone to stay with their grandparents. This time, because relationships between Nim and the Neubergers were now cordial, Nim had promised to go over for dinner occasionally, to be with the children.

Nim had also – in fulfilment of an earlier promise – arranged to take Karen Sloan to the symphony.

He had received, several days ago, one of Karen's notes which read:

Days come, days go.
On some you are in the news
With Begin, Sadat, Schmidt, Botha, Carter,
    Giscard d'Estaing and Bishop Muzorewa.
But of them all, one Nimrod Goldman
Merits *my* front page.

It is good to read of you,
But better still
To see, and hear, be touched, and share,
And personally love.

He had sighed on reading it because he genuinely wanted to see Karen, then had thought guiltily : any complications in his personal life were of his own making. Since the memorable evening when he and Karen made love, he had dropped in to see her twice during the daytime, but the visits were brief and hurried, with Nim on the way from somewhere to somewhere else. He knew that Karen craved a longer time together, with more intimacy.

Ruth's absence seemed an opportunity to be with Karen in a more satisfying way, and going to the symphony, instead of spending the evening in her home, was a compromise with his conscience.

When he arrived at Karen's apartment, she was ready, wearing a becoming dark red dress and a single strand of pearls. Her long blonde hair, brushed and gleaming, fell about her shoulders. The wide mouth and soft blue eyes smiled a warm greeting. The nails of her long fingers, which rested on a lapboard, were manicured and shining.

As they kissed, letting their closeness linger sweetly, Nim felt his desire for Karen, which had only been dormant, unmistakably revive. He felt relieved they were going out.

A minute or two later, after Josie had come in and was busy disconnecting the wheelchair from a power outlet so it could become more mobile, Karen said, 'Nimrod, you've been under strain. It shows.'

'A few things have happened,' he admitted. 'Some you've read about. But tonight there's only you and me and the music.'

'And me,' Josie said, coming around to the front of the wheelchair. The aide-housekeeper beamed at Nim, who was clearly one of her favourites. 'But all I'm doing is driving you both. If you'll come down with Karen in a few minutes, Mr Goldman, I'll go ahead and bring Humperdinck around.'

Nim laughed. 'Ah, Humperdinck!' He asked Karen, 'How *is* your van with a personality?'

'Still wonderful, but' – her face clouded – 'what I worry about is my father.'

'In what way?'

She shook her head. 'Let's leave it now. Perhaps I'll tell you later.'

As usual, Nim marvelled at the dexterity with which Karen, using only her sip-blow tube, piloted her chair out of the apartment, along a corridor, and towards the elevator.

On the way he asked, 'How long is your battery good for?'

She smiled. 'Tonight I'm fully charged. So, using the battery for the chair and my respirator, probably four hours. After that, I'll need to plug in again to dear old GSP & L.'

It fascinated him how tenuous was Karen's hold on life, and that electricity kept her living.

'Speaking of GSP & L,' she said, 'how are your problems?'

'Oh, we always have a new assortment. They sprout like weeds.'

'No, seriously. I want to know.'

'Well, suddenly, oil is our biggest worry,' he told her. 'Did you hear that the latest talks between OPEC and the United States broke down today?'

'It was on the radio before you came. The oil exporting countries say they won't take any more paper money. Only gold.'

'They've threatened that several times.' Nim was remembering his conversation with Eric Humphrey and Mr Justice Yale shortly before Christmas. Then the oil situation had been worrisome; now, in March, it was gravely critical. He added, 'This time it looks as if they mean it.'

Karen asked, 'If imported oil stops coming, how bad will things be?'

'Far worse than most people believe. More than half the oil America uses is imported, and eighty-five per cent of that comes from OPEC countries.' He went on, 'Even now, though, an oil shortage is being thought about mainly in terms of cars and gasoline, not electricity.'

Nim reflected again, as he had on the way over tonight: the most dramatic confrontation yet with the OPEC oil nations, with a potential far more devastating than the Arab embargo of 1973-74, had happened abruptly within the past forty-eight hours. It was a possibility that everyone had known about but comparatively few took seriously. The eternal optimists, including some in high places, were still hoping a final showdown could be avoided, that one way or another the Niagara of imported oil would keep on flowing. Nim didn't share their belief.

A thought occurred to him concerning Karen. Before he could express it they came to the elevator and the doors opened.

Already inside, the only other occupants were two small children – a boy and a girl, cheerful and fresh-faced, their ages probably nine and ten. 'Hi, Karen!' they both said as the wheelchair, followed by Nim, moved in.

'Hello, Philip and Wendy,' Karen said. 'Are you going out?'

The boy answered. 'No. Just downstairs to play.' He looked at Nim. 'Who's he?'

'My date. This is Mr Goldman.' She told Nim, 'These are two of my neighbours and friends.'

As the elevator descended, they all said hello.

'Karen,' the small boy asked, 'can I touch your hand?'

'Of course.'

He did so, moving his fingertips gently, then asked, 'Can you feel that?'

'Yes, Philip,' she told him. 'You have gentle hands.' He seemed interested and pleased.

Not wanting to be outdone, the girl enquired, 'Karen, do you want your legs changed?'

'Well . . . all right.'

Carefully, apparently knowing what to do, the girl lifted Karen's right leg until it was crossed over the left.

'Thank you, Wendy.'

In the downstairs lobby the children said goodbye and ran off.

'That was beautiful,' Nim said.

'I know.' Karen smiled warmly. 'Children are so natural. They're not afraid, or mixed up, the way adults are. When I first came here to live, the children in the building would ask me questions like, "What's the matter with you?' or "Why can't you walk?" and when their parents heard that, they would tell them "Shush!" It took a while, but I got them all to understand I don't mind the questions, in fact welcome them. But there are still some adults who can never be comfortable. When they see me, they look the other way.'

Outside the apartment front door, Josie was waiting with the van. It was a Ford, painted a pleasant light green; a wide sliding door on the near side was already open. Karen manoeuvred her wheelchair so it was facing the door and a few feet away.

'If you watch,' she told Nim, 'you'll see what your Mr Paulsen did to help me get into Humperdinck.'

While Karen was speaking, Josie lifted down two lengths of steel channel from the van's interior. Attaching both pieces of channel to fittings at the base of the doorway, she lowered the other ends to the ground. Between the van's interior and the ground there was now a double ramp, the width matching the wheels on Karen's chair.

Now Josie stepped inside the van and reached for a hook on a steel cable; the cable was attached to an electric winch on the far side. She brought the hook to the wheelchair, snapped it through a steel eye, then returned to the winch. Josie touched a switch and held it down.

'Here we go!' Karen said. With her words, the wheelchair was pulled smoothly up the ramp. Once inside, Josie swung the chair around, the wheels slipping neatly into two recesses in the floor, where bolts secured them.

Josie, grinning, told Nim, 'You ride up front, Mr Goldman. With the chauffeur.'

As they eased out of the apartment house forecourt into traffic, Nim turned around in the front seat to talk with Karen. He returned to what he had been about to say when they reached the elevator.

'If we do have a serious oil shortage, almost certainly there will be rolling blackouts. You know what those are?'

Karen nodded. 'I think so. It means electric power will be off in different places for hours at a time.'

'Yes, most likely three hours every day to begin with, then for longer periods if things get worse. If it happens, though, I'll make sure you get warning in advance, then you'll have to go to a hospital with its own generator.'

'Redwood Grove,' Karen said. 'That's where Josie and I went the night those Friends of Freedom people blew up the sub-stations and we had a power failure.'

'Tomorrow,' Nim told her, 'I'm going to find out how good their generator is at Redwood Grove. Sometimes those stand-bys aren't worth a damn because they're not given proper service. When New York had its big blackouts, some of them wouldn't even start.'

'I'm not going to worry,' Karen said. 'Not with you looking out for me, Nimrod.'

Josie was a careful driver and Nim relaxed during the journey to the Palace of Arts, where the city's symphony orchestra performed. At the Palace's main entrance, while Josie was unloading Karen's wheelchair, help arrived in the form of a uniformed attendant who promptly whisked Karen and Nim through a side door and into an elevator which carried them to the grand tier. There they had front row space in a box, and a movable ramp eased the way for Karen. It was obvious that the Palace of Arts was used to wheelchair users among its patrons.

When they had settled down, and looking around her, Karen said, 'This is special treatment, Nimrod. How did you manage it?'

'Dear old GSP & L, as you call it, has some influence.'

It was Teresa Van Buren who, at Nim's request, arranged box seats and the facilities for Karen. When he had offered to pay, Tess told him, 'Forget it! There are a few executive perks left. Enjoy them while they last.'

Nim held a programme for Karen to see but, after a moment, she shook her head. 'I'll enjoy listening, but I always think music criticism and programme notes are written by people trying to prove how clever they are.'

He chuckled. 'I agree.'

As the house lights dimmed and the conductor ascended the podium amid applause, Karen said softly, 'Nimrod, things are different between us, aren't they?'

He was taken aback by her perception but had no time to answer before the music began.

The programme was heavily Brahms. *Variations on a Theme of Haydn* first. Immediately after: *Piano Concerto No 2 in B-flat Major*. The superb soloist was Eugene Istomin. The piano concerto was among Nim's favourites and, judging by her rapt attention, Karen's too. During the third movement with its moving, haunting cello melody, he reached out, putting a hand over one of Karen's. As she turned her head, he saw her eyes were wet with tears.

At last the music finished to sustained applause in which Nim joined – 'Please! For both of us,' Karen urged him – and house lights went up for the intermission.

While others left their seats to promenade, Nim and Karen remained where they were. Both were briefly silent, then she said, 'If you like, you can answer my question now.'

He had no need to ask which question and, sighing, said, 'I suppose nothing ever stays the same.'

'We're foolish if we expect it to,' Karen acknowledged, 'and I want you to know I never did. Oh, it's nice to dream sometimes, to long for the impossible and want everything good to last, but one thing I've learned is to be a realist. Be honest with me, Nimrod. What happened? What changed between last time and now?'

It was then he told her. Told her about Ruth, the invading malignancy which threatened her life, and how – because of it – she and Nim had found their way again, which for a while they had lost.

Karen listened in silence. Then she said, 'I knew the moment I saw you tonight that there was something different, something important and personal. Now that I know why, I'm glad for you in one way, and sad – of course – in another, especially for your wife.'

'We may get lucky,' he said.

'I hope so. Some people do.'

The orchestra was filing in for the concert's second half. Others in the audience were resuming their seats.

Karen said quietly, 'We mustn't be lovers any more, you and me. It wouldn't be fair, or right. But I hope we'll go on being friends, and that sometimes I'll see you.'

He touched her hand again, and managed to say, 'Friends, always,' before the music started.

On the homeward journey they were quieter than when they came.

Josie, too, seemed to sense the change, and said little. She had met them outside with Humperdinck, having been to visit friends while Nim and Karen were in the Palace of Arts.

After a while, again turning around in the front seat to face Karen, Nim said, 'Earlier on, you told me you were worried about your father. You didn't want to talk about it. Do you now?'

'I don't mind,' Karen said. 'Except there isn't a lot to tell. I do know Daddy is in some kind of trouble – financial, I think; he's dropped hints, but won't tell me exactly what. It does mean, though, I won't have Humperdinck much longer.'

Nim was shocked. 'Why?'

'The monthly payments are too much for my parents. I think I told you Daddy's bank wouldn't lend the money, so he went to a finance company and the interest rate was higher. I suppose that, and business things, have crowded in.'

'Look,' Nim said, 'I'd like to help . . .'

'No! I said once before I won't ever take money from you, Nimrod, and I meant it. You have your own family to look after. Besides, much as I love Humperdinck, I managed without a van before and can do so again. It's Daddy I'm concerned about.'

'I really wish,' Nim told her, 'there were something I could do.'

'Stay my friend, Nimrod. It's all I ask.'

They said goodnight – with a gentle kiss, not passionate any more – outside Karen's apartment building. At her suggestion, because she said she was tired, he did not go up, but walked sadly to his car, parked a block away.

12

In the last week of March, the dramatic, suddenly-erupting oil crisis overshadowed all else, dominating national and international news.

'It's like imminent war,' someone observed at a GSP & L management committee meeting. 'You keep thinking it won't happen, so that everything's unreal until the guns start firing.'

There was nothing unreal about the OPEC nations' unanimous decision. Members of OPEC – the Arab countries and Iran, Venezuela, Indonesia, Nigeria – had decreed a few days earlier: After tankers on the high seas and in United States ports had off-loaded their cargoes, no more oil would be dispatched to the US until the dispute over payment had been resolved.

The OPEC nations claimed to have ample dollar reserves with which to sit out their embargo, reserves far greater, they pointed out, than US stockpiles of oil.

'Unfortunately, too goddamn true,' a travel-weary Secretary of State snapped at Washington reporters in an undiplomatic, unguarded moment.

Within Golden State Power & Light, as elsewhere throughout the country, urgent policy decisions were being made. In GSP & L's bailiwick the question was no longer 'if' there would be widespread temporary blackouts, but 'how soon' and to what extent.

The two previous years of drought in California and the light winter snowfall in the Sierra Nevada were compounding the problem because hydro-electric reserves were significantly less than usual.

Nim, whose role as vice president, planning, placed him at the centre of activity, became engaged in a hectic succession of conferences, their purpose to review emergency plans and decide priorities.

Meanwhile, some national and state priorities had already been decreed.

The President ordered immediate gasoline rationing, and a standby coupon scheme already 'on the shelf' was to be activated within days. Additionally, all sales of gasoline were forbidden from Friday nights to Monday mornings.

Also emanating from Washington was an edict halting all major sporting events and other attractions which produced large crowds, and closing national parks. The objective was to reduce unnecessary travel, especially by automobile. Theatres and movie houses, it was stated, might have to be closed later.

All public utilities using oil were ordered to begin around-the-clock 'brownouts' by reducing their voltages five per cent.

Public utilities which produced electricity by burning coal – principally in the central United States – were instructed to transmit as much power as they could spare to the East and West Coasts, which would be hardest hit by the oil embargo, and where massive unemployment was expected because of power-short plants and businesses. The scheme was labelled 'Coal by Wire'. However, its effect would be limited, in part because the central US needed most of its electricity for local use, and also because long distance transmission lines were few in number.

Schools in many areas were being ordered to close now, and reopen in the summer when their heating and lighting needs would be far less.

Curbs on air travel were being worked out and would shortly be announced.

More drastic steps, the public was warned – including three- or even four-day weekends – were likely if the oil situation failed to improve.

Accompanying all official measures were pleas for voluntary conservation of energy in all its forms.

At Golden State Power & Light, every discussion was over-shadowed by the knowledge that the utility's own stored oil was sufficient for only thirty days of normal operation.

Since some new oil, from tankers now en route, would still be coming in, it was decided that 'rolling blackouts' would be de-layed until the second week of May. Then, initially, the elec-tricity cut-offs would be for three hours each day, after which more draconian measures might be needed.

But even the earliest power cuts, it was realized, would be disruptive, and damaging to the state's economy. Nim knew how grim the situation was; so did others directly involved. But the general public, Nim believed, had still not grasped, or perhaps didn't want to, the full significance of what was happening.

As well as Nim's planning duties, and because of his reinstate-ment as company spokesman, he was in demand to explain the current scene and outlook.

He found the two responsibilities a strain and told Teresa Van Buren, 'Okay, I'll handle the important occasions for you, but you'll have to use your own people for the small stuff.' She said she would.

Next day the PR director appeared in Nim's office. 'There's a midday TV programme called *Lunch Break*.'

'You may not believe this, Tess,' he said, 'but I never watch it.'

'Yeah, yeah; very funny. Well, don't be too quick to dismiss daytime television. There are a million housewives out there who do watch, and tomorrow the programme wants the elec-tricity crisis explained.'

'By me, I suppose.'

'Naturally,' Van Buren said. 'Who does it better?'

Nim grinned. 'Okay, but do something for me. All TV stations specialize in time wasting. They ask you to be there early, then keep you waiting for ever to go on. You know how busy I am so, for once, try to arrange a fast-in, fast-out.'

'I'll come with you myself,' Van Buren said. 'And I'll work it out. I promise.'

As it turned out, the promise was not fulfilled.

Lunch Break was a one-hour show which went on the air at noon. The PR director and Nim arrived at the TV studios at 11:50. In the foyer a young woman programme assistant met them; like so many who worked in television, she dressed and looked as if she graduated from high school the week before. She carried the standard badge of office – a clipboard – and wore her glasses in her hair.

'Oh, yes, Mr Goldman. You'll be on last, at ten to one.'

'Hey, hold it!' Van Buren protested. 'I was assured Mr Goldman would be at the top of the show. He's one of our senior executives and his time is valuable, especially now.'

'I know.' The programme assistant smiled sweetly. 'But the producer changed his mind. Mr Goldman's subject is rather *heavy*. It might depress our audience.'

'They should be depressed,' Nim said.

'If they are, and then switch off, our programme will be over anyway,' the young woman said firmly. 'Perhaps you'd like to come on the set while you're waiting. Then you can watch the rest of the show.'

Van Buren looked at Nim, putting up her hands in a gesture of helplessness.

Resigned, knowing how much urgent work he could have accomplished in the wasted hour, he told her, 'Okay.'

The programme assistant, who had played the same scene many times, said, 'Come with me, please.'

The studio set, colourful and brightly lighted, was intended to look like a living room. Its centrepiece was a bright orange sofa occupied by two regular interviewers – Jerry and Jean – young, vivacious, turned-on, Beautiful People. Three TV cameras prowled in front in a semicircle. Guests would join the interviewers under the bright lights, one by one.

The show's first ten minutes were devoted to a dancing bear from a visiting circus, the second to a seventy-year-old grandmother who had travelled from Chicago on roller skates. 'I wore out five pairs,' she boasted, 'and would have been here sooner, except the police wouldn't let me use interstate highways.'

Immediately preceding Nim was *Lunch Break*'s own 'House Doctor'.

423

'He's on every day and has a tremendous following,' the programme assistant confided in a whisper. 'People tune in especially, which is why, when you follow him, they'll be listening to you.'

The doctor, in his fifties, greying and distinguished, was a solid performer who knew every trick in television's manual, including how to smile disarmingly, when to act the fatherly physician, and at what point to use a simplistic diagram of a stomach. 'My subject today,' he informed his unseen audience, 'is constipation.'

Nim watched and listened, fascinated.

'. . . Many people worry needlessly. What *not* to do is take laxatives. Millions of dollars' worth are sold each year – a waste; many are damaging to your health . . . Most constipation is "imagined". A daily bowel movement can be a needless fetish . . . Let your natural cycle have its way. For some, five to seven days without is normal. Be patient, wait . . . A real problem : some folks don't heed the call of nature immediately. They're busy, they postpone. That's bad. The bowel gets discouraged, tired of trying . . . Eat high roughage food, drink lots of water to stay moist . . .'

Van Buren leaned across. 'Oh God, Nim! I'm sorry.'

He assured her softly, 'Don't be. Wouldn't have missed it. I only hope I'm not an anticlimax.'

The doctor was faded out, a commercial in. The programme assistant took Nim's arm. 'You're on, Mr Goldman.' She escorted him to the centre of the set, where he was seated.

While the commercial continued, Nim and the interviewers shook hands. Jerry, frowning, cautioned him, 'We're running late. Don't have much time, so keep your answers short.' He accepted a sheet of notes from a stagehand, then, as if a switch had been snapped, his smile went on and he turned towards a camera.

'Our last guest today knows a great deal about electricity and oil. He is . . .'

After the introduction, Jean asked Nim brightly, 'Are we really going to have electricity cuts, or is it just another scare, something which in the end won't happen?'

'It's no scare, and it will happen.' (*You want short answers,* Nim thought, *so, okay.*)

Jerry was consulting the sheet he had been given. 'About that alleged oil shortage . . .'

Nim cut in quickly. 'It is *not* alleged.'

The interviewer's smile widened. 'We'll let you get away with that one.' He went back to his notes. 'Anyway, haven't we had a glut of oil recently in California – oil coming in from Alaska, from the pipeline?'

'There have been some temporary local surpluses,' Nim agreed. 'But now, with the rest of the country desperately in need of oil, any extra will disappear fast.'

'It seems selfish,' Jean said, 'but can't we keep that Alaska oil in California?'

'No.' Nim shook his head. 'The federal government controls it, and already has an allocation programme. Every state, every city in the country, is pressuring Washington, demanding a share. There won't be much for anyone when the available domestic oil is spread around.'

'I understand,' Jerry said, referring to his notes once more, 'that Golden State Power has a thirty-day supply of oil. That doesn't sound too bad.'

'The figure is true in one sense,' Nim acknowledged, 'but misleading in another. For one thing, it's impossible to use oil down to the bottom of every tank. For another, the oil isn't always where it's needed most; one generating plant may be without oil, another have enough in storage for several days, and the facilities to move big quantities of oil around are limited. For both reasons, twenty-five days is more realistic.'

'Well,' Jerry said, 'let's hope everything is back to normal before those days run out.'

Nim told him, 'There's not the slightest chance of that. Even if agreement is reached with the OPEC oil nations, it will take . . .'

'Excuse me,' Jean said, 'but we're short of time and I have another question, Mr Goldman. Couldn't your company have foreseen what has happened about oil and made other plans?'

The effrontery, the injustice, the incredible naïvety of the question astounded Nim. Then anger rose. Subduing it, he answered, 'Golden State Power & Light has been attempting to do precisely that for at least ten years. But everything our company proposed – geothermal plants, pumped storage, coal burning, nuclear – has been opposed, delayed or thwarted by . . .'

'I'm truly sorry,' Jerry interrupted, 'but we just ran out of time. Thank you, Mr Goldman, for being with us.' He addressed a zooming lens. 'Among the interesting guests on *Lunch Break* tomorrow will be an Indian swami and . . .'

On their way out of the TV station building, Teresa Van Buren said dispiritedly to Nim, 'Even now, no one believes us, do they?'

'They'll believe soon enough,' Nim said. 'When they all keep flipping switches and nothing happens.'

While preparations for widespread blackouts went ahead, and a sense of crisis pervaded GSP & L, incongruities persisted.

One was the Energy Commission hearings on Tunipah which continued, unchanged, at their original maddening pace.

'A stranger from Mars, using commonsense,' Oscar O'Brien observed during lunch with Nim and Eric Humphrey, 'would assume, in view of our present power emergency, that licensing procedures for projects like Tunipah, Fincastle, and Devil's Gate would move faster. Well, Mr Commonsense Mars would be dead wrong.'

The general counsel moodily ate some of his lunch, then continued, 'When you're in there at those hearings, listening to testimony and the same old rehashed arguments about procedure, you'd think no one knows or cares what's going on in the real world outside. Oh, by the way, we have a new group fighting us on Tunipah. They call themselves CANED, which, if I remember it right, means Crusaders Against Needless Energy Development. And compared with CANED's accusations about Golden State Power & Light, Davey Birdsong was a friend and ally.'

'Opposition is a hydra-headed monster,' Eric Humphrey mused, then added, 'The Governor's support of Tunipah seems to have made little, if any, difference.'

'That's because bureaucracy is stronger than governors, presidents, or any of us,' O'Brien said. 'Fighting bureaucracy nowadays is like wrestling a sea of mud while you're in it up to your armpits. I'll make a prediction: when the blackouts hit the Energy Commission building, the hearings on Tunipah will continue by candlelight – with nothing else changed.'

As to the Fincastle geothermal, and Devil's Gate pumped storage plant proposals, the general counsel reported that dates to *begin* public hearings had still not been set by the responsible state agencies.

Oscar O'Brien's general disenchantment, as well as Nim's, extended to the bogus Consumer Survey distributed in the city's North Castle district.

It was almost three weeks since the carefully planned questionnaire had gone out and it now appeared as if the attempt to entrap the terrorist leader, Georgos Archambault, had been abortive, a waste of time and money.

Within a few days after the bulk mailing, hundreds of replies poured in, and continued to do so through the following weeks. A large basement room at GSP & L headquarters was set aside to deal with the influx and a staff of eight clerks installed there. Six were borrowed from various departments, the other two recruited from the District Attorney's office. Between them, they painstakingly examined every completed questionnaire.

The DA's office also sent photographic blow-ups of handwriting samples from Georgos Archambault's journal, and the clerks worked with these in view. To guard against error, each questionnaire was examined separately by three people. The result was definite: nothing had come in which matched the handwriting samples.

Now, the special staff was down to two, the remainder having returned to their regular duties. A few replies were still trickling in and being routinely examined. But it seemed unlikely, at this stage, that Georgos Archambault would be heard from.

To Nim, in any case, the project had become a lot less important than the critical oil supply problem which occupied his working days and nights.

It was during a late evening session about oil – a meeting in Nim's office with the company's Director of Fuel Supply, the Chief of Load Forecasting and two other department heads – that he received a telephone call having nothing to do with the subject under discussion, but which disturbed him greatly.

Victoria Davis, Nim's secretary, was also working late and buzzed from outside while the meeting was in progress.

Annoyed at the interruption, Nim picked up the telephone and answered curtly, 'Yes?'

'Miss Karen Sloan is calling on line one,' Vicki informed him. 'I wouldn't have disturbed you, but she insisted it was important.'

427

'Tell her . . .' Nim was about to say he would return the call later, or in the morning, then changed his mind. 'Okay, I'll take it.'

With an 'Excuse me' to the others, he depressed a lighted button on the telephone. 'Hello, Karen.'

'Nimrod,' Karen said without preliminaries, her voice sounding strained, 'my father is in serious trouble. I'm calling to see if you can help.'

'What kind of trouble?' Nim remembered that the night he and Karen went to the symphony she had said much the same thing, but without being specific.

'I made my mother tell me. Daddy wouldn't.' Karen stopped; he sensed she was making an effort to regain composure. Then she went on, 'You know that my father has a small plumbing business.'

'Yes.' Nim recalled that Luther Sloan had talked about his business the day they all met in Karen's apartment. It was the day on which both parents later confided in Nim their burden of guilt about their quadriplegic daughter.

'Well,' Karen said, 'Daddy has been questioned several times by people from your company, Nimrod, and now by police detectives.'

'Questioned about what?'

Again Karen hesitated before answering. 'According to Mother, Daddy has been doing quite a lot of subcontracting for a company called Quayle Electrical and Gas. The work was on gas lines, something to do with lines going to meters.'

Nim told her, 'Tell me that company's name again.'

'It's "Quayle". Does that mean something to you?'

'Yes, it means something,' Nim said slowly as he thought: it looked almost certainly as if Luther Sloan was into theft of gas. Though Karen didn't know it, her phrase 'lines going to meters' was a giveaway. That and the reference to Quayle Electrical and Gas Contracting, the big-scale power thieves already exposed and still being investigated by Harry London. What was it Harry reported only recently? *'There's a bunch of new cases, as well as others developing from the Quayle inquiry.'* It sounded to Nim as if Luther Sloan might be among the 'others'.

The sudden news, the realization of what it implied, depressed him. Assuming his guess to be correct, *why* had Karen's father done it? Probably for the usual reason, Nim thought: money.

428

Then it occurred to him that he could probably guess, too, what the money had been used for.

'Karen,' he said, 'if this is what I think, it *is* serious for your father and I'm not sure there's anything I'll be able to do.' He was conscious of his subordinates in the room, waiting while he talked, trying to appear as if they were not listening.

'In any event, there's nothing I can do tonight,' Nim said into the telephone. 'But in the morning I'll find out what I can, then call you.' Realizing he might have sounded unusually formal, he went on to explain about the meeting in his office.

Karen was contrite. 'Oh, I'm sorry, Nimrod! I shouldn't have bothered you.'

'No,' he assured her. 'You can bother me anytime. And I'll do what I can tomorrow.'

As the discussion on oil supplies resumed, Nim attempted to concentrate on what was being said, but several times his thoughts wandered. He asked himself silently: was life, which had thrown so many foul balls at Karen, in the process of delivering still one more?

13

Again and again, sometimes while sleeping, sometimes while awake, a memory haunted Georgos Winslow Archambault.

It was a memory from a long-ago summer's day in Minnesota, soon after Georgos' tenth birthday. During school holidays he had gone to stay with a farming family – he had forgotten exactly why or how – and a young son of the house and Georgos had gone ratting in an old barn. They killed several rats cruelly, using rakes with sharp prongs to spear them, and then one large rat became cornered. Georgos remembered the creature's gleaming, beady eyes as the two boys closed in. Then, in desperation, the rat sprang, leaping, sinking its teeth into the other boy's hand. The boy screamed. But the rat survived only seconds because Georgos swung his rake, knocking the creature to the floor, then slammed the prongs through its body.

For some reason, though, Georgos always remembered that

rat's defiant gesture before its inevitable end.

Now, in his North Castle hideaway, he felt a kinship with the rat.

It was almost eight weeks since Georgos had gone into hiding. In retrospect, the length of time surprised him. He had not expected to survive so long, especially after the outpouring of publicity, about himself and Friends of Freedom, which followed the Christopher Columbus Hotel bombing. Descriptions of Georgos had been widely circulated, and photos of him, found in the Crocker Street house, appeared in newspapers and on TV. He knew, from news reports, that a massive manhunt with himself as the objective had been mounted in the North Castle district and elsewhere. Daily since going underground Georgos had expected to be discovered, the apartment hideaway surrounded and invaded.

It hadn't happened.

At first, as the hours and days went by, Georgos' principal emotion was relief. Then, as the days extended into weeks, he began wondering if a rebirth of Friends of Freedom might be possible. Could he recruit more followers to replace the dead Wayde, Ute and Felix? Could he obtain money, locate an outside liaison who would become another Birdsong? Could they resume, once more, Georgos' war against the hated establishment enemy?

He had considered the idea, wistfully and dreamily, for several days. Then, facing the hardness of reality, he reluctantly abandoned it.

There was no way. No way a revival of Friends of Freedom could happen and no way, either, that Georgos could survive. The past seven-plus weeks had been an unexpected brief reprieve, a postponement of the inevitable; that was all.

Georgos knew he was near the end of the line.

He was being hunted by every law enforcement agency and would continue to be for as long as he lived. His name and face were known; his chemically stained hands had been described; it was only a matter of time before someone, somewhere, recognized him. He was without resources or help, there was nowhere else to go, and – most critical of all – the money he had brought with him to the hideaway was almost gone. Therefore, capture was unavoidable – unless Georgos chose to anticipate it by ending his life defiantly, in his own way.

430

He intended to do exactly that.

Like the rat he remembered from his boyhood, he would make one last fighting gesture and, if necessary, die as he had lived, doing harm to the system he hated. Georgos had decided: he would blow up a critical part of a GSP & L generating station. There was a way it could be done to cause maximum effect and his plans were taking shape.

They were based on an attack he had intended to make – aided by other freedom fighters – before Davey Birdsong's idea of bombing the NEI convention intervened. Now Georgos was reviving the original plan, though he would have to execute it alone.

He had already moved part way towards his objective by a daring risk he had taken on the same day he went into hiding.

The first thing Georgos realized that day, on reviewing his situation, was the need for transportation. He *had* to have wheels. He had abandoned the red *Fire Protection Service* truck because he could not have used it without being recognized, but a substitute was essential.

To buy a vehicle of any kind was out of the question. For one thing, it was too risky. For another, he had insufficient money because the bulk of the Friends of Freedom cash reserve had been in the Crocker Street house. So the only possibility, Georgos reasoned, was to retrieve his Volkswagen van, which might, or might not, have been discovered by the pigs and be under surveillance.

He had kept the van in a privately owned parking garage not far from Crocker Street. Aware of the risk he was taking, gambling on being ahead of the police, Georgos walked to the parking garage the same morning, using side streets as much as he could.

He arrived without incident, paid the garage owner what was owing, then drove the van away. No one questioned him, nor was he stopped on his way back to North Castle. By mid-morning the Volkswagen was safely inside the locked garage adjoining the hideaway apartment.

Emboldened by his success, Georgos ventured out again later, after dark, to buy groceries and a late edition of the *California Examiner*. From the newspaper he learned that a reporter named Nancy Molineaux had provided a description of his Volkswagen van and that police were searching for it. The next day's paper carried a further report on the same subject, disclosing that the parking garage had been visited by police only a half hour after Georgos left.

Knowing that a description of his van had been circulated, Georgos refrained from using it. Now he would use it only once – for what might be his final mission.

There were several other reasons why retrieving the VW had been important.

One was a secret compartment under the van's floor. In it, carefully packed in foam rubber to prevent vibration, were a dozen cylindrical bombs, each containing Tovex water-gel explosive and a timing mechanism.

Also in the van was a small, inflatable rubber dinghy, in a tight package, just as Georgos had bought it at a sporting goods store a month or so earlier, and scuba diving gear, most of it purchased at the same time. All the items were essential to the daring attack he now proposed.

In the days which followed his recovery of the van, Georgos left the apartment occasionally, but only after dark and, when he had to buy food, was careful never to use the same store twice. He also wore light gloves to conceal his hands and, in an attempt to change his appearance slightly, had shaved off his moustache.

The newspaper reports about Friends of Freedom and the hotel bombing were important to him, not only because he liked to read about himself, but because they provided clues as to what the police and FBI were doing. The abandoned *Fire Prevention Service* truck, found in North Castle, was mentioned several times, but there was also speculation that Georgos had somehow managed to slip out of the city and was now in the East. One report claimed he had been seen in Cincinnati. Good! Anything which drew attention away from where he actually was was welcome and helpful.

On reading the *Examiner* that first day, he had been surprised to discover how much was known about his own activities by the reporter Nancy Molineaux. Then, as Georgos read on, he realized it was Yvette who had somehow learned of his plans and had betrayed him. Without that betrayal, the Battle of the Christopher Columbus Hotel (as he now thought of it) would have been a magnificent victory for Friends of Freedom instead of the inglorious rout it had become.

Georgos ought to have hated Yvette for that. Somehow,

though, either then or later, he couldn't manage it. Instead, with a weakness of which he was ashamed, he pitied her and the manner of her death (as described by the newspaper) on Lonely Hill.

Incredibly, he missed Yvette more than he would have believed possible.

Perhaps, Georgos thought, because his own time was running out, he was becoming maudlin and foolish. If so, he was relieved that none of his fellow revolutionaries would ever know about it.

Something else the newspaper had done was dig deeply into Georgos' personal history. An enterprising reporter, who tracked down the record of Georgos' birth in New York City, learned he was the illegitimate son of a one-time Greek movie goddess and a wealthy American playboy named Winslow, the grandson of an auto industry pioneer.

Piece by piece, it all came out.

The movie goddess hadn't wanted to admit having a child, fearing it would destroy her youthful image. The playboy hadn't cared about anything except avoiding entanglements and responsibility.

Georgos was therefore kept well out of sight and, during various stages of his childhood, assigned to successive sets of foster parents, none of whom he liked. The name Archambault came from a branch of his mother's family.

By the age of nine, Georgos had met his father once, his mother a total of three times. After that he saw neither. As a child he wanted, with a fierce determination, to know his parents, but they were equally determined – for differing, selfish reasons – not to know him.

In retrospect, Georgos' mother appeared to have possessed more conscience than his father. She, at least, sent substantial sums of money to Georgos through an Athens law firm, money which permitted him to attend Yale and obtain a PhD, and later finance Friends of Freedom.

The former movie actress, now far removed from a goddess in appearance, professed to be shocked when informed by news reporters of the use to which some of her money had been put. Paradoxically, though, she seemed to enjoy the attention Georgos now brought her, perhaps because she was living in obscurity in a grubby apartment outside Athens and drinking heavily. She had also been ill, though she would not discuss the nature of her ailment.

When Georgos' activities were described to her in detail, she responded, 'That is not a son, it is an evil animal.'

However when asked by a woman reporter if she did not believe her own neglect of Georgos had been largely responsible for what he had become, the ex-actress spat in the questioner's face.

In Manhattan, the ageing playboy father of Georgos dodged the press for several days. Then, when discovered by a reporter in a Fifty-ninth Street bar, he at first denied any involvement with the Greek movie-star, including having sired her child. Finally, when documentary proof of his fatherhood was shown to him, he shrugged and delivered the statement: 'My advice to the cops is to shoot the bastard on sight – to kill.'

Georgos, in due course, read both comments by his parents. Neither surprised him, but they intensified his hatred of almost everything.

So now, in the final week of April, Georgos concluded that the time was near for action. On the one hand, he reasoned, he could not hope to remain in hiding, undetected, much longer – only two nights ago, when shopping for food at a small supermarket, he caught sight of another customer, a man, looking at him with what seemed more than casual curiosity; Georgos left the place hastily. On the other hand, the initial impact of all the publicity, and circulation of his photograph, should have moderated by now, at least a little.

The plan which Georgos had worked on was to blow up the huge cooling water pumps at the La Mission generating plant, the same plant where – nearly a year ago, and disguised as a Salvation Army officer – he placed a bomb which damaged the generator the newspapers called Big Lil. He had learned about those pumps while studying textbooks on power generation to determine where GSP & L would be most vulnerable; he also visited the Engineering School of the University of California at Berkeley, where technical drawings of La Mission, and other plants, were available for anyone to inspect.

Georgos knew – again being realistic – that there wasn't a chance of getting inside the main building at La Mission, as he had succeeded in doing before. It was now too well guarded.

But with resourcefulness, and some luck, he could get to the pump house. The eleven massive, powerful pumps there were essential to the operation of *five generating units*, including Big

434

Lil. In destroying them he would knock out the entire generating station for months.

It would be like severing a lifeline.

The best approach was from the Coyote River. La Mission was built directly on the riverbank, enabling the plant to draw water for cooling and return it to the river afterwards. Getting to the river side of the plant was where the rubber dinghy would come in. After that, Georgos would make use of the scuba diving gear, at which he was expert, having learned underwater demolition during his revolutionary training in Cuba.

Georgos had studied maps and knew he could drive to within a half mile of La Mission and launch the dinghy at a deserted spot. From there the current would help him get downstream. Getting back to the van, and escaping, would be more of a problem, but that aspect he deliberately ignored.

He would enter the pump house underwater, through a metal grating and two wire mesh screens in which he would cut holes; the tools to do it were stored with his underwater equipment. The cylindrical Tovex bombs would be strapped to his waist. Once inside, he would place the bombs, which were in magnetic casings, simply and quickly on the pumps. It was a beautiful scheme! – as it had seemed right from the beginning.

The only remaining question was – when? Today was Friday. Weighing everything, Georgos decided on the following Tuesday. He would leave North Castle as soon as it was dark, drive the Volkswagen van the fifty-odd miles to La Mission, then, on arrival, launch the dinghy immediately.

Now, the decision taken, he was restless. The apartment – small, dreary, sparsely furnished – was confining, especially during the daytime, though Georgos knew it would be foolish to take chances and go out. In fact, he intended to remain in the apartment until Sunday night, when the purchase of more food would become essential.

He missed the mental exercise of writing in his journal. A few days ago he considered starting a new one, now that the original was lost – captured by the enemy. But somehow he could summon up neither the energy nor the enthusiasm to begin writing again.

Once more, as he had done so many times already, he roamed the apartment's three cramped rooms – a living room, bedroom, and kitchen-dining area.

On the kitchen counter top an envelope caught his eye. It contained a so-called Consumer Survey which had come in the mail to the apartment several weeks ago from – of all sources – Golden State Piss & Lickspittle. It had been addressed to one Owen Grainger, which was not surprising because that was the name under which Georgos rented the apartment and paid three months rent in advance to avoid questions about credit.

(Georgos always paid rent and other bills immediately, by mailing cash. Paying bills promptly was a standard part of terrorist technique when seeking to be inconspicuous. Unpaid bills brought unwelcome inquiries and attention.)

One of the items on that stinking Consumer Survey had made Georgos so angry on first reading it that he threw a cup he happened to be holding against the nearest wall and shattered it. The item read :

Golden State Power & Light apologizes to its customers for inconveniences as a result of cowardly attacks on company installations by small-time, would-be terrorists who act in ignorance. If there are ways in which you think such attacks could be ended, please give us your views.

Then and there Georgos had sat down and written a forceful, scathing reply which began : *The terrorists you presumptuously describe as small-time, cowardly and ignorant are none of those things. They are important, wise and dedicated heroes. You are the ignoramuses, as well as criminal exploiters of the people. Justice shall overtake you! Be warned there will be blood and death, not mere 'inconvenience' when the glorious revolution* . . .

He had quickly run out of space and used an extra sheet of paper to complete a truly splendid response.

A pity not to have mailed it ! He had been on the point of doing so on one of his night excursions when caution warned : *Don't!* It might be a trap. So he had let the completed questionnaire remain where it was, on the kitchen counter-top.

The postage-paid envelope which had come with the questionnaire was still unsealed and Georgos took the enclosure out. What he had written, he realized again, was masterful. Why not send it? After all, it was anonymous; he had already torn off, and discarded, the portion of the questionnaire which had the name *Owen Grainger* and the apartment address. Even that had been printed by a computer, something Georgos recognized instantly, so it was impersonal, as mailings from computers always were.

Someone ought to read what he had written. Whoever it was would be jolted, which was good. At the same time they could not fail – even if reluctantly – to admire the writer's mind.

Making another decision, Georgos sealed the envelope. He would put it in a mailbox when he went out Sunday night.

He resumed his pacing and – though he didn't really want to – started thinking again about that long ago day and the cornered rat.

14

At approximately the same moment that Georgos Archambault made his decision to bomb La Mission for the second time, Harry London faced Nim Goldman.

'No!' London said. 'Goddammit no! Not for you, Nim, or anybody else.'

Nim said patiently, 'All I've asked you to do is consider some special circumstances. I happen to know the Sloan family . . .'

The two men were in Nim's office. Harry London, standing, leaned across the desk between them. '*You* may know the family, but *I* know the case. It's all in here. Read it!' The Property Protection chief, his face flushed, slammed down a bulky file.

'Calm down, Harry,' Nim said. 'And I don't need to read the file. I'll take your word about the kind of case it is, and how messy.'

A short time ago, remembering his promise to Karen the previous evening, Nim had telephoned Harry London to see if he knew of a theft of service case involving a Luther Sloan.

'You bet I do,' had been the answer.

When Nim disclosed his personal interest, London had stated, 'I'll come up.'

Now Harry London insisted, 'You're damn right it's a messy case. Your friend Sloan has been bypassing meters – lots of them – for better than a year.'

Nim said irritably, 'He isn't my friend. His daughter is.'

'One of your many women friends, no doubt.'

'Knock it off, Harry!' Nim, too, was becoming angry. 'Karen Sloan is a quadriplegic.'

He went on to describe the Sloan family, how both parents helped Karen financially, and how Luther Sloan had gone into debt to buy a special van for Karen's use. 'One thing I'm certain of. Whatever Karen's father did with any money he made, he didn't spend it on himself.'

London said contemptuously. 'So does that make thievery any better? Of course it doesn't, and you know it.'

'Yes, I know it. But surely, if we also know of extenuating circumstances, we could be less tough.'

'Just what did you have in mind?'

Nim ignored the caustic tone. 'Well, maybe we could insist on restitution, let Luther Sloan pay back whatever was stolen, giving him some time to do it, but not launch criminal proceedings.'

Harry London said coldly, 'So that's your suggestion?'

'Yes, it is.'

'Nim,' London said, 'I never thought the day would come when I'd stand here and hear you say what you just did.'

'Oh, for Chrissakes, Harry! Who knows what they'll say and do in certain situations?'

'I do. And I know what I'm saying now: the Sloan case will take its course, which means a criminal charge is going to be laid within the next few days. Unless, of course, you decide to fire me and do it your way.'

Nim said wearily, 'Harry, stop talking bilge.'

There was a silence, then London said, 'Nim, you're thinking of Yale, aren't you?'

'Yes.'

'You're thinking that old man Yale got away with power theft, or at least involvement in it, so why shouldn't Luther Sloan? You're figuring there was one law for the big cheese, now another law for the little guy – your friend's father. Right?'

Nim nodded. 'Yes, I was thinking pretty much along those lines.'

'Well, you're right. That's the way it is, and I've seen it happen at other times, in other places. The privileged, the powerful, those with money, *can* bend the law or get themselves a better deal. Oh, not always, but often enough to make justice unequal.

But that's the way the system works, and while I may not like it, I didn't make it. However, I'll also tell you this: if I'd had the solid evidence against Mr Justice Yale that I have against Luther Sloan, I'd never have backed down the way I did.'

'Then there *is* strong evidence?'

London gave a twisted grin. 'I thought you'd never ask.'

'Okay, so tell me.'

'Nim, in the Quayle set-up, Luther Sloan was *the gas man*. They gave him most of the illegal gas work which came their way, probably because he was damn good at it. I've seen some of the jobs he did, and there were plenty; we have details from the Quayle records *and* the goods on him. Something else: you talked just now about Sloan making restitution. Well, as far as we can estimate, the illicit work he did has cost GSP & L, in gas revenue losses, about two hundred and thirty thousand dollars. And from what you tell me, Sloan might not have that kind of dough.'

Nim threw up his hands. 'Okay, Harry. You win.'

London shook his head slowly. 'No, I don't. Nobody wins. Not me, not you, not GSP & L, and certainly not Luther Sloan. I'm simply doing my job, the way I'm supposed to.'

'And doing it honestly,' Nim said. 'Maybe more so than the rest of us.'

Nim found himself regretting what had just passed between himself and Harry London. He wondered if their friendship would ever be quite the same again. He rather doubted it.

'Be seeing you, I guess,' London said. He picked up the file he had brought with him, and left.

Nim supposed he would have to call Karen and deliver the bad news. He dreaded doing it. However, before he could pick up the telephone, his office door flew open and Ray Paulsen strode in.

The executive vice president of power supply asked brusquely, 'Where's the chairman?'

'He had a dental appointment,' Nim said. 'Anything I can do for you?'

Paulsen ignored Nim's question. 'When will he be back?'

Nim checked his watch. 'I'd say in an hour.'

Paulsen looked weary and haggard, Nim thought, his shoulders more stooped than usual, his hair and beetling eyebrows greyer than a month ago. It was not suprising. They had all been under strain – Ray Paulsen, because of his large responsibilities, as much as anyone.

'Ray,' Nim said, 'if you'll excuse me for saying so, you look like hell. Why not take it easy for a few minutes? Sit down, switch off, and I'll send for coffee.'

Paulsen glared and appeared on the point of answering angrily. Then, abruptly, his expression changed. Dropping heavily into a soft leather chair, he said, 'Do that.'

Nim buzzed Vicki on the intercom and ordered coffee for them both. Afterwards he went around the desk and took a chair near Paulsen.

'You might as well know what I came to tell the Chairman,' Paulsen growled. 'We've lost Big Lil.'

Nim's calm deserted him. 'We've what?'

Paulsen snapped, 'You heard me the first time.'

'We've lost Big Lil!' Nim repeated. 'For how long?'

'At least four months. More likely six.'

There was a knock and Vicki came in with two mugs of coffee. While she set them on a table, Nim stood up and began pacing restlessly. Now he could understand Paulsen's distress, and share it. Big Lil, La Mission No 5, the largest single generator in the system, supplied a massive million and a quarter kilowatts, equal to six per cent of GSP & L's maximum load. At any time the sudden loss of Big Lil would create major problems, as was demonstrated after the bombing last July. In the present circumstances it was calamitous.

'People!' Paulsen exploded. 'Son-of-bitching, stupid people! You think you have it all figured, spell out every procedure clearly, then some incompetent clown lets you down.' He reached for a coffee mug and drank.

Nim asked, 'What happened.'

'We've had Big Lil off the line for a week for routine maintenance,' Paulsen said. 'You knew that.'

'Yes. It was due back on line today.'

'So it would have been. Except for a damn fool operator.' Paulsen slammed a fist into his palm. 'I could skin the bastard alive.'

Angrily, gloomily, he spelled out the sorry details.

When a huge, steam-powered, oil-fuelled generator like Big Lil was started up, procedures were elaborate and precise. An operator, working in a control room with a multitude of instruments to guide him, was trained to follow instructions carefully, step by step. A printed checklist was provided, undue haste forbidden. Normally, the entire process took several hours.

With Big Lil, as with any similar type generator, the boiler which provided steam was activated first. Projecting into the boiler, at various heights, were rings of oil guns – burners which sprayed atomized fuel. These were ignited remotely by the control room operator, level by level, starting at the bottom. For safety reasons, before a higher level was ignited, the level below it had to be burning.

Today, the operator – failing to check his instruments – thought the lowest level of oil guns was alight. It wasn't.

As succeeding levels of burners came on, the lowest level continued to pour out unburned oil which pooled at the bottom of the boiler. Eventually the accumulated oil and vapour exploded.

'I thought there was a safety interlock . . .' Nim began.

'Hell! – of course there is.' Paulsen sounded as if he were about to weep. 'It's designed to prevent exactly what happened. But – can you believe this? – the damn fool operator overrode it manually. Said he wanted to bring the unit on line faster.'

'Jesus Christ!' Nim could understand Paulsen's anger and frustration. He asked, 'How much damage did the explosion do?'

'Plenty – to the internal boiler structure, much of the duct and flu work, more than half the water-wall tubes.'

Nim whistled softly. He felt sympathy for Paulsen, but knew that words would do no good. He also realized that a four-month estimate for repairs was optimistic.

'This changes everything, Ray,' Nim said, 'especially about rolling blackouts.'

'Don't I know it!'

Mentally, Nim was running over problems and logistics. Although Big Lil was an oil burner and eventually could fall victim to the OPEC embargo, it was by far the most economical oil-fuelled generator the utility had. Now, Big Lil's output would have to be made up by other units which would use more fuel. Therefore, suddenly, GSP & L's total oil reserves represented a great deal less electric power than before.

Thus it followed, even more than previously: all oil stocks must be used cagily, rationed strictly.

'Blackouts should start within the next few days,' Nim said.

Paulsen nodded. 'I agree.' He got up to go.

'Ray,' Nim said, 'I'll let you know as soon as the chairman comes in.'

'My recommendation,' Nim said at a hastily called conference on Friday afternoon, 'is that we begin blackouts on Monday.'

Teresa Van Buren protested. 'It's too soon! We've already announced they won't begin until the week after next. Now you're saying you'd advance that ten days. We've *got* to give the public more warning.'

'Warning be damned!' Paulsen snapped. 'This is a crisis.'

With wry amusement, Nim thought : for once he and Paulsen were in agreement, ranged against the others.

There were five of them, seated around a conference table in the chairman's office suite – J. Eric Humphrey, Paulsen, Van Buren, Nim and Oscar O'Brien. The general counsel had been called in to consider any legal implications of the blackouts.

Prior to this conference, Nim had had several meetings with department heads to review the latest figures on GSP & L's oil stocks. They showed supplies were diminishing faster than anticipated, probably due to unseasonally warm weather and heavy use of air-conditioners.

Nim had also telephoned a Washington, DC, lawyer-lobbyist who represented GSP & L on Capitol Hill. His report was : no breakthrough, or any sign of one, in the United States–OPEC deadlock. The lawyer added, 'There's talk around here of plans to issue a new currency – an external, gold-backed dollar to satisfy OPEC. But it's talk, no more, and not enough to get the oil moving.'

Nim had passed on the Washington report to the chairman and the others.

'I agree with Tess,' Oscar O'Brien said, 'that we ought to give as much advance warning about blackouts as we can.'

Eric Humphrey queried, 'Suppose we hold off until next Wednesday and start the blackouts then? That's five days from now, which should give people time to prepare.'

After more discussion they agreed on Wednesday.

'I'll call a press conference immediately,' Van Buren said. She addressed Nim. 'Can you be available in an hour?'

He nodded. 'Yes.'

The remainder of the day proceeded at the same frenetic pace.

Amid the rush of decision-making and conferences, Nim postponed his intended call to Karen, and it was not until late Friday afternoon that he found time to phone her.

Josie answered first, then Karen came on the line. He knew she would be wearing the special lightweight headband, earpiece and microphone which, with a microswitch close to her head, enabled her to use the telephone without assistance if she wished. By arrangement with the phone company, Karen was able to reach an operator directly and have any number dialled for her.

'Karen,' Nim said, 'I'm calling about your father. I made some inquiries to see if there was anything I could do, but I have to tell you that there isn't. What's happening has gone too far.' He added, hoping it would not sound banal, 'I'm sorry.'

'So am I,' Karen said, and he sensed her dejection. 'But I'm grateful to you for trying, Nimrod.'

'The only advice I can give,' he told her, 'is that your father gets himself a good lawyer.'

There was a silence, then she asked, 'Is it really that bad?'

There seemed no point in lying. 'Yes, I'm afraid it is.' Nim decided not to pass along Harry London's statement that a criminal charge would be laid within the next few days, or London's estimate of a two-hundred-and-thirty-thousand-dollar loss to GSP & L. Both items of news would be known soon enough.

'The strange thing is,' Karen said, 'I've always thought of Daddy as the most honest person I know.'

'Well,' Nim acknowledged, 'I'm not making excuses for your father. I can't. But I guess, sometimes, there are pressures which do strange things to people. Anyway, I'm sure that whatever was behind what he did will be considered in court.'

'But he didn't *need* to; that's the tragic thing. Oh, I've enjoyed the extra things my parents have made possible with money, including Humperdinck. But I could have managed without.'

Nim didn't feel like telling Karen that obviously her father had seen a way to expiate some of his guilt feelings, and had taken it. That was something a psychologist or the courts, or maybe both, would have to unravel and pass judgement on. Instead, Nim asked, 'You still have Humperdinck?'

'Yes. Whatever else is happening, Humperdinck hasn't been re-possessed yet.'

'I'm glad,' he said, 'because you'll need the van next week.'

He went on to tell her about the new schedule of rolling blackouts beginning Wednesday. 'In your area, power will go off at 3pm Wednesday and stay off for at least three hours. So, to be safe, you should go to Redwood Grove Hospital sometime during the morning.'

'Josie will take me,' Karen said.

'If there's any change,' Nim told her, 'I'll call you. Also we'll talk about other blackouts later. Oh, by the way, I checked on the Redwood Grove emergency generator. It's in good shape and the fuel tank is full.'

'It's truly wonderful,' Karen said, with a flash of her normal brightness, 'to be cared about so much.'

15

'I really do believe,' Ruth Goldman observed, turning pages of the *Chronicle-West* Sunday edition, 'that people are beginning to face reality about an electrical crisis.'

'If they'd listened to Dad,' Benjy asserted, 'they would have done it sooner.'

The other three – Ruth, Nim and Leah – all laughed.

'Thank you,' Nim said. 'I appreciate the loyalty.'

Leah added, 'Especially now it means you're vindicated.'

'Hey!' Ruth told her, 'that vocabulary class of yours is paying off.'

Leah flushed with pleasure.

It was Sunday morning and the family had gathered in Nim's and Ruth's bedroom. Ruth was still in bed, having recently finished breakfast, brought to her on a tray. Nim had got up early to cook poached eggs on corned beef hash, a family favourite, for everyone.

Two days ago Ruth had flown back from New York following her second visit there for treatments at the Sloan-Kettering Institute. She had appeared pale on her return, and still did, and there were dark circles under her eyes. She admitted to having experienced some pain as a side effect, as had happened on the previous occasion, and was obviously tired.

It was still too early to know the effect of the treatments, and she would go back to New York in another three weeks. Ruth reported cheerfully, though, that the doctors she had talked with were 'very hopeful'.

Nim informed her about the impending 'rolling blackouts' and that their own home would be affected, beginning Wednesday.

Characteristically, Ruth had said, 'No problem. We'll plan ahead, and manage.'

For a while, Ruth's mother, Rachel, would be coming in several days a week to help with the house and allow Ruth to rest.

'Listen to this.' Ruth had turned to the *Chronicle-West* editorial page and began reading aloud.

THE POWER STRUGGLE

This newspaper, which tries to be honest and forthright in its opinions, admits to having second thoughts about some stands we have taken in the past.

We have, like many others, opposed increased development of nuclear electric power. We have, because of concern about pollution, aligned ourselves with opposition to coal-burning electric generating plants. We have supported wildlife preservation groups who opposed building additional dams for hydro-electric projects on the grounds that wildlife, especially fish populations, might be diminished. We expressed doubt about permitting more geothermal electric plants, fearing they would upset the economies of established tourist areas.

We do not apologize for any of these stands. They represented, and still do, our conviction in specific areas.

But, viewed as a whole, we are forced – in fairness – to agree with the electric power companies of California which argue that their hands have been tied while we have demanded of them what they cannot now deliver.

Instead of compromising here and there, as a give-and-take society should, we have said 'no' to almost everything.

Let us remember that when the lights go out next Wednesday.

Perhaps we deserve what we are getting. Whether we do or not, the time has come for serious reappraisal of some long-held views – our own and others.

'There!' Ruth declared, putting down the newspaper. 'What do you all think of that?'

Benjy said, 'I think they should have mentioned Dad.'

Ruth reached out and mussed his hair affectionately.

'It's a smooth piece of writing,' Nim said. 'Unfortunately, that's all it is. Oh yes, and it's five years late.'

'I don't care,' Ruth said. 'I suppose I should care, but I don't. All I care about right now is being home, and loving you all.'

In the afternoon, despite it being Sunday, Nim went to GSP & L headquarters and his office. There was plenty of activity, and decisions needing to be made. In a way, with regular blackouts only three days away, the utility was entering new and uncharted territory. As the chief dispatcher put it when Nim dropped into the Energy Control Center, 'We assume everything will go smoothly and, as much as we can, we've all made sure it will. But there's always factor "u" – for the unexpected, Mr Goldman. I've seen that devil "u" bollock things too many times to believe it won't happen anywhere at any moment.'

'We've had quite a few unexpected things already,' Nim pointed out.

'Always room for one more, sir, sometimes two,' the dispatcher said cheerfully. 'Anyhow, that's the way I see it.'

On his way home later, Nim wondered about the week to come, and the dispatcher's factor 'u'.

An hour or two after Nim went home, Georgos Archambault ventured out from his North Castle apartment. Now that his day for action – Tuesday – was so near, Georgos was more edgy and nervous than at any time since going into hiding. He sensed an observer or pursuer around each corner and in every shadow. But it proved to be imagination only. He obtained food, without incident, at a delicatessen, buying enough to last him until his departure for La Mission on Tuesday evening.

He also bought the Sunday newspapers and, on his way back to the apartment, mailed the envelope which contained that stupid Consumer Survey from Golden State Piss & Lickspittle. Briefly, Georgos hesitated at the mailbox, wondering if he should mail the letter after all. But, observing that the box had already had its single Sunday collection, and would not be cleared again until mid-morning Monday, he dropped the envelope in.

16

Monday, relatively speaking, passed uneventfully. Tuesday, in the early morning hours, did not.

Nature, as if conspiring to embarrass GSP & L at a troublous time, mounted its own onslaught at the utility's geothermal field in the mountains of Sevilla County.

Deep in the earth beneath 'Old Desperado', the wellhead which had once blown out of control and was never capped entirely, a subsidence of rock and subsoil released new geothermal steam under enormous pressure. The steam rushed to the surface with the force of twenty locomotives. Then, in a spectacular display which rivalled Dante's Inferno, hot mud, stones and rock were hurled high into the air with apocalyptic force.

Obeying another natural phenomenon, namely, 'what goes up must come down', the tons of muck splattered widely over other portions of the geothermal field.

By sheer good luck, the blowout occurred at 2am when only a handful of workers was on duty, and all were under cover. Consequently, there were neither deaths nor injuries, which would have been inevitable if the blow had happened in the daytime.

But the geothermal field's switching and transformer yard was less fortunate. It was deeply covered in wet muck, as were transmission lines nearby. The muck was a conductor of electricity. As a result, everything shorted out and the flow of power from all geothermal-driven generators to the GSP & L transmission system was instantly cut off.

No great or lasting damage was done. All that was needed was a massive clean-up job which would take two days. As for Old Desperado, its bout of mischief over, it settled back to sporadic, harmless steaming like a simmering kettle.

But for forty-eight hours, until the cleaning was complete, GSP & L would be deprived of seven hundred thousand kilowatts from its normally reliable geothermal source, and would need to find an equivalent amount of power elsewhere. The only way it could be done was by bringing more oil-powered generators on line, and thus the utility's precious reserve of oil was further, and unexpectedly, depleted.

One other question mark hung over Tuesday's operations.

Because of the time of year, out of the Company's more than two hundred generating units, an unusually large number were removed from service and undergoing maintenance in preparation for the summer peak-load period. Thus, with the abrupt loss of Big Lil four days earlier, and now all geothermals, GSP & L's total generating capacity – irrespective of the oil shortage – would be stretched thin for the next two days.

Nim learned of the geothermal failure and the potential capacity shortage on coming in to work on Tuesday morning.

His first thought was: how uncanny that the chief dispatcher's factor 'u' – the unexpected – had intruded, precisely as the dispatcher said it might. His second was that until geothermal was back on line, GSP & L could not withstand and absorb another factor 'u' episode.

The realization made him decide, before he started work, to telephone Karen Sloan.

'Karen,' Nim said when she came on the line, 'you've arranged to go to Redwood Grove Hospital tomorrow. Right?'

'Yes,' she answered, 'I'll be there in plenty of time before the afternoon blackout.'

'I'd prefer it if you went today,' he told her. 'Could you do that?'

'Yes, of course, Nimrod. But why?'

'We're having a few problems – some we weren't expecting – and it's possible there could be a non-scheduled power cut. It may not happen, in fact it probably won't, but I'd feel easier if you were at the hospital and close to that standby generator.'

'You mean I should go now?'

'Well, fairly soon. It's just a long-shot precaution.'

'All right,' Karen said. 'Josie's here and we'll get ready. And, Nimrod.'

'Yes?'

'You sound tired.'

'I am,' he admitted. 'I guess we all are over here. It hasn't been the best of times, not lately.'

'Take care of yourself,' she told him. 'And Nimrod, dear . . . bless you!'

After Nim hung up, he thought of something else and dialled

his home number. Ruth answered. He told her about Old Desperado, the geothermal cut-off, and the doubtful capacity situation.

She said sympathetically, 'Things do seem to happen all at once.'

'I guess that's the way life works. Anyway, with all this, and rolling blackouts starting tomorrow, I'd better not come home tonight. I'll sleep in the office.'

'I understand,' Ruth said. 'But be sure you get some rest, and remember that the children and I all need you for a long time to come.'

He promised to do both.

The special staff which had been assembled to process the so-called Consumer Survey in North Castle had been totally disbanded two weeks earlier. The basement room at GSP & L headquarters, where returned questionnaires had at first flooded in, was now in use for another purpose.

Sporadically, a few completed questionnaires straggled in. Some days there were one or two, on other days none.

Those that did arrive were routed by the mailroom to an elderly secretary in public relations, Elsie Young, who had been on the special staff but had since returned to her regular job. The questionnaires, in their distinctive postage-paid envelopes, were placed on her desk and, when she had time and inclination, she opened and inspected them, still comparing each with a sample of the handwriting from Georgos Archambault's journal.

Miss Young hoped the damn things would stop coming soon. She found them tedious, time-wasting, and an intrusion on more interesting work.

On Tuesday, around mid-morning, Elsie Young observed that one of the special Consumer Survey envelopes had been dropped into her in-tray by a messenger, along with a sizeable batch of inter-office mail. She decided to deal with the inter-office stuff first.

Seconds after Karen concluded her conversation with Nim by touching the phone microswitch with her head, she remembered something she forgot to tell him.

She and Josie had planned to go shopping this morning.

Should they still do the shopping, and afterwards go to Redwood Grove, or should they cancel the shopping trip and leave for the hospital now?

Karen was tempted to call Nim back and ask his advice, then remembered the strain in his voice and the pressures he must be working under. She would make the decision herself.

What was it he had said about a possible power cut before tomorrow's scheduled one? *'It may not happen, in fact it probably won't . . .'* And later: *'It's just a long-shot precaution.'*

Well . . obviously! The sensible thing was to go shopping first, which Karen and Josie both enjoyed. Then they would come back briefly and afterwards leave for Redwood Grove. They could still be there by early afternoon, perhaps sooner.

'Josie, dear,' Karen called out in the direction of the kitchen. 'I just had a call from Nimrod, and if you'll come in I'll tell you about our new plans.'

Georgos Archambault possessed a certain animal instinct about danger. In the past, the instinct had served him well and he had learned to rely on it.

Near noon on Tuesday, as he paraded back and forth restlessly in the confined North Castle apartment, the same instinct warned him that danger was close.

A crucial question was: should he obey the instinct and, taking a large chance, leave immediately and head for La Mission and the cooling pumps he planned to destroy? Alternatively, should he disregard the instinct and remain until darkness, then leave as originally planned?

A second question, equally important: was his present instinct genuine or the product of a heightened nervousness?

Georgos wasn't sure as he debated, within himself, the pros and cons.

He intended to make his final approach to the La Mission plant pump house underwater. Therefore, if he could get safely on the river and reasonably close to the plant, he would submerge and, from then on, the likelihood of his being seen was minimal, even in daylight. In fact, daylight, filtering downwards, would help him locate his underwater point of entry more easily than in total darkness.

But could he launch the dinghy and get into it, wearing scuba

450

gear, unobserved? Although the spot he had chosen as a launch-point – a half-mile from La Mission – was normally deserted, there was always the possibility of someone being there and seeing him, especially during the daytime. Georgos assessed that particular risk as: fair.

The really big hazard in daylight – a horrendous one – was to drive his Volkswagen van through North Castle, and then to La Mission, another fifty miles. A description of the van, and undoubtedly its licence number, was in the possession of police, sheriff's departments and the Highway Patrol. If he were spotted, there was no way he could outrun pursuit. On the other hand, it was eight weeks since the description had been issued and the pigs could have forgotten, or be inattentive. Something else in his favour: there were a lot of beat-up VW vans around and the sight of one more would not be unusual.

Just the same, Georgos assessed the first part of his mission, if undertaken now, as: high risk.

He continued pacing and debating, then abruptly made up his mind. He would trust his instincts about danger. The decision was to go!

Georgos left the apartment at once and went into the adjoining garage. There he began what he had intended doing tonight: checking his equipment carefully before departure.

He hurried, however, the sense of danger still persisting.

17

'There's a telephone call for you, Mrs Van Buren,' a waitress announced, 'and I was told to tell you it's important.'

'Everybody thinks their call is important,' the PR director grumbled, 'and most times they're dead wrong.'

But she got up from the table in the GSP & L's officers' dining room where she was lunching with J. Eric Humphrey and Nim Goldman, and went to the telephone outside.

A minute or two later she returned, excitement in her eyes.

'One of those Consumer Surveys came back and we've got a match on the Archambault handwriting. A halfwit in my department has been sitting on the thing all morning. I'll ream her out later, but she's on the way to the Computer Center with it now. I said we'd meet her there.'

'Get Sharlett,' Eric Humphrey said, rising from the table. 'Tell her to leave her lunch.' The executive vice president of finance could be seen a few tables away.

While Van Buren did so, Nim went outside to the telephone and called Harry London. The Property Protection chief was in his office and, when informed of what was happening, said he would go to the Computer Center too.

Nim knew that Oscar O'Brien, the only other member of the 'think group', was out of town for the day.

He joined the others – the chairman, Sharlett Underhill and Van Buren – at the elevator outside the dining room.

They had gone through the usual security formalities in entering the Computer Center. Now, the four who had interrupted lunch, plus Harry London, gathered around a table as Teresa Van Buren opened out the Consumer Survey form and a photographed handwriting sample which a chastened Elsie Young had delivered to her a few minutes ago.

It was Eric Humphrey who expressed what was obvious to everyone. 'There's no doubt of it being the same handwriting. Absolutely none.'

Even if there were, Nim thought, what was written was a giveaway.

The terrorists you presumptuously describe as small-time, cowardly and ignorant are none of those things. They are important, wise and dedicated heroes. You are the ignoramuses, as well as criminal exploiters of the people. Justice shall overtake you! Be warned, there will be blood and death . . .

'Why the hell,' Harry London said to no one in particular, 'did he take so long?'

Sharlett Underhill held out a hand. 'Give that to me.'

Van Buren passed her the questionnaire and the finance chief took it to the portable 'black light' which Nim had seen used during his previous visit to the centre. Mrs Underhill snapped the light on and held the form under it. At the top of the sheet the number 9386 stood out.

She led the way to a computer terminal – a keyboard with a cathode ray screen above it – and sat down.

First, Mrs Underhill tapped in her personal code: 44SHAUND. (It was her age and a corruption of her two names.)

The screen instantly signalled: READY. ENTER REQUEST.

She typed in the project name – NORTH CASTLE SURVEY – followed by the secret code, known only to herself and one other, which would release the needed information. The words NORTH CASTLE SURVEY appeared on the screen; the secret code didn't – the computer's precaution against others observing and memorizing it.

Immediately the computer signalled: ENTER QUESTIONNAIRE NUMBER.

Sharlett Underhill typed in: 9386.

The screen flashed back:

OWEN GRAINGER

12 WEXHAM RD, APT B

The city's name and a zip code followed.

'I got it,' Harry London said. He was already running to a phone.

Slightly more than an hour later Harry London reported personally to Eric Humphrey and Nim, who were in the chairman's office suite.

'Archambault's flown the coop,' London said. 'If that woman had only opened the questionnaire when it came in this morning . . .'

Humphrey said sharply, 'Recriminations will do us no good. What did the police find at that address?'

'A warm trail, sir. According to a neighbour, a man who's been seen occasionally before, drove away in a Volkswagen van half an hour before the place was raided. The police have issued an APB for the van, and they have the building staked out in case he comes back. But' – London shrugged – 'that guy Archambault has slipped through their hands before.'

'He must be getting desperate,' Nim said.

Eric Humphrey nodded. 'I was thinking that too.' He considered, then told Nim, 'I want an immediate warning sent to all our plant managers and security personnel. Give them a report of what has happened and repeat Archambault's description; also get a description of the vehicle he's driving. Instruct our people everywhere to increase their vigilance and to report anything suspicious or unusual. We've been that man's target before. He may decide to make us one again.'

'I'll get on it right away,' Nim said, as he wondered : was there no end to what could happen in a single day?

Georgos hummed a little tune and decided that today his luck was holding.

He had been driving for an hour and a quarter and was almost at the point, near La Mission, where he planned to launch the dinghy. Apparently his VW van had attracted no attention, probably – in part – because he had driven carefully, observing traffic rules and speed limits. He had also avoided freeways where encountering a California Highway Patrol car would have been more likely.

Now he was traversing a gravel road, his first objective less than a mile ahead.

A few minutes later he caught a glimpse of the Coyote River through a tangled growth of underbrush and trees which bordered it in this area. The river was wide at the point he had chosen and soon he could see much more of it. He stopped, where the gravel road ended, about thirty yards from the riverbank.

To Georgos' relief, no other vehicles or human beings were in sight.

As he began unloading the dinghy and supplies, carrying them in a half-dozen trips towards the river, his excitement and a sense of elation grew.

After the initial trip, he removed the dinghy from its container and inflated it with the pump which was in the package. No problem. Then he pushed the dinghy into the water, tying the painter to a tree, and transferred the equipment into it. There was a compressed-air tank and regulator – the tank filled with an hour's air supply, a face mask, fins, a snorkel for use if he was near the surface, a waterproof flashlight, a mesh belt, an inflatable vest to give him buoyancy because of the weight he was carrying, a hydraulic metal cutter, and wire cutters.

Last of all, Georgos loaded aboard the cylindrical Tovex bombs. He had brought eight of them, weighing five pounds each, and they would be fastened to his webbed belt. Georgos had decided that eight bombs were all he could carry; to attempt to take more would be inviting disaster. As it was, the bombs would destroy eight of the eleven water pumps – putting most, if not all, of La Mission's four operating generators out of action.

The fifth La Mission generator was the one they called Big Lil. Georgos had been sorry, in a way, to read in Sunday's newspapers that Big Lil was already disabled and would require several months of repairs. Well, maybe after today it would be several months more.

When everything was in the dinghy, and secure, Georgos, who had already discarded his clothing and changed into a wet suit, untied the painter and eased himself aboard. The dinghy at once floated clear of the bank and began moving gently downstream. There was a small paddle, and he used it.

The day was warm and sunny and, in other circumstances, an excursion on the river would have been enjoyable. But he had no time for enjoyment now.

Staying fairly close to the shoreline, he kept a lookout for other people. So far he had seen none. There were some boats in the distance, a long way downstream, but too far away for him to be observed.

In less than ten minutes he could see La Mission plant ahead, with its high smokestacks and the big, functional building which housed boilers and turbine-generators. In another five minutes he decided he was close enough, and paddled into shore. There was a small, shallow-water cove. On reaching it, he slipped out of the dinghy, then, wading in front, tied the painter once more to a tree.

Now he donned the tank, mask, snorkel, belt and fins, and attached the remainder of his load. When everything was in place he took one làst look around, then waded out towards midstream. Moments later he slipped into deep water and began swimming, ten feet below the surface. He had already taken a sight on his objective – the plant pump house, a long, low, concrete structure, projecting into the river.

Georgos knew that the pump house had two levels. One, above the water and accessible from other portions of the plant, housed the electric motors which drove the pumps. The second level –

mostly underwater – contained the pumps themselves. It was this second level he intended to penetrate.

On the way into the plant, he surfaced twice, quickly, to check his bearings, then went under again to stay out of sight. Soon his forward progress was halted by a concrete wall; he had reached the pump house. Feeling his way along, he began searching for the metal grating through which he would need to cut his way. Almost at once, the pull of the water guided him to it.

The purpose of the grating was to prevent large objects from being drawn in with the cooling water and damaging the pumps. Behind the grating was a wire mesh screen, shaped into a large, horizontal cylinder. The cylinder caught smaller debris and was rotated occasionally to clean it.

Georgos began working on the grating with his hydraulic metal cutter, a compact tool about eighteen inches long and favoured by underwater treasure hunters. Soon he had opened a large circle and pulled the metal bars away. The cutout portion dropped to the riverbed. There was no problem about seeing. Ample daylight was coming in from above.

The wire mesh cylinder was now exposed. Georgos knew he would have to cut his way into it from the outside, then make a second hole on the far side to reach the interior pump bay. The distance between the two holes – the cylinder's diameter – would be about ten feet.

He began snipping away with his wire cutters, smaller than the hydraulic cutter and suspended on a looped cord from his wrist. After a few minutes, another hole was cut. Georgos pulled away the cut circle of mesh, then eased himself carefully through the hole, making sure that none of his equipment snagged. Swimming forward, he began cutting the further screen. Soon that, too, gave way and he passed through.

Now he was fully inside the pump bay. From light filtering down from apertures in the pump house floor above, he was able to make out the bulk of the first pump, directly ahead.

Georgos was not afraid of the suction of the pumps. From his textbook studies he knew that he would only be affected by it if he went deep, which he had no intention of doing.

Using the flashlight, he began looking for a place to locate the first bomb.

Just as he found one – a flat surface on the housing – he sensed movement behind him and turned. There was enough light to see that the wire mesh cylinder through which he had entered, and which had been still, was now rotating, continuously and steadily.

The plant superintendent at La Mission was a bright young engineer, Bob Ostrander. He had been second-in-command to Plant Superintendent Danieli when Danieli, Walter Talbot and two others were killed last July as a result of the bomb, planted by Friends of Freedom, which damaged Big Lil.

Bob Ostrander, ambitious and tough-minded, had wanted to be promoted – but not the way it happened. Danieli had been his good friend and they worked well together. The men's wives were equally close; their children still used each other's houses interchangeably.

Because of the manner of Danieli's death, Ostrander nursed a burning anger about terrorists in general and especially the mis-named Friends of Freedom.

Consequently, when a teletype message arrived in the early afternoon of Tuesday, warning that Georgos Archambault, the Friends of Freedom leader and prime suspect in last year's Big Lil bombing, might make a new attack on GSP & L property, Bob Ostrander put himself and all his staff on full alert.

On his instructions, the entire La Mission plant was searched immediately for possible intruders. When none were found, attention was directed outwards to the plant perimeter. A pair of two-man patrols, which Ostrander organized, was ordered to make continuous rounds of the perimeter fence and report by walkie-talkie any unusual activity or sign of break-in. Guards at the main gate were told : no one, other than company employees, was to be admitted without permission from the superintendent.

Bob Ostrander also telephoned the county sheriff and learned that the sheriff's department, too, had received information about Georgos Archambault and a Volkswagen van he reportedly was driving.

At Ostrander's urging, the sheriff diverted two of his patrol cars to search roads in the area of the La Mission plant for any sign of a VW van such as described.

Less than thirty minutes after Bob Ostrander's call – at 2 : 35pm – the sheriff reported back that a VW van, positively identified as Archambault's, had been found abandoned by the Coyote River, a half-mile upstream of the plant. Not far from it were a pump and a package which apparently had contained an inflatable rubber dinghy. An intensive search for Archambault by sheriff's deputies was now in progress. One deputy sheriff would shortly be on the river in his own motorboat.

Ostrander at once removed several staff members from other duties and sent them to patrol the river side of the plant, their instructions – to sound an alarm at the sight of any boat.

The superintendent remained at his desk, which had become a communications centre.

About ten minutes later the sheriff phoned again. He had just received a radio report that a rubber dinghy, with no one in it, had been discovered in a cove they both knew, around a headland from the plant. 'It looks as if the guy has come ashore and figures to get in through your fence,' the sheriff said. 'Every man I have on duty is over your way, searching, and I'm coming myself. Don't worry! We've got him bottled up.'

As he hung up the telephone, Bob Ostrander was less confident than the sheriff. On previous occasions, he remembered, the Friends of Freedom leader had shown himself to be devious and resourceful. Coming through the fence, especially in daylight, did not make sense. Suddenly, as realization dawned, Ostrander said aloud, 'Scuba gear! That's why he needed a dinghy. The son-of-a-bitch is coming underwater. The pump house!'

He left his office on the run.

A watch foreman was among those patrolling on the river side of the plant. Ostrander, arriving hurriedly, asked him, 'Have you seen anything?'

'Not a thing.'

'Come with me.' They strode towards the pump house. On the way Ostrander explained his theory about an underwater attack.

At the forward extremity of the pump house, where it projected into the river, was an open walkway. The plant superintendent led the way on to it. Midpoint on the walkway was a metal inspection hatch directly above the wire mesh cylinder through which water passed into the pump bay; the two men opened the hatch, then leaned over, looking down. The top of the wire mesh cylinder was visible below them. Nothing appeared out of the ordinary.

Ostrander told the foreman, 'Go inside and turn the cylinder slowly.' There was an electric mechanism to do so, operable both from the pump house and the main control room.

Moments later the wire cylinder began to revolve. Almost at once Ostrander could see the first large hole which had been cut. He remained where he was, watching as the cylinder continued turning. When he saw the second hole his fears were confirmed. Running into the pump house, he shouted, 'He got inside! Keep the screen going!'

At least, he thought, he would block Archambault's way out.

His engineer's mind was icy cool. He stopped, aware of the need for a fast decision, yet taking time to think deliberately, carefully, assessing possibilities.

Somewhere underneath where he was standing, Archambault was swimming, undoubtedly with a bomb or bombs. Where would he direct the bombing? There were two possible targets. One was the pumps, another the condensers further into the plant.

Blowing up the pumps would be damaging enough; it could put all of La Mission's generators out of use for months. But a bomb in the condensers would be far, far worse. Rebuilding them might take a year.

Bob Ostrander knew about explosives. He had studied them at engineering school and since. A five-pound dynamite bomb, no larger than a loaf of bread, could pass through the pumps and enter the condensers. Perhaps Archambault had released such a bomb, or was about to. All that he needed to do was set the timing mechanism and drop it: it would find its way through the pumps to the condensers.

The condensers had to be protected. To do so meant shutting down the entire plant. Now.

There was a wall telephone in the pump house. Bob Ostrander went to it and dialled 11 for the main control room.

A ringing tone and a click. 'Chief operator.'

'This is Ostrander. I want you to hit the trips on all units and stop the circulating water.'

Reaction was instant as the operator protested. 'You'll blow the rupture discs. Besides, we should warn Energy Control . . .'

'Goddammit! Don't give me an argument!' Ostrander gripped the phone and shouted, knowing that at any moment an explosion might rip apart the pump house or the condensers. 'I know what I'm doing. Hit those trips! *Hit them now!*'

Georgos knew nothing of what was going on above him. He only knew, as the wire mesh cylinder continued to revolve, that his escape route was cut off. Not that he had really expected to escape; he had known from the beginning of this mission that his likelihood of surviving it was slight. But he didn't want to die in here. Not this way. Trapped . . .

He thought, with mounting panic: maybe the mesh cylinder would stop. Then he could cut two more holes. He turned sharply to inspect it.

At that same instant, while turning, his wire cutters, fastened to his wrist by the looped cord, broke loose. The knot had opened . . .

The cutters were yellow, intended for easy visibility. He could see them falling . . .

Instinctively, Georgos rolled over, kicked hard and dived, following the glimpse of yellow. His hand was outstretched. He almost had them.

Then he felt a sudden rush of water and realized he had gone too deep and was being sucked into a pump. He attempted to turn back. Too late! The water engulfed him and held him.

He let his mouthpiece and air tube go and tried to scream. Water filled his lungs. Then the pump impeller blades, seven feet across, seized him and chopped him into little pieces.

The air tank was chopped up too; the bombs, unfused and harmless, passed through the pumps.

Only seconds later, all pumps slowed and stopped.

In the main control room, the chief operator, who had just punched four red trip buttons one after the other on separate consoles, was glad the responsibility wasn't his. Young Ostrander had better have a damn good explanation for taking La Mission 1, 2, 3 and 4 – producing three million two hundred thousand kilowatts – off the line without warning. To say nothing of blowing all the turbine rupture discs, which would take eight hours to repair.

As he logged the time – 3:02pm – the direct line phone from

Energy Control Center began ringing. When the chief operator picked it up, a voice demanded, 'What the hell's going on? You've put the system into blackout.'

Bob Ostrander had no doubt that his decision to shut down all generators had been the right one. He foresaw no problem in defending it.

Blowing the turbine rupture discs – a safety feature anyway – was a small price to pay for saving the condensers.

Immediately after giving the shutdown order, Ostrander and the watch foreman had inspected the condensers, leaving the pump house to do so. Almost at once they saw a series of metal objects – the cylindrical bombs. Not knowing if they were dangerous or harmless, the two men gathered them up and ran to the river, where they flung them in.

Now, having returned to the condensers, and taking a second look around, Ostrander had time to reflect that nothing yet had happened in the pump house. Presumably Archambault was still down there and capable of doing damage, though it was possible the revolving wire mesh cylinder had diverted him. Ostrander decided : he would get back to the pump house and figure what should be done next.

About to leave, he noticed some small pieces of debris which appeared to have come through the pumps and had collected on a condenser. He was looking at one of the pieces and reached out to pick it up, then stopped. Bob Ostrander swallowed and felt sick. It was a human hand, peculiarly stained.

18

Goodness! – how quickly the time had gone. Karen was shocked to realize it was well past 2pm.

It scarcely seemed any time at all since she had promised Nimrod she would go to Redwood Grove Hospital, yet several hours had gone by. Of course, the shopping had taken longer than expected – didn't it always? – but she had bought a pretty dress at a bargain price, a pair of shoes, various items of stationery she needed, and a necklace of crystal beads which caught her eye. The necklace, which fortunately was inexpensive, would be just right for her sister; she would give it to Cynthia on her birthday, which was coming soon. Then Josie had a list of drugstore items they needed and that consumed still more time. But it had all been successful and Karen really enjoyed the shopping, which they did in a big, colourful mall only two blocks from the apartment building. Another good feature of the shopping mall was that Karen could go there directly in her wheelchair, controlling it herself, which she preferred to do.

One thing they did not need to do today was buy food because Karen would be at Redwood Grove during the electric power cuts. It looked as if these were going to be frequent until the OPEC oil mess was cleared up, which she hoped to goodness would be soon.

She hadn't let herself think too much about all that time she would have to spend at the hospital, but knew she would miss greatly being at home in her apartment. The hospital was reassuring, especially now, with its reliable supply of electricity. Just the same, it was an institution, fairly spartan, and as for the food there – yech!

The hospital food was another reason they were running late.

Josie had suggested, and Karen agreed, that it would be more pleasant if they had lunch at the apartment before leaving and, in any case, lunch at Redwood Grove would probably be over by the time they got there. So, when they came back from shopping, Josie prepared a meal for them both while Karen continued writing a new poem she intended to send to Nimrod.

Now, with lunch over, Josie was busy putting into a suitcase the things Karen would need at the hospital.

With a sudden surge of affection, Karen said, 'Josie, what a dear, dear person you are! You do so much, never complain, and give me far more than I can ever give to you.'

'You give me enough, just being with you,' Josie said, without looking up as she continued to pack the suitcase. Karen knew that open displays of affection embarrassed her housekeeper-aide, but would not be put off.

'Josie, stop that and come here. I want to kiss you.'

With a shy smile, Josie came.

'Put your arms around me,' Karen told her. When she did, Karen kissed her and said, 'Darling Josie, I love you very much.'

'And I love you,' Josie said, then broke loose and went back to her packing.

As she finished, she announced, 'We're all set. I'll go down now and bring Humperdinck around. Will you be okay if I leave you?'

'Of course. While you're gone I'll make a phone call.'

Josie put the telephone headband on to Karen. Then a minute or two later, as Josie left, Karen heard the apartment door close.

Karen touched the telephone microswitch with her head. In her earpiece she heard a ringing tone, followed by a voice. 'Operator. May I help you?'

'I have manual service, Operator. Will you dial for me, please?' Karen gave the number of her telephone, then the number she was calling – her parents' house.

'One moment.' There was a series of clicks, then a ringing tone. Karen waited for the call to be answered – as it usually was on the second or third ring – but to her surprise the ringing continued. Karen had talked with her mother early this morning and knew that Henrietta Sloan was feeling unwell and did not intend to go to work today, nor did she plan to go out.

Karen thought: the operator had probably dialled a wrong number.

She broke the connection by moving her head against the microswitch and tried again. Again a continuous ring. Again no answer.

Karen tried another number – Cynthia's. Again, a continuous ringing tone, but no reply.

Unusually, Karen felt a vague unease. She was rarely alone in the apartment and, on the few occasions when she was, liked to be in touch with someone by telephone.

When she had told Josie she could go, she did so without thinking about it. Now she wished she hadn't.

At that precise moment several lights in the apartment went out, the window air-conditioner stopped, and Karen felt a slight break in rhythm as her respirator switched over from the building's supply to battery.

With a start, Karen remembered something which both she

and Josie had overlooked. The battery on the wheelchair, which had been drawn on considerably during her shopping jaunt, ought to have been replaced immediately after she came in. Instead, Josie had plugged in the chair to the building supply and switched the chair battery to 'charge'. However, the battery would need at least six hours of charging to recoup what it had lost this morning; it had had barely one, and now, with external power off, the charging would have stopped.

There was a spare, fully charged battery to the right of Karen's chair, ready to be installed before leaving for the hospital. Karen could see it. But there was no way she could connect it herself.

She hoped the power would come back on in a few minutes. And, more than ever, she hoped Josie would return quickly.

Karen decided to telephone Nimrod. It seemed likely that the non-scheduled power cut he had said was 'possible' and 'a long shot' had actually happened.

But when she pressed the phone microswitch with her head, all she got was a recorded announcement. 'All circuits are busy. Please hang up and place your call later.'

She tried again. 'This is a recorded . . .'

Once more. The same result.

Karen knew, from having read about it, that whenever there was a widespread blackout, phone lines became clogged because more people tried to use them than the system could handle. Also, many dialled 'Operator' to ask what was happening, making it difficult to reach an operator too.

She began to be really alarmed. *Where was Josie? Why was she taking so long?* And why hadn't the janitor, Jiminy, come in to see if she was okay, as he always did when anything out of the ordinary occurred?

Though Karen had no means of knowing it, a combination of events had contributed to her predicament.

At 10:45am, while Karen and Josie were getting ready to go shopping, Luther Sloan was arrested and charged with a total of sixteen offences, all felonies, under Section 693c of the California Penal Code, which deals specifically with stealing gas.

Since that time, Henrietta Sloan, shocked, despairing, totally inexperienced in the matter, had been trying to arrange her husband's bail. Shortly before noon she telephoned her elder daughter, Cynthia, appealing for help. Cynthia responded by asking a neighbour to take care of her one living-at-home child when he returned from school, then left to meet her mother. Cynthia's husband was at work and would not be home until evening.

While Karen had been trying to telephone her mother and sister, both were shuttling between a bail bondsman's office and the jail where Luther Sloan was held.

They were in the visitors' section of the jail when the power cut occurred, but were unaware of it. The jail had its own stand-by generator and, while lights flickered off briefly, they came on again at once as the generator started up automatically and took hold.

Only a few minutes earlier, Henrietta Sloan and Cynthia had discussed phoning Karen, but decided against it, not wishing to distress her.

Neither of the two women, nor Luther Sloan, would know about the power cut for another two hours when bail was finally arranged and the trio left the jail together.

A few minutes before the lights in Karen's apartment went out and her wheelchair and respirator switched over to battery operation, Bob Ostrander had shouted to the chief operator at La Mission plant, 'Hit those trips! *Hit them now!*'

When the operator did, the GSP & L transmission system was deprived, without warning, of three million two hundred thousand kilowatts of power, at a time when the utility was operating with a thin reserve, and on a warm May afternoon with load demand unseasonably high because of widespread use of air-conditioners.

The result: a monitoring computer, recognizing there was now insufficient power on line to meet demand, instantly opened high voltage circuit breakers, plunging a large area of the GSP & L system into blackout.

Karen's apartment building was in one of the areas affected.

Josie and the janitor, Jiminy, were trapped in the apartment building elevator and were shouting frantically, trying to attract attention.

After Josie left Karen she walked quickly to a service station close by where Humperdinck had been left overnight. The lessee knew Karen and allowed the van to be parked without charge. It took Josie less than ten minutes to collect Humperdinck and stop at the apartment house front door, where Karen's wheelchair could be conveniently loaded.

The wizened old janitor was touching up paint outside when Josie returned. He asked, 'How's our girl Karen?'

'Fine,' Josie answered, then she told him about going to Redwood Grove Hospital because of the next day's scheduled blackout. At that he put down his paint can and brush and said he would come up to see if there was anything he could do to help.

In the elevator, Jiminy pressed the button for the sixth floor and they began ascending. They were between the third floor and the fourth when the elevator stopped and its light went out. There was an emergency battery-powered lamp on a shelf and Jiminy reached up and switched it on. In its dim glow he pressed every button in sight, but nothing happened.

Soon after, they both began shouting for help.

They had now been shouting for twenty minutes without any response.

There was a small trapdoor in the roof of the elevator, but both Josie and Jiminy were short and, even perching on each other's shoulders – which they tried in turn – they could move it only slightly but had no chance whatever of getting through. Even if they did, it was unlikely they could escape from the elevator shaft.

Josie had long ago remembered about Karen's low battery, which made her cries more desperate and, after a while, her tears flowed as her voice became hoarser.

Though they did not know it then, Josie and Jiminy would remain in the elevator for almost three hours until electric power was restored.

The telephone company would later report that, while its emergency generators functioned during the blackout, for an hour after it happened, demand for its services was unprecedented. Thousands of calls went uncompleted, and many who tried to reach operators for information were unable to do so.

Nim Goldman, under pressure on several fronts because of the sudden power failure, thought briefly of Karen and was relieved she had agreed to go to Redwood Grove Hospital early this morning. He decided that later, when things eased a little, he would phone her there.

Karen was now white with fear, and sweating.

By this time she knew that something serious had happened to prevent Josie coming back.

She had tried to telephone again and again. Still, all that she could get was the recorded voice. She considered manoeuvring her wheelchair and causing it to bang against the outside apartment door in the hope that someone might be passing and would hear, but to move the chair at all would drain, even faster, whatever strength remained in the battery. Karen knew, through experience and calculation, that the battery could not last long, even to power her respirator.

In fact, there was barely a quarter of an hour's life remaining in the battery. On returning from the shopping trip, its power was even more reduced than Karen supposed.

Karen, whose religious beliefs had never been strong, began to pray. She begged God and Jesus Christ to send Josie, or Jiminy, or her parents, or Nimrod, or Cynthia, or anyone – *anyone!*

'*All they have to do, God, is connect that other battery. The one down there, Jesus! Anybody can do it! I can tell them how. Oh please, God! Please! . . .*'

She was still praying when she felt the respirator begin to slow, her breathing become slow and inadequate.

Frantically, she tried the telephone again. 'This is a recorded announcement. All circuits are busy. Please hang up and . . .'

A high-pitched buzzer, connected to the respirator and powered by a small nickel cadmium cell, sounded a warning that the respirator was about to stop. Karen, her consciousness already diminishing, heard it dimly, as if from a long distance away.

As she began to gasp, helplessly craving air she could not take in unaided, her skin turned red, then blue. Her eyes bulged. Her mouth worked wildly. Then, as air ceased coming entirely, she choked; intense pain gripped her chest.

Soon, mercifully, the battery died and, with it, Karen.

Just before her death, her head slumped sideways and, as it

touched the telephone microswitch, a voice responded. 'Operator. May I help you?'

19

In some ways, Nim thought, it was like the rerun of an old movie as he explained to the assembled press group, including TV and radio crews, what had happened at La Mission plant to cause the latest blackout.

He reflected: was it really just ten months ago that Walter Talbot and the others died, and Big Lil suffered bomb damage which caused last summer's blackout? So much had happened since, that the gap in time seemed wider.

Nim was aware of one difference, today. It was the attitude of the media people, compared with ten months earlier.

Today, there seemed a genuine awareness of the problems GSP & L faced, and a sympathy which had previously been lacking.

'Mr Goldman,' *Oakland Tribune* asked, 'if you get green lights to build the plants you need, how long will it take to catch up?'

'Ten years,' Nim answered. 'Oh, if we had a real crash programme, maybe eight. But we need a lot of permits and licences before we can even begin. So far there isn't any sign of them.'

He had come here, to a press conference in the observation gallery of the Energy Control Center, at Teresa Van Buren's request, shortly after the shutdown of all La Mission's remaining generators and the resultant blackout. Nim's first intimation that anything was wrong was when the lights in his office went briefly off and on. That was because special circuitry was protecting the utility's headquarters, and vital installations like the Energy Control Center, from loss of power.

Nim, guessing that something was wrong, had gone to Energy Control at once where Ray Paulsen, who had arrived a few minutes earlier, filled him in on what had happened.

'Ostrander did the right thing, and I'll back him up on it,'

Paulsen said. 'If I'd been there, I'd have done the same.'

'Okay, Ray,' Nim acknowledged. 'When I talk with the press I'll take that line.'

'Something else you can tell them,' Paulsen said, 'is that we'll have all power back on in three hours or less. And by tomorrow, La Mission 1, 2, 3, and 4 will be on line again, *and* all geothermal units.'

'Thanks. I will.'

It was noticeable, Nim thought, that, in the press of events, the antagonism between him and Paulsen seemed to have evaporated. Perhaps it was because both of them were too busy for it.

Now, in the press conference, Nancy Molineaux asked, 'Does this change any of the scheduled blackouts?'

'No,' Nim responded. 'They'll have to begin tomorrow, as planned, and continue every day after that.'

Sacramento Bee inquired, 'Will you be able to restrict them to three hours only?'

'It's unlikely,' Nim said. 'As our oil supplies diminish, the blackouts will have to be longer – probably six hours a day.'

Someone whistled softly.

A TV newsman asked, 'Have you heard there's been some rioting – demonstrations against the "anti's"?'

'Yes, I have. And in my opinion it doesn't help anybody, including us.'

The demonstrations had happened last night. Nim read about them this morning. Stones were hurled through windows of the Sequoia Club and headquarters of the Anti-Nuclear League. Demonstrators at both places, who described themselves as 'Ordinary Joe Citizens', had clashed with police and several demonstrators were arrested. Later they were released without being charged.

It was being freely predicted that there would be more demonstrations and rioting, presumably across the country, as unemployment increased because of power cuts.

Amid it all, GSP & L's former critics and opponents were strangely silent.

Finally at the press conference, somebody asked, 'What's your advice to people, Mr Goldman?'

Nim grinned weakly. 'Switch off everything you don't need to survive.'

It was about two hours later, shortly after 6pm, when Nim returned to his office.

He told Vicki, who was working late – it was getting to be a habit – 'Call Redwood Grove Hospital and ask to speak to Miss Sloan.'

She buzzed him a few minutes later. 'The hospital says they have no Miss Sloan registered.'

Surprised, he queried, 'Are they sure?'

'I asked them to make sure, and they checked twice for me.'

'Then try her home number.' He knew that Vicki had it, though he found it hard to believe that Karen would not have left her apartment for the hospital.

This time, instead of buzzing, Vicki opened his office door and came in. Her face was serious.

'Mr Goldman,' she said, 'I think you'd better take this call.'

Puzzled, he picked up the phone. 'Is that you, Karen?'

A choked voice said, 'Nimrod, this is Cynthia. Karen is dead.'

'Can't we go any faster?' Nim asked the driver.

'I'm doing my best, Mr Goldman.' The man's voice was re-proachful. 'There's a lot of traffic, and more people than usual on the streets.'

Nim had ordered a company car and chauffeur to be at the main doorway, rather than lose time getting his Fiat and driving himself. He arrived on the run and had given the address of Karen's apartment building. They were on the way there.

Nim's thoughts were in turmoil. He had obtained no details from Cynthia, only the bare fact that the power cut had been responsible for Karen's death. Nim already blamed himself – for failing to follow through, for not checking sooner to be sure Karen had gone to Redwood Grove.

Though knowing it was too late, he burned with impatience to arrive.

As a diversion, looking through the car's windows at the streets in gathering dusk, he considered what the driver had just said. There were many more people out than usual. Nim recalled reading about New York City during blackouts – people came out-of-doors in droves but, when asked, few knew why. Perhaps they were seeking instinctively to share adversity with their neighbours.

Others, of course, had taken to the New York streets to break

470

the law, and burn, and plunder. Maybe, as time went on, both things would happen here.

Whether they did or didn't, Nim thought, one thing was certain: patterns of life were changing significantly, and would change still more.

The city's lights were either on or coming on. Soon, the few remaining pockets without power would have theirs restored too.

Until tomorrow.

And the day after.

And, after that, who knew how prolonged or drastic the departure from normal life would be?

'Here you are, Mr Goldman,' the driver announced. They were at Karen's apartment building.

Nim said, 'Please wait.'

'You can't come in,' Cynthia said. 'Not now. It's too awful.'

She had come out into the corridor when Nim arrived at the apartment, closing the door behind her. While the door was briefly open, Nim could hear someone inside having hysterics – it sounded like Henrietta Sloan – and a wailing which he thought was from Josie. Cynthia's eyes were red.

She told him as much as she knew about the series of misfortunes which added up to Karen's terrible, lonely death. Nim started to say what he had already thought, about blaming himself, when Cynthia stopped him.

'No! Whatever the rest of us did or didn't do, Nimrod, no one in a long time did as much for Karen as you. She wouldn't want you to feel guilt or blame yourself. She even left something for you. Wait!'

Cynthia went back inside and returned with a single sheet of blue stationery. 'This was in Karen's typewriter. She always took a long time with anything like this and was probably working on it before . . . before . . .' Her voice choked; she shook her head, unable to finish.

'Thank you.' Nim folded the sheet and put it in an inside pocket. 'Is there anything at all I can do?'

Cynthia shook her head. 'Not now.' Then, as he started to leave, she asked, 'Nimrod, will I see you again?'

He stopped. It was a clear and obvious invitation, just as he remembered the same invitation once before.

'Oh Christ, Cynthia,' Nim said. 'I don't know.'

The damnable thing was, he thought, he wanted Cynthia, who was warm and beautiful and eager to give love. Wanted her, despite his reconciliation with Ruth, despite loving Ruth devotedly.

'If you need me, Nimrod,' Cynthia said, 'you know where I am.'

He nodded as he turned away.

In the car, going back to GSP & L headquarters, Nim took out, and unfolded, the sheet of Karen's familiar stationery which Cynthia had given him. Holding it under a dome light, he read:

Is it so strange, my dearest Nimrod
That lights should be extinguished?
Rush lights have failed;
All fires that men have started
Burn low, and die.
Yet light, like life, survives:
The meanest gleam, a flaming brand,
Each holds a

What did they hold? he wondered. What last sweet, loving thought of Karen's would he never know?

20

A rollaway bed had been brought into Nim's office. It was there when he returned, made up with sheets, a blanket and a pillow, as he had asked for it to be.

Vicki had gone home.

Thoughts of Karen still filled his mind. Despite Cynthia's words, his sense of guilt persisted. It was a guilt, not only for himself, but for GSP & L, of which he was a part, and which had failed her. In modern life, electricity had become a lifeline – for those like Karen, literally – and it should not be broken, no matter what the cause. Reliability of service was, above all, the first duty, a near-sacred trust, of any public utility like GSP & L. And yet the lifeline would be broken – tragically, sadly, in a sense needlessly – again and again, beginning with tomorrow. Nim was sure that as rolling blackouts continued, there would be other losses and hardships, many unforeseen.

Would he ever shake off his guilt about Karen, he wondered? In time, perhaps, but not yet.

Nim wished there were someone he could talk to at this moment, in whom he could confide. But he had not told Ruth about Karen, and couldn't now.

He sat at his desk and put his face in his hands. After a while, he knew he must do something which would divert him mentally. For an hour or two, at least.

The events of the day – trauma piled on trauma – had prevented him from dealing with the accumulated papers on his desk. If he failed to clear some of them tonight, he knew there would be twice as many tomorrow. But as much for mental relief as any other reason, he settled down to work.

He had been concentrating for ten minutes when he heard the telephone in the outer office ring. He answered it on his extension.

'I'll bet,' Teresa Van Buren's voice said, 'you thought you were through being the company's mouthpiece for today.'

'Since you mention it, Tess,' he told her, 'the idea had occurred to me.'

The PR director chuckled. 'The press never sleeps; more's the pity. I have two people over here who'd like to see you. One is AP, who has some supplementary questions for a national story on our rolling blackouts. The other is Nancy Molineaux, who won't say what the hell she wants, but wants something. How about it?'

Nim sighed. 'Okay, bring them over.'

There were moments – this was one – when he regretted the defection and departure of Mr Justice Yale.

'I won't stay,' the PR director said a few minutes later. She introduced AP, an elderly male reporter with rheumy eyes and a smoker's cough. Nancy Molineaux had elected to wait in the outer office until AP was through.

The wire service man's questions were professional and thorough and he scribbled Nim's answers, in his own version of shorthand, on a batch of copy paper. When they had finished, he got up to go and asked, 'Shall I send the doll in?'

'Yes, please.'

Nim heard the outer door close, then Nancy entered.

'Hi!' she said.

As usual, she was stylishly, though simply, dressed – tonight in a silk shirtwaist dress, coral-coloured, a perfect complement to her flawless black skin. Her handsome, high-cheekboned face seemed to have lost some – though not all – of its haughtiness, Nim thought, perhaps because she had been friendlier, ever since their meeting in the Christopher Columbus Hotel, and the shattering events which followed it.

She sat down opposite him, crossing her long, shapely legs. Nim regarded them briefly, then looked away.

'Hi!' he acknowledged. 'What can I do for you?'

'There's this.' She got up and placed a long strip of paper on the desk in front of him. He saw it was a carbon copy of a teletype.

'It's a story that just broke,' Nancy said. 'The morning papers will have it. We'd like to develop it with some comments – yours for one – for the afternoon.'

Swinging his chair to where the light was better, Nim said, 'Let me read this.'

'Be hard to comment if you don't,' she said lazily. 'Take your time.'

He scanned the news story quickly, then went back to the beginning and studied it carefully.

WASHINGTON, DC, MAY 3 – IN A DRAMATIC MOVE TO RESOLVE THE CURRENT OIL CRISIS, THE UNITED STATES IS TO ISSUE A NEW CURRENCY, TO BE KNOWN AS THE NEW DOLLAR. IT WILL BE BACKED BY GOLD AND BE WORTH TEN EXISTING DOLLARS.

THE PRESIDENT WILL ANNOUNCE THE NEW DOLLAR AT A WHITE HOUSE PRESS CONFERENCE TOMORROW AFTERNOON.

SOME WASHINGTON OFFICIALS HAVE ALREADY DUBBED THE NEW CURRENCY 'THE HONEST DOLLAR'.

THE OIL EXPORTING NATIONS OF OPEC WILL BE ASKED TO ACCEPT PAYMENT FOR THEIR OIL IN NEW DOLLARS, WITH PRICE-ADJUSTMENTS TO BE NEGOTIATED.

INITIAL OPEC REACTION HAS BEEN CAUTIOUSLY FAVOURABLE.

HOWEVER, OPEC SPOKESMAN SHEIK AHMED MUSAED STATED THAT AN INDEPENDENT AUDIT OF UNITED STATES GOLD WOULD BE SOUGHT

BEFORE ANY AGREEMENT BASED ON THE NEW DOLLAR COULD BE CONCLUDED.

'WE WOULD NOT GO SO FAR AS TO SUGGEST THAT THE UNITED STATES HAS LIED ABOUT ITS GOLD RESERVES,' SHEIK MUSAED TOLD REPORTERS TONIGHT IN PARIS, 'BUT THERE HAVE BEEN PERSISTENT RUMOURS, WHICH CANNOT BE BRUSHED ASIDE LIGHTLY, THAT THEY ARE NOT AS LARGE AS OFFICIALLY STATED. THEREFORE WE WISH TO MAKE SURE THAT GOLD BACKING OF THE NEW DOLLAR IS REAL AND NOT ILLUSORY.'

THE PRESIDENT IS EXPECTED TO INFORM AMERICANS THAT THEY CAN ACQUIRE NEW DOLLARS BY SURRENDERING THEIR OLD DOLLARS AT THE RATE OF TEN TO ONE. THE CHANGE WILL BE VOLUNTARY AT FIRST BUT, UNDER PROPOSED LEGISLATION, COMPULSORY WITHIN FIVE YEARS. AFTER THAT, THE OLD DOLLAR WILL BE PHASED OUT, HAVING VALUE ONLY AS A COLLECTOR'S ITEM.

AT HIS NEWS CONFERENCE THE PRESIDENT WILL UNDOUBTEDLY BE ASKED . . .

Nim thought: so the possibility which GSP & L's Washington lobbyist had mentioned last week had become reality.

He was aware of Nancy Molineaux, waiting.

'I'm no financial genius,' Nim said. 'But I don't think you need to be one to know that what's happening here' – he tapped the teletype sheet with a finger – 'has been inevitable for a long time, since inflation started and, after that, we let ourselves get dependent on imported oil. Unfortunately, a lot of decent, middle-class folk who've worked hard and accumulated savings, are the ones who'll be hurt most when they line up to trade their dollars ten for one. Even now, though, all that this does is buy us some time. Time until we stop purchasing oil we can't afford, stop spending money we don't have, and begin developing our own, untapped energy resources.'

'Thanks,' Nancy said, 'that'll do nicely.' She put away a notebook she had been writing in. 'Over at the paper, by the way, they seem to think that you're Sir Oracle. Oh yes, and speaking of which, you might like to know that in Sunday's edition we're reprinting what you said at that hearing last September – the one where you blew up and got yourself in the shit. Suddenly it all makes more sense than it seemed to then.' A thought occurred to her. 'Do you want to tell me – for the record – how you feel about all that?'

On impulse, Nim opened a drawer of his desk and took out a folder. From it he extracted a sheet of blue stationery and read aloud:

Be, at that harvest moment, forgiving, gracious,
Broad of mind, large-purposed,
Amused by life's contrariness.

'Not bad,' Nancy said. 'Who wrote that?'

'A friend of mine.' He found he was having trouble speaking. 'A friend who died today.'

There was a silence, then she asked, 'May I read it all?'

'I don't see why not.' He handed her the paper.

When Nancy had finished, she looked up. 'A woman?'

He nodded. 'Yes.'

'Was that the reason you looked the way you did when I came in here tonight – like you'd been swept up from a stable floor?'

Nim smiled briefly. 'If that's the way I looked, I suppose the answer's "yes".'

Nancy put the sheet of stationery on top of the folder on his desk. 'Want to tell me about it? Off the record, if you like.'

'Yes,' he said, 'it'll be off the record. Her name was Karen Sloan. She was a quadriplegic, and had been one since she was fifteen.' He stopped.

'Go on,' Nancy said. 'I'm listening.'

'I think she was the most beautiful person – in every way – I've ever known.'

A pause, then: 'How did you meet her?'

'Accidentally. It happened right after that blackout last July . . .'

Barely an hour ago Nim had longed for someone to talk to, to confide in. Now, he poured it out to Nancy. She listened, interjecting an occasional question, but was mostly silent. When he described the manner of Karen's death, she stood up, moved around the room, and said softly, 'Oh, baby! *Baby!*'

'So you see,' Nim said, 'I guess looking like something from a stable floor wasn't all that surprising.'

Nancy had returned to the desk. She pointed to his spread-out papers. 'Then why are you bothering with all that crap?'

'I had work to do. Still have.'

'Bullshit! Dump it and go home.'

He shook his head and glanced towards the bed. 'Tonight I'm sleeping here. We still have problems, and tomorrow – remember? – we start rolling blackouts.'

'Then come home with me.'

He must have looked startled because she added softly, 'My

476

pad is five minutes away. You can leave the phone number, then if you have to, you can get back here fast. If you don't get called, I'll make breakfast in the morning, before you leave.'

They stood facing each other. Nim was aware of a musky perfume, of Nancy's slim, willowy, desirable body. He had an urge to know more about her. Much more. And he knew – as had happened so often in his life, and for the second time tonight – he was being tempted by a woman.

'You won't get the offer again,' she said sharply. 'So make up your mind. Yes or no?'

He hesitated for the briefest second. Then he told her, 'Okay, let's go.'

Arthur Hailey
Airport £1.50

Nonstop reading excitement as Arthur Hailey probes the hidden nerve-centre that controls a great modern airport.

'Supercharged' CHICAGO SUN-TIMES

Hotel £1.50

The scene is the St Gregory Hotel, New Orleans. Through this totally fascinating novel move vividly drawn characters involved in robbery and blackmail, a near-disastrous orgy and a take-over battle . . . There is courage too, and a love story that will remain etched on the reader's mind.

The Moneychangers 95p

The genius of Arthur Hailey combines Money, People and Banking in an absorbing story of the financial and personal crises seething behind the dignified bronze doors of a major US bank. Interwoven with the dreams, passions, rivalries and guilty secrets are currency and credit-card frauds, embezzlement, a prison gang-rape, Mafia torture and the call-girl sex that sweetens irregular business deals.

Richard Ben Sapir
The Far Arena £1.25

Eight metres down in the Arctic ice an oil drill strikes into human flesh – the icebound body of a man nineteen centuries old, suspended between life and death by a freak of metabolic chemistry. Modern medical technology slowly restores to life the body of Lucius Aurelius Eugenianus, greatest of the Imperial gladiators. A tale of gripping complexity unravels the political confrontations of Ancient Rome and the moral dilemmas of a modern world where science has advanced too far for its own good . . .

Ashley Carter
Panama 95p

Philippe Jean Bunau-Varilla — by profession a skilled and
ambitious engineer, by inclination a sensualist and womanizer.
The strange and lovely Madelon enters his life. Unwanted wife, a
ravishing beauty scarred by love, she comes to dominate Philippe's
every moment . . . But he was destined to build a waterway
between two mighty oceans, a project bedevilled by disease and
disaster in a hostile land of vicious voodoo warriors.

Frank Yerby
Speak Now £1

Harry is eloquent, upright, intelligent, earnest — and black. Kathy
is rich, young, naïve, refreshing — and white. This is their story, set
in riot-torn Paris of the late sixties — a truthful story of the love
between a black jazz musician and a white American girl from the
Deep South. Surrounded by inbred prejudice, sexual conflict, the
bitterness of student rebellion, Harry and Kathy are forced to come
to terms with their oppressive heritage.

Frank Ross
The 65th Tape £1.25

It began with a letter from the grave . . . a dying man's confession
that could not be publicly revealed. The message : a group of
powerful men responsible for the three most cold-blooded
assasinations of the century are within sight of putting their
candidate in the White House. For Washington Intelligence, there
is only one solution — their only weapon that snatch of recorded
conversation, a terrifying recital of political murder and top-level
corruption.

'One of the most exciting, intricate and clever thrillers of the year'
DAILY MAIL

Wilbur Smith
Cry Wolf £1

Two men, one girl and a batch of decrepit armoured cars . . .
running the gauntlet of an Ethiopia in the grip of the Wolf of
Rome. 'Mussolini has all the guns, aircraft and armour he needs.
The jolly old Ethiop has a few ancient rifles and a lot of
two-handed swords . . . It should be a close match.'

'Another cracker . . . Africa, arms dealing, armoured cars,
strong men with stronger women all combine beautifully for
real entertainment' DAILY MIRROR

Eagle in the Sky 95p

In Israel's nerve-stretching struggle for survival, David Morgan's
brilliance as a Mirage pilot is his passport to Debra's love.
But terrorism and tragedy spawned by the violence that drew
them together threaten to tear them apart. From savage air-fights
over the desert to hand-to-hand conflicts on a South African game
reserve, this unforgettable story blends intense excitement
with a tender, sensual love . . .